Forever a Dragon

Book IV of The Dragon Archives

Linda K. Hopkins

FOREVER A DRAGON

LIST OF MAIN CHARACTERS

Lleland Seaton: Master of Philosophy; father was killed by a dragon when he was six

Anabel Seaton: Lleland's mother

Edith: Lleland's sister

Alan: Edith's husband

Aaron Drake: Master of the dragons; powerful dragon whose father was killed by humans; married to Keira

Keira Drake: Aaron's human wife

Zachary (Zach) Drake: Aaron and Keira's son; Lydia's twin brother and a student in Lleland's philosophy class

Lydia Drake: Aaron and Keira's daughter, and Zach's twin sister

Anna Brant: Keira's sister

Max Brant: A member of Aaron's clan who helped Aaron defeat Jack; married to Anna

Jack: A black dragon that terrorized Civitas until being killed by Aaron

Zachary Drake: Aaron's father. Not to be confused with Zach, Aaron's son

Eleanor Drake: Aaron's mother

Richard Carver: Keira and Anna's father

Syngen Gail: King Terran's ambassador to Civitas; kidnapped Keira during the war against Terran; was raised by a dragon father

Edmund Hobbes: A young man who expected to marry Keira; kidnapped Anna before she was rescued by Aaron; was killed by the dragon

Matthew Hobbes: Edmund's younger brother

Thomas: Aaron's steward

Favian Drake: Aaron's cousin

Cathryn Drake: Favian's wife

Will Drake: Cathryn and Favian's son

CHAPTER ONE

Lleland Seaton, Master of Philosophy, closed his book and placed it atop the pile of papers on his desk. Leaning back in his chair, he stared out through the window. The glass was uneven, distorting the view of the gardens beyond which were damp from the steady drizzle that had fallen all morning. The rain had finally stopped, and reaching over his desk, Lleland lifted the latch and pushed the window open, allowing the fresh, rain-clean air to flow in and drive away the stale mustiness of his chamber. A breeze stirred his papers, and a shaft of light, breaking through the clouds, shimmered on the gold lettering of the book on the desk: Aristotelis De Caelo: *On the Heavens, by Aristotle*. Lleland gathered his papers and rose to his feet. It was early afternoon, and the first class of the semester was about to begin. His students would already be gathered to hear Aristotle's work read aloud and the lecture that would follow. Grabbing his cape and cap, Lleland headed out the door.

As he walked, Lleland glanced over his list of students. He already knew most of them: fine young men who had proven their commitment to the rigorous training offered at Kings College. It was a prestigious university, and many vied for one of the coveted spots, although only the most conscientious were awarded a place. The students in Lleland's class had already received their Bachelor's degree in Arts, and were about to embark on the next stage of training to earn their Master's, as Lleland himself had done some years before. Out of the ten students, two were new: Thomas Bell and Zachary Drake. They must have already earned their Bachelors elsewhere: St Mary's, perhaps, or Eastbridge. The name Drake seemed familiar, and Lleland turned it over in his mind as he walked down the stairs to the ground floor.

"*Bonum mane, Magister.*"

"*Bonum mane,*" Lleland muttered absent-mindedly to the student on the stairs. Latin was the only language allowed within the college precincts, whether it be in classrooms, the dining hall, or chambers, and an infraction could earn the guilty party a fine, or even an expulsion. He reached the bottom of the stairs, still searching his memory for the name Drake, and then put the matter out of his mind as he followed the passage towards the classroom.

No sound came from behind the door as Lleland approached, and he smiled to himself. Clearly, the students were heeding the Dean's admonishment made that morning in the opening assembly to behave like "young ladies, with dignity and propriety, refraining from laughter, murmurs and hissing at their Masters." Lleland stepped into the room and glanced around. Two rows of narrow wooden benches faced the small desk at the front of the room. The walls were bare, except for the window that overlooked the college gardens. It was closed, of course, since the sounds of the outside world might prove too distracting for serious scholarship.

The students, young men ranging in age from eighteen to twenty, turned their attention to Lleland as he surveyed them. His gaze slid over those he recognized, but stopped on the two newcomers for a moment to take their measure. The first man glanced up, his eyebrows lifting as he took in Lleland's form. With his youthful appearance and large, muscular stature, Lleland did not fit the mould of a typical scholar, and he was used to the expressions of surprise. He turned to the second newcomer. Light-brown eyes, almost golden in color, met Lleland's, and he stiffened as their gazes locked. There was something unsettling in this student's gaze, and Lleland had the uncanny feeling that he was the one being measured. Turning away, he stalked to his desk. "*State nomen tuum.*"

One by one the students rose and gave their names as Lleland marked them against his list: Henry Baxter; Aubrey Ferrier; Simon Mortimer; Zachary Drake. Drake was the student with the golden eyes, and Lleland watched as he stood. He was tall, taller even than Lleland, who usually topped his students and colleagues by a few inches. Drake was also lean, but Lleland knew that only a fool would think that indicated a lack of strength. The man exuded power and confidence. Lleland frowned and returned his attention to his list as the students continued to state their names.

The class ended two hours later, and Lleland rushed from the room to a meeting in the Dean's office, where he spent the rest of the afternoon. It was only after supper had been served to students and staff at six o'clock that Lleland finally had a moment to reflect on his class. He had sat next to Rutherford, Master of Divinity, during the meal, and asked Rutherford what he knew of the new students. Rutherford only knew them by name, but he had revealed one important piece of information. Drake's father had contributed a large sum of money to the college to ensure that his son was given a private chamber. This was interesting news, since as a matter of policy all students were expected to share with at least one other student, so that "they did not become accustomed to private solitude and reflection, but rather had the opportunity at all times to share their insights and learnings."

So the Drakes were a wealthy family but jealous of their privacy, Lleland mused as he sat in his chamber later that night, his daybook open on his desk. He turned the name

3

over in his mind again. Drake. There was definitely something familiar about it – something that played around the edges of his memory, but what, he could not quite capture. Ah, well. It would come to him in due course. He turned his attention back to his diary and completed his notes for the day.

A few hours had passed by the time Lleland made his way to his bed, the light from the candle casting shifting shadows along the wall. His chambers consisted of two small rooms – the first with a desk and chair beneath the window, a small shelf stacked with books, and a bench in the corner; while the second had a narrow bed, a table with a ewer and basin, and a chest where his clothes were stored. A small three-legged stool completed the furnishings. He placed the candle on the floor, a few inches away from the wooden bed. The mattress was stuffed with straw, and a single spark would be enough to make it go up in flames. A thick fur covered the mattress, over which was spread a quilt, made for him by his mother, and as he lay down, he said a short prayer for her health and well-being, before snuffing out the light and closing his eyes.

Fires were not allowed in private chambers, and Lleland pulled the quilt closer as he slept. A monster was stalking the edge of his dreams – a creature of the night that had long been held at bay, but was now determined to haunt Lleland once more. Outside his window the long, solemn cry of an owl broke through the silence, and the beast drew a little closer. Danger tracked Lleland as he slept, and he tossed restlessly through his dreams.

It was warm in the early summer sunshine, and Lleland looked up at Father as they walked along the streets of the city. There was no-one as strong or brave as Father, and the boy was proud to be at his side. They were on a secret mission to find the tortoiseshell comb that Mother had seen the previous day in the market. It would be a gift for her birthday. Lleland was excited to be part of the secret. Only six years old, there were not many things he knew that his mother did not.

4

Usually, his parents were trying to keep secrets hidden from him. Secrets like the dragon that had been terrorizing the city. But Mother and Father were unable to prevent the older neighborhood children from frightening the younger ones with stories of the monstrous beast that stalked the streets from above. Lleland glanced up as they walked, but saw no horrible creatures. He still drew closer to Father, and Father wrapped a calloused hand around the boy's shoulder. As long as Father was with him, there was nothing to fear.

When the dragon plunged from the sky, there was no warning. One moment the sun had been shining kindly on them, and the next, huge wings, black and terrible, blocked the light, casting the street into shadow as the beast landed on the hard dirt road a few feet away. People screamed and ran in terror, but the dragon blocked all escape for father and son. As black as the darkest night, from the dangerous horns that rose from its skull to the long, spiky tail that swished across the ground, it was truly a terrible sight to behold. Orange flames spewed from its mouth and licked along the dry ground, burning leaves and refuse which smoldered into ashes.

Lleland stared in horror, unable to move, until rough hands grabbed him and sent him flying through the air. "Leave my son be," Father shouted at the dragon. "Take me." Lleland slammed into an abandoned cart, his shoulder catching the rim of the wheel, before he slipped between the spokes. A nail tore his skin and a searing pain shot through his arm, but he clamped his lips against the cry that threatened to spill out. He would not be a baby. Blood poured from the open wound, and tears sprang into his eyes. A sob broke free and he squeezed his eyes shut against the panic that was settling in. When he opened them again, the dragon was looking at him, an amused expression on its beastly countenance. "Please," Father pleaded, "spare the boy."

The dragon turned back to Father. "Why? You would both be a tasty treat, and young flesh is always more tender."

"He's just a child. My only son. You've feasted in the city for days, so you can easily spare this one." Lleland stared at Father in confusion. What did he mean, asking the dragon to spare him? Spare him from what?

"Your only son, hmm? And how will he feel, watching his father *die?"*

"Father?" Lleland said.

"Lleland! Run! Get away from here!"

"Enough!" Flames lit the air as the dragon roared. "I'll spare the boy," it said, "but he'll watch as I kill you."

"No! Spare him that!"

"Spare his life! Spare him suffering! Enough of your whining, human. You make me reconsider."

"Close your eyes, son," Father shouted. "You're the man of the house now." Lleland wrenched himself free of the wheel, ignoring the searing pain, and stumbling to his feet, ran towards his father.

"Father!" he screamed.

"No!" Father cried out. A heavy claw caught Lleland across the chest, the thick talons ripping his flesh, and sent him sprawling against the cart once more as blood poured from the gash. The dragon swung back and crashed his claws into Father's back. He staggered and fell to his knees, his eyes on Lleland, imploring him to look away. The beast's tail whipped around, smashing into Father and flinging him to the ground. Father cried out, but the sound was quickly cut off as talons swiped over his neck, staining the street with a spray of blood.

The dragon sank its claws into Father's belly and ripped as a sickening sound filled the air. Entrails spilled onto the street as Lleland finally dragged his terrified gaze away. A sob rose in his chest and caught in his throat as he pressed his face against the rough planks of the cart. He could hear the dragon growling as it ripped his father apart, and he tried to block his ears as his stomach heaved convulsively, but the sounds continued unabated as the tears drenched Lleland's tunic.

Lleland woke with a start, his heart racing furiously as tears streamed down his cheeks. The quilt was wrapped around him like a rope, and he tugged at it with a shaking hand, loosening its hold. The damp bedclothes made him shiver. His throat was raw, and he knew he must have screamed in his sleep, but no footsteps could be heard running towards his chamber. He could feel the ache in his shoulder from the nail, and the pain in his chest where it had been ripped by a dragon's claws, but it was just the remnants of the dream. These wounds had long since healed.

Nearly thirty years had passed since that terrible day when Father was killed, and as a child Lleland had suffered from nightmares, waking sobbing night after night. As he learned to channel his fear and anger, the dreams had slowly subsided, and it had been a long time since the monster had shown itself. Something had brought the creature to the fore, and Lleland knew what it was. Drake. The dragon-slayer. He was surprised he hadn't immediately recognized the name, since it was a Drake that had killed the beast. Lleland had never met the dragon-slayer, but when he ran his sword through the heart of the creature, killing him and ridding the city of the monster, his name had been on everyone's lips, passed along the streets and around the marketplace, until even the smallest child could name their savior. Aaron Drake.

Lleland lay back against the quilt, trying to recover his breath. The latch on his window rattled as the wind blew against the glass panes. The new moon cast little light, and outside the window the sky was a relentless sea of black. Lleland stared into the darkness as his heart finally slowed its frantic beating, and the nausea in his belly began to subside.

CHAPTER TWO

Lleland peered through the mist, narrowing his eyes as he focused on the painted post a hundred paces away. The sun had not yet risen, making it harder to see the four-inch-wide marker. He shifted his hand on the grip of his longbow and pulled the string back to his cheek, keeping the arrow loose between his fingers. The bow, made from the finest quality yew, resisted the draw, but Lleland had spent years training on this weapon, and his muscles easily overcame the bow's resistance. He closed his eyes and shifted slightly to account for the faint stirring of a breeze, before opening his eyes again and letting his arrow fly. He reached for another and nocked it on the string, releasing it as the first found its mark. Six arrows sprang from the bow, and six soft thuds were heard as they hit the wooden stake. Lleland strode forward to examine his work, and grunted when he saw the six arrows in the post. Five were clustered around the thin red line that cut across the wood, but the sixth had hit near the base, away from the others. Lleland collected the arrows and measured out a hundred and fifty paces. On the horizon a faint smudge of light was growing, but cloud blotted out the sun, draining the color from the dawn landscape. The ground beneath

Lleland's boots was slick from the rain that had fallen overnight, and his breath hung in the cool damp air.

It was Sunday morning, the one day of the week that staff and students were free to follow their own pursuits following the pre-dawn service in the college chapel. Lleland had left the city and headed into the countryside, where the wide open fields provided an ideal place to hone his skill with the bow. The field and the forest which bordered it were all crown land, but commoners were tolerated, as long as they refrained from poaching, and other archers used the land to practise their skills as well. But on this silent dawn Lleland was alone, the distant church bells tolling the hour the only sound.

The first time Lleland had picked up a bow and arrow was just a year after his father's death. It had been nothing more than a child's toy, but with childish determination he had taught himself how to use the simple weapon. Each day, following his chores, he took his little bow and the sharpened sticks that served as arrows, and made his way to the green in front of the church where he tormented the cheeky squirrels and noisy blackbirds, using them as targets. Other neighborhood children had joined him at first, but they soon wearied of the game and wandered away, leaving Lleland alone. He didn't mind – serious and determined, he wasn't interested in the games of other children, and he grew used to his own company. Even Mother was too busy and weary to give him more than cursory attention. Only little Edith, barely more than a toddler, stayed with him, happy to play in the mud while he followed his own pursuits.

For the most part, the adults who hurried past the green gave Lleland little attention, but there was one man who would pause in his passage and watch young Lleland for a moment before continuing on his way. The man was not known to him, and Lleland paid no attention to this silent witness of his progress. Almost a year had passed when the man first approached him.

"Hey lad." The man towered over Lleland, with broad shoulders and arms as thick as beams. "That's a mighty small bow you have there. What do you plan to do with it?"

Lleland turned and stared defiantly at the man. "I'm going to be an archer!"

"Planning on going to war, are you?" the man said with a chuckle.

"No! I'm going to kill some dragons."

The man was standing before the sun, and Lleland did not see the change in his expression, but he noticed the man's form suddenly stiffen. "Dragons, eh? Not easy creatures to kill. Many have tried, but few have succeeded."

"Aaron Drake killed a dragon."

The man nodded. "So he did." He took a step closer. "You're going to need something bigger than that little bow if you want to follow in his footsteps. You need a longbow."

"A longbow?"

"Aye. But you'll need to build some strength in that puny chest of yours. I can help you, if you want."

"You'll teach me to use a longbow?" Longbows were huge weapons, as tall as a man, made with the strongest wood in the forest. It took a massive amount of strength to draw one – strength that took years to build.

"I will lad, as long as you're prepared to do all I tell you, and not question my methods. Think you can do that?"

"Yes," Lleland breathed.

"You'll also have to work at it every day. I can show you what to do, but you must practice whenever you find a few spare moments."

Lleland was astounded. "But I can't use a longbow at home!"

The man laughed. "You're not going to. Using the bow will only come after many years. In the meantime you need to build those muscles."

"How?"

"With this." The man held his staff towards Lleland.

"This is a quarterstaff. You're going to learn to fight with your own."

"With a stick?" Lleland said scornfully.

"In the right hands this stick can become a dangerous weapon, lad. It'll also build your strength so you can use a longbow. Are you prepared to learn with this, or am I wasting my time with you?"

Lleland stared at the man, then back at the staff in his hand. It was an inch and a half thick, straight as an arrow and taller than Lleland. "That will help me kill dragons?"

"If you work hard and train diligently."

Lleland thought about that for a moment. "All right."

The man ruffled the top of Lleland's head. "Good lad," he said. "My name's Grimald. You can call me Grim."

Grim lived outside of the city, in a small stone cottage in the center of the woods. As King's Verderer, he looked after the forest, cutting back deadwood, counting the herds of deer that ranged through the forest, and tracking down poachers. The next day, Grim sought and gained the permission of Lleland's mother to take him beyond the city gates for a few hours. When they reached the forest, he instructed the lad to help him find branches that would be suitable as a quarterstaff.

"About one inch thick, five feet long and as straight as a line," he said.

It had taken most of the morning, but eventually they had found three that satisfied Grim. "We'll strap them together to straighten them," Grim explained, "and they must dry out. In the meantime you can help me build a fence." Lleland had started to protest, but one look from Grim made him hold his tongue.

And so it was that each day, Lleland left the city and hurried to the cottage in the forest. For six weeks he dug, sawed and hammered the posts of a new fence, until one day Grim deemed that the rods they had collected were dry enough to be unbound. Lleland watched as Grim carefully removed the straps and inspected each staff, discarding one as too bent and a second as too brittle. The third, however, met with approval, and he handed it to Lleland, who received it as though it was the most precious item in the world. Bidding Lleland rise, he showed the boy how to balance the weight of the staff on his open hand, and the next stage of training began.

Day after day, Lleland had to balance the staff on his open palm as he twisted from his waist and slowly turned this way and that. The twist became a full rotation which increased in speed as he learned to maintain the balance of the staff. When Lleland was able to bend and circle without dropping his rod, Grim showed him how to place one hand at the quarter mark, the other at the half mark, and using the strength of his arms and momentum of the staff, turn it into a dangerous weapon. For hour upon hour he spun, hit and parried against his mortal enemy, the tree stump. More than a year passed before Grim deemed him ready to progress to a longbow. Lleland had chafed against the delay, but when Grim handed him his first longbow, made to his size, he was able to draw back the string without his muscles trembling at the effort.

When Lleland was twelve, Grim left to go to war. It was eighteen months before he returned, dirty and unkempt.

"I was taken by King Terran," Grim explained when Lleland asked why he had been gone so long. The war had ended almost a year before, with the death of King Alfred.

"You were captured?"

"I was."

"Were you locked in a dungeon?"

Grim looked amused. "No. I was set to rebuilding one of the town walls destroyed by our army. I'd still be there now, but found a way to escape. That was just the start of my problems, however, since I had to avoid the patrols that roamed the countryside. I would've been back months ago if I could've taken the road. Instead, I skirted through forests and across the mountains, until I finally reached home."

"What was it like, fighting a war?" Lleland wanted to know. "I heard Terran's men are cruel and vicious."

But Grim had shaken his head. "They're men, like you and me," he said. Lleland frowned as he considered that. "There were plenty of skirmishes," Grim continued, "but the two armies only faced each other a few times before the king and his brother were both dead."

"Was the king killed in battle?"

"Assassinated. They say it was done by Terran, but there are others who whisper that the king was killed by his own brother."

"Prince Rupert? Why?"

"No idea, lad. And I don't suppose we'll ever learn the truth of the matter, so there's no point wondering." He picked up his staff. "Now show me you haven't forgotten how to use this."

At the age of thirteen, Lleland could hit a target at sixty yards, pulling the bow taut against his cheek. At fifteen, his range had increased to a hundred and thirty yards, and by the time he was eighteen, he could hit his target at two hundred and fifty yards, matching Grim's range.

"Why do you want to kill dragons?" Grim had asked Lleland one day. They were sitting outside the cottage, stripping branches to make new arrows. Grim lifted one to his eye and squinted down the shaft as he waited for Lleland's reply.

Lleland bit his lip to stop his sudden trembling, his gaze on the ground. "You know my father was killed by a dragon," he said.

"Aye." Grim was silent a moment. "My niece was killed by the monster, too."

"Your niece? I didn't know that!"

"She was only eleven years of age. She was my sister's, and I loved her like my own."

Lleland stared at him. "How can you be so calm? Don't

you want to kill the monsters?"

Grim glanced up at him, then returned his attention to the arrow he was examining. "Aye, I do. But what good will wishing do?"

Lleland threw down his own arrow and started pacing. "You might not care, but *I* want to kill every single dragon that dares to walk our land. That ... that monster," he spat, "killed my father, and then made me watch as it ripped him apart. Even when I looked away, I could hear everything!" Turning to the bench, he kicked it violently, sending it flying. "It should have been me that killed that beast."

Grim nodded. "You'll have your chance. But not like this."

"Not like this? What does that mean?" Lleland's voice rose. "I'm training every day! Honing my strength! I listen to your instructions and do as you say, and now you tell me 'not like this!'"

Grim placed the arrow he was sharpening on the ground and looked up at Lleland. "Get your staff."

"What?"

"Get your staff." Grim rose to his feet and stalked towards Lleland. "Show me how ready you are to kill the dragon."

Lleland's staff was leaning against the wall of the cottage, and he seized it in his hand as Grim tightened his grip on his own.

"Why do you hate dragons?" Grim said. He brought up his staff. "You say you're going to kill them, but you're like a child, kicking the bench in a fit of anger. What good will that do when you're faced with a dragon?"

"I'm not a child!" Lleland lifted his staff. "I'll kill every dragon I see."

"Show me. Show me how you'll kill the monsters."

"Like this," Lleland yelled. He pulled back his arm and swung at Grim.

Grim stepped back easily. "Why do you want to kill

dragons?"

"Because a dragon killed my father," Lleland shouted, swinging the staff above his head and dropping down low, aiming for Grim's legs. Grim spun out of the way.

"Killed your father, like they did my Liza. The monster ripped them apart, didn't it?"

"Yes!" Lleland leaped forward, twisting the staff through the air and bringing it down towards Grim's back. Grim dropped to his haunches and met the blow.

"The monster ripped them apart then ate them limb by limb, didn't it?" Grim panted slightly, but his voice was calm.

"Yes!" Lleland screamed. "I hate dragons and will kill them all!" He struck again, and Grim's staff slid beneath his raised arm, striking him on the ribs. He fell back, then lunged once more. His staff connected forcefully with Grim's, slipped from his grasp and went sailing through the air. He ran towards it, but was caught short when Grim blocked his path.

"What are you doing?" Lleland spat.

"You're filled with anger, lad, and anger can be a good friend or a bad enemy. At the moment, it's your enemy, controlling you. At the moment your anger makes you as effective against a dragon as a maid would be. You must learn to control it so it can become your friend." He pointed at Lleland's staff lying on the ground. "You lost your staff, and I landed a blow on your ribs that you easily should have parried. But you were blinded by your rage."

Lleland ran his fingers over his chest, feeling his ribs. "That was painful," he said.

Grim grinned. "Of course it was." He placed his staff against the wall and sat down, picking up the arrow he had been working on. "It isn't physical prowess that'll enable you to kill a dragon, lad. Many have tried and failed. It's what's up here that matters." Grim tapped his forehead with one end of the half-finished arrow. "Dragons are wily and shrewd – as clever as any hunter. You must be focused and smart so you can outwit them. Only then do you stand a chance of success. Use your anger as a tool. As you train, raise the staff in your hand and think about what you wish to fight. Imagine your enemy. Tell yourself how much you hate it. Think about it ripping your father apart. Don't push the memories away. Embrace them until they no longer have the power to hurt you." Grim ran a finger down the shaft of the arrow, then laid it on the bench. "Let your anger motivate you," he continued, "but don't let it control you. And then imagine yourself killing the dragon, calmly and intentionally. Consider how you'll evaluate your enemy and discover its weaknesses. Think about the people who'll be saved when the monster is dead. Think about the love you had for your father. And face the dragon."

Lleland fell onto the bench and dropped his head in his hands. "I don't think I can."

"You can," Grim said. "You must. Or find a new goal. Because you'll never succeed if you cannot control what you feel."

Lleland remembered the lesson now as he notched another arrow. He closed his eyes for a moment and allowed the pain which was never far away to wash over him. The memory of his father pleading for his life made his eyes sting, and his stomach clenched at the horror of his death. He breathed in deeply, then slowly exhaled, gathering the pain into a cold shaft of anger. He opened his eyes and released the arrow. He glanced at the post. A perfect shot.

The memories of Grim continued to race through Lleland's mind as he sent his arrows to their target. It was because of Grim that he'd become so skilled with the bow, but he probably wouldn't even have picked up the weapon if Father had not been killed by a dragon. Instead, he would have followed in his footsteps and at the age of thirteen, apprenticed as a mason. Father had been a Master Mason, and his skills had been well sought after. He would have ensured that Lleland received the best possible training.

Lleland had watched as the neighborhood boys started their life in trade, sullenly trailing after their fathers each morning. Would he have been that reluctant to learn, he wondered? Occasionally a father and son would walk by in animated conversation, and Lleland would feel envy well up as the father ruffled his boy's hair, or laid a hand on his shoulder. A knot would form in his stomach as he was reminded, yet again, that he would never again experience the affection of his father, and his hand would tighten around the staff that he always kept near until it ached.

The sun was rising behind the blanket of cloud, but it did little to dispel the mist and gloom. Lleland shot the last arrow in his quiver, watching with satisfaction as it hit the mark, before collecting and carefully stowing them so as not to damage the fletchings. As he walked across the open field in the direction of the city gate, he glanced over his shoulder, imagining Grim standing beneath the trees. He had last seen him five years before. Grim had been shot by a poacher, and the wound had turned septic, poisoning the blood. He had died slowly and painfully, and Lleland had sat at his bedside for much of the time. In the last day he had drifted in and out of consciousness, but before he fell asleep for the last time, he had beckoned Lleland to come closer.

"Keep a hold of your anger," he rasped. He fell back against the pillows for a moment, but when Lleland started to speak, he held up his hand feebly. "It must serve both of us, now. Allow it to lead you to the monsters, and then kill them all. I'm counting on you."

CHAPTER THREE

Lleland strode across the cobbled street and turned into the mirey lane that ran alongside the river and past the docks. His destination was the home of his mother, Anabel Seaton. Lleland and his sister Edith had both been born in the narrow townhouse on Tottley Alley, and when Father died, Anabel had refused to leave, insisting she could find a way to earn the rent money, until finally the landlord relented and allowed her to stay.

Widowed in her late twenties, she was still a pretty woman when Father died, and more than one man had sought her hand. But despite being in the tenuous position of having to earn her own keep and support two young children, she had refused all offers. Instead, she took in mending and sewing jobs, often working long hours by the dim light of a single candle to earn a few pennies. It had been just enough to keep the landlord satisfied and hunger at bay, but the hard work had taken its toll on Anabel. Nowadays it was Lleland who paid the rent from the meager income he earned at the university, and his hunting skills put food on her table.

As Lleland rounded the corner into Tottley Alley, he saw Anabel hurrying from the opposite direction in her best

Sunday gown, her hand on her head to keep her veil secure. Her hand flew to her mouth when she caught sight of him, and he smiled wryly when she hastened her step.

"Oh, dear!" she said. "You're here already. Martha Turham would not stop talking, even when I told her I had to make haste." She glanced down the road. "And Edith will be here soon, too, with a brood of hungry children."

"Stop fretting, Mother," Lleland said gently.

"I'm not fretting!" She glanced up at him. "But the dinner is probably ruined! I told Eve to tend to it while I was gone, but she can be so careless!"

"The dinner will be fine," Lleland said, linking his arm into hers and leading her towards the door. Eve, the serving maid who helped Anabel with the household chores, was quite capable of handling the meal. In her mid-twenties, she had ably served Anabel for the past ten years.

"Yes, yes, of course. But the children will be here soon, and I wanted everything ready and I slept so poorly last night …" She quickly covered her mouth with her hand as she turned anxious eyes towards Lleland.

"You couldn't sleep?" Lleland could see the signs of her troubled night – red rimmed eyes, and dark rings beneath.

Anabel looked away. "Just restless. Don't worry about me, dear."

"Are you having bad dreams again?"

They reached the door, and Anabel pulled her arm from Lleland's as she stepped into the house. "I need to check the dinner. Edith will be here soon. I'm surprised she isn't already!"

Lleland watched as she bustled into the kitchen, undoing the ties of her cloak as she went. She disappeared into a haze of steam as Lleland turned towards the parlor.

In the corner was a small table with a single book. It had been Father's, and there wasn't a day that went by when Anabel did not sit down with it and carefully open the page to where Father had written the names of their children. She couldn't read the letters, but she knew which name was which.

Lleland opened the book and examined his father's writing, as he had many times before. Each letter had been carefully written by someone unused to holding a pen. But Father had been able to read and write, and Lleland could remember sitting at his feet, listening to him recite from this one precious volume. It was a rare thing to possess a book, and little Lleland had thought his father owned the only one in the entire world. It wasn't until after Father's death, when he stumbled upon the Abbey library, that he realized that wasn't the case. He smiled at the recollection.

Mother had sent him to the Abbey to deliver a package, and he had come across Brother Amos sitting at a desk, lit by a single candle, writing with a quill. He had stared at the shelves of books that lined the room, before turning his gaze on the man as he scratched his markings on a piece of parchment. He watched for a few minutes until Brother Amos finally lifted his head from the sheet and noticed him for the first time.

"Ah, Lleland, is it? Do you want to see what I'm doing?" Lleland nodded, and walked hesitantly to the man's side. "I'm writing down words," Brother Amos continued. "Do you know what words are?"

Lleland frowned. His mother sometimes spoke about right words and wrong words. "Things we say," he finally replied.

"Correct. Look, each word is spelled with letters. And each letter has a name. G. O. D. God. When you join the letters, and then the words, you have a story." He pointed out more letters, naming each one, then joined them to form each word. "Was; word; in; sun; moon."

Lleland frowned as Brother Amos spoke, then pointed to another word. "M ... ma." His eyes were screwed in concentration. "Man."

"Yes!" Brother Amos beamed. "You're a quick learner!

How old are you, boy?"

"Nine."

"Nine, hmm? Very good. Now give me your package and run along home."

Lleland did as he was told, and forgot about the incident until two days later when Brother Amos appeared at their door. "Brother Amos, what a surprise!" Mother wiped her hands nervously on her apron as she gestured for the man to enter. "Can I offer you some wine?"

"No, Mistress, but thank you. I wish to speak to you about your son."

"Lleland?" Mother's eyes darted to where he stood in the corner. "What's he done?"

"He hasn't done anything, Mistress. But I've noticed that he's a bright young lad. What are your plans for his future?"

Mother pulled back slightly in surprise. "His future? Well … I … I suppose he'll become a mason like his father."

"If your husband still lived, Mistress, that would almost certainly be the case. But who will train him? Do you know someone who will take him on as an apprentice?" He leaned forward. "Without his father, his opportunities are limited, Mistress. I'm sorry to distress you, but you must see the truth of what I'm saying."

Lleland saw with surprise that tears were gathering in Mother's eyes. He stepped forward. "Don't worry, Mother," he said. "I'm going to be an archer."

"An archer, eh?" said Brother Amos, leaning back in his seat. "And what will you fight?"

"Dragons," Lleland said. Anabel drew in a shuddering breath.

"No," she whispered. "Brother Amos is right. You need a future." She turned back to the priest. "What are you suggesting?"

"Every year the Abbey sponsors the education of boys that are intelligent and eager to learn. I believe Lleland would be an excellent candidate. We will teach him his numbers and letters, and if he chooses to continue his studies beyond that, we will provide him the opportunity to do so."

"He'll learn to read and write?"

"Yes! And more besides."

"I don't want to go to school!" Lleland had seen the long faces of the boys that trudged their way to the Abbey each morning. "I want to fight!"

"You'll do as you're told!" Anabel said. She turned back to the priest. "Can I think on it?"

"Of course! But don't take too long – there are other boys that would welcome such an opportunity."

"Father wouldn't send me to school!" Lleland shouted as soon Brother Amos left the house.

"Your father spent three years at school," Anabel said sharply. "Where do you think he learned to read and write? And Brother Amos is right, without some learning, you have no future."

"But –"

"Not another word, Lleland."

Anabel had made her decision by the next morning, and Lleland was sent to the Abbey to give Brother Amos the news. He didn't dare disobey Mother, but he scowled as he walked, kicking the stones along the dusty road. If only Father was alive, things would have been different.

The first few months of school had been torturous for Lleland. The restrictions of the classroom chafed his spirit, and many were the days when he stared out the window, longing for the freedom to roam as he chose. As he walked to class each morning he carried his staff, and leaping from rocks and fences, fought against an imaginary foe; in the evenings, when his mother finally released him from chores, he rushed to the green to practise. The days when there was no school were spent with Grim, trailing him through the forest, or improving his skill with the bow.

But as the months passed, the letters Lleland had to learn by rote began to take on new meaning as they formed words, and then sentences. Ideas leaped from the page, leading to new thoughts, and soon Lleland was devouring the books housed in the Abbey library as though his life depended on them. Religious writings, as well as the work of Aristotle, Socrates and Plato, broadened his mind, and like a sponge, he wanted more. He learned about the celestial beings and earthly creatures, and studied algebra and geometry. He read in amazement about strange and wondrous beasts, unseen in the civilized world – animals with two heads, pygmies that walked on their hands, monsters of the deep that swallowed whole ships, and sirens that lured sailors to their deaths. When he wasn't training his body to kill, he studied maps and trade routes plied by merchants as they skirted the end of the world, and when he was old enough, went to taverns that sailors were known to frequent to discover what he could about the lands that lay beyond his own. The sailors, coarse and ill-spoken as they were, spoke of realms filled with spices that kings were willing to give gold to acquire; lands where vines covered the hillsides, warmed by the sun all year long; places held in the grip of winter, no matter the season. Lleland eagerly recorded the accounts in his daybook, rereading them time and again; and at night, when he fell asleep, his body exhausted from its vigorous training and his mind spinning with new ideas, he had dreamt of these faraway places, of sailing across the oceans and seeing all the world's marvels. He jealously watched the birds in the forest leaving for warmer climes each autumn, and when they returned in the spring, he wondered what they had seen on their travels. Had they tasted the sweet nectar of fragrant islands or seen the leviathan of the deep? Did they know how fortunate they were that they had wings to fly?

His thirst for learning grew and expanded. As an adult, Lleland spent time traveling the southern reaches of the kingdom. He explored the coastal regions and fishing villages that dotted the shoreline, and marveled at the architectural wonders in the towns. He discovered artifacts left behind by ancient invaders, and traced his fingers over ruined walls, built hundreds of years before – a reminder of what had been. The scraps of knowledge that he gained left him craving more, and he expanded his travels to the west and east of the city. The only area still undiscovered was the north, where the Northern Mountains dominated both life and the landscape.

The sound of children's laughter pulled Lleland from his musings, and he replaced the book on the table before rising to greet his sister and her family. When Father had died, Edith was just a toddler, and as the years passed, she had served as the perfect recipient for his superior wisdom and knowledge. Her willingness to sit at her brother's feet had waned as the years passed, however, until her companions were other girls her age, whose ambitions in life were simple – to marry, manage a home and raise a family. She had accepted Alan's proposal of marriage when she was seventeen, and despite his being nearly twice her age, the marriage had been happy and fruitful.

Edith and Alan had been in the house for just a few minutes when Eve announced that dinner was served. By the standards of simple folk it was a feast – roast pheasant, baked turnips and spiced bread. None of it was burned, as Anabel had feared, and the bird was turned to perfection.

"Did you hear that Queen Matilda has taken another playwright under her wing?" Lleland said as Eve cleared away the plates. He caught her eye and smiled, and she blushed as she bustled from the room.

Edith kicked Lleland beneath the table. "None of us can possibly keep up with her favorites," she said. She turned to Anabel. "Did you hear about the latest scandal involving Denton, Mother? He's been insisting …" she paused. "Mother, are you listening?"

"What's that, dear?"

Edith shot Lleland a glance as Eve returned to the room, placing a tray of small desserts on the table.

"What about the spiced figs?" Anabel said.

"Spiced figs, mum? You said nothing about figs today, mum."

"I didn't? I must have forgotten." Her brow was furrowed. "Bring the mulled wine, then."

"Yes, mum."

Lleland watched as Eve left the room, then turned to his mother. "What's wrong, Mother?"

"Wrong? Nothing's wrong!"

"You're distracted."

"I'm not." Anabel gave a little laugh. "No, no, just a little tired. The wind kept me up last night."

Eve returned with the wine, and Lleland allowed the matter to drop. The meal ended and they retired to the parlor as the children went outside to play, leaving the adults to their conversation. The afternoon waned, and as the light began to fail, Edith gathered up her brood.

"Are you leaving, too?" she asked Lleland as Alan lifted her cloak around her shoulders.

"I'll stay a little longer," Lleland replied, placing a kiss on Edith's cheek. She smiled, and with a wave to her mother, left the house on Alan's arm. Lleland poured himself another glass of wine and took a seat in the parlor across from Anabel.

"What's wrong, Mother?" he said. "You didn't give me an answer when I asked if you were having bad dreams."

Anabel looked down at her hands, folded in her lap. "They started about a week ago." Lleland leaned back in his chair with a frown. After Father's death, Anabel's peace had been fragile. The loss of tranquility was always accompanied by vivid and terrifying dreams. Monsters stalked her nights and stole her rest.

"Why?" he asked gently.

The light caught the unshed tears in her eyes. "Your Father and I would have celebrated forty years last week," she said. "I suppose he's been in my thoughts more than usual." She sighed. "I miss him so much, even after all this time. We should have grown old together." Lleland's jaw clenched and his eyes narrowed. The dragon had not just taken Father's life, it had robbed Anabel of the love and support of a husband, and left himself and Edith without a parent.

"The dragon is dead," he said. "Don't give it the power to steal your peace."

"Something's going to happen, son. I can feel it in my bones."

"Nothing's going to happen," Lleland said.

"Please, Lleland, stay away from the dragons. I know how much you long for vengeance, but I cannot lose another I love to one of those beasts."

Lleland sighed. "I'll take great care to preserve my life to a ripe old age," he said. "Please stop this fretting." He patted her hand. "I must go, Mother, or I'll not be fit to teach anyone tomorrow."

She pressed her lips together and looked away. He watched her for a moment, then leaning down, kissed her cheek. "I'll see you soon," he said, before striding out the door.

CHAPTER FOUR

Lleland was eighteen when he killed his first dragon. It had been more chance than skill, but it had set his heart racing and fire spilling through his veins.

It had been late October, a beautiful autumnal day. The sky was a brilliant turquoise, and the leaves glowed in bright hues of red and orange. Lleland and Grim had left the city early that morning to travel into the hill country. On a fast mount, the distance could be covered in a couple of hours, and Grim had allowed Lleland to ride one of the hunters in the forest stables, kept there for the king's hunting parties. As chief verderer, it was up to Grim to ensure the horses were always ready for the hunt, and that the hunters found their game. He had received no formal education, and his skills in reading and writing were rudimentary, but there was nothing about the forest Grim did not know. He could name every plant and bird within the 20,000-hectare forest, and track an animal through any terrain. He knew where each herd of deer was currently grazing, and noted those that were sick and injured. He could point out fox lairs and badger dens, and could name the birds in the forest by their calls. He had never married, preferring the quiet solitude of the forest, and seldom went into the city, except to deliver a monthly report to the king's steward. It had been in pursuit of that task that he had first seen Lleland with his bow.

It was mid-morning when Grim and Lleland reached the rolling hills. They didn't stop, but pushed their way through the valleys until Grim finally called a halt on the banks of a river. The water was sluggish, as though preparing for the cold that would soon spread its icy fingers and freeze it into place. Rocks were strewn across the river bed, some rising above the level of the water. As always, Lleland carried his weapons. They had become an extension of him, and whenever he left the city, his bow was in his hand and his sword at his side. Both he and Grim also carried a staff, and Grim led Lleland into the river. "Come lad," he said, "show me how well you can fight on a slick, uneven surface!" Lleland followed as Grim sprang from rock to rock until they stood facing each other in the middle of the waterway, their staves extended.

"I'll show you, old man," Lleland replied with a grin. He lifted his rod and struck it tentatively against Grim's, gaining his balance as Grim blocked the blow. Lleland's next swing was more forceful, and the sparring increased in speed as both men parried and attacked as they hopped between the rocks. Some of the boulders swayed beneath Lleland's feet, and he had to concentrate to keep his balance as he avoided Grim's blows. The game ended when Lleland fell into the river, gasping as the cold water drenched him. His clothes were sopping wet, and he stood for a moment, dripping as Grim laughed.

"Take a hike up the hill, lad," he said. "That'll dry you out." Grim lay down on the sunny bank of grass and closed his eyes. Leaving his sword and staff, Lleland grabbed his bow and arrows and headed up the slope. By the time he reached the summit, his clothes were damp rather than dripping, and a sheen of sweat had built up on his brow. The hill was not high, and he could see Grim lying on the grass below. He turned to view the panorama that unfolded before him. Hills spread into the distance, like a wrinkled piece of cloth. A movement caught his eye, and he turned to see something circling high above. His first thought was that it was an eagle, but as Lleland watched, the creature turned and the sun glanced off shining scales. His heart started to race, and he dropped to his haunches behind a rock, keeping his eye fixed on the creature above.

With as much stealth as possible, Lleland strung his bow and notched an arrow. The dragon dropped a little lower, and he could see that it was not as big as the one that had killed his father. It also wasn't black, but rather a dark, rust color. It circled lower, and Lleland drew the bow tight against his ear, holding the weapon steady. He aimed his bow at the creature's chest and waited for a chance to release the barb. The dragon swept closer, and Lleland closed one eye. He judged the creature to be only two hundred yards away. He waited another moment, then released the arrow. It sang as it leaped off the string, flying straight and sure. The beast turned towards the shooting barb as it whistled through the air, and the breath caught in Lleland's throat. The arrow was going to miss its mark! But fate was guiding the arrow, and it struck the creature at the point where the wing met the huge body. It sank in, and a stream of flame escaped the dragon's mouth. The arrow in its side had rendered the wing useless, and it fell towards the earth as Lleland watched, open mouthed. Just yards from where Lleland still crouched behind the rock the dragon crashed into the ground, making the earth tremble. Dust, grass and bits of rock flew into the air in every direction. Lleland whipped out another arrow as the dragon lifted its head and looked straight at him. Its eyes were blazing, and it roared in pain and frustration as it rose to its feet. It snapped at the arrow in its side with its massive jaws, and Lleland notched the second arrow. He drew back the string as the dragon's tail swung through the air, narrowly missing him, then released it and watched as the iron tip sank into the dragon's leathery chest. It fell back to the ground with a stream of flame, and using its talons, clawed at the arrow that protruded beneath its heart.

"Kill it, lad!" Grim's voice came from behind, and Lleland turned, startled. "Now!" Grim yelled. "Before it kills you." Swinging back, Lleland pulled out another arrow. He notched, drew and released in one smooth movement, aiming a little higher than before. The arrow found its mark, and the dragon twisted on the ground. It turned to look at Lleland, and he could see the light dimming in its eyes.

"Why?" the creature whispered. A few sparks fluttered from its mouth. "I did nothing to you."

"You killed my father," Lleland said as Grim ran past him and plunged his sword into the creature's chest, burying the blade to the hilt. The light in the creature's eyes dulled, and then it was still.

"Well done, lad," Grim said. His voice was exultant. "You killed your first dragon." He walked around the beast, poking it with his foot. "Think how many lives you saved today." He took a hunting knife from his waistband and held it out to Lleland. "Take yourself a trophy."

Lleland looked at the knife, then back at the huge beast lying dead on the ground. The dragon was a monster that would surely have killed him, if he had not killed it first. He had done the right thing – ridded the world of a monster. He should be thrilled. But instead he felt empty and dull, as though the light that had faded in the creature's eyes had somehow cast his own soul into shadow. He pushed the knife away. "I don't want anything," he said, before turning and heading down the hill without a backward glance.

It was dark as Lleland walked along the narrow alleys and lanes back to the university. Anabel had always hated the thought of him hunting dragons. As a boy, he had hoped she would be pleased at his determination to rid the world of the beasts that had killed Father, but instead, his intentions had filled her with dread. She'd pleaded with him to put aside thoughts of revenge, but it was impossible to acquiesce to her demands. He'd not been able to stop the dragon that killed Father, but he would do all he could to ensure that others were safe from the monsters. He wondered what Father would have said about the matter. As a youth, he imagined his father's words: "Well done, lad," he would have said. "I'm proud of you." Father, he was sure, would have approved.

The fight was not easy, though. His first kill had been due to luck rather than skill, and most dragons were too wily and cunning to be defeated so easily. Further hampering the efforts was the fact that these days sightings around the city were few and far between. Even when dragons were spotted, only a very few in the city had the skills and training to conquer such beasts, and the dragons were rarely defeated. It amazed Lleland that God would endow such terrible creatures with so many advantages – speed, strength, flight and flaming breath. There was the occasional success, of course, and Lleland himself had killed three dragons in the last dozen years. The second had been an old male, trapped in a cave. It had lacked the will to fight, and Lleland had easily sent an arrow through his tough, old heart. The third kill was the one Lleland remembered with the most pleasure. It had been a bitter fight to the end, and more than once, Lleland had narrowly escaped the burning breath of the creature racing through the air above him. It took a dozen arrows and a few swipes from his sword before the creature had finally breathed its last, fiery breath. Lleland did not escape easily, either – he had burns to his legs, a sprained wrist, a cracked skull and three broken ribs, but the wounds had healed within a matter of weeks. These victories seemed insignificant, however, in light of the many dragons that had escaped, and Lleland despaired that they would ever win the war against the vicious beasts.

To make matters even more difficult, as dragon sightings

lessened, so had the fear of the people. Few remembered the horror that had gripped the city when the black dragon had attacked and killed its citizens. And with no new reports of missing maidens, they forgot that dragons were monsters of hell. But Lleland knew that it was just a matter of time before dragons once more emerged from their hidden lairs and started attacking humans. What frustrated him most, though, was the lack of knowledge about the beasts. Who knew how long the creatures lived, or where they kept their lairs? No-one had ever seen a baby dragon, so where did they keep their young? Did they grow in the swamps and emerge fully formed, or were they nurtured by their dragon mothers?

A cold wind had picked up during the afternoon, and Lleland pulled his cloak tighter around his chest as he pondered the questions that plagued him. There was only one person who might have the answers, but that one person was almost as elusive as the dragons. Aaron Drake had revealed none of his knowledge over the years. But now Zachary Drake was in Lleland's class. Perhaps fate was lending a hand.

The sound of laughter spilling onto the street interrupted Lleland's musings, and he stopped outside the door of a crowded tavern, left open to allow fresh air to pass into the smoky interior. A group of students was gathered around a table, shouting and laughing, and Lleland recognized some from his class. A tawny head, towering over the others, caught his attention, and he watched as Zach Drake laughed at something. Standing with his fellow students, his strength and power were even more evident than in the classroom, and Lleland shivered, whether in anticipation or trepidation he wasn't sure. As he watched, Drake lifted his head and turned in Lleland's direction. Their gazes clashed, and Lleland drew in a sharp breath, as though he had been dealt a physical blow. Drake raised his eyebrows and inclined his head slightly towards an empty table in the corner, and Lleland nodded. Fate was definitely on his side.

CHAPTER FIVE

It was noisy in the tavern, and the air was heavy with smoke. The stench of tallow mingled with the smell of cooking, stale ale and unwashed bodies. Scraps of food and the shells of nuts littered the wooden floor, while a rat peeped through a crack in the wall, its nose twitching as it eyed a precious morsel. A cat, its gleaming coat catching the light of the fire, crouched in the corner and watched the rodent intently.

Lleland ducked under the age-darkened timber beams as he made his way between the crowds towards the table where Drake was taking a seat. The wooden surface was marred with gouges, made over the years by those wanting to leave a permanent mark of their passing, and worn to varying degrees of smoothness. Lleland glanced down as he ran his hand over the deeper scratches, his fingers quickly finding the mark he had made more than fifteen years earlier when he had frequented the tavern as a student.

"Are you weary of your friends?" he asked.

Drake raised his eyebrows and grinned. "Would I be revealing too much if I said they can no longer converse in Latin?"

Lleland snorted in amusement. "I'm not surprised," he

said. "Like dogs let off a leash."

A pair of mugs were slammed onto the table by an elderly crone. A few strands of greasy, gray hair escaped her cap, and she pushed it aside with dirty fingers as she cast a toothless leer in Drake's direction. "'Ere you go, luv. Give us a kiss, an' you can 'ave it for nuffin." She leaned closer, but instead of pulling away, Drake leaned forward and planted a kiss on her puckered lips. Her eyebrows flew up and she drew back. "Ay, wot's this? Why you so 'ot?" She eyed Drake suspiciously. "You got a fever! Trying to kill me or sumffin?"

Drake laughed. "I was standing by the fire, Mistress. And a student needs all the free drinks he can get." He gave her a shameless grin as she scowled and marched away.

"She might be the one with something catching," Lleland said, lifting the mug to his lips. The ale was tepid and stale, but it warmed his belly after the cold outside. "She's been offering free drinks in exchange for a kiss since my student days. It appears nothing's changed!"

"I have a strong constitution," Drake replied. He took a drink of ale. "Have you always lived in Civitas?"

"Born and bred. You?"

"I grew up in the Northern Mountains, although I spent a fair amount of time around the city when I was growing up."

"The Northern Mountains? You're a long way from home. From what I've heard, it's very remote."

Drake shrugged. "We enjoy our privacy."

"Yes, so I've heard!" Drake looked at Lleland in surprise. "You have your own chambers, don't you?"

"Ah!" Drake leaned back in his seat and crossed his arms. "So I do."

Lleland waited for Drake to offer more, but he was silent. "Do you fence?" he asked.

"I've had a little training. Why do you ask? Are you a fencing Master as well as Master of Philosophy?"

Lleland smiled. "No. But it seems to me that you are

skilled in the art of weaponry. Perhaps you'd like to cross swords with me some time."

"Are you challenging me to a duel, Master Seaton? Would it be in my best interests as your student to accept or decline?"

Lleland laughed. "When we step on the field, I'll no longer be your Master. But I'm not challenging you to a duel. There are few opportunities for me to practise with someone with skill."

"You're assuming I'm skilled with a blade?"

Lleland answered slowly. "I am. In fact, I think your form belies your strength." Drake's eyebrows lifted a fraction. "My preferred weapon is actually a longbow. Have you trained in archery?"

"A longbow? No." Drake leaned back in his seat. "So you're a scholar and an archer?"

Lleland shrugged and smiled wryly. "I suppose I am."

"What made you take up archery? I understand it takes years of committed training. Your studies must have left you with little time for such rigorous instruction."

"It started as a childish interest, but I enjoyed it. The strength and discipline of the sport suit me, and I was fortunate to have a skilled archer take me on as his pupil. I found that my bow and my books worked together to hone my mind and sharpen my intellect. And it's a useful skill to have when you travel as I do."

"You travel a lot?"

"I do. Like most scholars, I seek knowledge."

"What are your main areas of interest?"

"History. The study of people, and where they came from. The events that make them who they are. Everyone is shaped by events of the past, whether they be recent or distant."

"And what events shape you, Master Seaton?"

Lleland was silent for a moment. "The death of my father," he finally said. He glanced up at Drake, who was watching him intently.

"Was he an archer as well?"

"No. A mason. He died when I was a child."

"I'm sorry," Drake said.

"It was a long time ago." Lleland waved for another round of ale. "Do you have family in Civitas?"

"Not in Civitas, but thirty miles hence, near the hills."

"The hills? There used to be dragons in the hills."

Drake watched as the crone sloshed ale over to the table. "You have an interest in dragons?"

Lleland waited a moment before replying. "Nearly thirty years ago Civitas was attacked by a dragon. Perhaps you've heard the tales. It was killed by a man name Aaron Drake." He paused, waiting for a reaction from Zach, but received none. "Is he a relation?"

Drake stared into the fire. The light of the flames made his skin glow. "The dragon-slayer? You know him?"

"Just his name," Lleland said. "I was a boy when the black dragon attacked Civitas. It was before your time, but maybe you've heard tales of the hellish creature that wrought horror and destruction in our streets. They are monsters that sate their appetites with human flesh, and once they've killed, they continue to bring destruction with their blazing breath." His gaze wandered over to the fire, and he stared into the flames. "They lure you with their words, spoken in human tongue, but they're cunning and sly. I remember the beast that terrorized our streets, claiming its victims without care or concern for the misery it created." He pulled his gaze from the blaze. "Aaron Drake's name was celebrated through the streets, the one who conquered the beast and returned it to Hades."

Drake cocked his head. "Do you know how he did it?"

"He ran a sword through the monster's heart, then ripped it out with his bare hands." He paused a moment. "But you must know this story."

Drake shrugged. "As you said, it was before my time." He

threw back the last of his mug and rose to his feet. "Now if you'll excuse me, I have a hard taskmaster who expects me to read three more chapters of *Aristotelis De Caelo* before tomorrow." He grinned, and with a nod, headed towards the door. Lleland watched him leave with a frown. He seldom talked about the dragon, and never before had he spoken so freely to a student. There was something about young Drake that had loosened his tongue. It was only after Drake disappeared into the darkness that Lleland realized he had not answered his question.

CHAPTER SIX

"Philosophy is the study of truth," Lleland said, pacing the front of his classroom. It was the last day of class before the Christmas break. "Is it possible to know all truth? Socrates taught that the only knowledge is in knowing that you know nothing. And Aristotle suggested that it is impossible to know anything in its entirety." His eyes swept over his students. "What do you think?"

"It depends on whether the object being investigated is animate or inanimate," Dodds said.

"What do you mean?"

He held up a book. "I know the truth of this book. It is rectangular in shape. It has pages, filled with words. The cover is brown leather, and I can measure its dimensions. But it's harder to know the truth of a person."

"I agree," Drake said. "You might know a person as … a murderer, for example, but that person's mother knows him as a good son, while his lover knows yet another facet of him."

"What you say is true," Lleland said. "But what about moral truths. Is it wrong to lie?"

"Of course."

"What if the lie saves someone's life?" There was silence. "Consider the question while you're away," Lleland said, "and come prepared to discuss it more fully when you return. Class is dismissed."

The students filed past him, leaving Lleland alone in the room as he gathered his things. He was looking forward to a break from the classroom. There had been little free time in the past few weeks as he spent the evenings marking papers and exams. He had managed to squeeze in a few hours with Anabel each Sunday, knowing how she depended on his weekly visits. The nightmares had continued unabated, and she was looking worn and pale.

The mood was festive as Lleland made his way towards the hall late that afternoon for the evening meal. Some of the students had already left for the break, but most would leave the following morning to travel to their homes in the country. As always, there were some who would remain in their lodgings for the season, the distance home too far to travel in ten days. Lleland reached the bottom of the stairs and turned the corner, narrowly avoiding a collision with Drake.

"*Mea culpa, Magister*," Drake said, stepping back.

Lleland waved the apology away. "I wasn't looking where I was going." They fell into step as they walked along the passage. "Do you remain here during the festivities?" Lleland asked.

"No. My sister and I travel to family tomorrow."

"You have a sister in Civitas?"

"She's just here for a few days. We have a townhouse in the city, and she stays there." He paused for a moment. "I'll be joining her for the evening. Would you care to join us?"

Lleland stopped walking in surprise. "Join you? Well, uh …"

"Unless you have other plans, of course."

"No." Lleland continued down the passage. "Thank you, I would like to join you." Drake nodded and the two men entered the hall. To celebrate the end of term, the Dean had relaxed the rules regarding speaking at meals, and the mood in the hall was celebratory. Lleland walked to the dais and joined the other Masters as the priest intoned a blessing and the meal was served.

It was cold and drizzly when Lleland stepped outside a few hours later, where he had arranged to meet Drake. He pulled his cloak around his chest as Drake stepped from beneath the shelter of a tree.

"Drake House isn't far," Drake said as they started walking. "I sent a message ahead to Lydia to let her know I'm bringing a visitor."

"Lydia's your sister? Is there anyone else?"

"Just the servants."

"She stays alone?" Lleland was surprised. "How old is she?"

"The same age as myself," Drake said. "She's my twin."

They walked in silence for a while, before Lleland addressed Drake again. "I've heard the villages in the Northern Mountains are few and far between."

"They are. We didn't grow up in one of the villages, though. My family has a home deep in the mountains. The closest village is thirty miles away."

"I've also heard there are dragons in the Northern Mountains."

There was a moment of silence, and Lleland glanced at Drake, waiting for his reply. "You're not very fond of dragons, are you?" Drake finally said.

Lleland looked away. "No." He paused. "My father was killed by the dragon that attacked Civitas." Lleland heard Drake's surprised intake of breath. "I was just a boy. The dragon killed my father while I watched." There was silence, and Lleland turned slowly to look at Drake. His eyes were narrowed, his expression set like stone.

"I'm sorry," Drake said. "Please know how very sorry I am. I wish there was something I could do to ... to make amends." His voice shook slightly as Lleland listened in confusion.

"It was a long time ago, Drake."

Drake nodded. "Of course. I just … I cannot imagine how that must have affected you." They walked in silence for a few minutes. "If you don't mind," Drake said, "please don't mention this to my sister. I'm afraid it will distress her."

"Of course," Lleland replied. They rounded a corner, and Drake stopped before a tall townhouse. Using his fist, he thumped on the door, and a moment later it was pulled open from within by a large, matronly woman.

"Hannah," Drake said. "This is –" He was cut off when a young woman flew out the door and flung her arms around him.

"Zach!" He returned the embrace with a laugh.

"Hello, sister. It's wonderful to see you again, too. I've brought our guest."

"Oh!" Lydia pulled herself out of Zach's arms and turned to Lleland with a blush, her eyes lowered. "Please forgive me, Master Seaton, but it's been a while since I've seen my brother."

"Three nights," Zach said with a laugh. He threw a glance at Lleland, who raised his eyebrows. "Sorry, I've just made you complicit in my erring ways."

Lleland shrugged. "You ran into her in the street, I'm sure, since you know that entertaining someone in your chambers would lead to immediate expulsion, as would sneaking out at night."

Zach grinned. "Right you are."

"Let these men get out of the cold," Hannah interrupted. "My Sam lit a fire in the parlor in expectation of your arrival, and it should be cozy and warm by now." She pushed the door closed behind them and waited as they shed their cloaks. "Take the men into the parlor, dear," she said to Lydia, "and I'll be along with some wine and victuals in a few minutes."

"Of course, Hannah," Lydia said, leading the way down the passage. Her long hair rippled over her back as she walked, gleaming in the low light of the rush torches. Beneath the soft folds of a white gown swayed slender hips, and her bare feet passed over the stone floor with barely a whisper. She paused at the entrance of the room and turned to Lleland. He had been watching her graceful movements, but as he lifted his gaze to meet hers, the breath caught in his throat. All thoughts fled from his mind as he stared into her glowing eyes, shining like molten gold and more beautiful than anything he had ever seen. The eyes of a goddess.

"Please make yourself comfortable, Master Seaton," she said. He groped behind him and sat down heavily on a hard, wooden bench. Zach sat down next to his sister. "How go the studies?" she asked her brother.

"Ah," Zach said, leaning back in his seat. "We poor students are driven very hard. I've told you before that only Latin is allowed. A dry, dead language!"

"A hardship indeed," Lydia replied in that same language.

Lleland looked at her in surprise. "You speak Latin?" he said.

Lydia's forehead furrowed as she slowly turned to look at him. "Yes," she said. "Did you take me for an uneducated maid?"

"Lydia," Zach groaned. She turned to him with a glare, but then it was gone, and she gave a self-deprecating laugh as she turned ruefully back to Lleland.

"My apologies, Master Seaton, that was rude of me."

Lleland waved his hand. "The apologies are mine, Mistress," he said. "I didn't mean to insult you."

"Thank you," she said with a smile. "You're forgiven!" She caught his gaze, and Lleland smiled back, shaking himself when he realized he was staring.

"How, er, I mean, where did you learn to speak Latin?" he asked.

"Master Corbin. He was our tutor, growing up."

"Did he live in your remote mountain fortress?"

Lydia laughed. "Yes. And he sent us all over the mountain, searching for every specimen of flora that grew there, didn't he, Zach?"

Lleland had forgotten about Zach for a moment, but he glanced at him now, surprised to see Zach regarding him with a slight frown. It vanished as he looked at Lydia. "I think he was just getting back at us for hiding from him so often!"

"I don't remember you hiding very often," Lydia said playfully. "You were quite the student, always eager to please."

Zach flushed as Hannah entered the room, a large platter of sweetmeats in her hands. She placed it carefully on the table. "There now," she said, "a small morsel to keep you going." She picked up the wine and filled Lleland's cup. "You're Master Zach's tutor, I hear."

"That's correct," Lleland replied.

"It's good to have the children in Civitas. I remember when they were just youngsters, here for the old king's coronation." She turned to Lydia. "Remember how excited you were –"

"Thank you, Hannah," Lydia interrupted. "I think we have all we need." Hannah nodded and bustled out of the room. "Poor dear," Lydia said when she was out of earshot, "she's getting on in years, and sometimes gets a bit confused. She was thinking of our cousins, Bronwyn and Will."

Lleland laughed. "I was wondering about that. It must be…" – he paused to do a quick calculation – "…nearly twenty-five years since Alfred's coronation, so even if you had been born, you couldn't have been more than babes."

Lydia smiled. "A lady never reveals her age." She glanced at Zach. "And nor does a gentleman," she added.

Lleland laughed. "Very well, my lady, keep your secret, although I would hazard you are no more than twenty." She lifted her eyebrows, and he held up his hands in mock surrender. "But I'll say no more!"

"Have you heard from Father?" Lydia asked Zach.

"They arrived at the Manor yesterday. Anna and Max are already there."

Lydia smiled. "Anna's invited me to return home with them after Christmas."

"And are you going?"

"Of course!" Lydia turned to Lleland. "Anna is our aunt. Do you have family close by?"

"My mother and sister both live in Civitas. We'll spend the feast day together."

"What about your father?" Lydia asked.

Lleland shot a quick look at Zach before replying. "He died when I was a child."

"I'm sorry," Lydia said.

"It was a long time ago." He paused. "You know, the name Drake is well known in Civitas." From the corner of his eye, Lleland saw Zach stiffen. "Aaron Drake saved the city once from a terrible monster. Are you related to him?"

"Aaron Drake?" It was Lydia who answered. "He's our father."

"The dragon-slayer is your father?"

"Dragon-slayer?" Lydia's voice was sharp, and she turned to look at Zach, her eyes narrowed.

"Yes," Zach said. His gaze met Lydia's. "Remember the stories we heard about Father killing black, er, the black dragon?" He spoke softly, and in the silence that followed, Lleland shifted uncomfortably. Lydia finally leaned back in her seat.

"Of course," she said. "I was forgetting that's what they called him." She looked back at Lleland. "What do you know of dragons?"

"They are …" He was about to say 'monsters,' but something held him back. "They are large, winged beasts that breathe fire," he said instead.

Lydia smiled. "So I've heard," she said.

"You must have seen them, surely? I understand there are

44

some in the Northern Mountains."

Lydia laughed. "Oh, we see them all the time," she said.

"You do? They haven't attacked you?"

"Attacked us? Of course not! Why would they do that?"

"Because they're hunters."

Lydia harrumphed. "Really, Master Seaton, you shouldn't believe everything you hear! Dragons are not cruel monsters, you know!"

Lleland bit his lip and glanced at Zach, who shook his head, but Lydia seemed not to notice. "They are no different from you and me, really," she said. Lleland swallowed the harsh retort that sprang to his lips.

"Let's play a game," Zach said. "Lydia, you always have the best ideas. What do you suggest?"

Lleland glanced at Lydia to see her watching him curiously.

"How about charades?" she said.

CHAPTER SEVEN

Hannah and Sam were dragged from the kitchen to join in the game, and despite his earlier mood, Lleland found himself enjoying himself as the evening wore on. It wasn't the game, though, that kept him enthralled, but rather the beautiful woman sitting across from him. He watched Lydia as she acted her roles; and when she sat and watched the others, clapping and laughing, Lleland kept casting glances her way. Her golden eyes reflected the light of the flames, making them sparkle, and to Lleland it seemed that she glowed like an angel. Sometimes her eyes met his, and she smiled. Later, when the game was done, she asked his opinion about a book she was reading, and he could feel the heat from her skin caress his own as they spoke. It was a book of Roman history, and Lleland was surprised at the depth of her knowledge. When the church bells tolled the midnight hour, Lleland felt a sharp pang of disappointment that the evening was drawing to a close.

"Will you return to Civitas after Christmas?" he asked Lydia as Zach rose to take his leave.

"I'll be traveling with my aunt and uncle."

"Ah."

"But I come to the city often. I'm sure we'll meet again."

Lleland smiled. "I very much hope so, Mistress," he said. He stared into her eyes for a moment, resisting the urge to reach out and touch her, then reluctantly turned away and followed Zach through the door.

"We'll be gone at first light," Zach told Lleland as they walked through the dark streets. The rain had turned to snow, and large flakes, soft and silent, tumbled through the air to cling to their clothes and melt on the street. "I dare say Lydia will be happy to leave, as she isn't fond of the city."

"Oh?"

"She prefers the mountains." Zach glanced at Lleland. "I heard what she said, but the truth is she seldom ventures into Civitas."

Lleland nodded, disappointed. Despite her naiveté about dragons, he wanted a chance to know Lydia better. He could not remember when last he had been so fascinated by a woman. In addition to being the most beautiful woman he had ever laid eyes on, she was intelligent, self-assured and amusing, belying her youth. And her strange eyes had depths that demanded exploration. Zach had eyes the same color, Lleland mused, but whereas his were disconcerting, hers were mesmerizing. When he lay on his bed later that night, it was her smiling visage that rose in his mind as he drifted off to sleep.

Lleland left his chambers later than usual the following morning to find the passages a flurry of activity as students got ready to leave for the holidays, but by midmorning the last man had made his departure, and Lleland breathed a sigh of relief as peace and calm descended over the building. It was the eve of Christmastide, and Lleland had promised his mother to deliver some game for the Christmas feast. Removing his Master's cape, he pulled on some sturdy boots and left the building, bow in hand.

It was a dull day, with low clouds that threatened rain. Within the city the snow from the previous evening had already been churned to brown slush by the passing of many feet. Going through the city gate, Lleland crossed the open countryside and made his way into the forest. His thoughts, however, were not tending towards hunting. Rather, it was the memory of Zach's sister that rose in his mind, and once again he felt the pang of regret that he would have no opportunity to further his acquaintance with her. He laughed a little under his breath. He was no young lad, falling head over heels in love, but there was something – her beauty, grace and charm, not to mention her intelligence and confidence – that attracted him. The only flaw he had so far detected was her opinion of dragons. He smiled wryly. Of all the woman he'd ever met, she was the one who might actually fulfill his mother's hopes for his marriage, if only she didn't live so far away. It surprised him that Anabel still nurtured such a hope. He hadn't found anyone to marry in his first thirty-five years, so why did she think anything would change? It hadn't been for lack of interest, however. As a young man, Lleland had been eager for the warmth and comfort of a comely wife, and his eye had fallen on more than one pretty maid. But it never took long before he grew weary of their simpering ways and simple conversation.

"You expect too much," Anabel told him. "As long as she can cook and clean, she'll make you a good wife."

But try as he might, he could not put his expectations aside, until finally one day he realized that all the young, single maids were no longer young or single. He had given up the thought of marriage then, surprising himself with how easily he accepted the idea that he would remain a bachelor. There were a few passing fancies over the years, but no-one that he could seriously consider as an equal whom he wanted to marry. That was, until now. Despite having just met Lydia Drake, he was certain she was a woman who would prove to be more than just a pretty face. He sighed to himself. He would have enjoyed putting his theory to the test.

Lleland stopped to find his bearings. He had walked deep

into the woods, and was not far from Grim's old cottage. He tested the breeze and listened intently, then headed towards a low rise. There was a salt lick just beyond, and the wind was blowing the right direction for him to lie undetected and observe whatever creatures happened by. A half hour later he was rewarded when a small herd of deer wandered over to the lick. He watched them for a moment, then lifted his bow. He took aim and released the arrow. It was a clean shot and the creature was dead within minutes, averting any needless suffering.

Lleland skinned and cleaned the animal with a knife he kept tucked in his boot, then sliced the meat into large pieces for roasting, and wrapped them into pieces of cloth which he laid in a sack. Within a short time he was hefting the sack over his shoulder and heading back towards the city. He turned into Tottley Alley some time later and made his way to Anabel's house, knocking and pushing the door open at the same time.

"Mother?" he called.

"In here." He turned towards the kitchen, where he dropped his offerings on the floor. Anabel was sitting on a low stool peeling turnips, which she put aside as Lleland came in.

"Hello, dear," she said. "Have you brought us our Christmas feast?"

"I have," he replied with a smile. He bent down and kissed her cheek, watching as she picked up another turnip. Her hands were trembling as she applied a small knife to the pale surface.

"You're still not sleeping," he said.

She smiled back wearily. "It'll pass. Dame Thornton has given me a sleeping draught."

"You still dream of the dragon?"

"I dream of dragons, but they do not come for me. In my dreams they come for you."

Lleland dropped to his knees before her. "I'll kill any

dragon that comes after me."

"But that's just it, son. They surround you, but you don't see them." She dropped the knife and lifted her hands to her face. "I'm worried for you," she said. "I wish you'd leave the dragons be."

Lleland snorted. "And allow the monsters that killed Father to live? You're letting your fears play with your mind, Mother. How could dragons possibly surround me without me seeing them? You've nothing to worry about." He wrapped his arms around her and pulled her head onto his shoulder as tears slid down her cheeks. "Shh," he soothed. "You need to slow down and get some rest." He pulled away from her as he recalled something a colleague had once said about his wife needing to escape the city. "Do you remember Rutherford?" he said. "My colleague at the university."

Anabel nodded. "He was your Master before you graduated."

"Yes. That's him. He mentioned an inn in the country once, better than most. He sometimes takes his wife there when they need a break from the city. We'll go and stay there for a few days. The clean country air will be just the thing to chase away your fears."

"Go out of the city? Can we do that?"

Lleland laughed. "Of course. I have a little money set aside for just such a need as this. And with the college closed for Christmastide, the timing is perfect! We'll spend tomorrow with Edith, and leave the following morning. I'll arrange everything. You just need to be ready to go." He rose to his feet, sure of his course of action. It was exactly what Anabel needed to chase away her thoughts of dragons.

CHAPTER EIGHT

Christmas morning dawned clear and cold. Hoar frost clung to the trees, sparkling in the dull light of the winter sun. Lleland had risen later than usual, after accompanying Anabel to midnight mass the night before, and was now on his way to the house on Tottley Alley. The snow crunched beneath his feet as he walked, and cold seeped into his boots. By the time he reached the house, he could no longer feel his toes.

Edith was in the kitchen when Lleland arrived, helping Anabel and Eve prepare the Christmas feast. Eve would soon be gone, having been granted the afternoon hours off to spend with her family. Alan was seated in the parlor, perusing Father's book.

"Ah, Lleland, there you are. How goes the teaching?" Alan was a dozen years older than Lleland, and made a good living as a wine merchant. His marriage to Edith had been his second, his first wife having passed away in childbirth. The baby had not survived either, and Alan had turned his attention to building his business until he met Edith, barely more than a child at the time. He had been instantly smitten, and within months Edith was a married woman. The first of their offspring had arrived ten months after the wedding, and

Edith spent her days in perfect contentment as a devoted wife and mother.

"Teaching goes well, thank you Alan," Lleland replied. "But my concern lies with Mother. She hasn't been sleeping well."

Alan nodded. "Edith's also worried. It's the memory of that dragon, that's what it is."

"I think a removal from the city may help ease her mind. I'm planning to take her away for a few days."

"Good idea," Alan said. "Is there anything I can do? Do you need funds?"

"Thank you, but no. I have a few arrangements to make, and will leave once we're finished our meal."

"Let me pay for the hire of horses, at least." Alan dug into a purse at his side and pulled out a few coins. "Here."

For a moment, Lleland hesitated, before holding out his hand and accepting the offering. His own funds were meager, and Alan was, after all, a member of the family. "Thank you," he said.

"I'll walk Anabel over in the morning," Alan said.

Lleland nodded. "Thank you."

By late afternoon, everyone had eaten their fill and the house was a riot of noise and laughter as children ran in and out through the door, and around the adults' legs. Oranges and nuts were handed out, and the children grabbed their treats eagerly then scampered off to enjoy them outside. With a sigh, Anabel sat down in a chair in the parlor. She was wan, and Lleland noticed her hands shaking slightly.

"Alan will bring you to the university tomorrow morning," he said. "Have you packed a few things to take with you?"

"Packed?" Anabel looked confused.

"I'll help her," Edith said. "Why don't you go and finish your arrangements."

He nodded. "I'll see you in the morning, Mother." He smiled at Edith, nodded at Alan and left the house. His first port of call was the home of Master Rutherford to discover the name and direction of the country inn. Rutherford had married into money, and despite his modest college master's income he lived in a large house at the edge of the city. The door was opened by a footman, who stared at Lleland dispassionately before turning to fetch his master. Laughter and music rang from the hall, and a few minutes passed before Rutherford appeared. It did not take long for Lleland to apprise him of his plans, and within a few moments Lleland was in possession of the information he sought.

His next stop was the stables, where he arranged the hire of two horses: a docile pony for Anabel and a bay mare for himself. When he heard the price for the hire, he was glad he had set aside his pride and accepted Alan's offer, since it was money he could ill afford to spend. With the arrangements made, there was nothing more to do but pack a few belongings; these included a book, carefully bound in oilcloth, his daybook and a writing kit: a small wooden box with space for ink, quills, nibs and a pen knife. He would take his bow, of course, as well as a sword, since no sensible person traveled the roads unarmed.

The blue skies of Christmas Day had vanished by the following morning, and a thick blanket of cloud hung over the city. It was drizzling steadily, and when Anabel arrived shortly after eight, wearing a thick, woolen cloak, her bonnet was already sodden with rain. Alan carried her small pack, and he tied it to the pony before helping Anabel into the saddle. He handed Lleland a small package wrapped in oilcloth. "Edith packed some food for your journey," he said. "Travel safely, and I trust the country air will help relieve Anabel's fears."

"Thank you. We'll be back within the se'nnight."

Despite the dull, dreary weather, people were already teeming in the streets after their holiday. Lleland led Anabel through the crowds of merchants and hawkers entering the city with their wares, until they finally made it through the huge gates and beyond the city walls. Mud splashed up from the road, covering the hem of Anabel's cloak. It was late morning when they reached the crossroads which would take them south.

"We've traveled more than half the distance," Lleland told Anabel. Her cheeks were red with cold, but she smiled cheerfully.

"The city seems so far away," she said.

The path became steeper, and the mist grew thicker, until it was impossible to see more than a few yards ahead, and Lleland gave a sigh of relief when he saw the whitewashed walls of the inn suddenly appear ahead of them. It was two storeys tall, with blackened beams criss-crossing the white walls, and a black door with a brass knob. A sign, hanging over the door, squeaked on its hinges, the faded name barely visible: Duck and Bull. Lleland drew his horse to a halt and slid off the saddle, then turned to help Anabel alight.

"Go inside," he said. "I'll stable the horses."

The stables were at the back of the inn, and while Lleland was leading the horses across the uneven cobbles, a hostler stepped forward to take the reins. Lleland watched for a moment as the boy led the horses into the stables, then turned back to the building. He rubbed his cold hands in an effort to warm them as he pushed open the door with his shoulder, setting a bell jangling. A quick glance around revealed a small furnished hall, with a larger one beyond. A fire blazed in the larger hall, and Lleland could see Anabel standing before it. She had shed her wet cloak, and was holding her hands out to the fire.

"Good day, Master." Lleland turned around to see a short, portly man hurrying towards him, his balding pate shining in the light of the candle he held. "Are you the lady's son? She said you'd be coming in a few minutes."

Lleland nodded. "Master Seaton. We're in need of two rooms for a few nights. What do you have available?"

"You're in luck, Master," the man said. "Not many travel

the roads this time of year, and you have your choice of rooms. The one in the corner overlooks the gardens, with a view of the hills beyond, which I'm sure your parent would enjoy. The other offers a panoramic vista of the ranges."

"I'll take them."

"Very good, Master. My wife will lead the way. And when you come downstairs, we'll have some nice broth warmed up for you." The man glanced over his shoulder. "Mary," he shouted. A tall woman walked into the room a few moments later, a frown on her face.

"What you shouting for?" she said, but then she caught sight of Lleland. "We have guests?" she said. The man beamed.

"Show them to the hill rooms, my dear," he said.

Anabel had joined Lleland as he spoke to the innkeeper, and together they followed Mary up the stairs. The first room was Lleland's, and he dropped his small satchel of belongings on the floor before following Mary and Anabel to the second room. Like his own chamber, it was plain and simply furnished, with a narrow bed and small bedstand. A table held a ewer and basin, and there was a chair in the corner, placed near the window. As to the view, however, Lleland had to take the innkeeper's word that the windows overlooked the hills and gardens – all he could see beyond the glass was mist. But the room was clean, and there were quilts aplenty on the bed. An empty grate was built into the wall, and Mary waved towards it.

"We don't light the fires when there's no guests, but I'll send a maid to get it going."

"Thank you," Anabel said. She walked over to the window and glanced out, then turned to Lleland with a smile. "I think this is just what I need!"

Lleland left his mother to her ablutions as he returned to his room. It was cold, and he did not linger. The fire downstairs was calling him. He returned to the hall and glanced around. Long tables with benches beneath were arrayed in the large space, and Lleland guessed that it probably filled up at night with people from the nearby villages. He looked up as Mary walked into the room with two large bowls.

"This should warm you up," she said, placing them on the table. The bowls were filled with steaming broth, and Lleland's stomach growled as he waited for Anabel, who joined him a few minutes later. The soup was hot and hearty, and when he was done, Lleland sighed with satisfaction.

As Lleland had predicted, as soon as it grew dark outside the inn began to fill with farmers and laborers seeking a drink to warm their bellies after a day of work. The bell above the door jangled incessantly, bringing in a blast of cold air each time. The atmosphere grew thick and the innkeeper was kept busy carrying plates of food and tankards of stout, to the demands of his noisy customers. Lleland and Anabel sat in a corner, watching the goings-on until the crowd became too rowdy and he led her upstairs.

It was raining again the next morning when Lleland rose from his bed. The fire in his room had died during the night, and the room was cold. His fingers were stiff as he reached for his daybook and writing kit, and he rubbed his hands together before opening the journal and writing his notes for the previous day. He left the page open to allow the ink to dry, and headed downstairs with a book under his arm. The hall was much warmer than his chamber, and he pulled a chair up to the blazing fire and dropped into it with a sigh of satisfaction. The tables had been wiped clean from the night before, and as Lleland opened his book, he saw a maid carrying clean tankards to a long cupboard.

Lleland did not lift his head until Anabel came downstairs sometime later. He looked up with a smile. "Did you sleep well?"

"Very well! No monsters plagued my dreams!"

"Excellent," Lleland said. He closed his book and glanced out the window. A heavy mist still hung over the hills. "I see the rain has stopped. Perhaps you would like to take a walk with me?"

Anabel shivered. "I think I'd like to remain right here, where it's warm! I've brought some needlework, and will sit beside the fire perfectly content as you ramble the hills in the cold."

Lleland smiled. "Then I'll leave you in peace for a few hours."

The sky was still overcast when Lleland stepped outside a few minutes later, bow and arrows slung over his back as always. He stood for a moment, taking in his surroundings. The inn had been built at the base of a steep hill. Beyond the road were open fields, while behind the inn lay the gardens and a narrow path that led to a low peak. Skirting the building, Lleland gained the path and started walking up the hill. The going was easy at first, but as he continued, the path grew steeper and slicker with mud. After some scrambling, Lleland finally crested the summit. It was eerily quiet until the silence was broken by the lonely cry of an eagle. He watched as the bird circled, dropping lower, before it suddenly swooped into the sky with something clasped in its talons.

He looked across the hills, wondering which direction to take. He was familiar with the area, having traveled here before in the hopes of finding a dragon's lair. He shifted the bow on his back, glad of the familiar weight. He had not brought it to hunt, but habit would not allow him to leave it behind. He took the path to the left, where a small forest lay at the foot of the hill. It was damp in the woods and water dripped from the trees. The flash of crimson holly offered a bright respite from the sea of green, while a stream wound its way between the trees, rushing noisily over stones. Birds flitted silently between the trees as Lleland walked by. The stream finally broke into the open, and Lleland headed up a hill to the next summit. The inn could no longer be seen, hidden behind the gentle slopes.

When Lleland returned to the inn sometime later, it was

to the sound of laughter coming from the kitchen. He paused a moment, smiling, then followed the voices to find Mary and Anabel chopping vegetables. She looked up at Lleland as he entered.

"You're supposed to be resting," Lleland scolded as she scraped some peels into a large pail.

"I can't just sit around when there is work to be done," she said. "Besides, I'm keeping Mary company. How was your walk?"

"Wonderful. You should join me tomorrow."

"Yes, I should."

Lleland left the two ladies and returned to the hall, where he called for the innkeeper to bring him a mug of ale. He sat next to the fire as his chilled hands began to thaw. Two men entered the hall, calling for drinks, and took a seat near him.

"Bitter cold, ain't it?" one of them said. "Spent the day mending a broken fence. Damn bull!" The other man laughed and slapped him on the back.

"Did you some good," he said. He looked at Lleland. "Ain't seen you 'ere before. From the city, are ye?"

Lleland nodded. "That's right. Brought my mother here for some rest. Spent the day in the hills."

"That right, eh? Well, ain't much to see around these parts."

They chatted some more, and were soon joined by others as the evening passed away. Despite Lleland's efforts to draw Anabel from the kitchen, she'd waved him off with a laugh. "I'm perfectly happy passing the evening in womanly conversation. Go enjoy the evening with the men. Just don't drink too much!"

The rings around Anabel's eyes were starting to fade by the following morning, and her smile came easily when Lleland entered the hall. But when he reminded her of her promise to go walking, the smile quirked guiltily.

"Oh, dear," Anabel said. "I'd quite forgotten! I told Mary

I'd go with her to the market. She's taking the horse and cart."

"Then you should go, Mother."

"But I said I'd go with you!"

Lleland smiled and patted her hand. "I don't mind the solitude. Aristotle believed it's only for gods and wild beasts, so perhaps I have a touch of wild beast about me."

Anabel frowned. "The only thing 'wild' about you is the beasts you hunt."

"Well then, maybe I am a god!" He laughed at Anabel's look of consternation, and leaned down to kiss her on the cheek. "But since I can be quelled by the frown of a mere mortal, I suppose not!" He grinned as Anabel smacked his arm. "Enjoy your trip to market, Mother," he said.

With his bow and arrows slung once more across his back, Lleland took the same path as the previous day, but when he reached the summit of the first hill, he turned in the other direction and headed towards the next peak. The cloud that had hung over the hills for the past few days was finally lifting, and Lleland could see the hills stretching into the distance. As he walked, he glimpsed the brook he had seen the previous day, winding between the valleys. It would lead him back to the inn if he lost his bearings.

His stride lengthened as he hiked deeper over the knolls and through the valleys, and he could feel the prickling of sweat at the base of his neck. A fallen log lay across his path, and using it as a seat, he pulled open the small sack Mary had pressed into his hand that morning. A hunk of bread, some cheese, an apple and a jar of ale had been placed within, and Lleland thanked Mary silently before tucking in to his repast. Spread out before him was a panoramic vista of hills. In the distance, the stream sparkled as it wound along the valley floor, then disappeared into a copse of trees. He wondered in which direction Drake Manor lay. Had Lydia ever tramped through these hills? Maybe she had even stood on this very spot. He imagined her striding across the hills, her long hair flowing as her golden eyes sparkled. He allowed his mind to wander for a while, until he finally pushed his musings aside and gathered his bow.

Lleland continued towards the next summit, which he was determined to reach before returning to the inn and its dull, smoky interior. The steep path zig-zagged up the slope, and when he gained the top, he took a moment to catch his breath as the cold air filled his lungs. His gaze swept the vista as a shaft of sun broke through a parting in the clouds. Something glimmered in the distance, and he shaded his eyes as he stared at it. Golden wings stretched out wide from a huge body, while a long neck reached through the sky. A thick tail, armed with spikes, trailed out behind a massive frame, and a thin stream of flame flowed from the creature's mouth.

In an instant, Lleland had his bow strung and an arrow notched. As he lifted the weapon, the creature turned, its gaze landing on Lleland. He released the arrow, and immediately cursed himself for his stupidity. The monster was too far away for a shot. He watched, waiting for the creature to turn and start racing towards him as he notched another arrow and held it ready. The creature swept closer, its eyes never leaving Lleland as it soared through the sky. Its tail flicked from side to side, while massive wings stretched out like a canopy. Lleland lifted his bow. He could see the blazing yellow of the creature's eyes, but it was still beyond his range. He waited. The creature rose higher in the air and broke its gaze, turning its head in the direction of the distant hills as it started flying away.

Lleland lowered the bow and watched in confusion. Another dragon joined the first, its wings and body a dark, flaming red, and he lifted the bow once again, but beyond a quick glance, the dragons paid him no more attention as they flew away from him and into the distance.

Lleland stared at the two retreating forms until they vanished from sight, his confusion mounting. Dragons never retreated from an attack. Perhaps they were after other game – such as women. He turned towards the inn and started to run. Mary and Anabel had traveled to the market alone. They could be in danger, and he was too far away to do anything about it. He pushed himself to move faster, tripping over rocks and logs in his haste. It took him close to an hour to reach the inn, and he rushed through the door, panting and breathless as the bells over the door clanged violently.

"You're back!" The innkeeper, coming from the kitchen, was laden with a tray of broth and ale, which he was taking to the hall.

"My mother! Where is she? Is she back?"

"Your mother? No, she and Mary haven't returned yet."

"What?" Lleland grabbed the man by the arm, sending the contents of the tray flying across the floor and down the innkeeper's tunic. "What do you mean, they haven't returned?"

"Hey, what'd you do that for?" The innkeeper shook off Lleland's hand and turned to him with a glare.

Lleland pointed at the door. "There're dragons out there."

The innkeeper looked at the broth seeping between the wooden floorboards. "You're paying for that."

"I saw them! The dragons! The women could be in danger!"

"Dragons, eh?" The man took a towel from around his waist and started wiping his arms.

"I know what I saw," Lleland replied impatiently.

"There are dragons hereabouts all the time! That's no reason to make me spill the broth." He headed back towards the kitchen as Lleland followed.

"What do you mean? You've seen dragons before? And you're not worried?"

The man shrugged and glanced over his shoulder. "They've been around since I was a child. I'm alive, aren't I?" He disappeared through the door as Lleland felt the frustration rising again. He could not leave Anabel at the mercy of the monsters. But he had not even taken a step when he heard a clatter in the yard. He opened the door and breathed a sigh of relief when he saw a small cart, drawn by a single horse, coming to a halt. Anabel sat beside Mary on the narrow seat, and she waved when she saw Lleland at the door.

"Did you just get back, too? We spent a delightful day at the market. I'll tell you all about it, but first I need to change my gown."

"Are you all right? Did you see anything strange?"

"What are you talking about?" Anabel lowered herself to the ground.

"Nothing. I'm just glad you're back safely. I'll see you inside."

Lleland watched the ladies for a moment as he regained his breath, then headed back indoors, towards the large hall. What he needed was a large tankard of stout. He pushed his way towards an empty table in the corner but paused when he heard someone call his name. He turned in the direction of the voice, and met the gaze of Zachary Drake.

CHAPTER NINE

Zach sat at a long table, crowded between other revelers. To his right was a young man with auburn hair, who turned to look at Lleland as he approached. Zach said something to his companion, and with a nod, he rose and walked away, leaving an empty space.

"Master Seaton, come join me. Imagine seeing you here!"

"The surprise is mine," Lleland said, pushing his way to the table. "Although you did say you were visiting family in the area." Lifting his feet over the bench, he slid into the vacated spot. "Is your sister here?"

"Lydia? Definitely not! By the time I'm ready to leave, it'll be no place for a lady!"

"But she's doing well?"

"She's well."

"Did you come alone?"

"No, my cousin Will came with me." He took a sip of his ale as the innkeeper slammed a tankard in front of Lleland.

"I see the women returned home safe and sound," the innkeeper said to Lleland with a scowl.

"Yes," Lleland said. "My apologies."

"Hmph!" With an angry glare, the man moved away.

"Joseph doesn't seem very happy with you," Zach said as the man retreated.

"No, I'm afraid I caused him to spill the contents of his tray."

"Ah! A grievous mistake indeed."

"Indeed! And I'm afraid no amount of restitution will take away the humiliation of having broth spilled down his tunic!"

Zach smiled. "Do you stay in these parts for long, Master?"

"Just a few days. My mother needed a change of environment. She's been having nightmares. I thought the fresh, country air would be beneficial."

"And has it helped?"

"I believe it has. She hasn't suffered from bad dreams these past two nights."

"Good news, then."

They drank in silence for a moment, listening to the shouts of laughter and demands for more ale that rang through the hall.

"I saw some dragons today," Lleland said. He glanced up as Zach slowly lowered his tankard to the table.

"In the hills?"

"Yes. Two, in fact."

"And yet you escaped alive!" Zach said wryly.

"As you see. Although I cannot understand why. The beasts didn't come near."

"They weren't interested in you."

"I thought they might be after the women, but they arrived back here safely."

Zach frowned. "You don't seriously think that, do you?"

"Why not? Perhaps they prefer female flesh."

Zach leaned back and crossed his arms. "Well, clearly the dragons weren't interested in hunting any of you."

"So it would seem, but why?" Lleland tapped a finger against the wooden table. "After all, I launched an arrow at the first dragon, so it should have attacked."

"You came here to hunt dragons?"

"No. I always carry a bow. But I wasn't looking for dragons. They weren't even on my mind." Lleland took a long swig of ale. "But you of all people should know how dangerous these beasts are. You're the son of the dragon slayer!"

"My father killed a dragon that was terrorizing a city. The dragons you saw today have not harmed anyone."

"How do you know?"

"I just ... know."

"No, you don't! I've seen what dragons do, and they're not sweet little kittens. They are monsters."

"No. The one my father killed thirty years ago *was* a monster. But he was the exception."

"You're deluding yourself, Master Drake. Just as a wild boar will attack anything that moves, so too does a dragon. You cannot change the nature of a creature just by wishing."

"And yet the dragons today did not attack."

"There must be a reason beyond my understanding."

"Perhaps, Master Seaton, it's time to seek the truth. To question your own beliefs and explore other possibilities."

"The truth is that they're monsters."

"You're closing your mind to the evidence before you. Evidence that suggests your conclusions are wrong." Lleland frowned. "Everyone makes mistakes," Zach continued, his voice low, "but only a fool persists in his error."

"You're calling me a fool?"

"I'm sorry, Master, but when it comes to dragons, you're blinded to the truth."

"I've seen the truth of dragons, Drake," Lleland said, his voice hard. "I watched as my father was killed by one."

"You saw the truth of one dragon. But one dragon does not determine the actions of all."

"We're talking about beasts. A creature driven by natural instinct. An instinct to hunt and kill. It was that instinct that led the black dragon to attack Civitas all those years ago. And it's the same instinct that will lead to it happening again."

"Seaton –"

"Lleland! There you are!" Anabel's voice rang across the room, cutting through their conversation. Lleland turned to see her weaving her way towards them. He took a deep breath, and exhaled slowly through clenched teeth.

"Hello, Mother," he said as she approached. "Have you recovered from your day's exertions?"

"Oh, I wouldn't call them exertions! Look," she pointed to her hair, "I bought some new combs."

Lleland smiled tightly. "They're lovely." He glanced at Zach. "This is one of my students, Mother. Master Zach, may I introduce my mother, Dame Seaton." Zach's face was set in rigid lines, mirroring Lleland's, but he managed a semblance of a smile.

"Good evening," Zach said.

"Are you staying here, too?"

"No. Now, if you'll excuse me, I must find my cousin." Zach glanced at Lleland. "Master."

Lleland nodded and watched as Zach left the hall, weaving his way through the crowds.

"He's not very friendly," Anabel said.

"We were expressing a difference in opinions."

"Well I'm sure whatever it was, you were right!"

Lleland smiled. "Let's see if we can find a quiet corner away from these crowds." He led Anabel across the room, and saw Zach standing against the wall, the auburn-haired man beside him. Both men were watching him closely, their heads cocked to one side in a familial gesture. Zach's golden eyes glowed strangely in the low fire-light, and Lleland was struck once again by the strength and power that seemed to exude from the young man. He turned away, suddenly uncomfortable. Zach's stance had not been threatening, but there was something about the young Drake that both drew and repulsed him, leaving him perplexed – a most confounding feeling.

The feeling of uneasiness clung to Lleland throughout the evening, and when he climbed into bed later that night, his mind was still disturbed. When sleep finally came a strange man was waiting for him, just beyond his conscious mind. At first Lleland thought it was Zach, but as the man drew closer, Lleland could see that he did not have Zach's tawny hair and golden eyes. Instead, his hair was as black as pitch, and his eyes gleamed with a pale silver light. He was dressed in black from head to toe, and as he drew closer, he smiled sardonically. "Ah, Lleland," he said. "I've been waiting for you." *No*, Lleland wanted to shout, but instead he smiled and nodded. "You're mine," the man said. "You'll never escape me." He beckoned Lleland forward. "Come," he said. Lleland moved towards the man, but a crashing sound behind made him spin around, and he woke as a log fell in the fire grate. His heart was racing furiously, pounding against his chest as he fell back against the pillow. Already the dream was fading, the man in black just a shadow. There had been something about him Lleland needed to remember, but it slipped through his mind like sand. It was a long time before his heart slowed its frantic racing and he passed into a fitful doze.

Lleland woke late the next morning and stumbled down the stairs in search of a cup of ale. He was surprised to see that Anabel had already arisen, and was seated before the fire in the hall. She was staring out the window and did not notice his approach until he was almost at the chair. She turned with a start.

"Oh! You gave me a fright!" She turned back to the window, but not before Lleland noticed that the dark rings had returned.

"Couldn't you sleep?" he asked, pulling a bench closer to sit beside her.

"We're surrounded by dragons," she whispered. Mary entered the room and handed Anabel a cup of mulled wine, which she took with shaking hands. "They're everywhere," she said. "We cannot see them, but they're here." She grabbed Lleland's arm and pulled him close. "They're after you," she hissed.

Lleland glanced at Mary, who shrugged. "She's been speaking like this since she awoke."

"Get one of the maids to pack her things," he said. "We're leaving." He turned back to Anabel. "I'm taking you home, Mother."

She nodded. "Yes, home. They can't get you so easily there." She opened her eyes wide. "But you must be careful, son. They'll come when you least expect it."

"I'll be careful," he said. "Stay here next to the fire while I make things ready."

"It's this cold weather," Mary said as Lleland left the hall. "The rain and mist keeps one awake and plays tricks with the mind."

"Do you often see dragons?" he asked her, pausing at the bottom of the stairs.

"Not as often as when I was girl. We saw them all the time then."

"You must have lost a lot of people to the beasts."

"You mean the dragons killed them?" She laughed. "No, they never killed anyone. I used to watch them soar through the sky, and thought how wonderful it must be to be a dragon."

Lleland shook his head and climbed the stairs. Perhaps Mary was right: the rain and mist did affect the mind.

CHAPTER TEN

"'Anybody can become angry,'" Lleland read. "'That is easy, but to be angry with the right person and to the right degree and at the right time and for the right purpose, and in the right way – that is not within everybody's power and is not easy.'"

Classes had resumed. It was a miserable, blustery Monday. The halls and classrooms were cold and dank after being closed up for a week. Lleland had spent the weekend in the field near the woods, practising his aim and twirling his staff until his muscles ached. A narrow log across a small stream, slick with rain, had provided a perfect platform to twist, swing and jump with the weapon. He had fallen into the water once, but had climbed back and resumed his exercises in sodden clothes that clung to him and impeded his mobility. Zach's words bothered him more than he wanted to admit, and pushing his body helped him push the words from his mind. He knew that he was right, and that Zach was wrong.

Lleland paced the classroom, his long gown fluttering behind him. He turned to face his students. "How can anger be right?" He swept his hand in a gesture of enquiry and felt his fingers touch the smooth surface of his ink pot. He swung around in dismay as the jar started tumbling from the desk. The black liquid flew from the open jar as it tumbled top over end and landed on the hard floor, sending ink splashing over his clothes, his shoes, and across the floor. Shards of ink-black glass flew in every direction as the ink seeped over the stone, running into cracks and along the joints. He stared at the spreading stains for a moment before glancing up at the class, who were staring at him with expressions that ranged from horror to stifled amusement. Zach Drake was looking away, but he was definitely hiding a grin.

"Drake," Lleland snapped in annoyance, "would you be good enough to find some water and a cloth to clean this mess." Zach looked back at Lleland, eyes glinting with suppressed humor.

"Of course, Master," he said, striding to the door and into the corridor.

Lleland crouched down to collect the shards of glass as the students watched, and a short while later Zach returned with a maid hauling a bucket of steaming water. Lleland waited for her to finish before he continued with his class, but his train of thought had been disrupted, and he was relieved when the clock chimed four and class was dismissed.

The ink was dry on Lleland's breeches, and he regarded them with a sigh. He only had three pairs suitable for teaching, and he'd noticed the previous day that one of the others had a hole in the knee. He had planned to ask Anabel to mend them, but with this fresh disaster he knew that the purchase of a new pair was required. He glanced out the window. It was late afternoon, which meant there was still enough time to order a pair from the tailor before he closed for the day. Throwing a cloak around his shoulders, he hurried out the building and into the dismal, damp weather.

Within a few hours Lleland was on his way back to the university, relieved to have the ordeal of being measured, pricked and prodded behind him. The tailor had wheedled him into ordering a second pair, and Lleland was regretfully considering the sudden lightness of his purse.

Despite the wet weather, the high street was a hive of activity. The university was close to the Old Market, with its collection of cloth, leather and ironwork, and Lleland kept his hand on his purse as he walked through the closely-pressed crowds. A pie man stood on a low box, his tray of quickly cooling pies slung around his neck, while further along a hawker was standing over a fire, scooping roasted chestnuts into a sack on the ground. Small shops lined the street, and ahead of Lleland the door to the mercer's opened. A slim figure stepped onto the street, and Lleland paused.

"Mistress Lydia," he called out in surprise, hastening his step. Lydia turned, smiling when she saw him.

"Master Seaton! Imagine running into you!"

"I thought you weren't returning," Lleland said, falling into step beside her.

"It was a last-minute decision. I'm traveling with my aunt and uncle, and they wanted to come into Civitas to make a few purchases before returning home. We leave again in the morning."

"So soon? Have you seen your brother?"

"No, I'm on my way there now. He doesn't know I'm here, so I thought I'd surprise him with a quick visit." Lydia frowned. "I will be able to see him, won't I?"

"The university doesn't encourage visitors, but I can help get you a few minutes together."

"Then it's a very good thing I ran into you!"

Lleland smiled. "A very good thing!" He held out his arm, and Lydia wrapped her hand around it. She was warm, despite the cold weather, and Lleland found himself drawing closer to her. She met his gaze with her golden eyes, and the breath caught in his throat. He coughed and dragged his gaze away.

"So you leave tomorrow. Do you have far to go?"

"My aunt and uncle live on the coast."

"That's a few days' journey. Not as far as the Northern Mountains, though."

"I'm used to the traveling. We Drakes always seem to be on the move."

A woman selling muffins stepped onto the road ahead of them, and Lleland pulled out a coin from his purse. He purchased two of the treats, and handed one to Lydia. They ate as they continued walking, passing stalls selling furs and linen. They were nearly at the end of the street when Lydia paused to examine some embroidered cloth, woven with birds in flight.

"How lovely," she said. She glanced up at the woman selling the fabric. "Does it come from the Orient?"

"It does, Mistress," she said.

"Isn't is beautiful?" Lydia said, turning to Lleland. His eyes weren't on the fabric but on her.

"Quite beautiful," he replied, and she blushed.

"How come you never married, Master Seaton?" she asked as they continued walking.

Lleland glanced at her, surprised at the directness of the question. "I haven't met anyone I wanted to spend my life with."

"You must be a difficult man to please!"

"Not really. I have no need for a servant. I want a wife I can respect as well as love. Someone who'll be my equal."

"Ah! A very difficult man, indeed!" She smiled. "Have you always lived in Civitas?"

"I have," he replied. "But in the summer when I'm not teaching, I try and travel as much as I can."

"Have you been to the Northern Mountains?"

"No. I've heard they are very beautiful, but it's a long way."

"They're magnificent," she said. "So high, the snow lingers all year round. Our home is deep in the mountains, and the vista spreads in every direction. And in the summer, the forests are filled with birds and animals, and waterfalls tumble from the peaks. It's simply breathtaking. You must see it one day."

"Should I take that as an invitation?" he asked teasingly.

"I'm sure Zach would be happy to welcome you as his friend," she replied primly.

He laughed. "I'm not too sure about that. Besides, Zach may not be the one I want to visit."

She smiled, her eyes twinkling. "My father would enjoy meeting you," she said.

"And I would enjoy meeting him – the famed dragon slayer."

Lydia's smile faded. "I wish you wouldn't call him that. To me, he's just 'Father.'"

"I'm sorry, Mistress," Lleland said. He paused. "I didn't know my father. To me, he's just a vague memory."

"How old were you when he died?"

"Six. As a child, I'd dream of all the things we'd do together. In my mind, he'd always have time for me. Perhaps reality would have been different."

She touched his hand. "I'm sorry," she said.

He smiled. "No, I'm the one who should apologize. I'm being morose." Her gaze caught his, and any further words vanished as he stared at her. "Look, we're here," she said. "Do you have a key for the gate?"

Lleland glanced around to see that they were standing before the heavy iron gates of the university.

"We don't need a key. There's another entrance." He led her to a small wooden door in the wall and pushed it open. A narrow path led towards the large arched doorway of the university building, and Lydia's shoes rang against the stone as they walked up the path and stepped through the entrance. The entry hall was deserted, but down the passage came low murmurs from the dining hall; supper was being served. Lleland gestured towards a bench.

"Wait here," he said. "I'll find Zach for you."

"Don't tell him I'm here," she said. "I want to surprise

him."

"Well …"

"Please?" She turned her face up to his with a coy smile. He laughed softly.

"Do you always get your way?"

"Absolutely!"

"I can see why! Very well, I'll keep your secret."

Lleland watched as Lydia took a seat before turning towards the hall. Conversation was discouraged during dinner, and the sounds from the end of the passage were muted. He paused when he reached the threshold, his eyes sweeping the room for Zach, until he spotted him near the front of the hall. With a sigh of resignation, he threaded his way between the tables. The Dean would not be impressed if he caught sight of his tardy Master. He reached Zach unobserved and tapped him on the shoulder.

"You have a visitor," he said softly when Zach glanced around.

"Who?" Zach rose to his feet.

"I've been asked to keep their identity a secret," Lleland replied.

"Then it must be Lydia." Zach glanced at Lleland as they walked together out of the hall. "Why are you the one delivering the message?"

"I ran into her at the market, and when she told me her plan to see you, I offered to help."

"You walked with her from the market?" Zach's voice sounded strained.

"I did. I could not leave her unattended, especially when I learned her direction."

Zach sighed. "No, of course not." They reached the entry hall and Lydia jumped to her feet when she saw the men coming down the passage.

"Lydia!" Zach said. "Dear sister. What are you doing here?" Lleland was impressed with the surprise Zach infused into his voice.

"Anna wanted to stop in Civitas before returning home. We leave tomorrow, but I could not pass up the chance of seeing you while I was here. Who knows when we will be together again?"

Zach laughed. "You saw me last week. Besides, you had no idea you would even gain admittance."

"Ah, but I had Master Seaton to help me!" She smiled at Lleland.

"And it was my pleasure to do so!" he said. "Now, if you'll excuse me, I must return to the hall and see if I can take a seat unobserved by the Dean." He smiled. "Mistress, have a pleasant journey."

"I will. And perhaps we'll meet again in the future."

"I certainly hope so," Lleland said. He walked away, but as he reached the door he glanced over his shoulder. Zach was saying something to his sister, his face close to hers. Lydia was frowning at his words, her hands on her hips as she met his angry gaze. Lleland turned and continued down the hall.

Lleland's hope that he would take his place at the table unobserved was in vain. The Dean saw him as soon as he entered the hall, and watched him with a frown as he stepped up to the dais. He leaned towards the Chancellor and said something beneath his breath, and the other man turned to watch Lleland as he sat down. There were only scraps left on the platter at the center of the table, and he scraped what he could onto his own plate with a sigh. His afternoon exertions had left him hungry. He had just taken his first bite when a servant, clearing the plates from the table, deftly slipped a note beneath Lleland's cup. One glance was enough to tell Lleland who it was from. He slid it into his palm and tucked it into his tunic, before taking a long quaff of wine.

CHAPTER ELEVEN

The missive Lleland had received at supper was not unexpected, and he was in no hurry to open it. It was a summons from the Dragon League, and he waited until he was alone in his room before breaking the seal and spreading it open.

'Come to the Guildhall tomorrow night at midnight,' it read. Signed 'G.'

'G' stood for Grant, Lord Bartholomew Grant, Head Master of the Dragon League. The Dragon League had been founded twenty-two years earlier by Grant's father, Lord Bart the elder, at the behest of King John, although it was well known amongst the members that it had really been at the urging of the Lord Chamberlain. The League was cloaked in secrecy and tasked with discovering all they could about dragons, with the aim of ensuring that all possible threats against the kingdom were eliminated.

It had been from Grim that Lleland first learned about the existence of the League. As King's Verderer, one of his tasks was to organize and lead the king's hunting parties. The young king had only been on the throne for a few months when he ordered Grim to organize a hunting party for the noble lords who had served his father during the war. The hunt had been considered a great success when King John, only ten years old, hit a stag in the hindquarters with an arrow launched from his short bow. Grim had quickly dispatched the poor creature with a second arrow through the throat, killing it instantly, but the praise went to the young king, who was hailed as the hero of the forest.

As the triumphant party wound its way back through the woods and towards the palace, Lord Grant had fallen in beside Grim.

"You're a good shot, Master Verderer," he said. Grim shrugged off the praise. "I wonder whether you would be able to fell a dragon with that bow of yours," he continued. Grim glanced at Grant in surprise, but said nothing. They rode for a little while, until Grant spoke again. "I've heard whispers that perhaps someone you knew was killed by the dragon," he said.

Grim took a while to answer. "My niece," he finally said.

Grant nodded. "We need to stop these monsters from ever hurting our people again. Do you agree?"

Grim pulled his horse to a halt, and turned in his saddle to face Grant. "What are you saying, my lord?"

Grant glanced around, saw that they were alone. "I'm looking for dragon-slayers," he paused a moment, "to serve a secret mission. Does this interest you?"

"You want to hunt and kill dragons?"

"Yes."

"And how will you do that?"

"Can I trust you?" Grim nodded. "The Dragon League has sworn to locate the dragons' lairs and kill every last one of them."

"I've heard that they are difficult to find, and even harder to kill."

"Aaron Drake has set the precedent. If he can kill a dragon, then so can we. We will not rest until every last dragon has been removed from our realm."

Grim took a moment to consider this. "I'm not the only skilled archer. Why are you approaching me?"

"You have something the others lack. Something that will ensure you have success where they have failed. Motivation." Grim was silent. "We meet Thursday next. Think about what I am proposing, and if you're interested, join us. If not, forget this conversation ever took place."

Grim nodded. "Very well." A sound in the forest indicated the approach of others, and the conversation ended. But the following Thursday Grim made his way to the home of Lord Grant, and pledged his life to following the call of the League.

Lleland had only learned of all this many years later, when he was already a skilled archer himself. He remembered the day Grim told him about the League. They were tracking an injured boar.

"Why am I only learning about this now?" Lleland had asked in frustration. "I've already killed two of those monsters. And you know how much I want to kill them all!"

"Aye," Grim had replied, "but you weren't ready to share that goal. You wanted to find and kill them on your own. Until you could work with others, you were not ready to join the League."

"And how many dragons has this League of yours killed?"

Grim crouched down to examine a track. "A few. But the beasts are more cunning than we thought."

"But they're still just animals, and lack the intelligence of humans. If we learn their ways and habits, we'll outsmart them."

"True. But that takes time and observation. We've not had that opportunity."

"So if you had someone skilled in observation and analysis, then you might be closer to finding them."

"Yes. Perhaps that's a skill you can bring to the League."

That had been ten years ago. Lleland had been tasked with collecting whatever was discovered about the dragons, but it amounted to very little. All sightings were recorded and numbers tallied, but even back then dragons had started disappearing. There were those who believed that dragons were dying out, but Lleland believed differently; they were still around, just more adept at hiding. He had no evidence to support this conclusion, however; just a feeling in his gut.

Lleland reached the outer precincts of the Guildhall as the clock struck midnight. He pulled his cloak closer around his chest and peered into the surrounding darkness. The grounds were deserted. Through a crack between the doors fell a faint shaft of light, and Lleland entered a circular hall. A single torch burned in a sconce on the wall, its flickering light reaching no more than a few feet. Pushing the door closed behind him, Lleland walked over to the torch and held a reed, dipped in tallow, up to the flame, watching as it flared with light.

Hidden in the shadows opposite the entrance was a low, narrow doorway, and Lleland made his way over to it, twisting the iron handle and pulling the door open a crack. Holding up his reed light, he glanced around the hall he had just crossed, ensuring that there were no prying eyes, before opening the door more fully. A small, stone landing lay just beyond, from which a narrow staircase spiraled downward. The murmur of voices rose from below, and descending the steps, Lleland found himself outside a large storage room. Wide, double doors stood open, revealing a room well-lit with torches and lanterns. Hessian-wrapped bales lined the walls, while in the center of the room was a circular table, scratched and stained from years of use. Long shadows played over the bales, casting the men who sat at the table in caricature – here, a long, beaked nose and thick eyebrows; there, a loose, flabby neck and rotund belly.

Facing the doorway sat Lord Grant of the beaked nose, with his graying hair pulled into a queue at the back of the neck. A wealthy man with the ear of the king, Lord Grant was the leader of the League. Although skilled with weapons, he seldom accompanied the others in their hunting missions, preferring to arrange the details and finances. He nodded as Lleland entered the room. Around the table sat another seven men, six of them members of the League. Lleland knew them well – he had hunted the hills with them many times as they searched for signs of dragons. The seventh man was not a member of the League, but Lleland recognized him as Lord Hindley, until recently Lord Chamberlain to the King. He'd held that position for over forty years, and in that time had served three monarchs. His failing health was cited as the reason for his retirement, although it was rumored on the streets of Civitas that King John was eager to appoint his latest favorite to the coveted position. He had granted Hindley a handsome pension, however, and estates in the south.

Lleland took a seat beside Durwin Scott and leaned towards him. "What's Hindley doing here?" he asked softly.

Scott shrugged. "Grant says he has information that might prove useful. He wouldn't say more until you arrived." The faint smell of untanned leather rose from Scott's skin, and Lleland pulled away slightly. Scott was the youngest member of the League, and when he wasn't hunting dragons, he worked as a tanner. It was hard work, and his hands were stained and calloused, but he had a handsome face that women seemed to find attractive. His dark, curly hair hung loosely around his face, and on his head sat a felt cap, rakishly set over one ear. Unlike the other League members, he had never seen a dragon, and had certainly never killed one. Lleland had often wondered about his admission into the League. While it was true that his father had served Lord Grant on his estates, and that Scott was a skilled fighter, his yearning to hunt dragons lay not in ridding the world of the monsters, but rather in the chase after a superior beast. In fact, Lleland had often mused, the League could have been hunting any behemoth and Scott would have been equally enthusiastic.

Grant banged his fist on the table to get everyone's attention. "Let's begin. You're all familiar with Lord Hindley." He turned towards the older man. "Welcome, my lord."

Hindley nodded. "Thank you." His eyes were a startling blue, clear and alert despite his advancing years. He was dressed in a black doublet over a crisp, white shirt, and from where Lleland sat, he could see black breeches, black stockings and black, pointed shoes. A memory stirred, but Lleland could not quite capture it.

"My Lord Hindley has asked to join us tonight," Grant continued. "I'm sure we can all agree that that's acceptable." He was met with silence. "Before we give him the floor, are there any updates, Seaton?"

Lleland took a moment to look around the table. "I saw two dragons in the hill country last week."

The men around the table leaned forward, and Grant clasped his hands. "You saw two dragons, you say? Did they see you?"

"Yes. I loosed an arrow – foolishly, as they were beyond my range, but they did not retaliate in any way."

"Maybe they'd already hunted," Scott suggested.

Lleland shrugged. "Perhaps."

Baric Callaway, seated across from Lleland, tapped his chin thoughtfully. "Did you see them more than once?"

"No. But I understand from the innkeeper that dragons are not unknown in the area."

"Did you ask him about a lair?"

"No. But clearly these two animals did not see me as a threat, so if there is a lair, I doubt it was close by." Callaway nodded, his long, thin face thoughtful as he considered Lleland's words.

"It would still behoove us to search the hills," Branton said. He leaned back in his seat and rested his crossed arms over his large stomach. Branton was a merchant who spent part of each year across the water, seeing to his business interests. He had been away from the city when the black dragon attacked, but the monster set fire to one of his warehouses, destroying the merchandise stored within. Branton had managed to salvage the business, but lost a large sum of money. Along with Grant, he funded many of the League's activities.

"I agree," said Grant. "Channing? Elliott? Perhaps you can undertake a trip to the hills?" He waited as the two men nodded. "Good. Now let's move on to the reason Lord Hindley is gracing us with his presence." He turned to the older man. "Would you care to explain?"

"Thank you, Bart." Hindley looked around the table. "As you probably know, it was my influence that helped establish the League and set the goals of this august group of hunters. However, I am well aware that the fight has been difficult. You are battling an enemy that is shrewd and cunning, and although you have had successes, they have been few and far between. Even when the black dragon attacked Civitas, we knew we were dealing with a monster unlike anything ever seen. We lost many to the beast, until one man stepped forward to battle it. You all know I am referring to Aaron Drake. He alone was able to lay a trap that would be the creature's undoing."

Callaway tapped his long fingers impatiently on the table. Like Lleland, he had lost a person he loved to the black dragon. His older brother was a guard who fought to stop the beast from killing a young woman, and been killed by the creature.

"Since my retirement from service," Hindley continued, "I've spent my time writing down the details of my time at court, recalling long-forgotten events." He crossed his arms on the table. "After Drake killed the dragon, he met with the king. I was not present, but I remember that Alfred seemed particularly distressed when Drake left. He refused to relate the particulars, but was distracted for quite a few days.

"Drake's name seldom came up after that, until the eve

of the war with Terran, when Alfred passed the affairs of state into my hands. We had many meetings before his departure, and one of them involved the threat of dragons. He indicated that there was something particular he needed to tell me, but at the last minute, he changed his mind. 'Perhaps some things are better left unsaid,' he said. As you know, Alfred died in the war, and whatever he was going to tell me died with him. But I believe Aaron Drake is the key."

Callaway leaned forward, eyes narrowed as he looked at Hindley. "What makes you think that?"

"He mentioned Drake by name."

"And do you have an inkling of what he was going to say?"

"I cannot be certain, but I think Aaron Drake knows more about dragons than he's revealed – knowledge that would help us defeat them."

"Be that as it may," Grant said, "how does it help us?"

"You need to speak with him."

"Aaron Drake has already shown himself unwilling to aid us in our cause," Grant said, "and if he is keeping secrets, then that would suggest he's actively hindering us. When my father invited him to join our ranks, Drake informed him that should another dragon threat arise, he would deal with it himself, but was unwilling to hunt dragons that were not attacking. I doubt he has revised his position."

"That must have been thirty years ago!" Hammond Elliott snorted incredulously, lifting his thick, bushy eyebrows. "He's well beyond the age of dealing with dragons now. He must tell us what he knows!"

"And without the information he possesses, you may as well give up the fight," added Hindley.

"Never!" The word was softly spoken, but none could doubt the vehemence in Lleland's voice. "We must never give up."

"No, we'll never give up," agreed Grant. "But even if Drake were prepared to reveal his knowledge, actually speaking to him could prove impossible."

"Why?" said Elliott.

"Apart from his reluctance to serve the League, he values his privacy more than anyone I know," Grant explained. "He seldom ventures into the city, and when he does, it's only for a few days. We know he lives in or near the Northern Mountains, but that doesn't help us much because the region is so vast."

"I can discover where he lives," Lleland said. Seven pairs of eyes turned to look at him. "His son is a student in my class."

"Ah!" Grant leaned back in his chair as a slow smile spread over his face. "Your student, eh? That gives us something to work with." He tapped his chin. "Yes, hmm…" He leaned forward. "You're a traveler, Seaton, always exploring different towns and ruins. Have you ever been to the Northern Mountains?"

"I haven't," Lleland said. He thought of Lydia and her enthusiasm for her childhood playground. It had been she who suggested he visit Zach and explore the terrain. "But I think a trip in the summer would be most enlightening."

"I believe it would," Grant said.

CHAPTER TWELVE

"'The wise are instructed by reason, average minds by experience, the stupid by necessity and the brute by instinct.'" Lleland looked at the bored faces in his class. It was a gloomy, gray day. Outside, the rain beat a steady tattoo against the window, while shrubs and trees dripped incessantly. Cold crept through the thin pane of glass and wormed between the cracks in the walls, while the stone floor made the room even colder. As Lleland spoke, his breath hung in the air for a moment before slowly dissipating. Only Zach Drake appeared to be interested in the lecture. "Cicero," Lleland continued, "that great Roman philosopher, understood that not all minds are equal." He glanced around the room. "He also understood that 'knowledge which is divorced from justice may be called cunning rather than wisdom.'"

Zach cleared his throat. "Cicero also tells us," he said, "not to 'listen to those who think we ought to be angry with our enemies, and who believe this to be great and manly. Nothing is so praiseworthy, nothing so clearly shows a great and noble soul, as clemency and readiness to forgive.'"

"True," Lleland said. "Clemency and forgiveness are

certainly right and worthy. But sometimes our enemies are of lesser minds, and 'hatreds not vowed and concealed are to be feared more than those openly declared.'" His gaze swept over the other students, one or two of whom were shivering. "I expect an essay from each of you by the end of the week on the relationship between reason and forgiveness." The students knew better than to voice their objections, but dismay was clear on their faces. Lleland picked up his book and continued reading.

As the winter months dragged by, Lleland paid close attention to Zach Drake. There was something about the young man that both repelled and attracted him, but when he tried to pinpoint what it was, he was at a loss. Sometimes he felt an inexplicable aversion to Zach, but just as often felt drawn towards him, like a fly to the shimmering strands of a spider's web. It was strange and disconcerting. Sometimes he would catch Zach watching him, his head cocked curiously, and he wondered what the young man saw in him.

Zach's comments at the inn still bothered Lleland, but the more time he spent in Zach's company, the more he realized that Zach was a man apart. Unlike other students, he was eager to learn, and would not hesitate to contribute his opinion in the class, often reciting an obscure text to support his argument. He was well read and familiar with other areas of study as well. He spoke as many languages as Lleland – French, Italian, and Greek – and they would often converse in a different tongue. Their conversations were usually a battle of wits, as each strove to prove a certain point. One particularly dreary night, Lleland challenged Zach to a game of chess. He won the game, and the next week Zach demanded a rematch. Zach won that game, bringing them to an even score, and a routine of a weekly game was established.

The cold months of winter slowly gave way to the warmth of spring, and the dark, dank air of the college began to lighten as laughter and conversation filled the corridors. In the classrooms, sunshine spilled through the windows which a few weeks before had revealed only cloudy skies, and in the evenings Lleland threw open the window in his chamber and allowed the fragrant spring air to clear out the mustiness of winter.

One sunny morning, shortly after dawn, Lleland left his chambers and headed outside, bow and staff in hand. He had just stepped over the threshold when he saw Zach walking towards him, dressed only in his breeches and tunic. He stopped in surprise as Zach drew closer.

"Drake! What are you doing out so early?" he said.

Zach smiled. "I wanted to watch the sunrise."

"I'm heading out to do some training. Why don't you join me? We could spar a little."

"I would, but I have no weapons."

"I'll wait while you fetch them."

"I have only a dagger, but that's not really suitable, is it?"

Lleland's eyebrows rose in surprise. "Hmm. You can use my staff, and I'll look for a suitable branch."

Zach nodded. "Very well." He fell into step with Lleland. "Do you train often?"

"Whenever I have a chance. I like the discipline and control."

They reached the field, and Lleland scoured the edge of the forest in search of a suitable weapon. He soon found a long stick and stripped off the twigs and leaves. He handed his staff to Zach. "Ready?"

Zach gripped the staff and nodded. Lleland twirled the stick above his head. It wasn't as smooth as his staff, but he was adept with the weapon and easily overcame the difficulty this presented. He brought it down without his usual force, aware that Zach did not have his skill and training, but when Zach easily parried the blow, he realized he had underestimated his opponent. He increased his speed, but Zach easily kept pace.

At the end of twenty minutes, Lleland was panting and he

could feel his strength beginning to wane. Zach, most frustratingly, wasn't even out of breath. Lleland dropped the stick to the ground and leaned over his knees. "I thought you hadn't trained with a staff," he said.

Zach shrugged. "I haven't. Perhaps it comes from growing up in the mountains."

Lleland looked at Zach skeptically. "Somehow I doubt that," he said. "How do you maintain your strength?"

Zach lifted his eyebrows in amusement. "It runs in the family," he said.

As the spring progressed, Lleland turned his thoughts to the journey he was to make that summer to the Northern Mountains. He had not mentioned his intentions to Zach, concerned that he would veto his plans. He did, however, ask Zach about his childhood home, and discovered that Storbrook Castle was set deep in the mountains, far from other human habitation. The closest village, Zach told him, was on the northern side of the mountains, thirty miles away. And he learned that the most direct route – and most treacherous – was straight over the vast mountain range. Further information was gained from the abbey library, where the records of scribes who had traveled the kingdom were carefully stored. Lleland made his own notes in his daybook, recording the names of towns that he would pass through, and any details he found interesting. A number of the towns boasted old Roman ruins, while others could trace their roots even further back to the Celts. From Civitas the journey to the mountains would take five weeks on foot, while crossing the mountains themselves would take another week, at least. Despite searching through the records, Lleland could find little evidence that the trip across the mountains had been accomplished – the only note he found was that any thought of attempting the crossing was foolishness.

The warmer weather also brought about a change in Anabel. The morbid dread of dragons that had gripped her throughout the winter months finally abated as the warm, spring sunshine pushed aside the cold drear. Lleland was relieved. He had been concerned about leaving her for such a long period of time while she still suffered. He continued to visit her every week, and was glad to see her skin gain more color as the weeks progressed.

Time continued to fly by as Lleland made his final preparations for his journey. He planned to travel on foot, unwilling to incur the expense of a horse. The weather would be fine, the roads well-traveled, and with his years of strength training, the distance would not wear him out.

The primary motivation for the trip was to meet Aaron Drake and discover what he knew about dragons. But as a seasoned traveler, Lleland found himself anticipating the journey for other reasons. The scholar in him wanted to learn more about the history of the northern towns, the fighter in him longed to be free of the confining restrictions of city and school, and the romantic in him looked forward to seeing pastoral scenes and sweeping landscapes. Of course, the fact that he would see Lydia again and maybe even have a chance to further their acquaintance added a certain piquancy to the adventure.

Lleland had marked a day in mid-June as the date for his departure, after his responsibilities at the college were done for the term. The weeks of May and early June sped by as students wrote their exams, handed in papers and finished their assignments. Lleland continued to meet Zach every week over the chess board, and one sunny evening Zach asked him about his plans for the summer.

"I'll do some traveling around the countryside."

"Are you going to the hill country in search of dragons?"

Lleland glanced at Zach in surprise. Since their meeting at the inn, neither of them had raised the subject of dragons. "No," he said, "I actually thought I'd travel north."

"North?" Zach leaned back in his seat and regarded Lleland closely. "You think you'll find dragons to the north?"

"This is not a hunting trip. More a trip of … exploration."

"But you do hunt dragons?" Zach's tone was filled with disgust.

Annoyance goaded Lleland into a rash reply. "Yes," he said, "as do others!" He bit his lip in frustration. "I'll defend my life against any beast," he added.

Zach stared at him a moment longer, then made his move, taking Lleland's queen. A few minutes later the game was done, and Zach strode from the room without another word.

Lleland saw Zach only in class for the remaining week of term, but he was aware of a wariness that hadn't been there before. When the last class finished, Lleland stopped Zach before he exited the room.

"*Ave et vale*," he said. "Farewell, and have a good summer."

"Thank you, Master."

"You travel to the Northern Mountains?"

"I do."

"Well, I'm sure you have a swift mount to get you there quickly."

A glimmer of a smile played around Zach's lips. "Indeed," he said. "Enjoy your travels, and I look forward to renewing our games of chess when classes resume." He paused a moment. "If you see any dragons, keep an open mind. Truth has many facets." He nodded, and left the room.

The day before he was due to set out, Lleland made his way across the city to Anabel. He had not mentioned his plans for the summer, but with the moment at hand, he needed to tell her that he would be gone until September. He sat down in the small parlor across from her and asked her about her week. They chatted for a while, until Lleland brought up the reason for his visit.

"I'll be going away for a while," he said. "I'm traveling north. I leave tomorrow."

"Exploring again," she said with a smile. "How far do you go?"

Lleland shrugged. "Perhaps as far as the mountains."

Anabel's face paled. "The Northern Mountains. It's said there are dragons in the mountains."

"I'm not going to hunt dragons, Mother."

Her eyes narrowed. "Then why are you going?"

"I've never explored that region of the kingdom."

"You're not going to look for dragons?"

"I want to discover more about them." He thought of Zach. "Perhaps there's more to learn."

"Please, Lleland, be careful. Dragons are dangerous — sometimes in ways we cannot imagine."

Lleland laid his hand over hers. "Nothing will happen, I give you my word," he said.

"If only it were within your power to keep it," she whispered. "But you won't even recognize the danger until it's too late!"

"I'll take great care, Mother." He rose to his feet. "I must go. But I promise to return, safe and sound."

Anabel nodded. "I'll pray for you every night," she said.

CHAPTER THIRTEEN

The new day promised clear, sunny weather as Lleland slung his cloak around his shoulders, hefted his quiver onto his back and lifted the strap of his satchel over his arm. He wore a new pair of sturdy brown leather boots that would withstand a pounding on the hard, dirt roads, and a straw hat which would offer protection from both sun and rain. A small dagger had been tucked into his boot, and his bow was in his hand. After much internal debate, he had decided to leave his sword and staff, aware that they'd be more to carry. His skill with the bow should give him ample protection, and he kept a dagger tucked in his boot. He stepped into the road and headed along the busy streets in the direction of the north gate, leading over the river. He glanced back at the city when he reached the far bank, then putting his back to Civitas, started striding along the road that led to the Northern Mountains.

Lleland maintained a brisk pace throughout the day, stopping only to have a bite to eat and a drink of watered-down ale from his canteen. The road was well worn from people hauling produce into the city from the countryside each morning, and he weaved his way between women hefting crates of eggs and workmen dragging carts filled with carrots, peas and an assortment of fruit. Chickens squawked from covered baskets. Even children did their share, carrying bundles of kindling. As the day wore on the crowds thinned, and as the sun was beginning to near the horizon he saw a small town in the distance. He knew there was an inn on the town's northern outskirts, and Lleland stopped outside The Dancing Hind an hour later. The inn bordered the courtyard on three sides like a horseshoe, and on the opposite side a wide, double door stood open, beyond which patrons could be seen gathered around long trestle tables. Lleland stepped through the doors and looked around until he espied the innkeeper in his leather apron. He waved at the man, who ambled over with a frown.

"I need a bed for the night," Lleland said.

"Where's yer 'orse?" the man said. He was short and rotund, with a balding head.

"I walked."

The man's eyes narrowed. "Ya got coin?"

"Of course!"

"'Coz I don't got no bed for a thief."

"I'm not a thief! I'm a scholar."

"A scholar, hmm? But ya walked 'ere? No 'orse?"

"As you see, I have no horse. Surely I'm not the only traveler on foot!"

"Most people 'ave a 'orse."

"I have no horse." Lleland glanced around. The inn, while clean, was neither grand nor luxurious. "Now do you have a bed or not?"

"Only if you show me yer coin."

Lleland sighed in frustration. "I'll show you my coin when you show me your room!"

The man gave Lleland another scrutinizing look, then nodded. "Follow me." He took a candle from a shelf and led Lleland outside, up some stairs at the far end of the building, and along a dingy passage before pushing open a door. "'Ere yer go. A penny for the bed and two more if ya want food. 'Nother ha'penny if ya want wine."

Lleland stepped inside and glanced around. There were a half-dozen beds, three on each side of the room. Next to each was a wooden chest, and in the corner stood a small table with a basin and jug. A man sat on one of the beds, and he glanced at Lleland, his eyes narrowing slightly when he saw the bow. Turning away, Lleland dug a copper penny from his purse and tossed it to the innkeeper. "For the bed. I'll eat here, so send up a plate of food with a glass of wine, and I'll pay for it when I'm done." The man fingered the coin, then with a nod, left the room, taking the candle with him. Choosing one of the beds, Lleland dropped his satchel and bow onto the floor as the other man looked at him.

"Think I'll steal your things if you leave them unattended?" he said.

Lleland shrugged. "Only a fool would trust a man he's never met before."

The man laughed and rose to his feet. "I'm Adam," he said, walking towards the door. "So now we've met!" He slipped out of the room, and Lleland watched as the door closed, before sitting down on the bed and slowly easing off one of his boots. The leather the shoemaker had used was soft and supple, but still, twenty miles of walking had taken its toll. He groaned slightly as he flexed his toes, then eased off the other boot, carefully placing them beneath the bed where they were not easily spotted. New boots might prove too much of a temptation for someone with light fingers. He lay down on the lumpy mattress and closed his eyes, and in a moment dozed off.

A soft scraping next to his bed brought Lleland awake with a start. For a moment he was confused. The sun had set, and the room was dark, with just a glimmer of moonlight coming in through the open window, but in the next instant he was alert as he felt a movement beside him and saw a dark shadow rummaging through his belongings. He shot out his hand and smiled grimly when he heard a grunt. He started to rise from the bed, but the thief was not to be taken easily. A swinging fist caught Lleland above the ear, and he loosened his grip as pain shot through his head. In the next instant the thief was running, but Lleland immediately gave chase. The thief was quick and nimble and had the advantage of a clear head, but as he slipped out the door, the moon caught his face for an instant, and Lleland recognized his roommate, Adam. He clattered down the stairs, then swung over the rail and ran into the dark night. With a growl, Lleland made his way back to the bed. His purse still hung at his side, and a quick check assured him that nothing had been taken. He sat down on the bed and pulled on his boots as a knock sounded on the door.

"Aye," Lleland said, looking up as a maid pushed open the door, a tray in her hands. "The master said ta brung yer food 'ere," she said.

Lleland relieved her of the tray. "Please send up your master. A man just tried to rob me. And fetch a candle, please." He withdrew a farthing and gave it to her, and she bobbed a quick curtsey before hastening away. It took a while for the innkeeper to arrive, and when he did so, he was scowling.

"Wot's this 'bout a thief?"

"The man who was here when I arrived. He tried to rob me as I slept," Lleland explained.

"'Ow you know it was 'im?"

"I saw him."

"Thought ya said yous was sleeping."

"I was," Lleland said. "I woke while he was robbing me. I tried to catch him, but he escaped."

"Ya didna give chase?"

"And leave my things here so he could circle around and rob me while I was chasing a ghost? Don't be a fool, man!"

"Aye, well, he's prob'ly long gone."

"Did you make him pay in advance, too?" The man

looked away in discomfort as Lleland snorted. "You make the honest man pay, and let the thief get away." The innkeeper looked back with a scowl.

"Well, I didna know he's a thief, did I now? And ya betta not be making any trouble, either."

"I'll be gone by first light," Lleland assured him.

The maid had brought Lleland a meal of cold beef, bread and cheese, which he ate hungrily. The wine was sour and had been watered down, and he swallowed it with a grimace before wiping his sleeve across his mouth. As he ate, two more guests were brought to the room, but Adam didn't return, and no items remained in the box next to his bed. The innkeeper was probably right and the man was long gone.

The rest of the night passed without incident, although Lleland slept with his boots on, his bow and arrow at his side, and his hand on his satchel.

CHAPTER FOURTEEN

Lleland spent the first few hours of the next day exploring the small town, but there was little to discover that interested him. It did not have a market, and although The Dancing Hind had stood on the same spot for nearly two hundred years, there was nothing to mark it as different to any other inn. By mid-morning Lleland was back on the road, continuing his journey north.

The days where there was nothing to investigate, Lleland traveled about twenty miles. The countryside was flat, with open fields and sheep dotted across green hillocks bleating plaintively as he walked by. Farmhouses could be seen from the side of the road, and often a farmer would wave Lleland over to share the latest news.

"Comin' from the city, are ya?" they would ask. "What's happening there, then?" And Lleland would tell them about the king, and the grand new palace he planned to build, the troubles merchants were having with taxes, and the fire that had burned a ship in the harbor. In return, the farmer would have his wife pack some food, and would share a tankard of ale before sending him on his way.

As the distance between Lleland and the city increased,

so the towns and roadside establishments become less frequent. A few times Lleland sought shelter within the humble walls of a monastery. The furnishings were sparse and the meals meager, but the beds were clean and comfortable, with quilts to keep the sleeper warm. As payment for their hospitality, Lleland would hunt a deer in the surrounding woods which he delivered to the kitchens. Other times, the only roof over Lleland's head was the leafy canopy of a rowan or the spreading branches of beech or horse chestnut. At these times, his satchel served as a pillow and his cloak as a blanket. He collected herbs along the way that could prove useful on his journey – St. John's Wort, for the cleansing of open wounds, and yarrow to stop bleeding.

He had been on the road for a week when he awoke to rain: a heavy, drenching downpour that continued all day. The rain collected in the brim of his hat and dripped into his eyes, and the clothes beneath his cloak were wet. The road turned to mud as he walked, and rivers of water cut across the path, filling the ruts and seeking the ditches. It was late afternoon when the sun finally pushed the dismal clouds away and opened the world to blue skies. The ground was sodden, and Lleland's boots squelched through a morass of mud. He continued until it was dark, hoping to find an inn where he could procure a dry bed and hot meal, but no buildings rose to greet him, and he saw no other travelers. The moon was already high when he finally turned off the road and looked for a place to make a bed for the night. A low stone wall ran alongside the road, and climbing over it, he felt the ground on the other side. It was damp, not sodden, and Lleland spread out his cloak and lay down.

He passed an uncomfortable night, but when he awoke the sun was shining brightly. A sound near his ear had him reaching for his dagger, but he relaxed a moment later when he saw a sheep staring at him placidly as it chewed a clump of grass. He stretched his arms and his cramped muscles protested at the effort. Picking up his belongings, he climbed over the wall. His cloak and hat were still wet, but he pulled them on, knowing they would dry quickly. His boots were also damp and the leather was tight around his feet, chafing his heels and toes. He had spent the night at the base of a small hill, but he easily gained the summit and looked down at the vista before him with a groan.

A quarter mile away lay the town of Roxton, nestled in the valley. He could see the church with its squat stone tower, and further down the road lay an inn built around a cobbled courtyard. It gleamed in the clean air as hostlers scurried about, carrying loads of hay and leading horses to their well-rested travelers. The town was small, but it had once been a Roman settlement, and the road into Roxton passed beneath the ruins of an ancient Roman aqueduct built of stone. The tall arches towered overhead, and Lleland could not help gaping at the impressive feat of engineering. A trickle of water, caught in the fold of Lleland's hat, spilled over the brim and down his neck. Dropping to the ground alongside the road, he pulled out his daybook and made some notes, before continuing into the town.

The Clearbrae Inn was not much further, and he stopped for a meal and an ice cold cup of ale. The ale, he learned from the innkeeper, was stored in a pool behind the inn. Hidden behind trees, the warmth of the sun never reached the pool's cold depths, making it the ideal place to store casks of wine and ale.

A short distance beyond the town Lleland was excited to discover another Roman find – an ancient milestone. A tall column of etched stone, it topped his height by a foot, although Lleland guessed it probably stood even higher before being worn down by the elements. Much of the writing was worn beyond reading, but he traced the letters that were still visible with his fingers, and pieced together the names and distances of nearby towns. Along the base of the column was a dedication to the Roman Emperor Septimus Servius. In the ground below, the outlines of paving stones were visible, and Lleland used his dagger to scrape away the surface of the dirt, grinning when he saw the neatly cut stones resting just an inch below. Finding a place to sit, Lleland opened his daybook and drew a crude rendition of the stone and its markings. He wondered for a moment about the person who had carved it, before packing away his daybook and writing kit and continuing along the road.

Throughout the early days of walking, the Northern Mountains loomed in the distance, a smudge of purple and gray that stretched across the horizon, but before Lleland reached the mountains, he would have to travel through the Magnus Silvum, the Big Woods. It stretched in front of the mountains like a vast shadow, extending to the east and west as far as the eye could see, and three weeks into his travels, Lleland reached the first towering trees. He had read that the forest was nearly sixty miles deep, and anyone foolish enough to leave the road could land up hopelessly lost, unable to trace their bearings beneath the thick canopy of leaves.

Little sun reached beneath the trees, and moss wrapped around the trunks of oak, beech, elm and yew, along with firs and pines. Large webs crossed the path, the silvery strands gleaming in the dull light, and Lleland broke through them with reluctance. Bluebells clustered around the base of the oaks, a carpet of green that had long since lost its blooms, while ferns blanketed the dells. Paths led in all directions from the main road, and once Lleland saw a solitary house nestled between the trees, but no-one was about. Fairy rings poked through the dark mulch of the forest floor, while overhead squirrels and birds chirped and chattered as Lleland walked by. A small stream babbled beside the road for some of the way, and Lleland used his dagger to spear a fish in the shallow waters, cooking it over a small fire he made in a clearing; and when night came, he stepped off the road and slept beside the trunk of some large tree.

On the second day, Lleland caught the sound of rustling

as something large moved between the trees. Wild ponies roamed through the woods, but this animal was much larger. With the skill of a hunter, he headed upwind of the creature and crept stealthily through the trees, stopping with a small gasp of surprise as the creature came in sight. Although he had never seen one before, Lleland knew from the huge, dark body and massive horns that he was looking at one of the few remaining aurochs. The aurochs had once been as numerous as the deer, but over the years it had slowly disappeared from the countryside until only a few remained. They were protected by the Crown, and hunting them was punishable by death. As quietly as possible, Lleland drew his daybook and writing kit from his satchel, eager to capture the lines of the magnificent animal. It stood grazing on the leaves of trees for a few minutes, until it slowly ambled away; but for a long time, Lleland stared at the spot where the beast had been, thrilled at what he'd just witnessed.

The day after his encounter with the aurochs, the trees opened up into a wide meadow, with a small cluster of houses built of gray stone. The back wall of each house had been built into a low, sloping hillock that ran the length of the meadow. The roofs were covered in sod, and on a few of the houses, goats nibbled on the green grass of the roofs. On the other side of the path was a tavern – so small it could fit only a few people at once, and beside it, a wattle and beam house. Jasmine and honeysuckle covered the walls of the house and wound around the large front window. The shutters had been thrown wide open, and as Lleland walked by, a woman stuck her head through the window and waved her hand.

"Oi! I have fresh bread and pastries for sale. The best you'll ever taste!"

Lleland ambled up to the window with a smile, breathing in the mouth-watering scent of fresh baking.

"What is the name of this village?" Lleland asked as he eyed the tray of pastries set before him.

"Name? We don't have a name."

"But surely you must have a name to tell people who don't live here." He selected a fruit bun and loaf of bread, and handed over a ha'penny.

"We just tell 'em to come to Middle House."

"Middle House?"

"Aye. The house in the middle of the woods."

"Oh. Well that makes sense." He took a bite of the bun and smiled with pleasure.

"Is it the best you've ever eaten?" asked the woman.

Lleland nodded. "Absolutely!"

Five days after first entering the forest, Lleland emerged on the northern side of Magnum Silvum. The Northern Mountains were no longer distant shadows but distinct peaks, with green forests climbing up the lower elevations and waterfalls cascading down the rock faces. Glaciers clung to the summits, and Lleland shivered slightly at the thought of crossing them to reach the other side. The mountains loomed over the road and villages, casting long shadows over travelers. Even the trees and flowers seemed different this close to the towering peaks. Lleland knew from his notes that once he reached the mountains the road would fork, and he would travel west along the foothills for a few days before he found the path that would lead him into the mountains. From there, he would have to pick his own route over the lofty range.

As the mountains drew closer, the landscape changed to undulating hills and dales, and the road twisted and curved around knolls and between small lakes. Lleland met many other travelers on the roads – farmers and housewives making their way to market – and he would fall in step with them. He shared news he had picked up along the way, and learned more about the surrounding countryside. Sometimes he asked about dragons, but the subject was usually met with a shrug. He'd had one such conversation with a farmer who was taking some sheep to market.

"Oh, aye, we see them time to time, flying between the mountains."

"What do you do?"

"Do?" The farmer look at Lleland in surprise. "Nothing. They don't bother us."

"But ... surely they must hunt?"

"I s'pect there's enough animals in the forest for them to hunt." He paused. "Although ... my neighbor's-uncle's-wife's-cousin lost a cow to a dragon once!"

"You see! They're thieves! Surely that should worry you! You're a sheep farmer."

The farmer chuckled. "Well, here's the thing. That man – my neighbor's-uncle's –"

Lleland waved a hand. "Yes, him."

"Well, he wanted to get rid of that cow, anyways. It wasna a very good milker, and he was goin' to sell it. Well, the dragon takes the cow and leaves payment for the animal!"

"Payment? What do you mean?"

The man started laughing. "The dragon left a bag of silver, twice what the cow was worth!"

Lleland stared in confusion. "The dragon left money?" This man was trying to make a fool of him. "That's impossible."

The farmer wiped his eyes and looked at Lleland, humor still clear on his face. "God's truth. That's exactly what happened."

Lleland narrowed his eyes suspiciously. "Did you ever talk to the man himself?"

"Course I did. He's my brother-in-law."

Lleland sighed. Of course.

Occasionally, a coach or carriage would rumble along the road, creating a cloud of dust that hung in the air for hours afterwards. One afternoon a carriage rushed past Lleland, covering him in a thin layer of dust, before it vanished around a bend in the road. He spat the grit from his mouth as he glared after the offending vehicle, then continued walking. The next town was still a few hours away, and he hoped to reach it by nightfall. It was a hot day, and sweat gathered on his brow and dripped into his eyes as he walked. He reached a bend in the road a short while later, and stopped when he rounded the corner. In the middle of the road, lying on its side, was the carriage that had rushed past him earlier, the wheels still slowly turning. One of the horses was struggling against the harness to gain its footing, but the second was lying still, foaming at the mouth. The coachman lay on the ground, moaning as blood poured from a wound to his head. From within the carriage came the sound of crying and banging.

Lleland rushed forward to help the occupants get free of the trap. The door to the carriage had ripped from the leather hinges and hung loosely over the opening. Lleland dragged it off and tossed it aside, then peered into the carriage. A young woman lay slumped against the bench. A small cut bled on her forehead, and when she looked up at Lleland, silent tears coursed down her cheeks.

"Mistress, are you all right?" Lleland asked as he reached into the carriage. The woman was shaking as she grasped his hand.

"Please, help me," she whimpered. Lleland gently took her by the waist and lifted her clear of the wreckage. She had lost a shoe, and the skirt of her gown was ripped.

"You're fine," he said. "You'll be fine." She nodded. "What's your name?" he asked.

"Muriel Gail."

He pulled out a canteen and offered it to her. "I'm going to check on your coachman, Mistress Gail," he said. She took the canteen and he walked over to where the man was slowly rising to his feet. "How badly are you injured?" Lleland asked.

"I hit my head." He grasped Lleland by the arm. "How's Mistress Muriel?"

Lleland glanced over at the woman. "She's not dissolving into hysterics."

"She's a fine one, that's for sure."

"What happened?"

"A rock. You can see it beneath the carriage. It hit the wheel and sent the carriage flying, dragging the horses down with it."

The rock was large, and Lleland looked around, wondering whether it was the result of deliberate sabotage. There was no-one in sight, however. Using the knife he kept in his boot, he cut the first horse free and led it off the road, then turned his attention to the second horse, still lying on the ground. A brief examination confirmed a broken leg, and he used his dagger to quickly end its life. He heard a soft sob and turned to see Muriel watching, her eyes wide as she stared at the dead horse.

"I'm sorry, Mistress," he said.

"I know. It's just …" She stopped with a sob and dropped her head into her hands.

"You've had a terrible scare," Lleland said gently. "And I'm afraid your carriage is in need of repair. Do you think you can walk to the next town?"

"I think so." Her voice wavered.

"Good. First we need to get the wreck off the road before it causes another accident." He turned to the coachman. "Do you think you're up to lifting with me?"

"I'll manage."

Together they placed their hands beneath the fallen side and heaved. The carriage began to pivot upwards, one inch at a time, until it reached the tipping point and crashed onto its wheels. The wood trembled and the wheels rolled, but Lleland braced his hand against the carriage and brought it to a shuddering halt. The coachman looked at him in amazement.

"That's some strength you've got there."

He shrugged. "I'm an archer."

Apart from the broken door, the axle of the carriage was shattered, one of the wheels had buckled, and the roof had split apart. The straps holding the trunk at the back of the carriage had broken, and it had fallen onto the ground, spilling gowns and shawls into the dust. "We'll need to find a wainwright in the next town to come back and effect repairs," Lleland said. He turned to Muriel. "Do you have some more suitable footwear you can change into? You've lost one of your slippers, and even if you hadn't they'd soon be wrecked if you walked in them."

"Yes." She turned to the fallen trunk and rummaged through the jumble of garments before pulling out a pair of boots. She laid them to one side, and then removed a small, gilded box, which she placed next to the boots. Turning back, she started folding the garments and placing them back in the chest. Lleland watched in silence. "Will my chest be safe out here?" she asked as she closed the straps.

"We'll hide it beneath a bush and hope that it's overlooked by anyone passing by." He hefted it onto his shoulders and walked along the hedge, looking for a suitable hiding place. In one place the hedge was deeper, with more tangled undergrowth, and he pushed the chest between the branches.

When he turned back, Muriel had donned the boots and was clasping the box she held close to her chest.

"Do you want me to carry that?" the coachman asked.

"No, John," she replied. "I think I would like to carry them myself." She turned to Lleland. "My jewels."

Lleland nodded. "Very wise to take them, Mistress," he said. "Are you ready?"

"Yes," she said. John had taken hold of the reins of the remaining horse. "Let's be off."

CHAPTER FIFTEEN

"Where are you traveling from?" Lleland asked Muriel as they walked.

"The city. We received word that my mother is very ill, and I'm on my way to be at her side."

"You have a far way still to travel?"

"We go to Terranton."

"That's a long way. Where's your maid?"

"She fell ill a few days ago. Given the urgency of my journey, I would not be delayed, so I decided to continue alone. Besides, I have John." She smiled at the coachman.

"Aye, that's right. She has me."

"What will your family say?"

She sighed. "Uncle Syngen won't be happy, but he'll understand I had no other option."

"Her uncle is Terran's ambassador," John said. "Perhaps you've heard of him?"

"Yes, of course."

"You have?" Muriel looked at him in surprise.

"I also live in the city, Mistress."

"And you've traveled all this way on foot?" She clutched the box she was holding tighter. "Do you sleep in the bushes and hunt your own food?"

"Yes." He laughed. "But only when I can't find an inn."

It was dark when they finally reached Dragolea, a small town nestled in a valley in the foothills of the Northern Mountains. A few enquiries led Lleland to the Flying Duck, an inn that offered private rooms and a hearty meal, and he left Muriel in John's care and went in search of a wainwright. He was at supper with his family when Lleland finally found him.

"Can't do nothing 'til morning," the wainwright said when Lleland explained the situation. "And from what you say, it'll take a few days to fix."

Lleland nodded. "I thought as much. I'm leaving in the morning, but you can find the lady at the Flying Duck. John, her coachman, will be able to direct you to the wreckage, and will assist you."

"Very well."

He walked back to the inn, and joined Muriel and John where they sat at one of the benches. Despite the fine summer weather a fire burned and crackled in the fireplace, the flames sending shadows dancing on the walls. Lleland watched Muriel as she ate. She had solemn brown eyes that reflected the burning flames, and her hair, golden like Lydia's, was neatly pinned at the nape of her neck. She had already finished her meal, and sat with her hands folded in her lap.

"Were you able to find someone to lend assistance?" she asked.

"I did, Mistress. It'll take a few days for repairs to be effected."

"A few days?" She stared down at the table for a moment. "I see."

"I'm sorry," Lleland said. "I know you're anxious to be on your way."

"I understand," she said, nodding, then paused. "And what of yourself, Master Seaton? Do you leave in the morning?"

"I do. I still have a long way to travel."

"We can give you a ride when the carriage is repaired."

"Thank you, Mistress. But I must keep going."

She nodded and dropped her eyes to her lap. "Of course. And I thank you for your assistance."

Lleland smiled. "It was nothing, Mistress. I'm happy I could be of service."

"I'm glad it was you," she said, blushing slightly as she stared at her hands. "You behaved like a perfect gentleman. Others might not have been so ... considerate."

"John would have protected you," Lleland said, casting a glance at the coachman.

"Yes," Muriel said. "Of course."

When Lleland was done eating, he went for a walk, taking his daybook and writing kit along with him. An ancient wall ran around the town, and he climbed the rampart to the walkway on top. The town had been built on the top of a mound, and in every direction were uninhibited views of the surrounding countryside. Towers rose from the wall every five hundred yards, and Lleland took care to examine the materials and design of the formidable fortress, before committing them to the pages of his daybook. To the north the mountains loomed above the town. Chatting with a guard, Lleland discovered that the town was the last outpost before the towering range.

"How well do you know the mountains?" he asked.

The guard shrugged. "Well enough, I s'pose. When we were younger, my brother and I did some exploring."

"Did you ever find a route across the mountains?"

"We never went that far. The terrain is demanding. If you plan to attempt a crossing, make sure you have rope and an ax."

Lleland nodded. "Thank you, I'll purchase some. Did you ever see dragons?"

"Often. But only ever in the distance."

Lleland made his purchases the next morning, and then was on his way. The road climbed steeply, then dropped into yet another valley. In the distance he could see where the road forked, flanking the mountains in either direction, and with each summit gained, it grew closer.

He reached the fork in the late afternoon. The mountains stretched out before him, as far as he could see. He had bread and cold meat in his satchel, and he sat down to eat as he gazed at the towering peaks. In the summer sunshine they looked as if they had been rendered with an artist's brush, with their medley of greens, blues and purples splashed with reds and yellows. A waterfall tumbled down the rock face of the closest peak, the spray creating a cloud of mist, while the more distant summits glistened with unmelted snow. Lleland felt a stirring in his heart – a mixture of trepidation and excitement. The mountains were calling to him, inviting him to come and learn their secrets. He had been aware of the stirring for a few days now, and the closer he drew to the mountains the more the excitement grew. He searched the sky, as he had done on previous days, for signs of dragons – longing for some sign of the beasts – but the blue sky was empty. Taking out his daybook, he sketched the mountains, but his efforts did not capture their sweeping grandeur and majesty, and he laid the book aside in frustration.

Rising to his feet, Lleland dusted off bits of grass and twigs and started down the west road. He had only gone a few miles when long shadows started to take the place of bright sunshine, although it would not be dark for a few hours yet. As he walked, Lleland searched for a place to sleep – he did not want to be stumbling in the dark. Large rocks lay scattered over the ground, as though flung by some giant hand in a fit of temper. Lleland picked his way over the ground until he found a large enough spot, clear of stones, where he could lie down in comfort. A big boulder stood close by, and he laid his possessions beside it. As the last light vanished the air quickly grew cool, and he spread his cloak over himself as he stretched out on the ground. The mountains gathered closer around him as night began to fall, and even in the dark he could sense their looming presence. The air was thick around him, and it coursed through his blood, making him aware of every sound, the slightest movement of air, the scent of the rock. He felt as though his blood was thrumming to a silent beat, responding to the crags before him.

When Lleland opened his eyes the next morning, the pale light of dawn had bathed the mountains in a soft pink. He lay for a moment and admired the majestic peaks, drinking in their beauty, before rising to his feet and continuing on his way.

There was little sign of habitation along the mountain road, and the next two nights found Lleland camping in the open again. On the third day he heard a rumbling behind him and turned to see a carriage traveling slowly along the undulating road. It came to a halt a few yards away, and John waved from atop the driver's seat.

"Want a ride?" he called.

"How's she going?" Lleland asked. A dappled gray replaced the horse that had been put down.

"As good as new," John said, smacking his hand on the carriage roof.

The door opened and Muriel peeked out. "Master Seaton," she said, "I'm so glad we caught up with you! As you can see, the wainwright you found for us did a very fine job."

"So I see," Lleland said.

"Can we offer you a ride? I'm sure John would enjoy the company, and it's the least we can do after all your help."

"I'm only going as far as the next village," Lleland said. "From there I head into the mountains."

"Hop on," John said. "We'll be there before nightfall." Muriel withdrew into the carriage with a smile and closed the door as Lleland laid his bow and arrows along the footboard before swinging himself onto the bench.

"You're familiar with this road?" Lleland asked.

"I've traveled it a few times. The highway is more direct, bypassing the mountains to the west, but I prefer the quieter roads."

The village, which consisted of a church, a tavern and a collection of shabby cottages, was reached in the late afternoon. John pointed out the narrow path that led from the main street. "That's the path you're looking for," he said. It was little more than a footpath, and it meandered through a field before disappearing between the trees. "It's quite a climb," John said. "Sure you don't want to come with me and go around the mountains? Once you reach the trees, there's no path. You could get lost."

"I won't get lost. And what better way to experience the mountains?"

John shook his head. "Well, what can I say? It's a lonely place to die."

Lleland smiled. "I have no plans to die," he said.

He was on the path again at first light, before the others were even awake. The village soon disappeared from view as Lleland entered a forest of pine trees. The ground was carpeted in a thick layer of needles, which made walking difficult when the path became steep, and more than once Lleland had to grab the sticky trunks to prevent himself slipping down the smooth surface. The forest finally petered out sometime in the afternoon. By now there was no path to follow, and Lleland took a moment to get his bearings and decide on the best way to proceed. Long shadows lay over the ground, and the sun was beginning to slip towards the horizon. He continued north for another hour, scrambling along a shallow ravine as he kept an eye open for a level place to stop for the night. A narrow ledge of outcropping rock offered the only option, and Lleland carefully crawled onto it, pressing himself as far as he could against the rock face before pulling out his daybook. The light was quickly fading, and he only had time to make a few notes before it was too dim to see clearly. He returned the book to his satchel and closed his eyes.

It was the sun shining directly onto his face that woke him the next morning. A shimmer in the sky caught his eye, and he turned to see a dragon soaring high above the highest peaks. It was the first time he had seen a dragon on this journey, and he watched it as it circled lazily, its tail streaming out behind the huge body and wide-spread wings. The early morning light lit the scales, making them gleam like burnished gold. It would almost be beautiful, Lleland thought to himself, if it wasn't so dangerous. He watched until it disappeared behind the peaks before pulling out his daybook. 'Early morning,' he wrote, 'single dragon observed above mountains. Did not see me. No sign of lair.' He waited a moment for the ink to dry, then closed the book and packed it away.

The route grew steeper, and many times Lleland had to inch along to avoid tumbling to his death below. His path zigzagged across the face of the mountain as he found crevices and cracks where he could climb his way to the summit. It was late afternoon when Lleland finally reached the top of the first peak. Before him, spreading as far as he could see, mountain after mountain stretched into the distance, connected by ridges and valleys. Lleland dropped his belongings and crouched down, staring into the distance. It was colder at this height, but even so, it seemed a good place to stop for the night and allow his body the rest it craved after two days of climbing.

The next eight days were a test of strength and determination as Lleland climbed the rocky heights. At the end of each day, he cleaned the gashes and scratches that covered his arms and legs with water from the mountain streams and the herbs he had collected along the way. He survived on berries, fish from the cold, glacial waters, and the small animals that scampered with ease over the rocks; and when darkness fell he checked the stars to ensure that he was still on the right course. Once he stripped off his clothes and dived into the frigid water of an alpine lake, yelling when the freezing water hit his skin. He climbed out a minute later, shivering but exultant. He reached the first glacier on the third day, the ice field covering the side of the mountain in a dazzling blanket. The air was cold, and when darkness fell, Lleland used the ax to dig a hole into the hard ice to serve as a meager shelter. Eagles made these rocky heights their home, and Lleland would often see one soaring through the sky in search of prey, then diving at dizzying speeds to snatch some small creature in its talons.

Every morning the golden dragon soared high above the peaks, sometimes on its own, sometimes with another. If it noticed Lleland, huddled on the ground below, it gave no indication.

Eventually the mountains began to fall away, and in the distance he saw sweeping valley, through which a turbulent river surged. It took another day before he began his descent into the valley, and he picked his way down the slope until he met a path which led to the river's banks. It was the final obstacle, and Lleland approached it cautiously. He did not want to come so close to reaching his destination only to drown in a raging river. He walked along the riverbank until he found a spot where the surging waves were forced through a narrow gap of rock before crashing over a waterfall a few feet high. He waded through the shallow water to the rocky gap, holding his boots and other possessions above the current, and jumped. When he landed on the opposite side he smiled with satisfaction. From there it did not take long to reach the road that led to the village, and Storbrook.

The village was still a dozen miles down the road, and it wasn't until the next day that Lleland finally saw the first houses on the village outskirts. There was no sign of life at the first house he passed, but outside the second house a man sat on a stool in the sunshine, sanding a large, shallow bowl to a gleaming smoothness. He glanced up and nodded a greeting before returning his attention to his project.

Lleland continued along the high street to the village inn. It opened directly onto the muddy road, and Lleland ducked his head as he stepped down into the dingy interior. A long bar ran the length of the room, and seated in the corner was the single patron of the establishment. A man was standing behind the bar, his elbows crossed as he leaned against the surface, but he straightened as Lleland entered.

"What be your pleasure?" he asked.

"Ale," Lleland replied. He waited as the barman filled a wooden tankard with the brew. He had his choice of seats, and he picked one near the window. As he sat down, the man in the corner rose to his feet and made his way over to Lleland's table. He was tall and lanky, with thinning hair and a graying, scraggly beard. He nodded at Lleland.

"Mind if I join you?" he asked. Lleland waved at the chair across from him, and the man sat down. "You don't look like a pilgrim," he said.

"I'm not," he said.

"I'm Matthew Hobbes," the man said, stretching his thin lips into a smile. "Are you just passing through?"

"I'm looking for a man named Drake. You know of him?"

Matthew's features hardened. "I know him."

"He lives in the mountains, does he not? Can you direct me to him?"

"What do you want with Aaron Drake?"

"That's my business."

Matthew turned away for a moment and looked out the window. "Do you know there are monsters in those mountains?" he said.

"The dragons? Yes, I know that." Lleland leaned forward on the table. "What can you tell me about them?"

"When I was a boy there was just one, but it's spawned more. I've seen as many as a dozen at once terrorizing the area. No-one in the village is safe, and people are too scared to venture anywhere near the mountains."

"They hunt in the village?"

"Those monsters are too cunning for that! No, they hunt further afield, trying to lull us into a sense of security. But I know better."

"You've seen them hunt, though?"

Matthew glanced away. "No. But my father was attacked by the first monster. He was trying to protect the village."

Lleland felt his stomach clench. "I'm sorry," he said. "I lost my father to a dragon, too."

"So you know what they're like?"

"I do."

Matthew glanced at the huge longbow leaning against a bench. "Do you hunt them?"

"Yes."

"Are there others?"

Lleland nodded. "There are."

"I'm just one man, but for a long time I've wanted to rid the mountains of those monsters. Maybe you can send some hunters."

Lleland leaned back, considering. "We have a league in Civitas," he finally said. "Perhaps we can help you."

"A league, eh?" Matthew rubbed his chin. "You know that Aaron Drake aids the dragons?"

"Aids them? That's impossible! He killed the dragon that was terrorizing Civitas. He's the dragon-slayer."

Matthew snorted. "I don't care what happened in the city, but I do know that Master Drake" – he spat out the name – "protects those monsters."

Lleland rubbed his chin as he considered what Matthew was saying. "Why would he do that?" he finally said.

Matthew shrugged. "The man is arrogant and proud. Everyone knows that the dragons live in caves below the castle, and that Drake even allows the monsters to use Storbrook as a prison for captured maidens." He leaned forward, his eyes hard and cold. "They are imprisoned and ravaged, day after day, and when they're too weak to serve a useful purpose, they're eaten."

Lleland frowned as the images of Zach and Lydia crossed his mind. "Do you know where the castle is?"

"Still determined to see Drake? I hope you kill some monsters along the way." The door of the tavern opened, and a man stepped over the threshold. Matthew snorted and turned to Lleland. "That man is as bad as the rest of them, but if you still want to go to Storbrook, he's the one who could show you the way." Lleland turned around to look at the newcomer, and recognized the man he had seen earlier, sanding his wooden bowl.

"Who is he?" Lleland said.

"Richard Carver. His daughter is married to Aaron Drake."

CHAPTER SIXTEEN

Lleland swallowed the last of his ale and pushed himself away from the table. Richard Carver was leaning against the bar, talking to the barman as he filled a tankard.

"I'll get that," Lleland said, laying a coin on the table. Richard turned to look at him in surprise. "Who are you?" he said.

"My name's Lleland Seaton," he replied, "and I'm Zach Drake's college master."

Richard's eyes widened slightly, and he glanced over at Matthew Hobbes. "I see our friend has told you who I am." He held out his hand. "Richard Carver at your service." Lleland shook the proffered hand.

"Can I speak with you for a moment?" Lleland asked. He indicated a table away from Matthew, and Richard nodded. As they sat down, Lleland gave Richard a closer look. He had worn, calloused hands, and his hair was graying at the temples, but his step was sure and his back straight.

"So you're Zach's Master?" Richard said. "What are you doing all the way up here?"

"I wanted to explore the area," he said, "and I've heard the mountains are spectacular."

Richard nodded. "That they are."

"Zach has spoken to me about Storbrook, and since I've traveled this far, I thought I'd seek him out." He paused. "I'm also eager to meet his father."

Richard glanced once more at Matthew, and a sardonic smile twisted his lips. "You're prepared to take such a risk?" he asked. "I'm sure you've already heard that Aaron Drake is no better than a monster himself."

Lleland smiled. "So I was told," he admitted, "but I was unable to reconcile that piece of information with what I know of my student or his sister."

"You've met Lydia?"

"Zach invited me to spend an evening with them at Christmastide."

"I see. And does he know you're coming?"

Lleland looked away. "Er, no. He was gone for the summer before I had a chance to speak of my plans."

"Hmm." Richard glanced out the window. "Zach's away at the moment, and the Drakes are very protective of their privacy."

Lleland leaned back in his seat as he considered this information. "I'd still like to meet Master Drake," he said. "It was Mistress Lydia who urged me to visit the mountains – perhaps she'll convince her father to give me a welcome. If you'd just set me on the road to Storbrook, I'd be most grateful."

"It's thirty miles away," Richard replied. "If you plan to travel by foot, it will take you two days to get there."

"I've traveled much further than thirty miles, Master," Lleland said.

Richard nodded. "Very well. Come stay the night with me, and I'll show you the path in the morning. I'm sure you can do with a hearty meal and a warm bed after all your days on the road."

Lleland thought of where he had slept the previous eight nights. "Thank you, Master," he said. "I'll gladly accept your offer."

Lleland collected his belongings as Richard finished his drink. He eyed the longbow for a moment, but remained silent as he gestured for Lleland to follow him. Matthew Hobbes had disappeared, but other patrons were arriving, keeping the barman busy. Richard led the way back to his house at the end of the street. "It's just me," he said. "My wife passed a long time ago. There's a girl that comes to clean and cook every day, but she goes home in the evenings." They reached the house and Richard pointed to the staircase. "There's a room up top where you can sleep. Go put down your things and we can share the food that Agnes has left."

The room that Richard indicated was a loft room, with two narrow beds. Dried flowers hung on the wall, dusty and colorless, and Lleland guessed that at some time the room had been occupied by Richard's daughter. He returned downstairs to find Richard spooning some meat and vegetables into a bowl from a pot hanging over the fire. He nodded at a jug on the table. "Help yourself to wine," he said.

The evening passed pleasantly as Lleland heard about Storbrook from Richard. He learned it was a splendid castle, with an army of servants that worked very willingly for their master.

"What about the dragons?" Lleland had asked, surprised.

"What about the dragons? They don't bother anyone, and no-one minds seeing them."

"They don't attack people in the mountains?"

Richard shook his head. "You clearly don't know very much about dragons," he said.

"Matthew Hobbes said that Master Drake is in league with them. Is that true?"

Richard took his time in replying. "Aaron Drake knows that, like humans, not all dragons are the same. A few are evil, but most are not."

"I've never heard of a good dragon," Lleland retorted.

"Then you haven't come across many dragons," Richard

replied. He sighed. "They can be elusive, and tend to keep to themselves, so there aren't many opportunities to observe them. But if you were attacked by a rabid dog, would you assume that all dogs are rabid?"

"Are you saying the dragon that attacked Civitas was rabid?"

"You'll have to ask Aaron."

Lleland slept soundly that night, on a straw mattress that felt as soft as down. When he awoke the next morning Richard was gone, but Agnes was puttering around in the kitchen.

"Master says you're to eat and he'll be right back," she said when Lleland poked his head into the room. "There's bread, cold meat and ale."

Lleland was still working his way through his meal when he heard sounds in the yard. Grabbing his cup, he went outside to see Richard tying a horse to the fence. "Good. You're up," Richard said as Lleland walked into the sunshine. "I've just been to the inn to get you a horse. I only have the one mount, you see."

"I don't need a horse," Lleland protested. "I'm happy to walk."

"You may be," Richard said, "but I'm not traveling thirty miles on foot! And you'll slow us down if you're walking."

"You don't need to accompany me the whole way," Lleland said, surprised. "Just point me in the right direction."

Richard grinned. "You may need some protection from those dragons you keep mentioning," he said.

"I think I can defend myself against a dragon," Lleland replied stiffly.

"Perhaps," Richard said. "Nevertheless, it's about time I paid my daughter a visit."

They were on the road shortly after, and Richard led the way through the village and past the inn. Matthew Hobbes was leaning against the wall, and he nodded in Lleland's direction before scowling at Richard.

"He doesn't like you much," Lleland said.

"No. He doesn't like anyone connected with Aaron."

"He said his father was killed by a dragon."

Richard snorted. "His father was injured by a dragon when he tried to kill it."

"Good for him!" Lleland said.

Richard led his horse onto a path that ran behind the churchyard. "You'd better keep those thoughts to yourself at Storbrook. The older Hobbes rounded up a group of villagers to kill the dragon. He took my wife and daughter hostage to force Aaron's hand, and when the dragon arrived to ensure the release of the women, he attacked with his sword. Even then, the dragon showed restraint and didn't kill Hobbes, although his legs were burnt quite severely."

"How do you know all this?"

"I was there."

"Then you also wanted to kill the dragon?"

"No. I was trying to talk reason into Matthew's father. As it turned out, the dragon saved my life."

"It did? How?"

"I was injured and ..." Richard stopped.

"And?"

"The dragon carried me to safety. But Matthew Hobbes' animosity towards Aaron has more to do with his brother than his father."

"Was *he* killed by a dragon?"

"Edmund Hobbes thought he was going to marry my daughter, and was angry when she chose Aaron."

"So this brother nurses a grudge."

Richard was silent for a moment. "Edmund vanished many years ago," he finally said. "He kidnapped my other daughter, Anna, in an attempt to hurt Keira after her marriage. Anna was rescued by a dragon, and Edmund was never seen again."

"So he *was* killed by the beast?"

"Perhaps. If so, he was receiving his just due. But the

dragon returned Anna unharmed."

Lleland frowned. "You sound as though you admire the creature."

Richard shrugged. "I do."

Lleland fell silent, his mind troubled. They crossed a field and entered a copse of trees where the path became steeper. Richard rode ahead, leaving Lleland to his musings. They continued riding throughout the morning, and the air was thick and muggy when they finally stopped to rest the horses on the bank of a river.

"How much further?" Lleland asked as Richard passed him a heel of cheese.

"We're about halfway," Richard replied. "We'll be there mid-afternoon."

They were on their way again a half hour later, and the path grew narrower and steeper as they climbed the mountain. When they finally broke through the trees, Lleland glanced upwards to see Storbrook Castle towering above them, built on a wall of sheer, solid rock.

"There it is," Richard said with a note of satisfaction as Lleland stared in silence. "The castle covers the whole mountain."

"It's massive! How do we get up there?"

"The path leads around the back," Richard said. "There's a lot of shale and loose rock, so we'll need to go slowly." He nudged his horse, and they continued along the path. They rounded a corner, and for a while Storbrook was lost to sight as the path led them through a small stand of trees, but then the canopy of leaves opened for a final time, and the huge castle loomed above them. They walked the horses the last few yards up the gravelly path, then passed beneath a portcullis, with its wickedly gleaming spikes, and entered an enormous cobbled courtyard. Lleland looked around in amazement. The castle donjon rose at the far end of the courtyard, while along one side were stables and workshops. In the corner near the entrance was a squat tower with barred windows, and in the opposite corner stood a small stone chapel with a priest house attached. Green lawns could be seen beyond the courtyard, bordered by bright flashes of color. The courtyard was busy as people hurried between the buildings, and near the stables, two men were deep in conversation.

As Lleland took in the scene, Richard took the reins from his hand and walked both horses over to a stablehand. "Quite something isn't it?" he said.

"Remarkable," Lleland said. "How did they manage to build all this at such a great height?"

Richard shrugged. "Storbrook has stood here for many generations." He gestured with his hand. "Come, let's go find Aaron."

They started across the courtyard, but they hadn't gone very far when they were stopped by an elderly man coming from the donjon. "Master Reeve," he greeted Richard. "We weren't expecting you."

"Thomas! Good to see you again." Richard slapped the man on the back and he grimaced slightly. His white hair was pulled back with a ribbon, hanging down a slightly stooped back, and when he glanced at Lleland, he could see the deep creases that lined the man's face.

"This young man is Zach's tutor," Richard said. "He's traveled from the city to explore the mountains, and expressed a desire to see Storbrook."

"Master Zach's away," Thomas said.

"Yes, I know. But Master Seaton also wishes to meet Aaron."

Thomas turned bright blue eyes on Lleland and looked at him closely. "You've come a long way," he said.

"Yes."

Thomas glanced at Richard, then turned towards the building. "Come wait in the hall while I advise Master Aaron of your arrival. I'm sure he will be happy to meet you, and provide a bed for the night."

Lleland nodded. "Thank you," he said humbly. He and Richard followed Thomas as he arduously climbed the stone stairs that led to the hall. He left them there for a few minutes, and when he returned he beckoned Lleland and Richard to follow him.

"Master Aaron will receive you in the solar," he said. He led them up a wide, curving staircase and along a passage, stopping at a thick wooden door. He pushed the door open and gestured for Lleland and Richard to enter, then pulled the door closed behind them.

CHAPTER SEVENTEEN

The first thing Lleland noticed as he entered the room were the two women seated on a long, cushioned bench across from the door. One of them was Lydia, and he smiled when he saw her. Next to her sat a woman too young to be her mother. Lydia returned the smile, but was silent; she glanced at the man standing near the window.

"Master Seaton." The man stepped forward and held out a hand. "I've heard Zach speak of you. I'm Aaron Drake."

Lleland took the outstretched hand in confusion. The man before him looked to be only a few years older than himself – far too young to be the dragon-slayer. He glanced at Lydia for a moment, then back at Aaron. "I'm pleased to make your acquaintance."

"And this is my wife, Keira," Aaron continued, gesturing to the woman beside Lydia, "and I believe you've already met my daughter, Lydia."

Lleland looked back at Lydia in confusion. "Master Seaton," Lydia said. "I see you took my advice to explore the Northern Mountains."

"I did," Lleland said.

"And are they as beautiful as I said?"

"They are indeed, Mistress."

"We are very pleased to welcome you to our home," Keira said, speaking for the first time. "As Aaron has already mentioned, Zach has spoken of you many times."

"Thank you, Mistress," Lleland said.

Aaron was speaking with Richard in earnest, his brow furrowed. He turned back to Lleland. "As Richard has already told you, Zach is away at the moment, but we welcome you here, and invite you to spend the night at Storbrook. You've traveled a long way and must be exhausted. I'm sorry you've come so far for nothing, but I'm sure Richard will be happy to accompany you back to the village on the morrow."

Lleland felt his heart sink, but before he had a chance to respond, Lydia was on her feet. "Papa! As you said, Master Seaton has come a long way, not just to see Zach, but also to see the mountains!"

"Lydia, Master Seaton doesn't know our ways," Aaron said softly. He met Lydia's narrowed gaze for a moment, but before either of them said anything, Keira spoke.

"Master Seaton," she said, "we'd be delighted if you remain here as our guest." She ignored Aaron's furious expression. "Storbrook is so remote, we tend to forget our manners when strangers arrive, but we hope you'll enjoy our hospitality for as long as you wish to stay."

"Keira, what are you doing?" Aaron strode over to Keira and glared down at her. "He cannot stay here!"

"He can, and he will," she said quietly.

"Besides," Richard interjected, "he also came to meet you, Aaron."

Aaron stared at Richard for a moment, then turned back to Keira with a look of frustration. "The men and women of my clan obey my every command, but when it comes to my own home, my wishes are completely disregarded. I trust you're prepared to accept the consequences of this foolish decision."

Keira placed her hand on his arm as she smiled up at him. "Something tells me we need to do this," she said. Aaron stared at her for another long moment, then nodded.

"Very well, my sweet. I trust you." He turned to Lleland. "Please don't think I've taken offense to you personally, Master Seaton, but there are many other factors at play here. However, since my family seem determined that you remain within these walls, at least for now, then I hope you'll enjoy your stay and make yourself comfortable. I must warn you, though, that you may see things that will make you wish you hadn't set foot in Storbrook."

"Are you referring to the dragons?" Lleland said. Matthew's words about maidens being imprisoned at the castle flashed through his mind, but he pushed the thought away as his glance fell on Lydia.

"Yes, the dragons. They're not our enemy, Master Seaton. We live peacefully with them and welcome them to Storbrook."

Lleland dropped his gaze. If this was the dragon-slayer, how could he not be an enemy of the monsters? For himself, he knew that the only fate suitable for a dragon was death. He nodded. "Thank you for the invitation to remain."

Aaron stared at him for a moment, then turned away. "Lydia, pour our guest a glass of wine."

Lydia did as she was bade, and when she handed Lleland the glass, she smiled. "I'll show you some of my favorite places in the mountains while you're here, if you like."

"I'd like that very much," he replied. She was only a few inches shorter than him, and he looked into her golden eyes with a smile. "I look forward to it," he added.

"Zach has spoken of you often," Aaron said as Lleland took a seat. "He enjoyed your discussions about the great philosophers."

"Zach is a brilliant young man," Lleland replied, "whose intellect challenges my own. It's always a pleasure to talk with him. I'm sorry he's not here."

"He'll be disappointed to hear he missed you," Keira said.

"Do you expect him to return soon?"

"He'll return when he's ready," Keira said with a wry smile. "But you've traveled a long way. Tell us about your journey. How long has it taken you to cover the distance from Civitas?"

The rest of the evening passed as Lleland related his journey, but he could not help staring at Aaron whenever he had an opportunity. Apart from his youthful looks, there was something about him that was different, although Lleland couldn't quite pinpoint what it was. He had the same tawny eyes as Zach, darker than Lydia's. His hair was a light golden brown, without any trace of gray, and his face was smooth and unlined. He was tall and lean like Zach, and the same sense of power exuded from him. In fact, Lleland would have guessed he was Zach and Lydia's brother, not father. But he spoke with authority, and Lleland noticed that Richard, the older man, treated him with deference.

A few hours had passed when Aaron turned to Lleland. "You have something on your mind, Master Seaton. What is it?"

Lleland colored slightly, embarrassed that his stares had not gone unnoticed, but he returned Aaron's look steadily. "Are you the dragon-slayer?"

Aaron's brow furrowed slightly. "If you're referring to the black dragon that was terrorizing Civitas several years ago, then, yes, I'm the one that killed him."

"How can that be? It was thirty years ago, and you don't appear much older than me."

Aaron glanced at Keira with a definite expression of admonishment, before turning back to Lleland. "I'm older than I appear, Master Seaton. Youthfulness is a family trait." He paused. "You yourself don't appear old enough to be a Master of Philosophy."

Lleland flushed. "My apologies, Master Drake. You're correct, and I've been rude."

Aaron nodded, then turned to Lydia. "I'm sure Master Seaton's weary after all his traveling. Why don't you show him the blue chamber?"

Lleland rose to his feet, recognizing the dismissal. "I don't wish to impose on your hospitality," he said to Aaron. "If you'd prefer I leave tomorrow, I'll do so."

Aaron cocked his head slightly and stared at him. "You may stay," he finally said, "until you're ready to leave. You're a scholar, with an enquiring mind. The mountains can be a strange and mysterious place to those who are not familiar with them. Keep your mind open, and don't jump to hasty conclusions."

Lleland was silent as he considered the words. A sense of foreboding washed over him, and for a moment, Anabel's dream about dragons surrounding him came to mind. He pushed the thought aside and nodded. "Goodnight, Master Drake," he said.

Lydia led Lleland past the wide, sweeping staircase and down a long, dark passage before stopping at a wooden door. She pushed it open and stepped inside, waiting as Lleland walked past her, his eyes widening at the size of the chamber with its high ceilings and large shuttered window. The shutters were closed, but Lleland guessed that every window in the castle had a view of the mountains. A large bed stood against one wall, while thick furs covered the stone floor. On the opposite side of the room was a table and chair, and another long table stood in the corner, with a basin and ewer and a pile of linens. His possessions, taken earlier by one of the servants, had been unpacked and neatly laid in a chest at the foot of the bed, while his staff, bow, and arrows stood in a corner.

"Will this do?" Lydia asked, turning to him.

"Perhaps," Lleland replied with a grin. "It's a little small, don't you think?"

She laughed as she wagged a finger in his face. "I've seen

how small the chambers are at Kings College, so none of your complaining, Master Seaton."

Lleland lifted his eyebrows. "You've seen the chambers at Kings? How did you manage that, I wonder?"

Lydia's eyes widened and she pulled in a deep breath. "Oh, no! I shouldn't have said that! Please forget I said anything."

Lleland laughed. "Since you've promised to be my mountain guide, I promise to keep your secret. Although keeping your secrets is becoming something of a habit!" She smiled, and Lleland had to tear his gaze away. "Your father's not very happy about me being here," he said.

"My father is a very private man, distrustful of anyone he doesn't know. It's not that he doesn't like you, just that he doesn't know you." She walked over to the door. "I'll see you in the morning. Goodnight."

And before Lleland could respond, the door closed and her footsteps were fading down the passage. He sat down on the bed, wondering at all that had passed that evening. Despite Lydia's assurances, he wasn't sure that Aaron would ever accept him. There was something strange and unsettling about him, something otherworldly. He could almost believe that Aaron Drake belonged to the ancient race of gods, but then, he didn't believe in mythology. For a moment he wondered at the wisdom of coming to Storbrook, before chiding himself. He was acting like an uneducated and suspicious peasant, rather than a well-educated and enlightened scholar. He had come with a purpose – to speak with Aaron Drake and gather information about the dragons. And then there was Lydia – he was willing to suffer through her father's animosity if it meant getting to know her better. No, he decided, it was a good thing he was at Storbrook. And in the light of a new day, he would laugh at the foolish fancies he had entertained.

Sleep was a long time in coming. The castle was silent, and his chamber was pitch black. He tossed and turned in the darkness, until finally he rose from his bed and pushed open the shutters. His room overlooked the courtyard, and in the corner he could see a small fire pit and a guard staring into the flames. He wondered why the Drakes had need of a guard. The moon was high overhead, and stars littered the sky, their little pinpricks of light chasing away the darkness. He lay down on his back and stretched out his limbs as he stared out the window, until finally his exhausted body fell into a deep sleep.

It was late morning by the time Lleland finally awoke to shouts and clanks from the courtyard. It took him a moment to remember where he was, but then he was on his feet, scratching through the chest to find a clean shirt, tunic and breeches. Someone had been in the room and removed his dirty garments. He pulled on the clothes and washed his face with water from the ewer. It had been placed next to the fire, which had been stoked and was pleasantly warm. He walked over to the window and glanced out. He could see Lydia standing near the portcullis, waving as Richard rode under the gate, leading the horse Lleland had ridden the previous day. He turned away from the window and pulled on his boots – which had been cleaned – before opening the door to his chamber and stepping into the passage.

There was no-one else in the dingy shadows as he walked in the direction of the stairs. Beyond the stairs a door opened, and Aaron stepped out and waved Lleland over. "I've been waiting for you to emerge," he said as Lleland approached, and Lleland flushed, embarrassed at his tardy appearance. "Come join me in my study," Aaron said.

He waited as Lleland stepped inside, then closed the door behind them. A large, ornate desk stood across from the door, with windows on either side of it. Papers were strewn across the table, the ink still drying on some of them.

"Wine?" Aaron asked, walking over to a small table with a pitcher and some glasses.

"Thank you," Lleland said, taking the glass from Aaron's

hand. He watched as Aaron walked over to the window and gazed out at the mountains beyond.

"Beautiful, isn't it?" Aaron said, waving Lleland over. Standing beside Aaron, Lleland looked out at the mountains spreading out as far as the eye could see.

"Yes," Lleland replied.

Aaron took a sip from his glass as he continued to stare at the vista. "Do you know that I attended Kings College?"

Lleland glanced at him in surprise. "No, Master," he said.

"Many years ago, of course, so things have probably changed." He paused to take another sip of wine. "In my day, a Master would never travel to visit one of his students." Lleland had been about to take another sip of wine, but he paused, the glass at his lips, before taking a deep gulp. "Was Zach aware of your plan to travel here?" Aaron continued, his gaze still focused on the view.

Lleland turned away from the window and placed his glass on the table. "No," he said.

Aaron turned around to face him. "Why are you here, Lleland?" he asked.

"I ..."

"Is it because of the dragons?"

Lleland took a deep breath before meeting Aaron's gaze. "I wanted to speak to you and learn what I could about them."

"Zach told me you hate dragons."

"Did he also tell you what happened to my father?"

Aaron's gaze didn't waver. "Yes. Your father was killed by the black dragon. But that dragon is dead and gone. You've allowed your anger to blind you." Lleland was silent. "Do you hunt dragons?"

"Yes."

There was a crackling sound in the fireplace, and flames leapt within the hearth. Lleland frowned. He hadn't noticed a fire there before. Aaron's face was set when he turned to Lleland. "I've allowed myself to be swayed by my family and agreed that you may remain here, much against my better instinct. Perhaps you've been sent here by a greater power for some specific purpose. But as long as you remain at Storbrook, you are forbidden from using your weapons against any dragon you may see."

"Can you vouch for my safety from those beasts?" he demanded.

"I can," Aaron replied. "You'll not be harmed by any dragon that you see in the mountains."

"How can you be so sure?"

"You'll have to trust me," Aaron replied. He passed a hand over his brow. "What is your interest in my daughter?"

"What?" The sudden change in subject took Lleland by surprise.

"She's a pretty and good-natured woman, if a little stubborn. If you choose to remain at Storbrook, I'll not prevent you from spending time with her, as much as I am tempted to do so. My wife's mother tried to interfere in her affairs, and in doing so caused a great deal of mischief. I'll not repeat her mistakes, but will trust Lydia to not act foolishly. She's a grown woman who must make her own choices. But you must not, on any account, discuss your dislike of dragons with her, nor tell her of your occupation as a dragon-hunter. It'll only cause her distress." Aaron's eyes narrowed. "I'm quite certain nothing will come of your friendship, and that when you leave, she'll bid you goodbye without any regrets. But if you do anything to hurt my daughter, or take advantage of her in any way, you'll suffer the consequences. Is that clear?"

Lleland felt a wave of annoyance as he crossed his arms over his chest and met Aaron's gaze. "I have no intention of hurting your daughter, Master Drake," he said. "I agree that she is both beautiful and good-natured, but I'm not so cavalier as to toy with her feelings. Nor am I a young boy looking to seduce a pretty, young woman. At this point I'm only interested in furthering our acquaintance, but if my feelings deepen or change, I'm a man of honor and integrity, and would treat her thus. I trust that you know that, despite our difference of opinion regarding the beasts that roam these mountains."

Aaron nodded slowly. "That difference of opinion sets us completely apart, but I cannot deny that Zach has spoken highly of you, and I do believe you're a man of honor and integrity. If I thought otherwise, I wouldn't allow you to remain here." He paused. "You're a scholar, a seeker of truth. Don't allow what happened to your father to blind you to the truth about dragons." He walked around his desk and sat down. "Thomas will be here soon to write my letters, and I believe Lydia is in the hall, wondering if you plan to sleep the entire day away." He took up his quill with a nod, then bending his head, applied himself to his notes as Lleland exited the room.

CHAPTER EIGHTEEN

Lydia was in the Great Hall as Aaron had predicted, and she smiled as Lleland walked into the room. "I don't know how you covered the distance from Civitas to Storbrook in just six weeks when you spend so much time sleeping."

"It's your fault for giving me such a comfortable bed," Lleland said with a laugh.

"Well, come along. The day is wasting away, and I want to show you the mountains."

"All in one day? You're right, no time for a meal!"

"Oh, you're hungry! We'll sneak into the kitchen and steal something."

"Is that something you do often? Sneak?"

"Oh yes, and I'm very good at it, too! Come along." She waved him forward and tiptoed dramatically across the floor, pausing to place her finger on her lips when Lleland made a sound. "Shh," she hissed, "we don't want to be found out." She led Lleland out the hall through a small door behind the dais, down a steep, narrow staircase and into the kitchen below, where they were greeted with savory aromas that made the mouth water.

"Mistress Lydia, what are you doing here?" A woman of

middle age looked up at their entrance, her hands on her hips as she scowled at Lydia.

"Master Seaton, this is Cook," Lydia said, her tone rueful. "Nothing gets past her. I know, I've been trying for years!"

Cook smiled grimly. "I've been wise to your ways since you were a wee one, Mistress, as was my mother before me. Now what is it you're wanting?"

"Master Seaton is hungry," Lydia explained.

"Dinner'll be served in an hour," Cook said, turning to a pot bubbling over the hearth.

"Well that's just it. Master Seaton is here to explore the mountains. He's a scholar, you know. And we won't be here in an hour."

"Hmph!" Cook turned and faced them once more. "Fine. I'll give you some bread." She glanced at Lleland. "Plain."

"Couldn't you spare just a little stew," Lydia pleaded. "It smells so good, and you make the best stew in the world. Better than anything in the city."

Cook harrumphed again, but Lleland could see she was pleased. "Very well, I suppose I can spare a little. It isn't quite ready, though!"

"Oh, thank you," Lydia said, throwing her arms around the older woman.

"Yes, well." Cook patted Lydia on the back, then pulled out of Lydia's embrace and reached for a bowl. "I suppose you'll be wanting some too."

"Oh, yes please!"

"Of course you do! Never known you to say no to food!"

Lydia threw Lleland a quick grin before taking a bowl from Cook's hands and passing it to him. "Tell me this isn't the best stew you've ever tasted."

Lifting the bowl to his nose, Lleland took a long sniff. "It certainly smells wonderful," he said. He took the spoon Cook held out and dipped it into the bowl. "Delicious!"

"Hmph," was Cook's response, but she was definitely smiling. He winked at Lydia and ate another mouthful. It was better than most stews he had tasted – almost as good as his mother's. He finished the hearty meal and handed the bowl back to Cook with a smile of thanks, waiting as Lydia finished hers.

"Ready?" she said as she scraped out the last remnants of meat and vegetables.

"Yes! Let's go exploring!" he said. He followed Lydia out the door and into the courtyard. "Where are we going?" he asked when she stepped onto the lawn.

"There's a door at the back of the gardens," she said. "Zach and I used to use it when we wanted to sneak out."

"Are we sneaking again?" he asked. She threw back a grin but didn't reply. They walked along a winding path laid with stone, past a huge, spreading oak and wide swaths of flowering shrubs and bushes. They had lost sight of the courtyard when Lydia stepped off the path and onto the lawns, leading Lleland beneath a low tree and past a huge rhododendron, beyond which could be seen a high, stone wall with a narrow wooden door set into the stone. Lydia turned the iron ring and pushed the door open, and Lleland drew in a deep breath. The door opened onto a narrow ledge, about ten inches wide, beyond which was nothing but air. Wind gusted through the open door, whipping strands of Lydia's hair across her face.

Lleland looked at Lydia in disbelief. "You don't mean to walk out there, do you?"

"And why not?"

"Well, for one thing, it doesn't seem very safe, and for another, it's hardly appropriate for a lady!"

Lydia cocked an eyebrow at him. "Master Seaton," she said, "I have grown up in these mountains, with no companion but my brother, and although my mother is a woman of great determination and strength, the one area she failed in was teaching me some decorum. It is not my intent to impress you with airs and graces. Rather, I prefer to be myself, especially in my own home, and around people with whom I share a friendly acquaintance. Somehow I had conceived the notion that you found the ladies of the city dull and boring, but perhaps I was wrong?"

Lleland listened to this speech in astonishment, then laughed. "Mistress Lydia, my apologies. You've put me in my place! I would far prefer you to be yourself, and if clambering over the mountains is what you do, then I'll gladly join you in your pursuits." He glanced towards the ledge. "But perhaps we should just use the main entrance?"

"You won't fall," Lydia assured him.

Lleland pulled back. "As you pointed out, you were born and bred in the mountains," he said, "and probably have the feet of a goat. I come from the city, where there are only tiny, little hills, and the ladies are quite happy to flounce along a small stretch of nice, paved road as they go from one store to another."

She laughed. "Come on," she said. "You can do it."

Lleland looked at Lydia, who smiled playfully. Her eyes were glowing, and her hair was mussed from the wind. "Fine," he said. "But if I fall to my death, these mountains will be forever haunted by my ghost."

"I've always wanted to see a ghost," she said. "It's all settled then. Let's go." She stepped through the door and onto the ledge, and moved along a few feet to give him space. "Come on," she said.

Lleland glanced over the edge once more, then taking a deep breath, tentatively placed one foot on the ledge, while his hand gripped the door frame. Placing his other foot next to the first, he carefully slid along until he was standing beside Lydia, his back to the wall. His toes overhung the ledge by an inch, and below them the mountain plunged into a valley, far, far below. Ahead of him lay peak after peak, spreading in every direction. Snow covered the towering summits, while the valleys were blanketed in green. In the distance he heard the thundering of a tumbling waterfall. He looked for it from the side of his eye, but it was outside his line of sight. A blast of wind blew the hair around his face, and he pressed his back against the wall.

Lydia smiled at him encouragingly, then walked another few feet, while he sidled along slowly, pausing whenever a gust of wind whipped his tunic. "It's not far," she said. "Just a few yards until we reach the ridge." Lleland gave a slight nod, his eyes focused on the edge of the ledge.

"Right behind you," he said. It was a little further than a few yards, but inching slowly along the reassuring face of the wall, Lleland finally made it to where the ledge met the ridge. He took a deep breath as he jumped down to solid ground, and glanced at Lydia. "Perhaps we can return through the front gate," he said.

She smiled – wickedly, Lleland thought with an inward groan – then pointed to a cliff a short distance away. "There's a good view of Storbrook from up there," she said.

"No more ledges?" he asked.

"None," she promised.

"Lead on," he said. They reached the foot of the cliff which was covered in scrub and scree. Lydia led him along the base of the cliff, stopping at a crack in the rock face. It was about two feet wide at the bottom, narrowing to a point about three feet from the ground. "There's a funnel we can climb through," she said. "We just need to squeeze through the crack."

"I'm not sure I can," Lleland said, eyeing the opening skeptically. Lydia turned to look at him, her eyes narrowed as she inspected him.

"Zach can get through with a few inches to spare, and you're about the same size," she said. Lleland frowned. "It opens up inside," she assured him. He nodded and gestured with his hand for her to lead the way. She dropped to her haunches and shuffled through sideways. Following her lead, Lleland also crouched down, but it was immediately evident that he wouldn't fit. With a sigh he lay down on the ground and stretched his legs through the hole, edging his way over the ground on his back. The gap opened into a small cave and he rose to his feet and looked around. Above his head the roof narrowed into a long chimney that reached all the way to the top of the cliff. It was wide at the bottom, nearly five feet across, but tapered towards the top.

"How do we climb up?" he asked Lydia, gazing into the funnel.

"You have to brace yourself against the sides," she said.

He looked at her doubtfully. "Have you done this before?" he asked.

"Oh yes, many times," she said, loosening the ties of her gown.

"What are you doing?"

"I can't climb in this," she said, shrugging the offending article off her shoulders and down to her feet. Beneath the gown and over her chemise she wore a shirt and a pair of breeches. Lleland looked at her outfit dubiously. "That isn't really appropriate apparel for a lady," he said.

She ignored him. "Lift me up, please," she said, turning her back to him. He stared at her for a moment, then slowly wrapped his hands around her waist. They settled on her hips, which curved gently. She reached up her hands and he lifted her the full length of his arms. Her hands settled on the stone walls of the funnel, and she lifted her feet to brace herself, then shuffled upwards.

"How do I get up?" he asked.

"Jump."

"I can't jump that high! How does Zach get up there?"

She glanced upwards. "If we had some rope, I could throw it down to you and pull you up."

"You? Pull me up?" Lleland snorted. "Besides, we don't have any rope!"

"We can use this!" Lydia dropped back to the floor of the cave and picked up her gown.

"No!" Lleland grabbed the gown from her hands, his expression horrified. "Absolutely not!"

She lifted her eyes to his and smiled. "It's just a gown," she said. Lleland dragged his gaze away.

"No," he said, more gently this time. "It's not right that you destroy your clothes on my account. Maybe we can find another way up. Perhaps there's a path."

Lydia shook her head. "There's no path, but we can try scrambling up the side. There're a few small bushes that might give us some leverage."

"We don't have to make it to the top," Lleland said.

"You'll be glad if we do," Lydia said. "The view of Storbrook is breathtaking."

Lleland nodded. "Then let's give it a try."

They scrambled their way out of the cave again, and walked once more around the base of the cliff, searching for another route. The dead stump of a tree provided a boost up the first few feet, and from there it was little more than a scramble. The side of the mountain was covered in loose scree that slipped as they climbed, and more than once Lleland grabbed rocks and bushes to stop himself falling. By the time they reached the top his hands were scraped and his breeches had a rip in the knee, but these inconveniences were forgotten when he rose to his feet and stared out at the surrounding vista. Storbrook Castle lay below them, a massive golden palace that glittered in the sunlight. Beyond the castle the mountains stretched in every direction, disappearing into a haze of purple and white. He turned and saw an alpine lake shimmering in the distance, while further to the left a high waterfall cascaded down the mountain. Other waterfalls caught his eye as he continued to turn, and occasionally he could see the river that twisted its way down to the valley below, more than half a mile away.

"It's a long way down, isn't it?"

Lydia peered over the edge. "Not really." She glanced back at Lleland with a smile. "It's all just a matter of perspective."

"Well, from my perspective it looks very far!"

Lydia laughed. "Perspectives can change. If you were an eagle, then the distance from here wouldn't seem very far."

"Ah! But I'll never be an eagle."

"True!" Lydia cocked her head slightly. "Then let's say an eagle – a very big eagle – swoops you into its talons and flies you to its eyrie way up there." She pointed to a mountain peak in the distance. "You'll think the distance to the valley from here quite short after that."

Lleland laughed. "I'll concede that you're right, Mistress Drake. If that were to happen, then I'd find this a quite comfortable height." She grinned and turned back to the view. "Which way is the village?" he asked, but when she pointed north, he could only see more mountains.

"Have you ever seen such a view?" she asked him, and he shook his head.

"No," he replied.

"Was it worth the climb to this great height?"

"Absolutely!"

They stood in silence for a few minutes, drinking in the view. A ground squirrel scurried over the bare rock and Lleland glanced down, noticing the hole in the ground for the first time. He walked over to it and dropped to his haunches as he squinted into the shadows.

"We can go down through the funnel," Lydia said, watching him.

"After you," he said. She sat down at the edge and scooted forward, then lowered herself into the hole, using her hands and feet to brace herself.

"Are you sure you can manage?" he called as she dropped into the darkness. Her laugh echoed between the stone walls.

"Of course! I've done this many times," she said. "Come on." He waited for another moment, then carefully lowered himself to the edge. A small stone skittered into the darkness.

"Watch out," he called, relieved when she ducked out of the way.

"I'm fine," she said. He lowered himself into the funnel

and paused a moment as he braced himself against the walls, then slowly started his descent.

Lydia watched as he dropped the last few feet to the floor of the cave. She had already donned her gown. "There's a waterfall not too far away," she said. "We can go past it on our way back."

"Do we have to defy death to get there?"

She laughed. "I won't lead you into danger."

He looked at her skeptically. "Please forgive me if I don't find that reassuring! But lead the way. I'm right behind you."

She smiled. "You'll just have to trust me."

CHAPTER NINETEEN

It was a short hike to the waterfall, where Lydia waded in the shallows of a pool just below. From there she led Lleland through a forest, and finally back towards Storbrook, arriving just in time for the evening meal. It was served in the hall, and Lleland joined the Drakes on the dais. The priest said a blessing, then joined the servants as they sat below. When the meal was finished, someone brought out a fiddle, and an impromptu dance soon followed.

"Does this happen often?" Lleland asked.

"Almost every evening," Lydia said. "Come dance with me." She slipped a warm hand into his and pulled him to his feet. "Sometimes Cook or one of the others will sing, or Fritz will regale us with a story. His father was a traveling bard, and he knows plenty of tales."

"The servants don't mind living so remotely?"

"Most of them have been here for generations, and this is their home as much as ours." She led him into the middle of the hall, and they joined hands with the other dancers. She laughed as they circled around the hall, her hand in Lleland's. It was with reluctance that he let it go when the music ended and the servants started clearing the hall.

Lleland had no trouble falling asleep that night and was awake at dawn. It was a beautiful morning, full of the promise of summer, and he flung the shutters wide to allow the warm air into the room. A flicker of light through the open window caught his attention and he gazed into the distance. A pair of dragons were circling between the mountains, their scales glimmering in the morning light. Lleland grabbed a tunic and breeches and quickly pulled them on, his eye still on the dragons outside. He glanced at the bow and arrows standing in the corner, but turned away without taking them, Aaron's warning ringing in his mind.

All was quiet within the halls and passages as he made his way downstairs, but in the courtyard people were already bustling about, getting ready for the day. He nodded a greeting at those he recognized from the previous evening as he hurried towards the gate. He could no longer see the dragons, but hoped that once he was beyond the walls he would catch sight of them again. If he could get an idea of where they had their lair, perhaps he could persuade Lydia to take him in that direction.

He passed beneath the raised portcullis, and scrambled down the stony path that led to the castle. He had noticed a fork in the path the previous day which led to a higher elevation. He reached the summit of the next peak a half hour later. Behind him lay Storbrook, tall and proud on its rocky height, while soaring through the sky above him were the two dragons he had seen from his window. While both dragons were golden in color, one was lighter than the other and looked almost dainty compared to the huge beast beside it. Their tales streamed out behind them and massive wings glittered in the morning light. Dropping to his haunches, Lleland watched as they swept through the sky.

The dragons drew closer, and Lleland could see the bright yellow of their cat-like eyes. He wondered which of the beasts would be the bigger threat, before deciding they were probably equally dangerous. A slight breeze stirred, and

Lleland swore softly under his breath as both dragons turned towards him. The larger one drew to a stop, hovering in the air as it stared at him, and Lleland felt a clenching in his stomach as he returned the gaze. The smaller dragon did not slow down but continued flying towards Lleland. He had no weapons, but he grabbed a rock as he rose to his feet, and tightened his grip around it as the creature bore down on him. A roar split the air, and Lleland's gaze flew to the larger creature as it snarled at the smaller dragon. A fight seemed imminent when the smaller dragon turned away with a growl and headed in the direction of Storbrook. The larger dragon stared at Lleland for another moment, before it too turned and followed the other. The rock slipped from Lleland's hand as he watched them flying away. Although he had grabbed the rock, he had not really felt threatened. Instead, he had the strange impression that the dragon was just being friendly. He took his time retuning to Storbrook, thinking about what had happened. Aaron Drake had assured him that the dragons would not attack while he was in the mountains, but what kind of sway did the man have over the dragons that he could prevent them from harming Lleland?

It was late morning when Lleland arrived back at Storbrook. As he crossed the lower hall, he could hear the sounds of laughter and pots clanging in the kitchen beyond, but all was quiet as he mounted the staircase. He turned into the passage as the door to Aaron's study opened, and Lydia stepped out. She was frowning, and didn't notice Lleland as she started marching down the hall in the opposite direction.

"Mistress," Lleland called. She swung around, her expression startled, then gave a tight smile.

"My apologies, Master Seaton, I didn't see you there."

"I've just come from a walk," he said. He moved towards her. "Are you all right?"

Dropping her head, she covered her eyes with her hand for a moment. "I'm fine," she replied. She glanced up at him. "I was with my father."

"Ah! I'm sorry!"

She gave a reluctant smile. "Dinner will be served soon. Would you like to do some more exploring this afternoon?"

"I'd enjoy that very much," he replied.

She nodded. "I'll see you later," she said, before turning around and walking away.

Lleland returned to his room thoughtfully. Back in his chamber, he paced as he pondered the dragons, then opened his daybook and scratched out some notes about what he had seen. When he finally made his way to the hall below for dinner, Aaron and Keira were already seated at the table. There was no sign of Lydia.

Keira waved him over with a smile. "How are you enjoying your stay?" she asked. "I heard that Lydia shocked you with her unladylike behavior yesterday."

Lleland smiled. "She presented her case quite persuasively," he said. "I quickly realized that Mistress Lydia is a woman who marches to her own drum."

Keira laughed. "That's a polite way of putting it! She is determined, like her father. They're frequently in a contest of wills!" She turned to Aaron with a smile. "Perhaps she'll follow in his footsteps one day."

"She's too headstrong," Aaron said. He glanced at Lleland for a moment. "And too used to getting her own way. She's lived a very sheltered life."

A maid brought a tray of food to the table and the conversation ended, to Lleland's relief. Aaron did not linger at the table, but Keira chatted to Lleland as they ate, and by the end of the meal he had reached the conclusion that she was a woman of quiet charm and intelligence. "Enjoy your afternoon ramblings," she said as they left the table. "I think you'll find Lydia upstairs."

"Thank you Mistress." He followed her from the hall and started his way up the stairs to see Lydia standing on the landing.

"Are you ready to go?" she asked.

"I am. But you haven't eaten."

She smiled. "I ate earlier. You should bring your daybook."

"Where are we going?" Lleland asked as they headed down the passage towards his chamber.

"I have something to show you. I think the scholar in you will find it interesting."

He raised an enquiring eyebrow, but she just smiled. She waited at the door as he grabbed his daybook and writing kit and placed them in a small cloth bag which he slung over his shoulder, then led him outside.

"Did you write about the dragons you saw this morning," Lydia asked as they walked across the courtyard.

Lleland glanced at her in surprise. "How do you know I saw dragons?"

"You were out walking," she said. "Since the dragons always hunt at that time, I assumed you saw them. Did they scare you?"

"Scare me? No, but I would have felt a little safer with a weapon in my hand."

Lydia looked at him. "They'll never harm you," she said.

"Because of your father? He has some power over them, doesn't he?"

Lydia laughed dryly. "You could say that," she said. "But," she continued, "that's not why they won't hurt you. They just aren't interested in people – at least not in the way you're thinking. They want to live in peace."

"Really?" Lleland said dryly. He followed Lydia as she veered off the main path through the trees. "Do you know where they have their lair?"

Lydia stopped and turned to look at Lleland. "Why do you want to know?"

Lleland shrugged. "I want to learn all I can about them."

"Perhaps they don't want to be studied."

Lleland snorted. "Perhaps living so near them all your life has affected your perspective, Mistress, but they're just beasts!"

"You're wrong!" Lydia's eyes narrowed as she turned and stalked away. Lleland growled in frustration.

"Mistress!" he said. She continued walking, ignoring him. "Lydia!" he said. She stopped, and after a moment, turned towards him. "I don't want to argue."

Lydia frowned. "I don't want to argue either," she said. "But when it comes to dragons, I've had far more opportunity to observe them than you. You're just being obdurate."

He nodded. "I'll grant you that I'm stubborn, but I've experienced firsthand what dragons do. My father was killed by one."

"Oh." Her face softened. "I'm so sorry. I can understand why you're angry. But if your father had been killed by a human, would you hate all people?"

Lleland sighed. "Of course not. But this is different."

"It's not," she said gently. "Even though some people do wicked things, not all people are wicked. So it is for dragons."

"Lydia, dragons are hunters. Predators. They act on instinct. And their instinct is to kill."

Lydia shook her head. "No, you're wrong."

Lleland smiled cynically, but said nothing more. They hiked in silence for another hour between the rough trunks and prickly needles of conifers, before the trees started changing to birch and poplars. "We're nearly there," Lydia said. She led him off the path and through the trees, until they came to a clearing in the woods. Sunlight filtered through the leafy canopy and painted a dappled design on the mossy rocks that lay scattered beneath the branches, while dried leaves from the previous autumn lay between patches of green grass. The stones were uniform in shape and each stood about eighteen inches high. Someone once, a very long time ago, had placed them in a circle, about six feet in diameter. Lleland stepped forward, carefully walking towards the ring of rocks. Designs had been etched into each of them near the base, and he crouched down to examine one of them. Three spirals, joined together to form a roughly triangular shape. He traced them with his finger, then moved over to the next rock to see a similar design. He glanced up at Lydia.

"This is amazing," he said. "Do you know what it is?"

"Corbin, our tutor, told us it's a sacred grove. He said it's probably been here a thousand years."

Lleland nodded. "At least." He pointed to the spirals. "This is an ancient symbol thought to represent completeness."

"Corbin said it represented the three elements: earth, sea and sky."

Lleland nodded. "The complete universe. Do you come here often?"

"I like to come here to think. It's so peaceful."

"It does seem like a good place to contemplate life, doesn't it." Lleland sat down on a stone and reached into his cloth sack to withdraw his daybook and writing kit. He sharpened a quill, then dipped it into the ink. A fat drop splashed back into the jar before he lifted it to the page.

'Sacred grove in Northern Mountains,' he wrote. He made a few notes about the site then drew a rough sketch of the layout of the stones, which he examined critically. It showed the basic proportions adequately enough, but his talents did not lie in drawing.

"Would you like me to draw the designs for you?" Lydia asked. She was seated on the stone next to his. He glanced at her with a smile.

"That bad, eh? I'm not much of an artist, I'm afraid." He handed her the book, and watched as she swiftly copied the pattern from the rocks. "Much better than mine," he said when she was done. "Do you draw often?"

"Sometimes."

"Can you draw dragons?"

She glanced at him. "I think so."

"I saw two golden dragons this morning. You're probably familiar with them. Can you draw them?"

She stared at him a moment, then turned the page and started drawing, swiftly sketching an outline of two dragons. She turned the book towards him. "Like this?"

He bent down to examine the sketch. She had drawn the two beasts with their wings outstretched, tails streaming behind them, just as he had seen them this morning. Flames poured from the mouth of the larger, while the smaller one looked directly forward. "Incredible!" he said. "You've very talented," he said.

"I've had years to observe them," she said, placing the book on the ground so the ink could dry.

"Yes, I suppose you have." A shaft of sunlight fell on her, and he watched as the light played in her hair, making each strand look like spun gold. His gaze caught hers, and he drew in his breath. Her golden eyes, framed between long brown lashes, sparkled and shimmered. He glanced at her lips soft and pink. He pulled his gaze away and looked at his book. "I think the ink is dry," he said. He glanced back at her to see she was studying the stones.

"Are you an archer?" she said. "I remember you brought a bow to Storbrook."

"I am."

"Did you have someone to teach you?"

"Yes. His name was Grim." He told her about the man who had trained him in weaponry, omitting any mention of dragons. "I suppose in a way, I'm the person I am today because of him," he said.

"I suspect you had the makings of a good man before you even met him," Lydia said when he was done. "He just added the finishing touches." She smiled. "Since you've brought your bow all this way, why don't you do some hunting? Cook is always complaining her kitchen isn't stocked enough. There are plenty of fallow and red deer in these forests."

Lleland nodded. "I'd be happy to stock the pantry, and I

need to maintain my strength. I'll go in the morning."

"Cook will be pleased." Lydia rose gracefully to her feet. "We should start heading back to Storbrook if we want supper," she said. She turned to him with a smile as a single ray of sunshine shone down on her, casting her in a golden light.

CHAPTER TWENTY

Lleland took his bow and arrows and headed down the mountainside early the next morning. The two dragons were out again, and he glanced at them as he walked, until the canopy of trees blocked his view. He followed the path he had taken with Lydia the previous day, but veered to the west when he drew close to the clearing, heading deeper into the woods. The heat of the day had not yet reached the shadowed depths, and the air was thick with the damp smell of mulch. Birds twittered between the trees, fluttering from branch to branch as he walked beneath.

As he crossed a small meadow he noticed that the smaller of the two dragons was still soaring through the heavens. It circled above him, and he watched it for a moment before continuing on his way. He was surprised it hadn't returned to its lair, and the thought crossed his mind that the creature was tracking him. His hand tightened around his bow, its weight a comfort.

As Lleland walked, he checked the ground and bushes for signs that deer were nearby. A river roared in the distance, and he headed towards the sound, treading quietly. The cool scent of water reached him a short while later, and he paused, checking the lay of the land before continuing. The ground was higher to his right and he took that direction. The river came into view, and he paused once more. On the banks were small bushes and lush green grass. The roaring he had heard was from a waterfall further downstream, but here the river was flowing at a more sedate pace, and a calm pool of water made a perfect watering hole. He crouched down and rubbed dirt over his skin to mask his scent, then leaned his back against the trunk of a tree, partially hidden behind some bushes, to wait.

He was rewarded an hour later when a small herd of deer appeared from beneath the trees and walked into the sunlight. They moved forward cautiously, stopping to sniff the air every few feet. After a few moments, they lowered their heads to the sweet grass. Selecting a small doe, Lleland slowly raised his bow, an arrow already notched, to his cheek. He waited a moment, checking his sights, before releasing the arrow. It sprung from the bow with a slight whir. The doe raised its head as the arrow had sunk into its chest. It turned, trying to follow the rest of the herd as they leaped from the clearing, but the wound was fatal and it stumbled and fell. Running over to where it lay, Lleland plunged the arrow deeper into the heart, and watched as the light faded from the creature's eyes.

It did not take Lleland long to gut the animal, and after a quick rinse in the river, he hefted the carcass onto his shoulders and started the long hike back to Storbrook. He kept to the shade as he walked, but the sweat was pouring off his brow and down his back by the time the castle finally came into sight. His legs were tired, and his shoulders ached, but he kept a steady pace.

Marching across the courtyard, he made his way to the kitchens, where he laid his load on the table. Cook was busy stirring a pot over the fire, but at the noise she turned to stare at the bloody carcass.

"Take it to the storeroom," she said. "You're making a

mess." She turned to one of the girls. "Go find John," she said. She turned back to the fire as Lleland stared at her, torn between amusement and annoyance. He lifted the animal and carried it the storeroom, where he dumped it on another table, then headed back outside. A barrel of water stood near one of the castle walls, and using a ladle he sluiced the water over his back and arms to wash away the drying blood. He turned around to see Lydia watching him.

"It's going to take more than a few ladles to wash all that muck off," she said.

"Don't I know it," he said grimly. "And you said Cook would be delighted. She didn't even thank me."

Lydia laughed. "She's like that with everyone. But she was grateful."

"Hmph," was Lleland's only reply.

"I know a waterfall we can reach in a few minutes if you're interested," she said.

Lleland glanced at his arms, still stained with dried blood. "Lead the way, Mistress," he said. He fell into step with her as they crossed the courtyard. "Is there any part of these mountains you don't know?" he asked as they passed through the gate.

"Probably not," she said. "I spent my childhood exploring every inch."

"You never got lost?"

"Once," she admitted. "I was about ten, and had been searching for an eagle's nest. I wandered too far, and when I started for home, I didn't know which way to go."

"How did you get back?"

"Father found me."

"In these mountains? You must have been lost for days!"

Lydia shrugged and turned away. "My father has a talent for tracking. He was able to find me within hours." They headed out the castle and took a narrow path.

Lleland heard a faint splash of water, and when the trail curved, he could see the waterfall next to the path. It was little more than a stream tumbling over a wall of rock about seven feet high. Lleland stripped off his tunic and went to stand in the shower of water, pressing himself against the rock to catch as much of the flow as he could. The water was icy, and he shivered as it splashed over him, washing away the stains of his morning. He pushed his hair from his face and stepped from the water to see Lydia watching him. In the bright sunshine, her golden eyes looked like they were on fire. He swallowed hard.

"Feeling better?" she asked.

"Colder and cleaner," he replied.

"Good. You must be hungry. I saw some berries close by." Lleland's stomach growled as he remembered he hadn't eaten that morning, and Lydia laughed. "Definitely hungry," she said. She led him through some trees, then stopped in front of a large bush covered in berries, still green and ripening.

"They don't look ready for eating," Lleland pointed out.

"Not those," Lydia said. "But the berries at the back are ripe."

The back of the bush overhung a steep cliff, and Lleland looked at her in disbelief. "You cannot be serious," he said. She smiled, and hitched her gown to her knees.

"Look, there's a branch," she said, pointing above her head. Lleland looked up to see a thick branch reaching beyond the edge of the cliff.

"You can't climb that," he said aghast.

"Why not?" She kicked off her shoes and pulled herself onto the branch.

"Stop," he cried as she rose to her feet and started walking along the length of the limb. He tried to grab her foot, but she skipped past him with a laugh.

"I'm fine," she said.

"Please, Lydia, come down."

"I won't fall," she promised. She continued walking along the branch, passing the edge of the cliff, as Lleland watched in dismay. Dropping to her haunches, she reached out and grabbed a handful of berries which she tossed into her mouth. She grabbed another handful, then straightening, turned and walked back to where Lleland stood and dropped lightly to the ground.

"Would you like some?" she asked, holding a handful of berries out to him. Ire and relief mingled together as he stared at her. Her lips were stained from the berries, and they parted slightly as he glanced at them. He stepped closer, then leaned down and brushed his lips over hers, tasting the sweet juice. He pulled away a moment later and looked into her eyes. She stared back at him, her emotions unreadable. "I'm sorry," he said. "I shouldn't have done that."

A light shade of pink tinged her cheeks, and she glanced at the berries still in her hand. "You'd better eat these," she said as she held them out to him, and he could see the hint of a smile, "since I risked my very life to obtain them for you."

He stared at her another moment, then took one from her hand and popped it in his mouth. "Thank you, Mistress," he said.

Days stretched into weeks, but Lleland could not bring himself to leave. The daylight hours were spent exploring the mountains with Lydia. He did not kiss her again, but the memory of her soft lips beneath his lingered in his thoughts. Before he pressed any further, though, he wanted to be sure of her feelings for him.

There was one thing he knew for sure, however. Lydia was quite unlike any other woman he had ever met. Intelligent and well informed, she did not hesitate to speak her mind. She was clearly loved by the staff, many of whom had known her from childhood, and she loved them all in return. She was also fiercely loyal to the dragons, and Lleland soon realized that she would never change her opinion about them.

"You know that dragons are dangerous," he said one time.

"Such as those you've seen around Storbrook?"

"They're an exception."

"You have no objectivity when it comes to dragons," she scoffed. "Even in the light of contrary evidence, you won't countenance anything that contradicts your views."

He threw up his hands. "I cannot discuss this with you," he said.

She crossed her arms. "Not until you can admit that you're wrong. You're supposed to be a seeker of truth!"

"What is truth, Lydia? The way I see it, there's your truth, and then there's mine. Which is actually truth?"

"Mine, of course."

The evenings were spent in the company of Lydia and her parents, either in the hall, where the servants organized various entertainments to amuse themselves, or in the private solar, in more quiet pursuits. Whenever there was an opportunity for quiet conversation with Aaron, Lleland took it, but he learned little more about dragons.

"Do you know that you're hailed as the dragon-slayer in Civitas?" he asked Aaron one evening.

Aaron nodded. "So I've heard." Keira was sitting at his side, and he glanced at her. "I told someone once that I would like to be known as 'dragon-slayer,' but I confess it was a lie." He turned back to Lleland. "It is a title I greatly dislike."

"But you killed a monster!"

"Only because of what he was doing. Not because of what he was."

"Many others tried to kill the beast, but failed. Your knowledge of these creatures must be vast."

Thomas entered the room and gestured to Aaron. He rose, then glanced back at Lleland. "You have a splendid opportunity to observe and learn for yourself," he said, before following Thomas through the door.

Lleland had not allowed the conversation to deter him, but he continued to be frustrated in his efforts to garner knowledge from his host. One evening, however, when he had been at Storbrook for a few weeks, he found himself alone with Aaron in the parlor. A chessboard was set up on a table, and Aaron motioned towards it. "Are you up for a game?" he asked.

"I am," Lleland replied, taking a seat on the black side of the board.

"You've had many chances to observe the dragons around Storbrook," Aaron said as he opened the game by moving a pawn. "Have you learned anything?"

"They're always around Storbrook, so their lair must be close by," Lleland replied, mirroring Aaron's move with his own pawn.

"Hmm." They played in silence for a few minutes. "Have the dragons tried to attack you?" Aaron asked, moving his queen into the center of the board.

Lleland glanced at Aaron. "No." He returned his attention to the game and moved his knight. "You have some power over the beasts, don't you?"

Aaron shrugged. "Not power. Authority." He took a moment to consider his next move, then slid his queen forward another two spaces. "Was it Grant that sent you here?"

Lleland looked at Aaron in surprise. "Grant?" he repeated cautiously.

Aaron leaned back in his chair. "You're part of the League." Lleland's hand froze over the board, hovering above his rook. "I suspected it when you arrived here," Aaron continued, "and sought additional information about you. It came today, and confirms your membership."

Lleland leaned back, his mind racing. "Yes," he finally said. There seemed little point in denying it. "I'm a member of the League, and traveled here at their behest."

"You used your acquaintance with Zach to gain entry."

160

Lleland looked away. "I did. I apologize for the deception, Master," he said. He drew in a deep breath. "I'll leave in the morning." He started to rise, but Aaron waved him back down.

"Sit down, Lleland," he said. Lleland paused, then slowly resumed his seat. "I'm disappointed, but not surprised. When the League first formed, they tried to convince me to join their cause, and when I refused, they still tried to garner information from me." He smiled grimly. "Unsuccessfully, of course. I'm not demanding your departure," he continued, "but I do want the truth. Why is Grant coming after me again now?"

Lleland ran his fingers across his brow before answering. "Lord Hindley thought you had some information."

"The Lord Chamberlain? Hmm." Aaron leaned back in his seat, his gaze intent. "What information does he think I have?"

"Hindley told the League that King Alfred was agitated about something before he left for war. He believes you told the king something of particular interest about dragons."

"I see. And what is it that Hindley supposes I told the king?"

"He doesn't know," Lleland replied.

Aaron nodded. "It's your move," he said, glancing at the board. Lleland moved his rook up the side of the board. "So you were sent here to try and extract this information from me."

"Yes. I already had my suspicions on how much, or little, you'd be willing to share with the League, and when I met you, it did not take me long to realize you would never do anything to aid our cause."

"They'll expect a report when you return," Aaron said. "What are you going to tell them?" He moved took one of Lleland's pawns with his bishop.

Lleland shrugged. "The truth. That you told me nothing new, and do not seek to kill the beasts." He frowned. "Does

Lydia know?"

"That you are a member of the League? No. She is completely unaware that such a league exists." Lleland was surprised at how relieved he felt. "Are you still convinced you should be hunting dragons?" Aaron asked.

Lleland moved his knight, blocking Aaron's bishop, as he considered his response. "I've spent my whole adult life in pursuit of that same aim," he said. "Just because you've somehow managed to prevent these beasts from attacking does not change my mind."

"Tell me, Lleland," Aaron said, "how many times have you truly been in danger because of a dragon?"

"Many times."

"Name them."

"The first time was when my father was killed."

"You were there?"

"Yes." Aaron frowned, but remained silent. "The next time," Lleland continued, "I was alone on one of the hills near Civitas when a dragon flew overhead."

"Did it threaten you?"

"I didn't give it a chance to threaten me," Lleland said.

"You mean you killed it without provocation?"

"I killed it before it could kill me," Lleland said. The fire in the grate roared as Aaron steepled his fingers and stared at Lleland. Leaning forward, Lleland moved his bishop across the board.

After what seemed an eternity, Aaron turned his gaze to the game and stroked his chin with his fingers. He leaned forward and reached for his queen. "If I were to give you the information you so earnestly seek, it would either fill you with such rage it could drive you mad, or it could convince you to completely change your views. I wonder which way you would go."

Cold fingers wrapped around Lleland's heart as Aaron leaned back in his seat. "Check," he said. A quick glance at the board showed Lleland that his few remaining moves would still result in Aaron winning the game. He was, in fact, checkmated. He laid his king on its side, forfeiting the game, before glancing up at Aaron, who was watching him intently across the board.

The door opened, and Lydia and Keira entered the room laughing. Keira sat down on the arm of Aaron's chair and wrapped her arms around him. "Hello, my sweet," he said. He tugged her into his lap, tipping the chess board onto the floor in the process and sending the pieces flying as his hands slipped around her back and pulled her close, while Keira moved her hands to his cheeks and lowered her mouth to his. Lydia picked up one of the carved figurines and after a moment's hesitation, gave it to Lleland.

"A gift," she said, her voice low. Lleland glanced at the figure. It was the knight, but instead of a horse, the shape carved into the yellow wood was that of a dragon.

CHAPTER TWENTY-ONE

"Be ready to go out early tomorrow morning," Lydia told Lleland later that week. "And bring your bow."

"Where are we going?" Lleland asked.

"You'll see tomorrow," Lydia said.

As instructed, Lleland was waiting for Lydia in the courtyard shortly after dawn the following morning, bow in hand and arrows in his quiver. The morning air was chilly, and Lleland stamped his feet in an effort to stay warm. He glanced around the yard as he waited, watching the guard that stood in the corner outside a small, squat tower. He had not slept well the previous night, and he rubbed his forehead to chase away the mild headache behind his eyes. The whispers of vague dreams played around the edge of his memory – a man, dressed all in black. His presence had been ominous, but Lleland had willingly gone to him. There was something about the man that was important, but Lleland could not remember what it was. The dream had startled him awake, though, and left in its wake a feeling of dread that had chased away further sleep.

Footsteps rang across the courtyard, and he turned to see Lydia.

"Come along," she said, not pausing to wait for him. "No time for loafers." Lleland quickly caught up with her, and they passed beneath the portcullis together.

"What's in the guarded tower?" he asked.

She glanced at him. "Prisoners," she said.

"You have prisoners? Why?"

She shrugged. "We hold them for the king," she said.

She pointed across the mountains, where the clouds, painted pink by the rising sun, lay like a skirt beneath the mountain peaks, hiding the slopes. "Isn't it beautiful?" she said.

"Yes," he said, but he his gaze was on the woman at his side.

"Come," she said, blushing slightly. "We have a long way to go."

Lleland walked beside Lydia whenever the path allowed, and more than once his hand brushed against hers. He could feel the heat emanating from her skin, and when she looked at him, her golden eyes dazzled him. She wore a dark crimson gown, and her hair rippled over her back like a waterfall. She led him into a forest, and birds flittered from tree to tree as squirrels chattered.

"I'll miss this when I leave," Lleland said.

Lydia glanced at him. "You're leaving?"

"I must leave eventually." Lleland felt his chest tighten at the thought. "I have classes to teach."

"Are the mountains all you'll miss?"

Lleland looked at Lydia. Her eyes were blazing, reflecting the light of the sun as she gazed at him.

"No," he said softly.

She stared at him for another moment, then turned back to the path. "It isn't too much further," she said.

They broke through the trees and crossed an open meadow with rising slopes on either side. In the distance Lleland could hear the roar of a waterfall. They passed beneath another canopy of trees, then stepped into a clearing.

A dozen feet away was a small cliff where the river tumbled over a ledge of flat rock. The rock overhung the river, creating a small, calm pool behind the curtain of water.

"This is one of my favorite places," Lydia said. "Swimming behind a waterfall seems so private. As though I'm in my own little world."

"Do you come here with Zach?"

"No. Zach doesn't enjoy swimming. I'm not sure he even knows about it."

"And yet you brought me here."

Lydia looked at him, meeting his gaze. "Yes." She kicked off her boots and sat down at the water's edge. Lleland sat down beside her. "Ready to go for a swim?" she said.

He grinned, then wrapping his arms around her waist, flung them both into the cool current. He kept his eyes open as they plunged to the depths of the pool, watching as hers widened in surprise. She struggled to free herself from his grasp, and he brought them both back to the surface. She gulped in a deep breath, then placing her hands on his shoulders, pushed him back beneath the water with a laugh. He grabbed her around the waist once more, dragging her down with him. Her hair floated around her face, and he stared at her through the water. Her gown drifted to her knees, and her bare legs brushed against his. He lifted his hand to her cheek as he stared at her through the water, then dragged his fingers against her lips. Even in the water, her skin felt warm. His feet touched the bottom, and he pushed with his toes and sent them drifting upwards. They broke the surface and for a long moment they stared at each other before she placed her hands on his chest and pushed herself away. She swam to the bank and lifted herself out. He followed more slowly, watching as she squeezed the hem of her gown. She turned to him as he reached the edge.

"My gown's sopping wet," she said. The words were light, but her voice trembled. Lleland lifted himself from the water and walked over to her.

"Lydia," he said. Her hair hung in strands over her shoulders, and he touched it lightly.

"I can't even take it off," she said. "A wet chemise doesn't hide much, you know."

He stepped closer and moved his hand to her cheek. She stared at him wide-eyed. "Lydia," he said.

"I'll miss you when you go," she said, dragging her gaze from his.

"I don't want to go."

"You must."

"Lydia – I love you. I want you to be my wife."

"No." She stepped back. "You've only known me for a few weeks," she said.

"Months," he corrected. "From the first moment I met you, I wanted to know you more. Part of the reason I came to the mountains was to see you."

"We're friends. Very good friends. And I ..." She paused. "I hold you in great esteem. But you weren't supposed to fall in love. You told me yourself you couldn't love someone you didn't respect."

"Lydia, you're unlike any woman I've ever met. Smart, determined and beautiful. You are everything I could possibly wish for in a wife. Do I respect you? Absolutely! But more than that, I love you with my whole heart. I cannot bear the thought of losing you." He paused, watching her. "Is esteem all you really feel for me?" he said. "Have I been a fool?"

She glanced back at him, her eyes shimmering. "It won't work."

"Why?"

"Because there are things about me that you don't know. Things that will make you hate me."

"No! Nothing will ever change the love I have for you."

"You know how I feel about dragons. Do you love that?"

Lleland pushed a hand through his hair. "That's just a difference of opinion."

167

"Could you ever love a dragon?"

"I love *you*. What does it matter how I feel about dragons?"

"Because dragons are the reason we can never be together."

Lleland shook his head. "That's the most ridiculous thing I've ever heard." He dragged in a deep breath. "Tell me you feel nothing for me."

"Lleland, I ..." She looked away. "It doesn't matter what I feel. It won't work. The love you feel now will soon turn to hate."

"No. That's impossible."

Placing her hand on his cheek, she kissed him gently on the lips. Her eyes were shining as she turned and walked away. He reached for her hand, but it slipped through his. "Please, Lleland," she whispered. "I'm sorry. Go home. I need to be alone."

"Don't go," he said, but she continued to walk away and didn't look back.

CHAPTER TWENTY-TWO

Lleland stood in the clearing, staring at the spot where Lydia had disappeared through the trees. His mind was numb as he struggled to understand what had gone wrong. He'd been so sure Lydia felt more than mere affection – why had she pushed him away? He laughed wryly to himself. After rejecting so many other woman, he was the one now being rejected. And all because of dragons. None of it made sense, but one thing was clear – he could not remain at Storbrook. He sat down on a rock and stared at the bow lying on the ground. He did not doubt his view of dragons, but how could Lydia have it so wrong? How could her truth be so different from his own? And how could it matter so much? His eye wandered to the pool behind the waterfall, and stripping off his clothes, he dived into the cold water. He wanted to wash away the pain of Lydia's rejection, but her essence lingered in the cool current, and he pushed himself onto the bank in frustration.

He picked up his weapons, which he hadn't even used, and glanced at the sun. It was a little past noon. The thought of returning to Storbrook was oppressive, and he turned in the opposite direction, eager to delay as long as possible. His mind was blank as he strode through the trees, and he missed a rustling in the bushes two dozen yards away.

A loud snort had him spinning on his heel to see a wild boar charging in his direction. The string of his bow was loose, and he cursed as it slipped through his fingers before he finally had it hooked onto the bow. The boar was an old fighter, with one long tusk blunted from years of use and the second broken halfway down, its splintered end far more dangerous than the undamaged tusk. The animal was barely yards away when Lleland notched an arrow and drew his bow.

The arrow hit the boar squarely in the chest, causing it to stumble. It squealed in pain but rose back to its feet and continued to charge. The brief falter gave Lleland enough time to draw another arrow, and it flew through the air to hit the boar in the neck. The creature dropped to the ground, swinging its head wildly through the air as its high-pitched squeals echoed between the trees, making birds take flight from the branches. A third arrow through the heart killed the animal, and Lleland dropped onto his knees beside it. It had been a close call, the result of a distracted mind. The animal was too large for him to carry back to Storbrook, but he sliced a thick hunk of meat from the boar's flank before leaving the remains to the wolves and other animals that roamed the mountains. He carried the meat away from the carcass, then stopped to build a fire. He hadn't eaten at all that day, and despite the events of the morning, his stomach growled in hunger. The meat was tough and stringy, and without salt to season it, was tasteless. It relieved his hunger, however, and gave him the strength to turn toward Storbrook again. It was already mid-afternoon and the castle still lay a few hours away.

The path to Storbrook led north, but to the east rose a high ridge, beyond which the mountains fell away in a vast panorama. He did not make a conscious decision to climb the ridge, but he was aware of a desire to see the view spreading before him one last time before leaving Storbrook and the Northern Mountains. The climb was easy at first, but became gradually steeper, until he was climbing almost vertically. He gained the height and looked out over the sweeping vista that spread in every direction.

A narrow path led to the next peak, and Lleland started towards it. The slopes of the mountain fell sharply away on either side of the path, and as he walked loose pebbles went tumbling down the side. He reached the base of the next peak an hour later, a crag of bare rock face that towered over him. He pushed his boots off his feet and slung his bow over his shoulder. With searching fingers he found a small crevice that would serve as a finger hold, and swung himself upwards. His fingers found another crack, and slowly he inched his way up the side of the rock face, swinging his hands between the cracks while his toes gripped the rock below. A glimmer in the distance caught his eye, but he ignored it as he focused on the wall above him. Inch by inch, he scaled the height, until finally he reached the top and pulled himself up on his stomach, lying for a moment as the burning in his muscles slowly eased. As the pain ebbed away, he rose to his feet and looked around. The rock he was on was barely a dozen feet in length and width – like a small tabletop high above the clouds. He dropped his bow and arrows and walked to the edge of the precipice. A cool breeze lifted the hair from his neck, and he spread his arms, enjoying the feeling of absolute silence and space.

He gazed towards the infinite horizon, turning to take it in from all directions. An eagle soared on currents far below him, circling as it dropped lower. He watched it as it dived, disappearing between the trees. Storbrook's golden walls lay in the distance, and he raised a hand to shield his eyes from the sun's bright rays as he gazed at it. Another needle of rock rose even higher a short distance away, and he squinted to see a messy scattering of twigs covering the top. He walked to the edge and peered up, trying to spot an eaglet. He saw none, but before he pulled back, there was a whoosh from below, and the wing of an eagle brushed over his face as it soared towards its nest. He lurched back, his hands waving wildly as he sought to regain his balance.

Lleland's foot slipped over the edge of the precipice, sending a scattering of stones tumbling down the side. His backside hit the edge and slipped forward. He slapped his palms against the rock but his hands slid over the smooth surface, unable to find purchase. A yell escaped his mouth as he skidded from the rock and started falling through the air, his arms and legs flailing as his heart pounded furiously.

A roar filled the air a moment before a snake-like cord, covered with gold scales that glittered in the sunlight, lashed around Lleland's waist, halting his fall. The side wrapped around him was smooth, but facing outwards were sharp spikes that curved like the thorns on a rose. He groaned as his eyes followed the long, golden length to the large, sleek body it was attached to. "From one certain death into the jaws of another," he muttered. The dragon's long neck curved gracefully downwards, and above the clamped jaws, fiery eyes glared at him. He closed his eyes and prayed that his death would be quick and painless.

The dragon rose through the air, bearing its burden above the rocky tabletop. As they climbed higher, Lleland could see his bow lying where he had dropped it, arrows beside it. Hope surged through him. Force of habit had made him slip one heavy arrow into his quiver, even though he had not expected to hunt anything larger than a rabbit, and if his aim was true, one was all he needed.

He watched as the rock grew closer. The dragon was almost above it, and he could feel its tail grow slacker. He wriggled, testing the grip. If he could slide down and slip beneath the tail as the dragon landed, he could reach his bow, still strung, and notch an arrow in the space of a heartbeat. The table of rock was just a few feet below him now, and as the dragon dropped, Lleland gathered his focus. His toes touched the hard surface, and with an outward thrust, he pushed away the tail and slipped down, rolling in the direction of the bow. He grabbed the weapon and spun onto his haunches, notching the arrow in one fluid motion. The dragon had landed on the rock, and as he pulled back the arrow the beast was directly in front of him.

The arrow sprang from the string with a whirl, but the dragon was even faster. It launched itself into the air, rising above the passing barb with barely an inch to spare. The creature raced over Lleland's head, the tip of its tail knocking the bow from his hand and sending it plummeting down the precipice. The dragon soared away from the rock as Lleland dropped to his knees and scrambled over the edge. He had to get away before the dragon returned. His foot slipped, and he slid down the face of the rock a few inches, until his scrabbling fingers found a small hold. He was scratched and bleeding, but he barely noticed as he searched for another toehold.

The dragon circled around him, and he leaned into the rock as it passed, breathing a sigh of relief when it disappeared around the other side. He continued his descent, slipping and sliding over the unyielding surface. He finally neared the foot of the cliff, and jumping down, spun around to look for the dragon. It was still circling around the rock, but as he looked up, it blew out a single stream of flame then turned away. He watched as it vanished into the distance, then sank to his knees. He could hear the roar of his heart in his chest. He started to shiver despite the heat of the sun, and he pushed a shaking hand across his forehead to wipe away the sheen of sweat. When he finally pushed himself to his feet, he saw his bow lying a short distance away. Somehow, it had survived the fall.

CHAPTER TWENTY-THREE

It was almost dark by the time Lleland arrived back at Storbrook, bruised and aching. Supper was being served, but he walked past the hall and headed up the stairs. As he reached the passage a voice called his name, and he turned to see Aaron standing in the doorway of his study.

"Are you hurt?" Aaron asked.

"Just some scrapes and bruises."

"You'll join us in the hall?"

"No. I don't have much of an appetite. But I need to speak with you later."

Aaron nodded. "I'll be in the solar."

Lleland headed to his chambers and packed up his few belongings. He placed the chess piece Lydia had given him on the small table beside the bed. He saw it now for what it was – not a token of affection, but a sign that she could never be his.

Lleland waited until he heard sounds in the passage before heading out the door and towards the solar. He pushed open the door and paused when he saw Lydia. Keira was sitting beside her, holding her hand.

"Ah, Lleland, come in," Aaron said. Lleland stepped in

174

and closed the door. "Help yourself to some wine."

Lleland nodded stiffly and poured himself a glass, before taking a seat across from Aaron. "Master Drake, I'll be leaving at first light," Lleland said. He heard Lydia's sharp intake of breath.

"That's probably for the best," Aaron said. "I'd hoped that staying here would help you see the truth about dragons. But perhaps –"

The sound of heavy footsteps could be heard through the door. Aaron lifted his head, then glanced quickly at Lydia, who met his gaze with raised eyebrows. Aaron's eyes moved on to Keira. "Zach," he said in response to her questioning expression.

They both stood as the door flung open, and Zach marched in, his eyes sweeping over the room. They settled narrowly on Lleland.

"You," he snarled. "You have the temerity to come here!"

"Zach," Aaron said, laying his hand on Zach's shoulder. Zach shook it off and met Aaron's gaze with a growl.

"Do you know who that is, Father?" he said, pointing at Lleland. "That … that murderer."

"What?" Lleland said, rising as Lydia jumped to her feet.

"What are you saying?" she demanded.

"I just saw Grandfather. He said we have a visitor." Zach turned to glare at Lleland. "Imagine my surprise when I heard it was *you*!"

"What are you talking about?" Lydia demanded.

Zach's gaze swung to his sister. "You don't know, do you?"

"Know what?"

"I did a bit more digging into Master Seaton." He spat the name. "He's a hunter."

"Zach." Aaron's voice held a note of warning, but Zach ignored it. "He's a *hunter*, Lydia. A dragon hunter."

"No!" Lydia's gaze swung to Lleland. "Tell me it's not true."

Lleland flushed. "It's true. But I didn't come here to hunt."

"Just to learn how to hunt more effectively," Zach snarled. "You're despicable. You profess friendship, when all you want to do is kill and murder." He turned to Aaron. "You, of all people, should have known better!"

"Zach!" Keira's voice held a note of warning.

"Careful, son," Aaron said. "I know what he is. I hoped being here would help him see the truth."

"He's too blinded by hate to see the truth," Zach said.

"The truth?" Lleland said. He stalked towards Zach. "You want to know the truth? The truth is my father was killed by one of those monsters! He pleaded for my life, and the beast made me watch as it ripped my father apart and ate him, one limb at a time." Lleland's nostrils flared as he glared at Zach. "Even when I turned away, I could hear the breaking and crunching of his bones. I couldn't even cover my ears, because I was trapped and injured." He turned to Aaron. "Do you know how old I was? Six! So tell me that dragons are not monsters." Silence fell over the room, broken only by Lydia's soft sob as she dropped to the floor. It was Aaron who finally spoke.

"How much blood did he give you?"

Lleland looked at Aaron in disbelief. "What?"

"Blood. How much did the dragon give you?"

"What are you talking about?" Lleland took a step back.

"You said you were injured. When the dragon finished with your father, did he just leave you there?"

Lleland shook his head, trying to make sense of what Aaron was saying.

"The blood of a dragon is very potent," Aaron said. "It slows down the aging process. It gives a human incredible strength. And it also heals. Did the dragon heal you with his blood?"

"No!"

"How much did he give you?" Aaron asked again.

"I don't know," he said. Lleland closed his eyes as the ghost of a memory flitted through his conscious mind.

"Yes, you do. Think, Lleland. What happened when the dragon was done with your father?"

"I –"

"You said you were injured. Were you able to stand?"

"No. I was … there was blood everywhere. Some of it was mine, and the rest …" Lleland swallowed and looked away.

"Jack gave you some blood, didn't he?"

"Jack?"

"Black Jack," Zach said.

Black Jack. The memory of a man dressed in black rose in Lleland's mind. *You're mine.* "I keep dreaming of a man in black," Lleland said.

"What does the man do?" Aaron said.

"Nothing. He just watches me."

"The man's not a dream, he's a memory."

"No. I'd remember that."

"How did you get home, Lleland? After your father was killed?"

"I don't remember."

"Yes, you do. You don't want to, but the memory is still there. That's why Jack comes in your dreams."

"I don't know this Jack!"

"Think, Lleland. How did you get home?"

"I, uh …" Lleland closed his eyes.

"Well, come along," said the man. "I'll walk you home. You can introduce me to your mother." Lleland nodded and rose to his feet. The dragon had vanished, and the man was shrugging on a black doublet.

"Where's the dragon?" he asked.

"He asked me to take care of you," said the man. Again, Lleland nodded. That made sense. He took the man's hand. "My name's Jack," the man said. "What's yours?"

Lleland gasped as his eyes flew open. "You're right," he whispered. "That man – Jack – he was there." He swallowed.

"How did you know that?"

"He gave you some blood. Do you remember?"

"No." Lleland shook his head. "No. I'd never have drunk someone's blood."

"He gave you dragon blood." Aaron's eyes narrowed slightly. "You'd been badly injured. How else could you even manage to rise?"

Lleland's hand rose to his shoulder, feeling for the scar that should have been there. He skin was completely smooth, however, with no trace of the deep wound he'd received. He took a deep breath and stared at Aaron. His eyes seemed to be glowing. *The dragon was standing over him, its head bent to Lleland's eye level. There was a scratch on his chest, where a few drops of blood had collected. "Come on, boy," it said, "you need some blood."*

"No." Lleland turned his face away.

"Either you have some or I'll kill you." The dragon sounded amused. Reluctantly Lleland opened his mouth, and the dragon poked a long talon between his teeth. Liquid coated Lleland's tongue. It was sweet, like honey, but it was mixed with the coppery tang of blood.

"That's the way, boy," the dragon said. "Have a bit more." Lleland shook his head, but when the dragon brought the talon to his lips again, he opened his mouth and licked the drops. The dragon nodded, pleased. "That's the way."

The wound on the dragon's chest had closed, but he scored himself open again, going deeper than before, and blood sprang to the surface. Lleland leaned forward and the dragon bent closer. "That's right, boy," he murmured, "use your tongue and lick it off. The more you have the quicker you'll heal." Lleland rose onto his knees and lifted his face to the chest, using his tongue to lick away the drops. When it was gone, the dragon pulled away.

"More," Lleland pleaded.

"No." The dragon laughed. "That's enough for one day. You can have more tomorrow."

Lleland frowned. "I don't think Mother will let me see a dragon."

The dragon laughed. "Never fear. I'll come to your house every day, but it won't be a dragon you see."

Lleland's eyes flew open, and he stumbled back to the bench. "No," he whispered.

"Lleland, tell me."

"Every day. I drank his blood every day."

"For how long?"

"Weeks. And then he stopped coming. I didn't eat. I didn't sleep. I didn't spare a thought for my father. I just wanted the dragon. And then the feelings disappeared." Lleland closed his eyes. "Oh, God," he groaned, "I'd forgotten. I didn't care that my father was dead." He looked at Aaron, eyes wide. "How could I do that? How could I just forget my father? He loved me, and I didn't care."

Aaron pulled a chair over and sat before Lleland. "It wasn't your fault," he said.

"I should have killed that monster! It twisted my mind and made me forget the most important person in my life." He dropped his head into his hands. "If only I could tell my father how sorry I am."

"He already knows, Lleland. And you were only six. How do you think you could have succeeded when grown men failed?" Aaron said. "When Jack gave you his blood, he bound himself to you. Considering how much he gave you, and the fact that you were so young, it's amazing that your mind survived intact. It speaks of your resiliency."

"What do you mean when you say 'bind'?"

"The blood ties the person to the dragon, and the dragon can manipulate his thoughts and actions, if he chooses to do so."

"Then why did the feelings suddenly disappear?" Lleland asked.

"Because Jack was dead. The bond was broken."

"But ..." Lleland rubbed his forehead in confusion. "You killed the dragon. Who was Jack?" His eyes widened as he stared at Aaron. "Jack was the dragon," he whispered. "The dragon was a man." He frowned. "You knew this."

"Yes."

179

"Dragons can become human."

"Dragons can take on the form of humans, but they are still dragons."

Lleland shook his head. "No, that can't be. You're wrong." The air suddenly seemed thick as he struggled to breathe. "How do you even know? Have *you* been drinking dragon blood?"

"No."

"But you look much younger than you should." He looked around the room, and his gaze fell on Lydia. Had she been drinking dragon blood, too? That would explain her tenderness for dragons. He slipped onto his knees in front of her.

"Lydia, I'm sorry."

She shook her head. "And I'm sorry. I'm sorry Jack killed your father, and that he gave you his blood." She glanced at him, and her eyes were blazing, as though flames were smouldering in their depths.

"Come along, boy," Jack said. He smiled down at Lleland. "Do you like spending time with me?"

"Oh, yes," Lleland said.

"And do you miss your father?"

"My father?" Lleland was puzzled. "No."

Jack laughed as flames kindled in his eyes. "Good."

Lleland stared at Lydia as his heart started to pound in his chest. "Your eyes," he whispered. "You have eyes like Jack." He lurched backwards and fell onto the floor. "No!" He shook his head. "It can't be."

"Lleland." She reached out a hand.

"Don't touch me!" He jumped to his feet and his eyes darted around the room before settling on Aaron. "Tell me I'm wrong."

"Lleland …"

"Tell me!"

"I can't."

Lleland's eyes flew back to Lydia. "You're a monster! You

attacked me! You tried to kill me!" he shouted.

"No!" she cried, jumping up. "I saved you, and you wanted me dead!"

Lleland lifted his hands as if to ward her away. His eyes flew wildly around the room. "She's a monster!" he shouted. Keira lifted her hand to her mouth with a soft cry, but Aaron and Zach were silent, watching him intently.

Lleland stared at Aaron, then gasped. Flames were smouldering in his eyes, too. "No." His gaze darted to the others. "No. It can't be. You're all monsters!" He stumbled backwards, his hand reaching for the door as he fumbled for the latch. "I'm a fool!"

"Lleland! Stop!" Zach took a step towards him, but Aaron held him back.

"Leave him," he said.

Lleland wrenched open the door and stumbled into the passage. Somehow he made it to his own chamber, where he slammed the door behind him and dropped the bar. A wave of nausea washed over him and he grabbed the chamber pot, retching until his stomach was empty. He pushed it away in disgust and dropped into the chair, his head in his hands. He had come looking for more information about dragons, but what he'd learned horrified him. He laughed cynically. He had not just found the dragon's lair, he had walked right into it.

CHAPTER TWENTY-FOUR

"Master Seaton?" There was a knock on the door. It took Lleland a moment to recognize Thomas's voice. He rubbed his face with his hands.

"Can I come in?" Thomas called. Lifting the bar, Lleland opened the door and stepped aside as Thomas entered.

"Thomas," he said.

"I heard about your discovery. You're distressed."

"You could say that." He crossed his arms. "How can you work here, serving those monsters?"

"I'm an old man," Thomas said, "and have served Master Aaron for forty-five years. I can tell you he's no monster."

"He's a dragon," Lleland snarled, pacing the room. "They're the same thing."

"No. Jack was a monster. I know; I saw what he did. It was Aaron who stopped him."

"Why?"

"Why?" Thomas was surprised. "Because what Jack was doing was wrong." He walked over to the chair, and sank down with a sigh. "Do you mind? These old bones are not what they used to be."

"Why don't you drink dragon's blood?"

"Dragons are forbidden from giving a human their blood. Jack broke the law when he gave you his."

"So Aaron won't give you his blood?"

"No. And I wouldn't drink it, even if he offered."

"You don't want to be tied to him?"

"It's not that. I'm already tied to Aaron through friendship and loyalty, and he would never demand anything of me that I was not prepared to give. I have no desire to prolong my life unnaturally."

"I see."

"I don't think you do." Thomas crossed his arms and leaned back in the chair. "The Drakes may be dragons, but they are good people. And Aaron has more reason than most to hate humans."

"Why?"

"Both his parents were killed by humans."

"Dragon hunters?"

"No. A jealous villager. His name was Arnold Hobbes—"

"Hobbes? A relation of Matthew Hobbes?"

"Yes." Thomas nodded. "He was a bit simple, and Eleanor – that's Aaron's mother – was kind to him. He thought she loved him, and was furious when Zachary took her away."

"Zachary is Aaron's father?"

"Yes."

"And did Arnold know that the object of his affection was a monster?"

"Like Lydia, you mean?" Thomas said, and Lleland's eyes narrowed. "But Aaron's mother wasn't a dragon, she was human. She grew up in the village."

"Human?"

Thomas nodded. "Like Keira. Only human women can bear a dragon child."

"I see. Aaron's dragon father abducted a human woman, and the villager wanted to rescue her."

Thomas settled a narrow gaze on Lleland. "Eleanor loved

her husband, just as Keira loves Aaron, and she married Zachary of her own free will. Like the other villagers, Master Hobbes didn't realize that Zachary – whom he only saw in human form – was a dragon, but since the beginning of time, the villagers have known that there's a connection between the Drakes of Storbrook Castle and the dragons. One day Zachary landed closer to the village than he should have, and Master Hobbes saw him with Eleanor on his back. Hobbes flew at the dragon with a branch, but Eleanor stepped into his path and was felled with a mortal blow. When Zachary saw Eleanor was dead, he was overcome with despair. He lost the will to fight, and the villagers killed him. Aaron saw it all."

"But the villagers knew the dragon was dangerous. They were saving their village from a monster. He probably would have killed his human mate eventually."

Thomas laughed dryly. "Zachary loved Eleanor. Look at Aaron and Keira. Do you think he would ever harm her? They've been married for forty years, and he loves her more now than ever. Besides, they've been bound together in a way two humans can never be."

"So she's tasted his blood. I know what that feels like – she has no choice but to stay with him."

"When a dragon takes a mate, the bond goes both ways. He's bound to her as much as she is to him. It was the same with Eleanor and Zachary."

Lleland dropped down at the end of the bed. "Why are you telling me this?" he finally said.

"You came here with your mind made up about dragons, Master Seaton. But as a scholar you should know better than to close your mind off to other possibilities. I just wanted to give you something more to mull over before you leave in the morning." Thomas pushed himself wearily to his feet, his hand on the arm of the chair. "Aaron has ordered a horse be saddled for you in the morning. You can leave it with Richard when you reach the village."

"I have no wish to impose myself any further on Master Drake," Lleland said stiffly.

Thomas shrugged. "Suit yourself. It's a long way down the mountain."

"Thank you. I'll walk," Lleland said.

He waited as Thomas left the room, then dropped the bar over the door once more. He glanced at the bed. His body ached with weariness, but he knew his mind would allow him no rest. He sank into the chair where Thomas had sat a moment before, and stared into the fire. The woman he loved was also a monster. The words she had spoken earlier that day taunted him: could he ever love a dragon? He rose to his feet with a growl and started pacing the room. Did the woman he loved even exist? Lydia was the kind of creature he most despised in the world, and she'd kept that information hidden. His jaw clenched as anger surged through him. She had taken him for a fool. Led him on, let him fall in love with her, all the while hiding her black heart! She'd asked him if he could ever love a dragon. No! Lleland growled the word through clenched teeth. Never!

A log fell in the grate, and he turned towards it. The glowing embers seemed to mock him, reminding him of eyes that burned with flame. With a snarl, he kicked the pile of wood beside the hearth, sending logs scattering. He could not remain a minute longer in the monster's lair.

He gathered his small bundle, grabbed his bow and lifted the bar from the door. All was quiet, but he paused a moment, listening, before heading into the passage and towards the stairs. Dragons, he knew, had excellent hearing. He froze when a scratching came from the wall, then breathed a sigh of relief when he saw the small, beady eyes of a mouse. He continued down the stairs, and a moment later cautiously pushed open the door to the courtyard. There was no-one about except the guard, who was dozing on a wooden chair near the fire pit. Lleland glanced upwards – the moon was nearly full, allowing him to easily see the gate.

Skirting the edge of the building, he crossed the courtyard and passed beneath the portcullis. It was raised, as always, and it occurred to Lleland that he had never seen it lowered. Indeed, there seemed little need for it when the castle was filled with dragons.

With as little noise as possible, he made his way down the stony path that led from Storbrook, breathing a sigh of relief when he reached the woods. It was dark beneath the trees, but he had traversed this path enough times over the last few weeks to know the general direction he needed to go. He traveled as quickly as possible, eager to increase the distance between himself and the dragons' lair.

By the time the sun crested the horizon, Lleland had already traveled a fair distance. He paused midmorning to fill his canteen with water, and at the waters' edge he found a bush with a few small berries which he gulped ravenously. He had not eaten since the previous afternoon. Whenever he left the canopy of trees, he glanced heavenwards. He thought he saw a dragon circling high above him, but it wasn't until he saw the sun glancing off the scales that he was sure.

It was late afternoon when he saw the spire of the village church between the trees. His belly ached from hunger, his limbs were exhausted and his head was wracked with pain. He stumbled into the inn, and after ravenously gulping down two bowls of stew, he fell on the bed provided to him, and was asleep within moments.

CHAPTER TWENTY-FIVE

Despite his exhaustion, Lleland did not sleep well. The sounds of the inn settling startled him awake, and he tossed and turned in the bed until finally he fell into a restless sleep. He awoke to the sun streaming in through the small window above his bed, still exhausted. His body ached from the previous day's exertions, but he barely noticed as the recollections of the last few days flooded his mind. What had seemed so simple before – his love for Lydia and his mission to rid the world of dragons – had suddenly become very complicated. Not only was the woman he loved a monster, but she could hide herself in plain sight.

Lleland had heard rumors before that dragons could take on human form, but like the other members of the League, had dismissed them as old wives' tales. Knowing now the truth of the tales, he understood just how cunning the dragons were. They had outwitted the hunters for years by changing their appearance and taking on human form. But armed with this knowledge, Lleland knew that the tide could be turned, and the world could finally be rid of the beasts. He coldly pushed aside the memories of golden eyes and soft lips that rose in his mind. They were based on a lie, and there was a war to be won, whatever the cost.

When Lleland left his chamber a little later, he found the innkeeper seated at a table in the hall. He nodded at Lleland as he entered the room. "Some bread and ale, Master?"

"Thank you," Lleland said. He watched as the innkeeper shuffled away. In his haste to leave Storbrook, he had not given thought to the route he would take back to Civitas, but it occurred to him now that he should have some plan. He remembered John, the coachman, talking about a road that skirted around the mountains.

"How do I get to the road that leads to the city?" he asked the innkeeper when he returned with a board of bread and cheese.

"The city, eh?" The man scratched his head. "The west road joins the highway." He shrugged. "I guess that heads south."

"How far to the highway?" he asked.

"'Bout seventy miles."

Lleland finished his meal, and collected his belongings. As he stepped onto the street he saw Matthew Hobbes across the road, talking to some friends. He ducked his head, hoping to pass unnoticed, but when one of the other men stared at him, Matthew turned around.

"The dragon hunter!" he said. "Did you kill some beasts up in the mountains?"

Lleland sighed inwardly. "No," he said.

"But you saw the monsters?"

"I did."

"And yet you did not kill them. Why not?"

"I didn't come here to hunt," Lleland said. "I came to gather information and learn what I could about the dragons."

"But you'll be back with a hunting party?"

Lleland shrugged. "Perhaps. But the mountains are a long way from the city, and we must deal with threats closer to home first."

Matthew frowned. "Our village may be small, but those dragons are just as dangerous as the monsters close to the city."

"After forty years, it seems to me that the risk is minimal. I'd rather focus my attention on more serious threats."

Matthew's eyes narrowed. "That monster killed my father," he said.

"From what I heard, your father attacked the dragon unprovoked."

"What kind of hunter chooses to side with the beasts?"

"Those dragons are not a threat," Lleland snapped. "And as long as they live peacefully in the mountains, we'll leave them alone."

"You'll wait until they attack and kill us?"

"They won't." Lleland glanced up at the sky. "I see no dragons coming in to burn, kill and plunder." He nodded his head. "Good day."

"Those monsters must die," Matthew shouted as he walked away. "And if you won't do it, I will!"

The day grew hot as the sun rose higher, and Lleland's palm was slick from gripping his bow. There were few travelers on the road, but there were plenty of sheep, and they complained loudly as he walked by.

When the sun dropped behind the mountains, Lleland looked out for somewhere to spend the night. A small stand of trees offered some shelter, and he headed off the road towards them. In his satchel he had a hunk of bread and a slice of cheese, taken from the inn that morning, and he pulled them out as he made himself comfortable against the trunk of a tree. He had not been there very long when he saw someone walking along the road, traveling in his direction. He looked away, but the traveler, a young man, shouted out a greeting.

"Hello, there," he called. He left the road and headed towards Lleland. He was dressed in a well-cut doublet and scarlet breeches. His boots were clearly new, and at his side hung a sword with a jeweled hilt. "I thought I saw someone ahead of me," he said. "Was that you?"

"It was." Lleland paused. In his hand he held the bread and cheese. "Will you join me in my meal?" he said. "It's not much, but I'm happy to share."

The man dropped to the ground. "Don't mind if I do," he said. "The name's Francis Smythe."

Lleland shook the proffered hand. "Lleland Seaton."

Lleland shared out the bread and cheese, and passed Francis a bottle of ale. As they ate, Lleland discovered that the young man was the son of a wealthy landlord, sent on pilgrimage as penance for getting the daughter of a neighboring farmer with child. "That's why I travel on foot," he said cheerfully. "I must suffer for my sins." He finished his food and rose. "Well, I'm not going to tarry. I have no wish to sleep in a field, and the next village is only five more miles."

"You shouldn't travel the roads alone in the dark," Lleland warned. "There could be wild animals – or worse," he added darkly. "Stay here and we'll travel together in the morning."

"Not I. I have no fear for my safety. I know these roads – have traveled them since I was a boy."

Lleland shrugged. "Very well."

"Perhaps we'll meet again," Francis said. He waved and continued down the road, disappearing into the gray light of dusk.

Lleland stretched out on the ground and stared at the stars as they began to pierce the darkening sky. A trail of flame caught his eye and he watched it for a moment. It was far away, but he imagined he could feel the heat licking over his body. Hr turned over and closed his eyes as sleep silently washed over him. In his dreams he felt soft lips pressed to his own, and he whispered a name into the night.

He awoke before the sun appeared over the mountains, and after a few mouthfuls of stale bread, continued on his way. The sky was clear, promising another hot day. He wondered if Francis had found the bed he sought. With his charming smile and easy manner, he had probably procured both a bed and a comely maid to warm it for him, Lleland thought wryly.

The road dipped and curved as it followed the mountains, disappearing into valleys and reappearing further away as it climbed another steep slope. Lleland had just crested a summit when he saw a group of men in the valley below. It was difficult to tell from this distance what they were doing, but he picked up his pace, then started running when he heard a yell.

One of the men was swinging a club, and as Lleland drew closer he saw Francis surrounded by three armed men. The men were being kept at bay by a swinging sword, but as Lleland watched, the man with the club moved behind Francis and raised his weapon. Dropping to his knees, Lleland notched an arrow and sent it flying. It hit the man with the club in the chest, and there was a dull thud as he dropped to the ground.

The other two men paid no attention to their fallen comrade, but the noise distracted Francis and he glanced over his shoulder, giving his attackers the opening they were looking for. One of the men lunged at Francis with a dagger, but Francis was already turning back and the blade merely scraped his skin. Lleland released another arrow and the man dropped to his knees, the shaft sticking from his belly. As he fell he caught the tunic of the third attacker, slowing him down. The man shoved his wounded friend aside, but Francis was already swinging his sword above his head. It crashed down into the last man's skull, and he crumpled to the ground as blood spurted in every direction. Francis turned towards Lleland kneeling in the dust.

"Behind you," Francis shouted.

Francis waved towards the bushes at the side of the road, and Lleland spun to see two more men running towards him from the cover of the trees. He notched another arrow and hit one of the men in the shoulder, but there was no time to release another before the last man was on him. Clasped in his hand was a short dagger, and he struck Lleland in the chest with enough force to send both men tumbling to the ground.

The man rose to his knees, straddling Lleland, and yanked the dagger from Lleland's chest. He drew back for another blow as Lleland tried to shove him aside, but the wound had been deep, and his strength was already draining away.

Out of the corner of his eye he could see Francis running towards him, shouting something as he lifted his sword. He's too far away to do anything, Lleland thought. He could see the glint of the dagger raised in the air, poised to strike again. He stared at it, fascinated by the way it shimmered in the light, but then suddenly it was gone. The man disappeared, and a golden dragon filled his vision. The dragon dropped beside Lleland, its huge body blocking Francis.

"Lleland. Look at me." Lydia lowered her head, and Lleland lifted his eyes to meet her golden gaze. "I'm not going to let you die," she said.

"You must," he said. He shivered. Behind Lydia's hulking form, Francis was yelling for her to stay away.

"Why do humans think we want to hurt them?" Lydia said.

"Perhaps because that's what dragons do." Lleland coughed, and specks of blood flew from his mouth, landing on Lydia's scales.

"You should know better by now," she said. The dagger that had pierced Lleland still lay on the ground, and Lydia grabbed it with her talons and placed it against her hide.

"No," Lleland said, trying to reach her claw, but he had no strength, and his hand dropped to the ground. "Let me die." Everything was growing hazy, and black specks swarmed his vision. A blurry image appeared in front of him, and the sun glittered against the sharp end of a sword, pointed at Lydia.

"Leave him alone," Francis shouted. The words battered against Lleland's mind, and he closed his eyes. The darkness was growing as the humming increased. Lydia said something, but he could not make out the words. Instead he gave himself over to the darkness.

CHAPTER TWENTY-SIX

It was the sound of voices, raised in anger, that penetrated the fog that clung to Lleland's mind, arousing him to consciousness.

"What have you done?"

"He was going to die!"

"Then you should have let him die!"

Lleland forced his eyes open. For a moment he wasn't sure where he was, but as the last of the fog cleared away, he realized he was back in his chamber at Storbrook. He turned towards the voices. Lydia was standing with her back to him, blocking the faces of Aaron and Zach. Lleland stared at them, trying to remember how he had arrived back here. Francis was being attacked, he remembered, and he went to his aid, killing three of the attackers. But he had been stabbed.

"You gave me your blood," Lleland rasped. Lydia spun around to face him. "Zach's right, you should have let me die," he said.

Lydia crossed over to the bed. "Here," she said, handing him a cup of water. He lifted himself to his elbow and drained the contents. His throat burned like desert sand, and heat coursed through his body, which the water did little to relieve. He handed Lydia the cup and fell back on the bed.

"I told you let me die."

"I couldn't," she replied as Aaron and Zach left the room.

"So instead you gave me your blood," he said bitterly. He turned to look at the wall. "What happened to Francis?"

"Francis? The boy? He tried to kill me with his sword, and when I took you with me, he hurled rocks at me."

"Good man," Lleland said approvingly. He turned back to Lydia, meeting her golden gaze. "You should have left me to die."

Lydia pulled her gaze away with a sigh. "So you keep saying. Would you have left *me* to die?" Lleland looked away, unable to give her a reply. He was so hot, and his skin was itchy where he had been stabbed.

"I've been bound to a dragon once before," he said. "I have no wish to endure it again."

"You're not a child anymore," Lydia said. "You know your own mind, and can resist the desire to do something against your will. Not that I would make any such demands of you."

"No? I just wouldn't be able to trust any feelings I have for you."

"You have feelings for me?"

"No!" Lleland pushed himself into a sitting position, wincing when pain flared through his chest. "Certainly not!"

Lydia turned away. "Good! Because I feel nothing for you, either. Whatever I felt vanished the instant you revealed that you kill my people!"

"Your people? Good lord, Lydia, your people are monsters."

"Monsters, Lleland? You're the monster! You hunt us like animals!"

"And what did your 'people' do when they ripped my father apart?" Lleland pushed the blankets from his naked body and rose to his feet. He should be feeling weak, but he felt strong and powerful. "I loved you," he shouted, "and you deceived me. And now you've given me your blood, binding me to you." A wave of dizziness hit him, and he staggered slightly. "I don't want to be bound to you," he roared.

Lydia stared at him, her eyes wide as she backed up against the wall. "Papa," she shouted. Lleland snorted in disgust. Heavy footsteps could be heard pounding down the passage. The door was flung open and Aaron entered, Zach a pace behind him. They both stopped and stared at Lleland.

"Well, well," Zach said wryly.

"Zach!" Aaron's voice was sharp. He glanced at Lydia. "Leave." She opened her mouth to protest, then nodding, left the room, pushing past Zach who closed the door behind her.

Aaron turned back to Lleland. "Look at me," he said. Lleland snorted, annoyed. Who did Aaron think he was, storming in here? He turned to glance around the room, and his eye fell on the open window. Outside, the blue sky beckoned invitingly, but it was blocked a moment later when Zach stepped onto the window ledge. His wings were open behind him, a dull gold in the shadows, but Lleland barely noticed. He wanted to get away from this place. The heat was burning through him and he felt strong and powerful. If he dived at Zach, perhaps he could get past him.

"Lleland!" Aaron's voice cut through his thoughts, and Lleland reluctantly turned to look at him. Aaron's tone held a note of command that Lleland could not ignore. "Tell me your name," he said. Lleland glanced around the room, seeking another way out. Something swished over the floor, thick and black, but Aaron was speaking. "Your name," he demanded again. Lleland could not understand the need to give his name. Aaron already knew who he was. "Lleland! What is your name?"

"Lleland Seaton," he growled.

"What are you, Lleland?"

Lleland snarled. "A hunter," he said. He leaned forward.

"I hunt monsters like you." Behind him Zach snorted.

Aaron's expression was implacable. "What else?"

"What else?" This game was getting tedious. "I'm …" Who was he, again? He tried to think. "A Master," he said, "at … at Kings College."

"Good." Aaron nodded in approval. "What do you teach?"

Lleland closed his eyes. Who cared what he taught? "The classics," he finally said.

"Name them."

"Why?" Lleland leaned forward and glared at Aaron. "What's the meaning of this?"

"Lleland, I need you to remember who you are. Think."

Lleland turned away. He had no wish to remember such irrelevant details. His throat burned and he longed for something to soothe it. He looked around the room again, but saw nothing that would satisfy. Something else caught his eye. Reaching to the ceiling he saw a pair of wings, as black as the night. He stared at them for a moment. He could see at a glance that they were strong and powerful. He looked at the window again.

"Lleland! Look at me." Lleland turned back to Aaron. "Think about who you are," he said. "Close your eyes. Imagine yourself in your classroom." Lleland closed his eyes, but he could not picture his classroom. All he could think of was black wings. "Tell me what you see," Aaron said.

"Dark wings. Long black tail. The fiery breath of a monster." He opened his eyes. "I'm a monster," he said. He laughed, and flames filled the room, blackening the dark stone walls. He could feel their heat, and he basked in it. "I'm a hunter," he said. He turned towards the window and threw himself forward, but before he could even reach it there was a flash of light and Aaron was towering over him, his huge body blocking the window. Lleland roared in frustration. He wanted to escape. The tail swished over the ground, thumping against the walls, and flames filled the room once more.

"Lleland!" Through the haze, Lleland recognized the urgency in Aaron's voice. He recognized something else, too. Aaron was no weak dragon, easily overpowered. He was strong – stronger than Zach or any other dragon Lleland had seen. He lowered his gaze. "Remember who you are," Aaron said. "Think of your mother."

"No."

"Your mother. Tell me her name."

"Anabel," Lleland said reluctantly.

"Describe her to me."

Lleland shrugged. What did Aaron want to know? "A woman. In her sixties."

"You took her to the country."

"Yes."

"Why?"

"She …" Lleland paused, trying to remember. "She was scared of the dragons."

"You were worried about her?"

"Yes."

"Are you still worried about her?"

Lleland thought about it for a moment. "Yes," he finally said.

Aaron nodded. "Think of her, Lleland. Remember how much you love her and want to keep her safe."

Lleland closed his eyes as Anabel rose in his mind. Her face was pale as she stared at him. He threw back his head as something ripped through him, breaking him apart, and he fell to the floor on his hands and knees. His hands were shaking, and his body felt as though it was on fire.

"What just happened?" he whispered. He looked up at Aaron, still towering over him. "I saw wings, and a tail … oh, God, no." There was a flash of light, and Aaron was crouching in front of him.

"Lleland, look at me."

"I felt …" His voice trailed away.

"Lleland, you're a dragon."

Lleland's head snapped up. "Impossible! That's impossible!" He stood and stumbled back. "No, you're wrong!"

Aaron gave him a sympathetic look. "You know I'm not."

"But ..." Lleland glanced at Zach, watching impassively. "I'm human! I hate dragons."

Aaron gave a wry smile. "Yes, we know that. But that doesn't change what just happened. You took on dragon form."

"How could that happen?"

"I don't know. I've never heard of a grown man turning. Are you sure your father wasn't a dragon?"

"Of course not! Jack ate him."

"Hmm. Then I think it must have something to do with the blood Jack gave you." Aaron tapped the side of his leg with his fingers. "You were just a child, and from what you say, he gave you a vast amount of his blood. It must have started a change within you."

"Then why has nothing happened to me before?"

"Lydia's blood probably served as a catalyst."

"Of course," Lleland said bitterly.

Zach jumped down from the window. "It makes sense," he said. "He hadn't reached puberty when he met Jack."

"What does puberty have to do with it?" Lleland asked wearily.

"Dragons only assume their natural forms when they reach puberty," Zach said. "You must know that."

"How would I know that?" Lleland snapped.

Zach laughed. "I thought you were the expert on dragons," he said.

"Enough." Aaron glared at Zach and he fell silent. "Zach's right," he said to Lleland. "When dragons are born they are, externally at least, human. It's only as they reach puberty that they manifest the signs of their dragon-ness. The blood Jack gave you must have worked the same changes within you that a dragon child experiences. But since you were not fathered by a dragon, the changes could not reach fruition."

"Until Lydia forced me to have her blood."

"Yes."

"But it won't happen again unless I have more dragon blood."

Aaron shrugged. "I don't know. We'll have to see if the effects wear off."

"They will," Lleland said, with an assurance he did not feel. But contemplating himself as a dragon was just not an option. He sighed, wincing when flames filled the room. A wave of weariness washed over him. "You must rest," Aaron said. "You're still recovering from your injury, and now this. Zach will remain here."

"Why?"

"In case you fly out the window and attack the village." Zach grinned. "Perhaps a hunter will kill you."

"You'd like that, wouldn't you?" Lleland said.

"It seems like an appropriate kind of comeuppance," Zach said.

Lleland turned to Aaron. "Are you sure he won't murder me in my sleep?"

"Zach knows better than to incur my wrath. You're perfectly safe." Aaron walked over to the door, where he paused. "You belong to us now," he said, before disappearing down the passage.

Lleland dropped down onto the bed. "You don't have to babysit me," he said to Zach.

"Actually, I don't mind," Zach replied. "Tell me, what did it feel like?" He pulled himself onto the window ledge.

"Confusing. And hot." Lleland groaned. "Just when I thought things couldn't get worse."

"Well," Zach said cheerfully, "now you're also a monster, just like us."

"Never," Lleland growled. "I'll never be like you. This

won't last." Zach was silent. Lleland lay down on the bed and curled himself into a ball as sleep washed over his exhausted body.

CHAPTER TWENTY-SEVEN

Lleland awoke in the late afternoon to see Lydia sitting in a chair near his bed. He could smell her scent – like an alpine meadow filled with sweet berries and bluebells. He stared at her for a moment, breathing her in as heat washed over him. "This is your fault," he said, his voice low.

She lifted her gaze to his. "I had no idea this would happen."

"If you'd listened to me and not given me your blood –"

"You'd be dead," she finished.

"Rather dead than a monster," he snarled. He rose to his feet and pulled a blanket around his waist. "Get out," he said.

"Lleland –"

"I said get out." She stared at him for a moment, and he could sense her pain. His desire to comfort her battled with his anger, but it was the anger that won. "Go," he said. He watched as she slipped through the door, then let out a long breath. He shrugged his shoulders. His skin felt hot and itchy again, and his throat was dry. The door opened and Zach walked in. "My babysitter is back," Lleland said.

"It was me or Lydia, and clearly you don't want Lydia."

"If it wasn't for Lydia, this never would have happened,"

Lleland said.

"If it wasn't for Lydia, you'd be dead," Zach replied.

"I have a feeling you wouldn't have mourned my passing."

Zach shrugged. "Believe it or not, I actually like you. I was disgusted to learn you're a hunter, and when I heard you were here, I was furious. Still, I don't despise you, even though you tried to kill me."

"Kill you? When?"

"In the hills, just after Christmas."

"That was you?" Lleland rubbed a hand over his forehead. "Who was with you?"

"A relative."

Lleland nodded slowly. "The man at the inn. Your cousin."

"Yes. But it doesn't matter."

"You didn't know I was a hunter then."

"Not then. At first I thought you were nursing a resentment about your father, and I accepted your explanation that you hadn't gone to the hills to hunt."

"I hadn't."

"I did wonder why a scholar would spend so much time perfecting his skill with a longbow, but then, why shouldn't you? It wasn't until the end of term when we were discussing our summer plans. You mentioned something about other hunters, and I started to do some digging. But you conveniently omitted to mention that you were coming here."

"I knew you would dissuade me. I came here to see your father. The League thought he had information that could help us." Lleland laughed dryly. "This isn't quite what they had in mind!"

Zach walked over to the window. "They'll want to know what you discovered. What will you tell them?"

"I haven't decided."

"Our safety lies in your hands."

"I know."

Zach was silent for a moment. "Have you tried changing again?" he finally asked.

"No."

"Then how do you know if you're still affected?" He cocked his head to the side. "Come on, give it a try."

"How?"

"Just imagine yourself as a dragon. Feel the heat and power."

Lleland had no desire to take on dragon form again, but he saw the sense of Zach's suggestion. If he didn't try, how would he know whether the effects of Lydia's blood still lingered? He drew in a deep breath and concentrated his mind on the dragon form he had glimpsed earlier.

The heat within him pulled towards his belly, starting as a small circle of flame that began to blaze as the heat increased. He closed his eyes, focusing his mind on the burning intensity, then flinging his arms wide, pushed away the heat as it exploded outwards in a blinding display of light and flame. He opened his eyes and glanced down at his chest, startled to see how black it was, before twisting his long neck to look at his massive body. Sharp spines marched down his back and along his tail, which rested on the floor. He lifted it and thumped it against the ground. It gave a satisfying whack. His wings were folded over his back, and he opened them gingerly to the extent of the room. He could feel muscles straining that he had never felt before. His wings were as black as coal, like the rest of him, but shimmered in the light. Facing forward again, he bent down. He could see the long curve of his neck, smooth at the front, but with more spikes along the back. He lifted a hand to his face and examined the black talons that had been his nails. Four inches long, they curved like the blade of a scimitar, ending in wicked points. Within his belly, the embers that had been smouldering before he changed became a burning blaze. They filled him with power that sparked and pulsed throughout his huge frame. He opened his mouth and flicked his tongue. It was long, with a forked end like a snake. The air was filled with emotions that he could taste – his own excitement, and Zach's amusement. He swiveled his head to glare at him.

"I didn't need to change to know the blood was still affecting me," he snapped.

"Well, no," Zach admitted. "But now you know what you look like. If you've finished admiring yourself, let's go flying." He tugged off his tunic.

"No."

Zach raised an eyebrow. "You're being stubborn."

"I won't be like this for very long, so there's no reason for me to go flying."

"But in the interests of scholarly learning, shouldn't you at least see what it feels like?" Zach said.

Lleland sighed, and the room filled with flame. He would have to learn how to control that if he was going to remain like this for even a few days. Once again, Zach had made a good point. "Very well," he said. Zach tugged off his breeches and jumped onto the window ledge. Lleland could see raised ridges along Zach's back that he hadn't noticed before. Zach leapt, and a flash of light filled the air. A golden dragon hovered outside the window.

"Come on," he said.

Lleland looked at the window, then threw himself forward, folding his wings tight against his body. The window frame scraped his sides, and then he was through and falling like a rock. He opened his wings, and his descent abruptly stopped. Zach was already racing into the distance, and instinctively, Lleland pushed himself forward, gaining speed as he caught up. The ground below flashed by, but Lleland's senses were acutely tuned. He could hear the chittering of squirrels as they leaped between the trees hundreds of feet below, and when he glanced down, he could see the smallest detail, down to their twitching whiskers.

He glanced behind him, and already Storbrook was

disappearing into the distance, although he could still make out all the details clearly. Lydia was standing at one of the windows, but as his gaze fell on her, she turned away. His tail, thick and black, streamed out behind him, and his wings, stark against the blue sky, were opened wide like a canopy. The wind rushed over him, and he could feel the pressure beneath his wings as he lifted himself higher.

Lleland turned forward again. A waterfall roared up ahead, and he followed Zach as he dived through the falling torrent, spraying water in all directions. He opened his jaws as he plunged through the water, but it did little to ease the burning dryness in his throat. He passed an eagle and met its gaze before it suddenly veered onto a different course. The sense of freedom was exhilarating, and for a moment, Lleland could imagine soaring like this forever. Dragons were the most powerful creatures on earth, and he could feel that power pulsing through him, making him want to claim his place of dominance. He pushed the feeling away. He was not a monster.

He passed the peak where Lydia had rescued him, and saw the river twisting through the trees like a silver ribbon. A waterfall cascaded over a rock and behind the curtain of water lay a small pool of tranquility. The distance between himself and Zach was increasing, and Lleland beat his wings heavily as he tried to catch up. His muscles were unused to the new activity and he was growing weary. Zach glanced over his shoulder, then circled back to Lleland.

"I'm forgetting your wings aren't as strong as mine," he said, "and you haven't fed."

"Fed?"

"You need fresh blood to increase your strength." Flames flooded Lleland's mouth as a pang of craving wound through his belly.

"What kind of fresh blood?"

Zach glanced at him. "We hunt in the woods, Lleland. Elk, deer, wild boar."

Lleland felt himself relax. "What's wrong with human food?"

"Nothing. It just doesn't provide all we need." They soared languorously through the air, and after a while, Storbrook appeared in the distance. "We'll land in one of the upper chambers," Zach said. He cocked his head slightly. "Aaron knows we're coming. He'll meet us there."

"He does? How?"

"I'm bound to him," he said.

"What do you mean? I thought only humans could be bound."

"My father is the Dragon Master," Zach said. "All dragons in our clan are bound to him."

Lleland blinked. "The Dragon Master? Then ..." The implications of what Zach was saying stole the words from his mouth.

"He's the most powerful dragon in the clan," Zach said.

"How many dragons are in your clan?"

"Hundreds. All the dragons in the kingdom, and beyond."

"And Aaron is the Master of them all?"

"Yes."

"So Jack –"

"Jack was a rogue. He was kicked out of the clan, but was still Aaron's responsibility."

Lleland was silent for a moment. "If Aaron is Master, then all other dragons are beholden to him."

"They've pledged their loyalty and obedience. That's why dragons aren't a threat to humans. Aaron has ordered them to leave humans alone."

"But dragons eat people!"

"Occasionally. We need human flesh to survive. But we keep a supply for that purpose. We don't attack and pillage the countryside."

"The prisoners in the tower."

"Yes."

Lleland was silent. They neared Storbrook, and Zach led Lleland to a large window. He changed as soon as he landed in the room, and Lleland followed suit, stumbling a little as he gained his feet. He looked up to see Aaron watching him.

"Enjoy your flight?" he asked.

"It was educational," Lleland replied.

"You'll probably feel worn out after using your wings for the first time," Aaron said. "And your body is craving some natural food. You need to feed."

"No." Lleland swallowed hard. "These effects won't last long. All I want is human food and something to quench my thirst."

"You need blood," Zach said.

Lleland glanced away. "No."

"Very well," Aaron said. "We'll see what happens in the next few days. But if you do not revert to your human nature, you will need to feed. In the meantime, join us in the hall for dinner. I think Cook is serving venison."

A moment later, Lleland was alone in the chamber. It was twice the size of the one he had been in before, with soaring ceilings that could easily accommodate the natural owners of the castle. Windows lined the outside wall – huge openings that a dragon could easily pass through. A large bed was against one wall, and a table on another, but most of the floor was bare. A chest stood at the foot of the bed, and opening it, Lleland saw his possessions neatly stowed within. He pulled out a clean tunic and breeches, and pulling on his boots, headed out the door.

CHAPTER TWENTY-EIGHT

Lleland stood at the window the next morning and watched as the sun brightened the sky. In the distance he could see three dragons circling above the peaks. With his enhanced eyesight, he could easily make out Lydia. She was the smallest of the three, and the lightest in color, with creamy gold scales that glittered in the early morning sun. Her wings were even paler than her scales, and the light reflecting off them cast a rainbow of colors into the air. She glided gracefully as she flew, her tail streaming out behind her. Lleland watched as she soared and dipped, and felt the flames burning in the pit of his stomach.

He turned away and rubbed the small of his back. It ached after his flight the previous day. Down the length of his spine he could feel the ridge of bone and muscle that supported his enormous wings. He had hoped that a night's sleep would rid him of the dragon effects he was suffering, but he knew as soon as he had awoken that they lingered. The heat still curled within his belly, even though the dagger wound he had received was completely healed, and when he sighed, sparks crackled in the air.

Walking over to the table, Lleland scooped his hands

through the basin of water and splashed it over his face. He lifted the jug and poured the remaining contents into his mouth, but it did nothing to relieve his parched throat. A small looking glass lay beside the basin, and he used it examine his features, searching for an indication of the changes within. His eyes stared back, the same green-gray color they had always been, and his skin showed no signs of scales. He sighed, and watched in dismay as flames curled from his lips. He opened his mouth to examine his teeth, but they were flat and human, and his tongue was not forked like a snake's.

He lay down on the bed and stared up at the high ceiling as his mind grappled with all that had happened in the last few days. Not only had Lydia turned out to be a dragon, but now he was one himself! What was it about dragon blood that had done this to him? Surely the effects would not be permanent. A little part of his mind whispered that he had enjoyed soaring over the trees the previous day, but he pushed it violently from his mind. He would not be a monster. He rose from the bed and examined himself in the looking glass again. Nothing had changed. His human face still stared back at him. He looked down at his hand and examined his nails. Were they any harder than before? Did they seem more curved? But no, they were just the same. He held his hand to his open mouth, and after a moment's pause, blew a stream of flame over his skin. He stiffened, anticipating the burning pain he knew would follow, but instead, the flame felt like a soothing caress. He pushed up the sleeve of his tunic and blew over his arm. The flames wrapped around him and stroked his skin like a lover, and he froze at the pleasure of it.

With a growl, he pulled down the sleeve and strode over to the window and stared out. The dragons were gone, but he could make out details he hadn't noticed before. The plumage of the birds flitting between the trees was no longer muted and brown but distinct shades of gray, blue and purple. He could see the twitching whiskers of the squirrels, and a spider spinning her web a hundred feet away. He sat down on the window ledge and dropped his legs over the side. The stone he sat upon immediately grew warm at his touch. He could feel the heat that spread through him, like wisps of flame curling though his body. They were pushing outward, demanding release, but he resisted them, and forced them back into his belly. He stayed there for a long time, staring out at the mountains – staring but not seeing. His mind retreated into silence, wearied and confused.

Exhaustion washed over Lleland when he lay down on the bed that evening, and his mind finally found rest from its ceaseless wondering as he fell into a deep sleep.

He awoke the following morning with a start as a loud thud echoed through the room. He jerked up in bed, then fell back when he saw Aaron. It was still dark outside.

Aaron slapped his tail against the floor. "Come," he said. "You must feed. You're weakening. If you don't feed soon, you'll place people in danger."

Lleland sat up and swung his legs over the side of the bed. "I'll never attack other humans," he said angrily.

"Not by choice. But your need for sustenance will overrule your natural aversion."

"Never."

"Lleland, I've watched many young dragons take on their natural form. This is not something you can fight."

Lleland turned to look out the window. He could feel the heat burning in him, and his throat ached. He nodded. "Very well." He rose from the bed as Aaron leaped through the huge window.

Gathering the burning heat into his belly, Lleland held it for a moment, then pushed it outward in an explosion of light that ripped through him, splitting him apart. It pulled back into his dragon form, and he followed Aaron through the window. Aaron was hovering outside, waiting for him, but instead of heading away from the castle, he circled around and landed on the parapet. "What are we doing here?" Lleland asked.

Aaron stared down at the courtyard below, and following his gaze, Lleland turned to see what was happening. Thomas was speaking to the guard who stood watch outside the small tower. He was leading two men into the courtyard, their hands bound with ropes. The priest followed a few steps behind, and Lleland watched as he blessed each of the men in turn. "What's going on?" Lleland asked.

Aaron watched for another moment, then turned to look at Lleland. "Pick one and feed," he said.

Lleland leaned back in horror. "I will not."

"These men know they are about to die, and they know what will happen when they do. Provisions have been made for their families."

"You expect me to eat human flesh?" Lleland glanced back at the men. He could smell their fear. "Impossible."

"A dragon needs human flesh to survive," Aaron said.

"You said that humans are safe from you," Lleland snarled. "You were lying."

"These men are going to die, whether by gallows or dragon. They've been found guilty of a crime and sentenced to hang. They have chosen death by dragon."

"Who chooses to be killed by a dragon?"

"Someone who wishes to ensure his family's future. We make sure they're cared for. And we never shed innocent blood."

"Except my father's," Lleland said.

"Enough, Lleland! You know as well as I do that Jack's actions did not speak for the whole clan, and he paid for them with his life."

Lleland looked away. "I'm not eating human flesh," he repeated.

"Then watch me. Perhaps the smell of warm blood will change your mind." Aaron crouched on the parapet, then sprang forward, landing on top of one of the men. Lleland heard a snap, and the stuttering of the man's heart as it stopped. The second man looked nervously at Lleland, but he ignored him. Instead, he watched as Aaron ripped the body apart. The smell of blood rose in the air, and he breathed in deeply. The flames roared within him, and he felt his belly cramp with craving. He turned away, repulsed at the hunger he felt. He was not a monster.

He opened his wings and dropped from the parapet over the outside wall and soared away. He would not eat human flesh, but he was still a hunter, and the blood of the human had intensified his craving. He glided over the forests, staying close to the ground, and sniffed. A trace scent of deer reached his nose and he turned to follow it. He flew silently, his wings open wide, and scanned the forest floor. He was nearing the river, and on the banks he spotted a small herd. He banked and placed himself upwind of the animals. He could smell them strongly now, and once more he felt his stomach clenching. He stretched out his talons and silently dropped lower. A doe, standing in the water, looked up, signaling an alarm, and the creatures started bounding away, but one stumbled on a loose stone. Lleland dropped down and ripped his talons into the creature, feeling it fall beneath his weight. It hit the ground, and instinct took over as Lleland clamped his jaws around the creature's neck. Blood gushed into his mouth, hot and thick, and he swallowed. The dryness in his throat eased, and he drew more blood into his throat. The creature was completely drained when he dropped the body from his jaws and ripped open its stomach with his talons, burying his snout in the steaming flesh. His breath seared the meat as he tore it apart, and he growled with pleasure. His forked tongue sought out every last morsel, and when he was done he licked away the last few drops of blood from his snout, then cleaned his talons. He collapsed contentedly onto the ground, his hunger sated. He curled his tail around his body and slept.

When Lleland awoke some time later, the morning sun

was shining brightly, making his scales shine. He rolled onto his back and rubbed it against the sand, groaning in pleasure as his tail swished over the ground. All the weariness he felt earlier had vanished, and power coursed through him. He rose to his feet and lifted his long neck to sniff the air. A myriad of smells reached his nostrils – the remains of his kill, a wild boar rooting, the river winding through the forest; *Lydia*. Lleland turned towards Storbrook. He felt stronger than he ever had before, and flames wove through him, fueling his power. He lifted his head and roared, spilling flames over his huge, scaly body. They rolled over him, caressing his thick hide, and dissipated in the air.

In the distance Storbrook rose from the huge wall of rock it was built upon, its yellow stone shining dully in the sun. Lleland flew unerringly towards his chamber, and landed on the stone floor. He lifted his head and pushed the away the heat. Light exploded from his body, then gathered back into his center. He was standing in the middle of the room, arms outstretched and head thrown back, naked as the day he was born. A scent tickled his nose – berries and sunshine – and he breathed it in, before turning slowly to look at Lydia. She was sitting in a chair in the corner of the room, but rose as he looked at her. She stared at him, her golden eyes meeting his, and a wave of desire washed over him. He stalked towards her, and when he reached her, he twisted his hand into her hair and pulled her hard against his naked frame. He could feel her warmth through her clothes, and he slid his hand around her back, exploring her shapely frame. His mouth dropped to hers, and she opened her lips to him as her hands wrapped around his neck. He pushed her against the wall and invaded her mouth with his tongue, kissing her deeply as he pressed his hard frame against hers. He slid his mouth along her jaw and down her neck. Her scent was sharp, increasing his desire, and he moved his lips back to hers, tasting her. It wasn't enough, though – he wanted to feel her bare flesh against his own – and he tugged at her gown, impatient to feel her skin against his. He pulled away to gaze into the burning depths of her eyes, then spun around when he heard a low laugh.

"Am I interrupting something?" Zach asked. Lleland stared at him for a moment as the burning desire he had felt a moment before turned to a sinking feeling of shame. He had treated Lydia like some common whore. He grabbed the tunic Zach tossed him and hurriedly pulled it on before turning to look at Lydia. She was leaning against the wall, her eyes closed, panting slightly. An irrational wave of anger washed over him. She'd done nothing to stop him from pressing his demands. In fact, he wasn't even sure he could trust what he felt – perhaps it was only the cords that bound him to her that had made him act so.

"My apologies, Mistress," Lleland said stiffly. "I don't know what came over me."

"You've finally been hunting," Zach said, dropping down on the edge of the bed. "It raises other appetites."

Lleland dragged his hand over his face. "I see."

"It's worse when you first start changing. After a while, you'll be able to keep your desires in check."

"Of course." He glanced at Lydia. "Why are you in my chambers?"

"I wanted to find out how you are doing."

"Well, I'm quite fine." He turned and stalked to the window. "Good day, Mistress," he said over his shoulder.

Lydia was silent, and after a moment he heard the door close softly behind her.

"You cannot keep blaming Lydia for what happened," Zach said.

"She gave me her blood," Lleland said. "She created a monster!"

"True, but if you're going to blame anyone, blame Jack."

"I do. But Jack didn't use deceit and falsehood to gain my affection."

"Is that what Lydia did? I thought she was ensuring her

215

self-preservation. But no matter. You're still attracted to her, and it's clear she loves you, despite the way you're treating her."

"What just happened was nothing more than pure, primal instinct – the result of the monster she has created."

"Very well." Zach leaned against the window ledge, his arms crossed over his chest. "Aaron told me what happened this morning. That you refused to feed on a human. But you still hunted, and I can see you're much stronger than you were."

"Stronger? Perhaps. But also disgusted and ashamed. I hope this wears off quickly, so I can get on with my life."

"You realize that may never happen?"

"I can't even contemplate that." Lleland paced the room. "What I need is to get away from here. From all of you. Perhaps being near Lydia," he grimaced, "is keeping me this way."

"You want to leave?"

"Yes. I need to return to Civitas anyway. Classes resume in October."

"That's still six weeks away!"

"It took me six weeks to travel here."

"You traveled on foot. It only takes a few days to fly."

"I'm human, Zach, and I will travel on foot."

"That's ludicrous."

Lleland shrugged. "Call it what you want. It's what I plan to do."

Zach stood. "Well, I can't stop you. We'd better go talk to Aaron."

CHAPTER TWENTY-NINE

"You left this morning," Aaron said as Lleland and Zach entered the study. "You went hunting on your own."

"I couldn't stay and watch," Lleland said.

"The animal blood helped. You look stronger. But you'll need human flesh eventually."

"Why?"

"A dragon needs it to survive. We can survive on animal flesh most of the time, but eventually our bodies demand human flesh – the essence of humanity. Just a few times a year will suffice, but a new dragon needs it sooner."

"Well, since this change is temporary, I don't think I'll ever need a dragon diet."

"Clearly what you had this morning is sufficient for now." Aaron leaned back in his seat. "So you plan to leave Storbrook?" he said. "Getting away from Lydia is not going to make any difference."

Lleland glanced at Zach, who grinned. Was there no privacy amongst dragons? "I must return to Civitas anyway," Lleland said.

"We'll have to have an oath ceremony before you go. We'll keep it private, though. Just us."

"An oath ceremony? What's that?"

"It's when you pledge your allegiance to me. I drink your blood, and you drink mine."

"No. No more blood."

"You must," Zach said. "You cannot leave here without making Aaron your Master."

"First of all, Aaron is the Dragon Master, and I'm not a dragon," Lleland said. He looked at Aaron. "And if I drink your blood, it may strengthen the effects of Lydia's."

"There are many dragons in Civitas, Lleland," Aaron replied. Lleland's eyebrows rose fractionally at the thought. Had he been walking past dragons every day and not known it? "They'll recognize you for what you are as soon as they see you, and if you don't create a bond with me, they'll know that too. You'll be considered rogue, which means they are free to do with you as they will."

"Then let them know what happened," Lleland said.

"Absolutely not! The dragons of the clan have sworn their allegiance to me, but I cannot control all their actions, especially those further afield. If word got out that Jack created a dragon by giving a child his blood, who knows what will happen." He pushed himself from the desk. "This must remain between us. I won't even tell the elders."

Lleland paced over to the window. "I still won't drink your blood," he said.

Aaron was silent for a long moment. "I cannot force you to join the clan, Lleland. But if you don't, your life could be in danger."

"I understand. Let's see what happens."

"You're just delaying the inevitable," Aaron said. "When do you plan to leave?"

"At first light."

Lydia was not in the hall that evening, and Lleland was relieved. It was, after all, better not to see her again. It was because of Lydia that he had become a monster. She meant nothing to him anymore. Even if he did have feelings for her, he could not trust that they were real. Not after she bound him with her blood. And given his behavior that afternoon, her absence made things less awkward. No, he told himself, he definitely did not want to see her. But that conclusion did nothing to lift his spirits and relieve the melancholy that settled over him for the remainder of the evening.

He left as soon as the sun reached the horizon the next morning, following the path that led from the mountain castle. Aaron and Zach circled above him, a pair of huge, golden dragons. "Do you want a ride to the village?" Zach asked, dropping closer as Lleland scrambled down the path.

Lleland frowned. "No."

"Halfway down the mountain, then?"

When Lleland remained silent, Zach swooped away with a laugh. "Don't get sore feet," he said.

It was nightfall when Lleland reached the village, but he did not stop. Instead he skirted the buildings and headed to the west road. Even though it was dark he could see clearly, and despite a full day of walking, did not feel weary. The moon was waning but shone brightly in the night sky. Between the trees a nightjar chirred, while from farther away came the hoot of an owl.

It was already past midnight when Lleland finally stopped to rest. He found a tree a short distance from the road to lie beneath, and placed his things on the ground beside him. Sleep came easily, and he dreamed of soaring above the trees and climbing the heavens to reach the stars. He was powerful, and he threw back his head and roared his strength to the night sky. When he awoke, he saw that the trunk of the tree he lay beneath had been singed with flame.

He gathered his things and carried on walking. He soon passed the place where Francis had been attacked, and saw a broken arrow on the path. Had it only been three days ago? It felt like a lifetime had passed. The smell of human blood assailed his senses. He could tell that some of it was his, but the rest belonged to the other men that had been killed.

As Lleland walked, he thought of his mother, his students, and the work he needed to do to prepare for his classes. Anything other than dragons. And Lydia. He pushed himself to walk as far as possible each day, taking his body to the brink of exhaustion. As the days passed, he noticed his abnormal strength lessening. Did that mean he was becoming human again?

Lleland had been on the road for a week when he reached a large town. The first inn he stopped at was full, but he was directed to another a short distance away, and he stepped into a large hall filled with the scent of humanity. He waved over a barman and ordered an ale before dropping his bag and taking a stool at the bar.

"Lleland Seaton? Is that you?" Lleland turned around to see Francis pushing his way towards him, and he groaned inwardly. "I thought you were dead!"

"As you can see, I'm quite alive."

"But how did you escape?" Lleland could smell his confusion. "You were badly wounded and when that creature grabbed you, I was sure you were doomed."

Lleland shrugged. "It meant me no harm. As soon as I was well, it let me go."

"It let you go? And you traveled all this way with a stab wound?"

"It was merely a scratch."

"A scratch? I saw the blood gushing from your chest!"

Lleland turned in his stool and took a long swig of ale. "It must have been the other man's blood," he said.

"I didn't think he was wounded." Francis eyed him skeptically.

"Well, as you can see, I'm fit and hale."

"Yes, so I see." Francis studied Lleland for a moment, then turned and waved for another ale.

"How has your journey been?" Lleland asked.

"No more thieves or bandits, I'm sorry to say."

"That's a good thing," Lleland said.

"It makes the journey so dull and tedious."

"You're supposed to be doing penance."

"True." Francis grimaced for a moment, but then grinned. "There've been some rather accommodating barmaids along the way."

Lleland groaned. "That's what got you in trouble in the first place."

"Ah, but I'm not giving them my name! And my father is not around to know what I'm doing."

"I wash my hands of you," Lleland said, swallowing the last of his ale and standing. "I'm going to find a bed for the night."

"I'll see you in the morning," Francis said cheerfully.

Lleland left before first light and did not see Francis again. He had taken some bread and cold meat from the inn, and ate as he walked, but it did little to relieve the gnawing hunger that had been growing in the pit of his belly for the last few days. His throat was continuously parched, and no amount of ale or water could quench his thirst. Aaron would say he needed blood, but he refused to consider it. If he faltered in his resolve to resist the urge of the dragon, all would be lost.

The days passed. When he was able to find an inn, he slept there, but just as often he slept beneath the stars, under a tree or bush. He refused to think of Lydia as he walked, but he could not keep her from his dreams. Sometimes she came to him in human form, and she'd take him by the hand and lead him to a pool of calm water. Her lips would touch his, and he would wrap his arms around her and whisper her name. Other times she came to him as a dragon, her huge wings spread over him, until he too changed form and chased her into the skies. She was hugely, savagely beautiful. Her fiercely spiked tail would wind around his, and he would drag his forked tongue down her neck as her eyes flamed with heat. He woke from these dreams panting, longing to feel her in his arms, until he remembered that she was a monster and he could no longer trust the feelings he had for her, and he would push the thoughts away with a growl.

As the days passed, Lleland's legs began to ache, and his body was no longer able to endure long hours of walking. It was late one evening when Lleland stopped for the night near a river. He had not eaten since the previous day when he had enjoyed a bowl of stew at an inn. But there were no inns in the country that surrounded him now.

He placed his satchel on the ground and taking his bow and a few arrows, headed towards the water. His plan was to hunt a small animal to roast over a fire. He sniffed the air. Something was approaching downwind of the river. He crept forward with as much stealth as possible, then paused and sniffed again. The animal was coming closer. He notched an arrow on the string of his bow, and crouched behind some bushes. A large elk appeared from behind some trees and stopped to nibble the leaves. Lleland paused a moment; the creature was large, and he was just one man, but hunger gnawed at his stomach. He drew back the string and loosed the arrow, watching as it hit the animal in the neck.

Blood spurted from the wound as the elk fell, and instinct took over as Lleland dropped his bow and ran towards the kill. His wings opened on his back, shredding his tunic and propelling him forward, but he didn't notice. He fell to the ground next to the animal and yanked out the arrow before sealing his lips to the wound. Blood gushed into his mouth, and he swallowed with pleasure as the burn in his throat finally subsided. Using his knife, he sliced open the belly of the huge animal, then used his teeth to rip the warm flesh, burying his face in the carcass. In the distance he smelled a wolf approaching, and he growled, a deep sound at the back of his throat. He heard the creature turn aside as he tore off more flesh. Flames roiled within him, burning the fresh meat as soon as it hit his stomach, and he filled his belly. When he had finally had enough, he lay down on the ground beside the carcass and slept.

The sky was still dark when he opened his eyes, awoken by leaves crackling beneath the soft paws of an animal. The wolf he had smelled earlier stood on the other side of the elk carcass, watching him. It stepped forward, then back, clearly unsure what to make of the man lying on the ground. Lleland glanced at the remains of the elk, then turned away in disgust. His memories were hazy, but he knew that the bloodied carcass was the result of his frenzied eating. The taste of flesh and blood were still in his mouth.

He rose to his feet, and frowned at his bare torso. He glanced over his shoulders to see a pair of black wings spread out behind him, trailing on the ground. He stared at them for a moment before folding them onto his back. They disappeared beneath his skin, leaving only ridges that ran the length of his spine. The wolf edged closer, eyeing him warily.

"Go ahead," Lleland muttered. "It's all yours."

Despite his revulsion at his actions, he could not resist licking the dried blood from his fingers. Strength and power coursed through his body, and the gnawing hunger and burning thirst that had tormented him had disappeared. He collected his belongings and started along the road, walking late into the following night before pausing for a rest.

Another two weeks had passed when Lleland stood at the top of a hill and looked down at the city below. The pall of smoke had hung over the horizon the whole of the previous day, along with the smell of foul air. All around him people crowded along the road, dragging carts with their merchandise or lugging huge bundles as they headed into or out of the city. He wended his way through the throng and crossed the bridge. The city pulsed with life, and his senses were overwhelmed by the sights, sounds and smells that assaulted him on all sides. He still knew the streets and alleys, and recognized the hawkers and flower sellers who had been there before, but Civitas was a foreign place. He longed to return to the mountains, and felt their call pulsing through his blood. He turned towards the university.

The grounds of Kings College were quiet – there were still two more weeks before the start of the autumn term. The only sign of life was the groundsman tending bushes in a far corner. Lleland walked up the path and pushed open the wooden door. A few of the Masters, like himself, lived at the college all year around, and the building was not completely empty.

His boots echoed over the flagstones as he headed down the passage. He had just reached the stairs when a door opened and he saw the Dean emerge from his office. "Ah, Seaton, you're back from your travels. I look forward to hearing your report."

Lleland nodded. "Yes, Master." He mounted the stairs and made his way to his chamber. It was cool and smelled a little moldy, and he flung open the window, letting in the late summer air. The room seemed very small after the chambers at Storbrook, but as he glanced around, his eyes fell on his books which had been carefully stacked on the desk, and he smiled to himself. No matter what changed around him, it was reassuring to know that some things remained the same.

CHAPTER THIRTY

Lleland sat in his chamber, his daybook before him on his desk. The window was open and the smells of the city wafted through. He rubbed his bare back over the hard wood of his chair as he read, in an effort ease to the pressure that would not go away. There was nothing he could do to relieve his back, or the ache in his belly, which craved raw flesh and blood. The thought of feeding his animal nature repulsed him, and he denied these cravings: perhaps if he starved the monster within, he could kill it. The memory of his last kill brought conflicting emotions. His stomach tightened as he thought of the hot blood spilling into his mouth and the steaming flesh reaching his belly, but he was revolted by his wild, beastly instincts which had him tearing the carcass with his teeth. He had stopped all hunting so he wouldn't become an animal again.

The constant, gnawing hunger was one thing, but it was the dreams that troubled Lleland most. He dreamed of himself, huge, black and monstrous. As monstrous as Jack. He dreamed of blood spilling into his mouth, and the taste of human flesh as he ripped it apart with his talons. The screams of frightened people filled him with power, and he took delight in their fear. Sometimes Lydia joined him as he feasted, killing dozens in a single night, while other times he hunted alone. His appetite was insatiable, and he reveled in it, until he awoke, aghast. He took to sleeping on the floor after he woke up with his quilt ripped and mattress shredded. Sometimes when he opened his eyes his wings were unfurled, trailing over his back and across the floor, and he lifted them languorously, marveling at their power, until he remembered what they represented. As much as the dreams appalled him, it was the cravings which lingered long after he awoke that most shocked and revolted him. He could not allow himself to become that monster.

Lleland glanced at the book before him. It was open to the account of his first encounter with the Storbrook dragons, and Lydia's sketches stared at him from the page. He traced his fingers over the drawing of the smaller dragon, then slammed the book shut in annoyance. He did not want to think about dragons, and especially not Lydia. But even so, the memory of her soft lips could not be forgotten, and he groaned. It was a woman he wanted, not a dragon.

His mind wandered back to his visit to his mother a few days before. It was the first time he had seen her since his return to Civitas. He knew that his reluctance to visit had been caused by his dread that somehow she would know he was changed – that he had become the creature she most feared. She'd stared at him when he first arrived at the door, and for a moment he was sure that she knew, but then she smiled and took his hands.

"It's been so long since I've seen you, son," she said, "I just had to remind myself what you look like!"

He grinned in relief. "It hasn't been that long," he said.

"Long enough! And I wasn't even sure you'd ever return!" A shadow passed over her face, then was gone. "But here you are! Come, sit down, and tell me about the places you've seen!"

The clock in the church tower tolled three, reminding

Lleland of the time. Durwin Scott, one of the members of the League, had sent him a note the previous day. He had heard that Lleland was back in town and suggested they meet over a pint. Lleland straightened his tunic and headed outside. The heat of summer had given way to cooler temperatures, but the days were still clear and fine. He turned in the direction of the tavern near the Guildhall, passing the busy market where hawkers and vendors shouted out their wares. His senses were assailed by a multitude of smells – spices, leather, flowers and fabrics, while all around him he heard the loud and not-so-loud conversations of buyers and sellers. He passed the table of fabric that Lydia had admired so much, and turned away.

"Master Seaton!"

Lleland spun around to see a carriage slowing to a halt a few feet away. He recognized John the coachman, and waved his hand in greeting.

"You're back in town," he said.

"We arrived last week. Mistress was eager to get back to the city after her mother passed. I'm glad to see you made it back alive, and didn't die in the mountains!"

The door of the carriage opened, and Lleland saw Muriel lean forward in the dim interior. "Master Seaton! I was hoping we would see you sometime." She blushed and bit her lip as her eyes dropped to her lap. An elderly gentleman sat on the bench across from her.

"This is my uncle, Ambassador Syngen Gail," she said.

The man leaned forward, and Lleland met his gray eyes with a nod. "Master Seaton? I understand from my niece that we owe you a debt of gratitude."

"I did as much as any other gentleman would've done."

"Perhaps. But I'm still in your debt. We're having a small party next week. Why don't you join us?"

"Well …" Muriel peered at him from beneath her eyelashes.

"You would honor us if you accept," Syngen said.

"Thank you, Master. I look forward to it."

"Good." Syngen closed the door and the carriage pulled away. Lleland swallowed a sigh as he watched it go, before continuing on his way.

He reached the tavern a short while later, and immediately saw Scott seated at a table in the center of the room. He was talking to the barmaid, who was laughing at something he said. Lleland made his way to the table and sat down. Scott was a tanner by trade, and even as a human, Lleland could smell the odor of untanned leather that clung to him. Now, however, it almost overwhelmed his senses, and he turned away to take in a deep breath.

"You're a married man now," he said as Scott patted the barmaid while she walked away. "You shouldn't be flirting with pretty women."

Scott turned to Lleland with a sigh. "Don't remind me," he said.

"That bad, eh? It's only been, what, ten months?"

"Eleven," he said morosely. "Who would've thought my pretty young girl would turn into her mother so soon?"

"Come on, it can't be that bad," Lleland said with a laugh.

"It wasn't so bad at first, but now with the baby coming in a few months, she nags me from morning to night." Scott drained his ale in one gulp. "How was your trip?"

"Good."

"Did you see Drake?"

"I did. He told me nothing new."

"Grant didn't think he would. What was he like? He must be pretty old."

"He, er, hardly looks his age. I don't think he'd have any trouble slaying another dragon, if he wanted."

"But he must be at least fifty! Probably even older! Is it true there are dragons in the mountains?"

"Yes."

"And did you kill any?"

"No."

"So you're taking a hunting party?"

The barmaid retuned with two tankards, which she placed on the table with a smile in Scott's direction. Curly brown locks fell around his face, and he pushed them aside as he smiled back.

"The Northern Mountains are Drake's territory," Lleland said. "If there's a problem, he'll deal with it."

"But the dragons are still alive. And I still have to kill my first beast!"

"Well, it won't be one of those. Those dragons aren't a threat."

"From what I've heard, all dragons are a threat."

Lleland shrugged. "Not these. They've lived peacefully in the mountains for years."

"Then why do we hunt them?"

"I don't know," Lleland snapped. "Perhaps some are more dangerous than others."

Scott leaned back in his seat and stared at Lleland with eyebrows raised. "What's wrong?"

Lleland sighed and took a long draught. "Nothing. It's just ... I don't think all dragons should be hunted."

"You? Don't think all dragons should be hunted?" Scott laughed. "I never thought to hear such words from your lips." Lleland glanced away in irritation. "Was it something Drake said that made you change your mind?"

"You could say that."

"So it's true that he isn't interested in hunting dragons?"

"He's definitely not interested! In fact, he has quite a fondness for the creatures."

"Fondness? That's rich! Who could ever love such hideous monsters?"

Lleland watched as a fly landed on the table and walked across the scratched surface. "Who indeed?" he said.

Lleland received an official invitation to Syngen Gail's party two days later, written in fine script on thick vellum and stamped with the official seal. He carried it in the pocket of his doublet the following Friday as he made his way across the city to the Ambassador's residence. The house was built on the river, downstream from the royal palace. Hundreds of lanterns lit the walkway, and a pair of footmen waited at the door to usher the visitors into the towering hall beyond. As Lleland stepped through the door, his heart sank. What Ambassador Gail had described as a little party included a hundred people or more, filling the huge hall. The room glittered with hundreds of candles, tapestries covered the walls depicting various battles, and a huge fire roared in the center.

"Ah, Master Seaton, I'm glad you could make it." Lleland turned to see Syngen Gail making his way towards him. He was dressed in a gold silk doublet embroidered with red, which matched his bright red breeches. He had no need for padding on the shoulders, Lleland noticed, and his stomach was still flat and firm beneath the clothing. "Let me introduce you to some of the other guests." He led Lleland around the room, finally leaving him alone with a man named Wilson. Lleland nodded politely as Wilson talked about the weather, elucidated his views on the grip of power the city merchants exercised over the king, and then launched into a diatribe on the evils of taxes.

The dinner bell rang, and Lleland turned away in relief. He had only taken a few steps when a footman appeared at his elbow. "This way, Master," he said, indicating the main table on the dais.

"Are you sure?" Lleland said, surprised.

"Yes. Ambassador Gail pointed you out himself." He led Lleland to a chair, covered in silk, near the center of the table, and Lleland waited as the other guests assembled. Muriel mounted the dais a moment later on her uncle's arm, and she darted a quick smile at Lleland as she took the seat next to him. She was dressed in a dark red gown trimmed with white lace which reached her throat, while her golden hair had been braided and twisted around her head and covered with a net decorated with pearls. The shade of the gown reminded Lleland of Lydia, who had once worn a similar color. But her hair always hung down her back, like a shimmering, silky curtain. He swallowed and pushed the memory away.

"I asked Uncle Syngen to seat you beside me," Muriel said as Lleland took his place beside her. "Was that wrong of me?"

"Not at all, Mistress," he said with a smile.

She leaned back in her seat and carefully placed a napkin over her knees. "Uncle Syngen has arranged a minstrel to entertain us tonight," she said. "He can sing, dance, juggle and tumble!"

A platter of food was placed on the table before them, and Muriel helped herself to a small portion of roasted quail. "Uncle Syngen says you teach at Kings College," she said as Lleland loaded his plate. "What do you teach?"

"Philosophy," Lleland replied.

"You've studied the great masters," she said. "I only know a very little, and can speak Latin but poorly." Lleland smiled, remembering his surprise when Lydia conversed in the ancient language, and her annoyance at his astonishment. Muriel looked away. "You're laughing at me," she said. The color was rising in her cheeks.

"Forgive me, Mistress, you reminded me of someone. Please don't think I'm laughing at you."

"It's just that many people think I cannot be interested in philosophy and other such subjects."

"And are you?"

"Oh, yes! I wish I could attend university and read Aristotle and Plato."

"There's no reason why you can't study them on your own, Mistress. I'd be happy to lend you my books and direct you on where to begin."

"Oh, would you?"

"Certainly. I have a slim volume of writings that would be

a good place to start. It's all in Latin, though," he added. "Do you think you know enough to follow?"

"If I am unsure of something I could ask Uncle Syngen."

Another course of food was placed before them, and Lleland waited as Muriel took a spoonful of fish, before piling his own plate. There was a scraping of chairs, and Lleland glanced around to see a man nimbly flipping head over heels into the room while holding a fiddle in one hand. He landed on his feet and started scratching out a tune as the guests clapped their hands. It made him think of Storbrook. Lleland glanced at Muriel, who was watching the minstrel with eager enjoyment. Her enthusiasm reminded him of Lydia, but where Lydia was bold and forthright, unconcerned about the opinions of others, Muriel was quiet-spoken and demure. He turned to watch the minstrel, laughing with the other guests when he tumbled to the floor.

"Isn't this wonderful?" Muriel said, her eyes shining. "I'm so glad you could join us this evening."

"Thank you, Mistress," Lleland said.

Further entertainments followed, and when the meal was finally finished, the tables were pushed aside as the minstrel began to recite poems of love and love lost. With a shy smile Muriel left Lleland and joined her friends, and Lleland moved to the back of the hall, where a few others were lingering. Syngen wandered over and took a place beside him. "I understand you promised to lend Muriel one of your books," he said.

"That's correct. She expressed an interest in philosophy."

"She's lived a sheltered and protected life, Master Seaton. The kind of life, I think, that you're not familiar with."

Lleland glanced at Syngen, but his expression was inscrutable. "I'm well aware of our different stations. I seek only to provide guidance to someone eager to learn."

"You misunderstand me," Syngen said. "I'm not concerned about your station in life, as far as it extends to your helping her – I think it would be good for Muriel to pursue other interests. I merely wish to give you a better understanding of her character. I had thought of approaching the queen to discuss her entering court, but I'm afraid the queen dowager is a little, er, indisposed to me."

"You know her well?"

"We were childhood playmates. I believe she thought I'd offer for her hand, but I was not the marrying type. She got a king instead, but never managed to forgive me. But you're not interested in my personal affairs. Muriel mentioned you explored some of the old ruins when you traveled north. Was that your main area of interest?"

"I'm a curious man by nature, Ambassador, and am interested in anything new and interesting. I'd already traveled the southern part of the kingdom extensively, but this was the first time venturing so far north."

"And the mountains – did they meet your expectations?"

"Absolutely! They're magnificent."

"Yes. I'm very familiar with them. Did you see anything, er, especially interesting?"

"It was all interesting, Ambassador."

Syngen nodded. "Yes, indeed." He nodded his head, and turning on his heel, walked away, greeting guests as he moved across the vast, glittering hall.

CHAPTER THIRTY-ONE

Lleland gathered his books and headed down the passage to start his first class of the term. The fine weather of late summer had given way to rain, making the corridors dark and gloomy, but the lack of light did not bother him. He glanced at the book in his hands. Plato. Of course. The ancient Greek philosopher. He sighed to himself. He had never been so unprepared to teach a class before. Instead of organizing his lessons, he had wandered restlessly around the city, exploring nooks and crannies in places he hadn't visited before. He had seen dragons often, and it amazed him now to think how many were in the city, hidden amongst unwitting humans. He could tell from a quick glance the strength of each, and although he was more powerful now than he had ever been as a human, he knew he was weaker than most of the dragons he encountered. He avoided the areas he noticed they frequented, hoping to prevent the confrontation Aaron had warned him about, but he had been stopped by a dragon one time near the cathedral. The man was large, with a power level close to Zach's.

"I don't believe we've met," he said. "I'm Calder."

"Seaton," Lleland replied.

"Seaton?" Calder cocked his head. "I've never heard that name before. And you're not part of Aaron's clan. He'll want to know about a stranger in his territory."

"He already does."

Calder crossed his arms over his broad chest. "You've been in contact with him?"

"I spent some time at Storbrook. Aaron knows I'm here."

"I see." Calder cocked his head. "Well, I won't question the ways of the Master, but the last rogue in the city caused a great deal of mischief. There are some dragons who'd kill you despite what Aaron thinks, just to ensure it doesn't happen again."

Lleland nodded. "Thank you for the warning. But I don't plan to be here long."

"Well, take care." He tapped his chin. "Did you meet Aaron's son while you were at Storbrook?"

"You mean Zach? I know him."

"Good. He lives in the city, too, so he can vouch for you." Calder turned to look down the road. "I'm heading to Drake's Landing for a drink. Will you join me? I can introduce you to some others, and we can allay any fears they may have about you."

Lleland lifted his eyebrows. "Drake's Landing?"

Calder grinned. "It's owned by a human. But many of our kind like to drink there. Are you coming?"

"Thank you, but I have some, er, errands to run. Another time, perhaps?"

"Of course. Just come find me first before you go stepping into the Drake! Don't want anyone to do something foolish!" He laughed, and Lleland gave a weak smile. "My house is on River Row. Number ten," Calder said. He waved his hand as he turned away and strode down the road, and Lleland had watched his retreating figure with a mixture of relief and confusion. He could hardly imagine this man attacking innocent people in the street.

Lleland pushed open the door to the classroom and

stepped inside as his eyes swept over the students. He had forgotten to review the list beforehand, but there were none in the class he did not already know. Only Zachary Drake was absent, which Lleland hoped was permanent. He placed his books on the table and pulled out a sheet of paper, before opening his writing set and sharpening a quill. He dipped it in the jar of ink he had carefully placed on the corner of the desk, then looked out across the room.

"State your name," he said. He waited as the first student called out his name, then wrote it down on the sheet.

"Harold Dodd."

One by one the students gave their names as Lleland recorded them. The door opened then closed, bringing in a familiar scent.

"Thomas Bell."

"Zachary Drake."

Lleland wrote the name on the list, before finally laying aside the quill and looking up at the latecomer. "Class starts precisely at two," he said. "Please ensure you're on time in future."

"Of course, Master," Zach replied. His gaze caught Lleland's, and for a moment they stared at each other. Lleland cleared his throat, and opened his book.

"Plato," he started. "Who can tell me anything about him?"

The lesson dragged by, until finally the bells across the city tolled the fourth hour. Lleland laid down the book and leaned against the desk as the students filed out, until only Zach remained.

"I thought you might not be back," Lleland finally said.

"Why not? I've as much academic interest as your other students. You didn't seem quite on form today, though." Zach cocked his head. "I see the effects of your change have not lessened in any way, but you're weak. You're not eating."

"Of course I am," Lleland replied. "The food served in the hall is always very hearty."

"That's not what I meant. When last did you feed?"

Lleland glanced away. "Four weeks ago."

"Four weeks? Lleland, you're being foolish! I suppose that's also the last time you changed."

"I'm not being foolish, I just refuse to be a monster. And I haven't changed since leaving Storbrook."

"But you hunted?"

"It was a … lapse. I didn't intend to eat like an animal."

"It was your body demanding what it needed."

"It was the creature within making that demand. I won't make the mistake of letting it free again."

"It's what you are now, Lleland. You need to accept that."

"Accept that I'm a monster? No!"

"How far will you push yourself? To death? And then what? Who will take care of your mother when you're gone?"

"My father was killed by a dragon! Do you really think she would survive the shock of knowing her son has become a monster?"

"You think she'd prefer you dead? Another victim to a dragon? The only one you're fighting here is yourself!"

"I've spent years hunting dragons, Zach. If this be my last fight, so be it!" Lleland turned to gather his things. "I'll see you tomorrow, Master Drake," he said. "Please ensure you're here on time."

Zach walked towards the door, then paused. "I'm hunting tonight," he said. "Join me." He didn't wait for a response, and when Lleland looked up he was already gone.

Lleland exhaled angrily, and a stream of flame coiled around his head. His back itched, and he twisted his shoulders in an effort to relieve the irritation. Zach's words pricked at his conscience – did he really want to choose death over life as a dragon? He shook his head. Of course death was preferable! And under no circumstances would he hunt with Zach Drake. He picked up his papers and stormed out the door.

That evening at dinner Lleland sat beside Master

Rutherford. "You look a trifle peaked," Rutherford said. "Are you quite well?"

"A little tired, perhaps," Lleland said.

"You need an early night."

"Indeed." Lleland looked across the hall. Zach was seated at one of the tables close to the dais, and Lleland could tell he was following the conversation closely. "Getting an early night is exactly what I plan to do," he said.

But when the bells began to chime ten Lleland was wide awake. He listened as they tolled the hour, and paced around the room. In an effort to distract himself, he opened a book: *The Ballad of Roland*. The tale of Charlemagne's defeat by ambush in the Pyrenees had always fascinated him. The true story of the ambush was clouded in the mists of time, but the legends around Roland, the commander of the rear guard who was killed in the attack, had continued to grow. It was a story that Lleland had read many times and it never failed to interest him, but this evening his mind refused to focus on the details, and when he laid the book aside, he could not recall what he'd just read.

He lay down, longing for sleep but dreading the dreams, but both refused to come, and he began to pace once again. The conversation with Zach played in his mind. Did he really want to die? But then he thought of Jack and the horrific things he had done. Jack had definitely deserved death. Lleland stopped at the window. Of course, not all dragons were like Jack. Aaron and Zach, for instance. They did not hunt and kill as Jack had done. He thought of Lydia attacking someone in the city, and almost smiled. She'd never hurt someone if she could avoid it. Except himself, of course. She had bound him to her side and turned him into a monster. He frowned and turned his thoughts back to Jack. The black dragon had been a monster, but was Lleland? Jack's blood coursed through his veins – did that mean he was the same? He remembered his dreams, and the resultant cravings, and he clenched his fists. Sometimes sacrifices had to made.

Across the road the church bells tolled eleven. A breeze stirred and cool air washed over his back, but it did little to soothe the constant irritation. His throat was burning, and he threw back a cup of water, knowing as he did so that it would do nothing to ease the pain.

He stared into the dark night. The sky was inky black, the stars and moon hidden behind a curtain of cloud, but Lleland was able to see clearly. A mouse scurried along the length of the garden wall. There was a squeak, cut short as an owl dived out of the dark sky and caught the little creature in its sharp talons. Lleland turned away and reached for his daybook. Sitting on the bed, he opened it and started reading, hoping to distract himself. He turned the page and stared down at the sketches Lydia had made. The sacred grove where they examined the ancient carvings seemed so distant, the peace he had felt then shattered. He pushed the daybook away.

The church bells started tolling in the distance, and closer by, the town crier shouted out the midnight hour. Lleland rose to his feet and went over to the window, staring once more into the darkness. Zach's chamber was on the upper floor, one storey above Lleland's. He heard a rustling, and he glanced up to see Zach gliding from the window, dressed only in breeches. His golden wings spread from his back, visible even in the low light. He turned and glanced at Lleland. "Come with me," Zach said.

"No."

Zach stared at him for a moment then shot into the sky, disappearing behind the clouds. There was a muted flash of light. Lleland turned away from the window and blew out a long stream of flame, which curled around the blackened rafters. He glanced at the window, then reluctantly turned away and threw himself onto the bed. When he finally fell asleep, the eastern sky was started to lighten with the coming dawn.

CHAPTER THIRTY-TWO

Lleland carried a slim volume of writings against his chest as he walked in the direction of the Ambassador's residence. The days following the Gail party had slipped by, his promise to Muriel forgotten, until he saw the book lying on the shelf. He didn't need to deliver the volume himself, but an apology was in order for his tardiness. He had also written a page of notes and questions for Muriel to consider as she read the book which were easier to explain in person.

He announced himself at the Gail residence twenty minutes later, and after a short wait, was ushered into a small parlor where Muriel was seated in a chair beside the window. She looked up as he entered.

"Good day, Master Seaton."

"Good day Mistress. I've brought the book I promised to lend you."

She smiled. "Thank you."

"I also wanted to apologize for taking so long in bringing it to you. I'm afraid I got sidetracked by other matters." She flushed slightly as Lleland held out the slim volume. "You'll see I've written some points for you to consider as you read," he said as she took the book from his hand. Her fingers brushed against his, and her blush deepened as she dropped her gaze. He looked at her in surprise as the smell of her pleasure wafted through the air. He cleared his throat. "Er, perhaps we can go through them together so you understand what to look for," he said.

"Yes, please," she said. She gestured to a chair near her own. "Please sit."

Lleland sat as Muriel took the loose page from the book and smoothed it out over her lap. With a brief glance in Lleland's direction, she started reading the first question aloud.

Lleland was busy explaining when Syngen Gail walked into the room a short while later. He paused at the threshold as Lleland rose to greet him.

"Brought that book for Muriel, I see. Well, since you're here, why don't you join us for supper?" He rang a bell without waiting for a reply. "Master Seaton will be joining us this evening," he told the footman who appeared at the door. He looked back at Lleland. "So, what ridiculous ideas are you planting in my niece's mind?"

"A little Aristotle, Ambassador."

"Aristotle, eh?" He turned to Muriel. "Just don't start lecturing me about ethics, niece. Just one word about Aristotle, and I'll bar Master Seaton from ever entering this house again."

Muriel's eyes widened before she dropped her gaze. "Yes, uncle."

Syngen laughed. "You silly goose," he said. "I'm just teasing. You know I'll listen to you expound on Aristotle as long as you want." He turned to Lleland. "You must get heartily sick of philosophizing."

Lleland shrugged. "Not really. And I don't limit myself to the masters. I read other books, too."

"You do? Such as?"

"Books of exploration and discovery. There are so many things to learn! But I have other interests as well." Syngen raised his eyebrows questioningly. "I'm also a trained archer."

Syngen's expression turned incredulous. "A scholar and an archer. That's quite a combination."

Lleland shrugged. "Perhaps. Learning the bow was a childhood interest that I found I enjoyed. And it seems to me that honing the body as well as the mind makes for a well-rounded man."

"And what do you hunt, Master Seaton?"

Lleland opened his mouth to answer, then paused. Was he still a dragon hunter? "Food for the table, and whatever threatens my life," he replied.

"Ah." Syngen poured a glass of wine and held it out to him. "And did you encounter any threats in the mountains?"

Lleland stared into his wine, before taking a long draught. "No," he said.

The butler appeared at the door and bowed. "Supper is served, milord," he said.

Syngen nodded. "After you, my dear," he said to Muriel. He fell in step beside Lleland as they followed behind.

"You don't have other guests joining you tonight?" Lleland asked as they were ushered into a room with a table already laden with food. A junior footman stood behind each chair.

"Not tonight," Syngen replied with a grin. "Does that make you feel easier?"

Lleland smiled. "Absolutely," he said.

The first course was oyster pie, following by pheasant roasted with chestnuts. The dishes were cleared away, and Syngen leaned back in his chair, wine glass in hand. "I'm interested in learning more about your trip, Master Seaton. Tell me about the places you visited."

"Yes, I would love to hear about them, too," Muriel chimed in eagerly.

"I've a particular interest in history, so I enjoyed those towns with ancient ruins. Studying ruins is really a study of people, you know!"

The head footman returned bearing a large platter of succulent red meat and placed it on the table. "Please, continue," Syngen said, spearing a piece of meat with a fork. It was still attached to the bone, and Syngen grabbed his knife to cut it at the same moment that the footman leaned forward to offer his aid. The knife sliced through the footman's palm, making him jerk away in surprise as blood welled to the surface and dripped onto the table.

"Oh, my!" Muriel exclaimed, quickly pushing herself from the table and turning away. She drew a handkerchief from her gown and held it in the direction of the servant. "Please, go and attend to that at once," she said. The scent of blood filled the air as the servant pressed the cloth to the wound, quickly saturating the delicate linen. Lleland stared at the crimson cloth as a craving stronger than anything he'd ever felt slammed into him, making him clench his fists in an effort to control himself. He could taste the blood in the air, and it was only through a supreme battle of wills that he stopped himself leaping over the table and licking the man's blood from his hand. The heat was coursing through his veins, growing in intensity, and he closed his eyes against the burning flames, dousing them through sheer will.

When he finally opened them again, it was to see Syngen staring at him, his narrowed eyes watching him intently. Lleland gave a weak smile. "I'm not good around blood," he said. Syngen's eyebrows shot up in surprise.

"You're a hunter!" he said incredulously.

"Human blood," Lleland clarified cautiously. "It reminds me of my own mortality."

Syngen stared at him for another moment, then gave a dry snort of laughter. "Quite," he said.

"I don't enjoy the sight of blood, either," Muriel said, finally turning back to the table as the footman disappeared through the door. "It makes me feel quite ill."

"Well, the footman, with his blood, has gone, so you may

both rest easy," Syngen said, surreptitiously wiping the spot on the table with his sleeve. The smell still lingered in the air, however, playing havoc with Lleland's senses as he helped himself to some of the cooked meat on the platter.

A junior footman took the place of the man injured and served the next course, but when the sweetmeats were brought to the table, the wounded footman returned, his hand swathed in snow-white linens, with a note on a tray. "This just arrived for Mistress Muriel," he said.

Muriel took the missive with a nod and opened it. She looked at Syngen a moment later. "It's a note from Maude," she said. "A few friends are planning to go walking in the country on Sunday and she wants to know if I'll join her." She turned to Lleland. "Perhaps you'd like to come too?"

Lleland and Syngen both looked at Muriel in surprise. "I, er …" Lleland began, but he was cut off by Syngen.

"I'm sure Master Seaton has other things to occupy his time other than walking, my dear," he said. He turned to Lleland. "Isn't that so?"

Lleland met his gaze. "Actually, I think a walk in the country would be most enjoyable, thank you." Lleland said. Syngen's eyes narrowed slightly, but he turned to Muriel with a smile.

"It seems I was mistaken. Master Seaton is quite the man of leisure!"

Muriel smiled as the color rose in her cheeks. She looked down at the note. "If you'll excuse me," she said, "I'll go write my reply directly, and see you in the parlor afterwards." Clutching her sheet of paper, Muriel hurried from the room as Syngen leaned back in his seat and picked up his glass of wine.

"Do you think that was a wise thing to do, Master Seaton?" Syngen said, staring at the red liquid. "You don't want to give Muriel false hopes."

"I don't know what you mean, Ambassador," Lleland replied. "Mistress Muriel is an intelligent woman, eager to have someone treat her as an equal."

"Ah!" Syngen took a sip of wine. "But you're not her equal, are you? In intelligence, you're her superior, and in social standing, you're decidedly her inferior. I'm happy to indulge her when it comes to learning, but don't think for a moment I would approve of anything else." Lleland sipped and remained silent. "It's not that I don't like you," Syngen continued, "but I find you something of an enigma. The matter with the blood, for instance. I've never met a hunter with a queasiness for blood before. Now it may be that you are exaggerating the truth about your skill in weaponry, but it's clear that you're a strong man who has no need to resort to dishonesty." Lleland frowned. "And then there's something else … something I can't put my finger on. Almost as if …" He shook his head.

"I'm not sure what you're referring to," Lleland said, "but I'm not a dastardly individual who needs to be kept from your niece."

Syngen laughed. "Oh, I know that. But still, one can never be too careful. And I would never approve of a match between the two of you. Her mother would haunt me from the grave if I did. But I do intend to watch you closely, Master Seaton. There's a mystery about you that I intend to discover." He rose from his seat. "Let's retire to the parlor where we can be more comfortable."

As Lleland walked home that evening, he wondered what Syngen knew about dragons. Twice, now, he had intimated that there was more to be found in the mountains than Lleland had revealed he'd seen. Did he know about the dragons of Storbrook? And if he did, did he know that humans could drink their blood? Was that what he meant when he said there was something else about Lleland? It would behoove Lleland to be on his guard. The ambassador was just a little too suspicious for comfort.

Sunday morning dawned wet and rainy, and Lleland was not surprised to receive the note from Muriel informing him that the plans for the day had been canceled. He was disappointed – he'd hoped that spending time in her company would help push aside thoughts of Lydia. It seemed to him that no matter what he did, she invaded his thoughts and drove away his peace. It was because of the blood bond, of course, but knowing that did not make things any easier. If anything, it made it far, far worse.

CHAPTER THIRTY-THREE

Lleland sat down on the edge of his narrow bed as a wave of nausea washed over him. His head ached, his back itched, and his skin burned so badly that he wanted to claw it off with his nails. In his hand he held a note from Muriel. She had completed the book, as well as the questions he'd prepared, and wondered whether he would look over her answers. Included in the note was an invitation to join her and her uncle for the evening. He groaned, wishing he could crawl into a corner and die. Which could happen soon, he acknowledged to himself. He barely had enough strength now to walk down the road. He could see the wondering looks of his students, and heard the murmurings of the other Masters, but he ignored them all. The only one he couldn't ignore was Zach, who knew exactly what he was doing. But he was Jack's spawn, and if sacrificing his life meant saving others, it was a sacrifice he was willing to make.

The nausea subsided, and Lleland crossed over to the window. The shutters were open despite the rain, and cool, damp air filled the room. It did little to relieve the heat that burned through him, but it felt pleasant on his skin. He leaned against the window frame and stared out into the night sky. In the distance he could hear the call of a nightjar.

He was about to turn away when a soft sound caught his ear. He peered into the darkness, then stepped back when Aaron suddenly appeared before him, hovering outside his window.

"Aaron," he said. "What are you doing here?"

"We need to talk," Aaron said. "Can I come in?"

Lleland stepped back and gestured into the room as Aaron dropped through the window and landed on the floor. "Why're you here?" Lleland said.

"The Dragon Council starts tomorrow, and Keira and Lydia wanted to come into the city."

"Lydia's here? In Civitas?"

"Yes. We leave tomorrow for the hill country. Zach will be coming too. He tells me you're not feeding. And I can see how much you've weakened." He clamped a hand on Lleland's shoulder. "You must eat, Lleland, or you'll die."

"Being a monster is a fate worse than death," Lleland said. He stepped out of Aaron's grasp and turned away. "I won't shed innocent blood."

There was a moment of silence. "You're not Jack," Aaron finally said.

Lleland turned and stared at Aaron. "Jack's blood runs through my veins," he said. "I feel him, in my dreams. I see what he sees, and enjoy being a monster. I'm his dragon spawn, Aaron. You know that! I'm as black as the devil, just as he was."

"You're reliving Jack's memories from his blood. You're not feeding yourself, so you're not strong enough to resist them. But you're not Jack. And his isn't the only blood that runs through your veins. You're succumbing to your fears, but Lleland, you're a dragon hunter! You've killed dragons stronger and more powerful than yourself. Are you going to be defeated by Jack?"

"This isn't about being defeated by Jack! Am I scared? Of course! I'm scared I'll become just like him. You yourself admitted you've never seen a grown man turn into a dragon. You don't know what will happen!"

"I have faith in you, Lleland. It's when you overcome your fears that you're truly free. Didn't Aristotle say that fear is the anticipation of evil? Jack never overcame his fears, and he gave up hope. He lost the person he loved the most and gave into his despair. But you, Lleland, are not without hope. You're not a monster. You have people who love you."

Lleland turned away. "Are you willing to risk innocent lives to find out if you're right?" he said.

"If your actions result in one innocent human losing their life, I will hunt you down and kill you."

"And one person will be dead."

"Despite your low opinion of yourself, I don't believe for a single minute that you will be a threat to people." He paused. "When you encountered Jack, he was indeed evil. But that was after he lost his human wife."

Lleland turned and stared at Aaron. "He was married to a human? What happened to her?"

"Jack's father killed her in a moment of insanity. But Jack blamed me for her death." He shrugged. "I'd ordered him to leave his wife behind when we went to defend our borders."

"Jack attacked Civitas because of you?"

"He wanted to wrest mastership from me. He also kidnapped Keira and her sister. He was going to kill them."

"He killed my father because he hated you?"

"Yes."

Lleland nodded. "Goodnight, Aaron."

"I'll leave. But think about what I said. Don't become Jack's last victim."

A carriage, sent by Syngen Gail, arrived at the university a short while later, and Lleland climbed into it gratefully. He leaned against the plush velvet seats and closed his eyes as the carriage rattled along the cobbled roads. Because of Aaron, his father had lost his life. The cord of fate became more snarled and twisted. The carriage lurched to a stop fifteen minutes later outside the ornate ambassadorial residence. A footman led Lleland past the hall and up a flight of stairs into the parlor. Muriel smiled at him from her seat beneath the window, and the sweet scent of pleasure filled the air.

"Master Seaton, please come in," she said. She gestured towards a seat opposite her, and Lleland took it gratefully. "Are you quite all right?" she said. "You look a little pale."

Lleland forced a smile. "Quite fine, thank you Mistress."

"Uncle Syngen will be down in a moment." The book Lleland had lent her was on her lap, and she laid her hands over it as she spoke.

"How did you find the book?" Lleland asked. His head was pounding.

"I enjoyed it." She looked down. "Some of it was a bit difficult to understand."

"Were you able to answer any of my questions?"

Muriel held out a sheet of paper with an eager smile. "I tried! Look, here it is."

Lleland took the sheet. "I'll have a look some other time. But I've brought another book for you." He held up a much larger tome, and Muriel's smile faltered slightly.

"I'll start reading it tonight," she said.

Syngen walked into the room. "What? Another book? Trying to be a martyr to philosophy, Muriel? You know I've already been pushed beyond what any man would consider tolerable when it comes to hearing Aristotle night after night. And in Latin, mind you." Muriel flushed and looked at the book in her hands, and Syngen laughed. "I'm teasing you, Muriel. I'm glad you have something to occupy your mind. Although, if Terran ever learns I'm being instructed in philosophy by my niece, he'll recall me in an instant!" He grinned as he turned to Lleland. "How go your classes? Are your students all as eager to learn as my niece here?"

"Unfortunately not."

A footman appeared at the door to the dining room. "Supper is ready, milord," he said.

"Excellent." Syngen held out his arm to his niece. "Shall we?" She glanced at Lleland, but took the proffered arm as Lleland rose to his feet. A wave of dizziness washed over him, and he grabbed his chair. It passed in a moment, and he looked up to see that Muriel had dropped her uncle's arm and stepped to his side. "Are you all right?" she asked anxiously. "You look quite unwell. Perhaps you should sit."

Lleland moved his hand from the chair. "I think I stood too quickly! I haven't eaten since early this morning!"

"Are you sure you don't need to lie down? I could send for some wine."

"No, no, I'm quite fine."

Muriel glanced at Syngen, who shrugged, and after a moment she took his arm once more and headed through the door, glancing back over her shoulder as Lleland slowly followed. The room started spinning, bringing another wave of nausea, and Lleland grabbed the doorframe as blackness overtook him and he fell to the floor.

A sharp, acrid smell brought him to his senses, and he opened his eyes to see Muriel kneeling anxiously beside him, holding a burning feather beneath his nose. Syngen was speaking to one of the footmen. "Take him to the garden chamber," he said.

"No," Lleland said, struggling to rise to his feet, "I'm fine. I'll just return home, if you don't mind me using the carriage again."

"You're in no fit state to go anywhere," Syngen said. He nodded at the footman, who pulled Lleland to his feet and half dragged him up the stairs. Lleland had no strength to resist, and he clutched the man's arm as he was led down a passage and into a small chamber. Muriel followed them into the room.

"Lie down, Master Seaton," she said, indicating the bed.

Lleland sat down. "My apologies, Mistress," he said. "I'll

be fine in a moment."

"I will send for some wine." She left the room as Lleland reached for the chamber pot beneath the bed and retched. He fell back on the bed and closed his eyes. A few minutes passed before the door opened again and a woman entered the room. She pushed a strand of gray hair into the greasy cap on her head, and placed her hands on her stout hips.

"I was told to tend to you," the woman said. "I'm Jones." She placed a hand on Lleland's forehead. "You're burning up." She poked her head out the door and shouted for someone to bring cold water and rags. She turned back to Lleland. "We must get your clothes off."

Lleland pushed himself onto one elbow as the woman eased off his tunic, then fell back onto the bed. A maid brought in a pile of linens and a jug of water. Jones wet the cloths and laid them over his chest, her eyes widening as they quickly steamed dry. In silence she compressed her lips together and soaked more, placing layer upon layer over his chest and down his side, before looking down at his legs.

"Now your breeches," she said.

"I'll do it," he said weakly. "And pass me something to cover myself."

"I've seen plenty of naked men in my day," said Jones with a leer. "No need to worry about your dignity."

Lleland shivered. "I'll preserve what little I have left," he said.

The woman laughed and handed him a sheet before turning to face the door. He stripped off his breeches and stockings and covered himself as the woman turned around. She soaked more linens and wrapped them around his feet, then replaced those on his chest, which were dry. "You should be dead with such a fever," she said. Lleland was silent.

Syngen came by a short while later. "How's he doing?"

"He's alive, that's all I can say," said Jones. "Though for the love of God I cannot say why."

"He's dying?"

"He's burning such a fever, it's a wonder the bed's not aflame."

"Very well. Give me a minute alone with him." Syngen waited as Jones left the room, then walked over to the bed. "It's clear you cannot return to the university tonight. I've already sent word that you won't be back. Can I contact someone to take over your classes?"

"No. I must return. I'll be fine by morning."

"Jones says you're deathly ill. I cannot allow you to leave." Lleland closed his eyes. "I'll let you get some rest," Syngen said. "Are you sure there isn't anything I can do?"

"Open the window."

There was a creak as the shutters were pushed open and cool, fresh air flowed into the room. The door to the room closed as Lleland breathed in deeply and blew out a stream of flame.

CHAPTER THIRTY-FOUR

Lleland dozed. In the distance he heard a door open and the soft, muted sounds of voices, but his mind was too dull to follow the conversation. A few minutes later his own door opened, and a soft fragrance of summer and berries filled the room, tinged with something else. Anger. He opened his eyes to see Lydia standing at the foot of the bed, arms akimbo.

"What you are doing here?" Lleland said.

"Zach overheard the Dean saying you were ill. But the question is, what are *you* doing here?"

Footsteps hurried down the passage, and Muriel burst into the room. "I'm sorry, Master Seaton," she said. She brushed a loose strand of hair from her face. "This woman refused to leave. I told her you weren't to be disturbed, but she wouldn't listen. Should I send someone to escort her out?"

"It's all right, Mistress," Lleland said. "Mistress Drake is a, er, friend." He glanced at Lydia, who was watching him with eyebrows raised.

"I need to speak with Lleland alone," she said. Muriel's lips compressed into a thin line as she looked at Lleland. He nodded, and she left with a frown.

"How could you, Lleland?" Lydia said as soon as the door closed behind Muriel. "You're killing yourself! Giving in!" She pointed her finger at him. "You think you're a monster, but you're not! You know the truth, Lleland. You know that dragons are not monsters! But instead of facing up to it, you're hiding behind your anger. It's time to let it go!"

"You're right," Lleland said. "Not all dragons are monsters. But Jack was."

"You're not Jack!"

"How do you know? How do you know what I'll do if I give in to this animal nature?"

Tears started rolling down her cheeks, and she swiped them away angrily. "You're allowing your fears to make you weak." She started pacing.

"I'm not —"

"And what about Muriel Gail? What will she think when you're dead?"

"Muriel Gail? What does she have to do with this?"

Lydia turned to look at him. "She has feelings for you. Isn't that why you're here?"

"No." Lleland pushed himself up in the bed. "Of course not! I lent Mistress Muriel some of my books, and she invited me to supper."

"Oh. So you care for no-one? Not even yourself?"

"Lydia, I —"

She swiped away more tears. "I cannot listen to you! And I cannot watch you die! I'm going!"

"Lydia, please —" But Lydia was already out the door. Lleland fell back against the bed with a groan. If he only knew the effect Jack's blood would have on him! Lydia said he was weak — was she right? No! he growled. He was doing this because it was the right this to do. He closed his eyes as the thoughts raced around in his mind. Was he sacrificing his life needlessly? Aaron had said something about fear — that it was the anticipation of evil. He gave a mental nod. Even through his dullness he could see the truth of that. But to conquer his fears, he needed to face them. He'd told his students the same thing many times! Was that true, or false? Perhaps Aaron was right and he wasn't Jack. Which meant the question was, was he brave enough to face life and find out?

Lleland waited until the house was quiet before he rolled painfully off the bed. He landed on the floor with a thump and groaned. He was dying – he could feel his body shutting down – but as the shadow of death hovered over him, he knew he wanted to give life a chance. Aaron had said he would kill him if he became dangerous. He dragged himself to the chair and found the dagger he kept in his boot. He doubted he had the strength to change his form, but if he was going to live, he needed to hunt. He only hoped he would be able to catch his prey.

He pulled on his breeches and stumbled across the floor to the window. Cold air rushed through the casement, caressing his burning body. He sat down on the window ledge and slowly edged his legs over the sill. A wave of dizziness washed over him and he gripped the sill until it passed, then looked at the ground, twelve feet below. He breathed in deeply and pushed himself out the window. His wings opened slowly, but they caught him just before he hit the hard earth. He pulled himself to his feet and stumbled through the grass, weaving like a drunkard. His wings dragged on the ground, but he was too weak to fold them.

He stopped when he saw Lydia, standing in the moonlight. In her arms she held a small doe. He rubbed his eyes and blinked, wondering if he was dreaming, but when he opened them again, she was still there. The doe was quivering, but she stroked it gently, whispering soothingly into its ears. She looked up at Lleland, then knelt down, the doe still in her arms. He walked towards her and sank to the ground.

"Why?" he whispered.

"I couldn't leave. I stayed here, hoping." She looked

down at the doe, and slowly removed her arms. The creature stumbled to its feet and leapt away, but fast as it was, Lleland was still faster. He shot out his hand and drew the dagger across the creature's neck. Bright crimson spurted in every direction, and he pulled the animal to his lips, clamping his mouth over the wound. Blood filled his mouth for the first time in weeks, and he closed his eyes as he swallowed the healing liquid. He could feel Lydia's eyes on him, but he didn't care. All he cared about was the sweet elixir flooding through him, filling him with more strength with each passing moment. When the flow of blood stopped, he used the dagger to slice the creature's belly, then ripped the flesh away with his teeth. A growl rose in his throat as he ripped and chewed. His tongue sought the last traces of meat, then he flung the carcass away before turning to look at Lydia. He didn't care that he was splattered with blood, or that she had seen him eating like an animal. A wave of desire washed over him, and he reached out a hand to pull her closer.

"Stop." She placed her hands on his chest and pushed him away. "Do you love me?" she said.

He growled and grabbed her hands, pulling her close as he kissed her. She turned her head, breaking the kiss. Her eyes were flaming.

"You didn't answer me," she said.

"You gave me your blood," he snarled. "You bound me to yourself. How do I know what I feel?"

She pulled her hands from his and moved back a pace. "I cannot bind a dragon, Lleland, unless he wills it. I can only bind a human. And you're definitely not human."

"That's right! Because you made me into a monster!"

She rose to her feet and glowered at him. "Yes, Lleland, that's right. A monster. Just like me." She stared at him for a moment longer, then turned and walked away.

He wanted to call her back, but he didn't. Instead he watched as she walked away from him. Again. Only this time he had chased her away.

He lay on the cold grass for a long time. A bright flash of light lit up the sky, then slowly dissipated. Eventually he rose to his feet and walked back to the house. He was no longer weak – the blood and flesh had increased his strength to dragon proportions. He reached the building and stared up at the window. There was only one way to reach it. He opened his wings and shot into the air. He flew through the open window and walked over to the bed, then turned as another scent assailed him. In a chair in the corner, sword in his hand, sat Syngen Gail.

Lleland stared as Syngen rose, sword outstretched, and walked towards him. "You're a dragon," he said. "I should've known! You come into my home, befriend my niece and abuse my hospitality while shamming an illness. What I want to know is why? Does the Dragon Master know about this?"

"What do you know about the Dragon Master?" Lleland said.

"That's neither here nor there. But it seems unlikely that Aaron would lower himself with such a deception."

"He wouldn't," Lleland said. "And neither would I."

Syngen pressed the tip of the sword against Lleland's throat. "I'll ask you again. What are you doing in my house? You have to the count of three before I kill you." He twisted the blade slightly, and a drop of blood welled up on Lleland's skin. "Muriel won't be very happy when she finds out that you're dead at my hand, but she'll forgive me eventually. And I did tell you I'd never consent to a union between you."

"I didn't come to woo your niece. And Aaron certainly knows about me. I saw him just before I came here."

"He sent you here? Why?"

"He didn't. Please, take your blade away. I've just decided I want to live, and you're threatening to kill me."

Syngen pulled the sword back slightly, but kept it raised. "I'll ask one last time. What are you doing here?"

"I'm here because Muriel invited me. As you know, I

brought her another book."

"That doesn't explain your deception. We both know dragons cannot get ill."

"They can if they don't feed."

"You seem perfectly fine now."

"I've just fed."

"Ah! How convenient. I heard Lydia Drake was here earlier. Is she in on this, too?"

"She came here because I was dying." Lleland glanced away. "She was angry with me. She helped me when I was too weak to help myself."

"And what does Aaron have to do with all this?"

"Nothing. He came to me this evening to try and convince me to feed."

"Why wouldn't you feed?"

"I didn't want to be a monster."

"A monster?" He laughed dryly. "A dragon who thinks he's a monster. How ironic."

"I wasn't born this way. I was created."

Syngen stared at Lleland, then stepped away and lowered the sword. "How's that possible?"

"Aaron warned me not to speak of it."

"I see. So you somehow changed into a dragon, and decided to starve yourself?"

"In turning into ... this thing ... I've become the monster I've spent my whole life trying to kill."

Syngen's eyes widened, and he let out a long whistle. "You're a hunter!" He laughed. "What an interesting twist of fate!"

"You could say that."

"Our destinies are determined by a higher power than our own," Syngen said. "Don't waste the gift you've been given."

"You think being a dragon is a gift?"

"All life is a gift."

"Even the life of a monster?"

"You tell me."

Lleland picked up his tunic and walked to the window. "I should leave. But before I do, would you mind telling me how you know Aaron?"

"Oh, I belong to his clan."

"But you're not a dragon!"

"No. I'll tell Muriel that you started to improve and insisted on returning to your own chambers. And Master Seaton, I'd prefer it if you didn't show your face in my home again."

Lleland nodded. "Goodnight, Ambassador." He turned around and stepped through the window. The muscles in his back tightened and stretched as he pushed his wings against the air. The stress and tension that had lain coiled in his belly fled. Strength and power coursed through him, and for the first time in weeks he felt free. He filled his lungs with air and blew out a stream of flame. It rolled over his body, caressing his skin. The desire to change burned through him, but he resisted it. He had chosen life, but he wasn't ready to embrace the beast. As he flew, he thought about what Lydia had said. It was impossible for her to bind a dragon, unless he too desired the bond. Which meant that whatever he felt about Lydia had nothing to do with being bound to her. He groaned to himself – was that a good thing, or not?

It was almost dawn when Lleland walked the last few blocks to the university. He opened the door to his chamber to see a scrap of crumpled paper lying on the floor. He picked it up and smoothed it out on his desk. It was from Lord Grant.

'Master Seaton,' it read, 'the League meets Thursday at midnight. Signed, G.'

Lleland gathered the scrap into his hand and scrunched it into a ball. It was Thursday morning.

The passages and halls were dark and empty when he left for the meeting that night, and at twelve o'clock sharp, he stepped into the storeroom beneath the Guildhall.

"Ah, Master Seaton! Welcome back from your travels."

Lord Grant rose to his feet. "We have a newcomer in our midst, to which we owe you our thanks. Please welcome Master Matthew Hobbes."

CHAPTER THIRTY-FIVE

A cold hand crept around Lleland's heart as he turned to look at Matthew Hobbes.

"Master Hobbes," he said, "what a surprise."

Matthew smiled thinly. "I don't know why, Master Seaton. After all, it was you who first told me about the League. When I heard there were others who shared my goal of ridding the world of monsters, I knew I had to join their numbers." He turned to Grant. "The dragons in the Northern Mountains have been terrorizing the towns and villages in the area for years. With your hunters, we can finally be rid of the monsters."

"And how will we manage that?" Lleland asked. "The dragons know better than to approach hunters."

"I know where to find their lair."

"And tell me, Master Hobbes, where exactly is it?"

"Storbrook Castle, of course. The home of Aaron Drake."

"What?" Grant half rose from his seat as his hands gripped the table. Scott turned to stare at Lleland.

"Is that true, Seaton?" Elliott demanded. His thick eyebrows pulled together in a frown as he tugged his thick beard.

"No." Lleland folded his arms. Callaway was watching him intently, his fingers stroking his chin. "Master Hobbes is guessing. I've been to Storbrook, and there's no lair."

"Then why do the dragons always stay near the castle?" demanded Matthew.

Lleland shrugged. "How do you know they do? Have you seen them around Storbrook? Have you even been to the castle?"

"Everyone knows the dragons have a lair there. And I also know that Aaron Drake is in league with the beasts. How did he convince you to deny the presence of the lair? Did he threaten to feed you to the monsters?"

All eyes turned to Lleland, and Scott's eyebrows rose questioningly as his gaze settled on him. "Of course not," Lleland said. "Aaron Drake does not believe the dragons to be a threat. If he did, he would deal with them. And after seeing them in the mountains, I tend to agree."

"What's this? *You* don't think the dragons are a threat?" Callaway sounded incredulous. "Master Hobbes has just told us that they've been terrorizing the villages."

"Ask Master Hobbes when a dragon last attacked his village and killed its residents," Lleland said. He looked at Matthew.

"You already know my father was killed by the dragon, as was my brother."

Elliott slapped a beefy hand on the table. "That's all we need to know," he said. "Seaton, you know that the loss of even one life is too many. I don't understand why the dragon-slayer would tolerate this, but I say we go to the mountains and kill these monsters."

"I agree," said Callaway. He looked at Lleland. "What's gotten into you? We all know how much you hate dragons. Normally you'd be leading the charge! And if people are being killed –"

"Master Hobbes' father was not killed by the dragon,"

Lleland said.

"What's this?" Elliott turned to Matthew. "Was he, or was he not, killed by the dragon?"

"The dragon burned his legs so badly, he eventually died from his injuries. And my brother's body was never even found!"

"I think we've heard enough," Callaway said.

"Let's kill the monsters!" shouted Channing. A short man, with heavy peasant features, Channing could smell blood a mile away.

"The dragons aren't a threat!" Lleland said, raising his voice against Channing's.

"All dragons are a threat!" Edgar Brenton leaped to his feet, with an agility that defied his size and age. He pounded the table with his fist. "It isn't just loss of life that should concern us, but loss of property as well!"

"Aye, aye," shouted Channing. "Let's send some hunters immediately."

"I'll be the first to go!" Elliott said. His brown eyes swept around the table, challenging the others. "The League doesn't let a threat go unchallenged."

"The mountains are six weeks away!" Lleland protested.

"Not if we ride." Callaway looked at Grant. "Will you provide mounts for the men who have none?"

"Of course," said Grant.

"Then we should leave right away," Elliott said. "Who's with us?"

"I'm not going to pass up a chance to kill a dragon," Scott said. He glanced at Lleland. "Sorry."

Callaway tapped his fingers against the table. "You can count me in."

"I'll lead you," Matthew said.

Branton shook his head. "I cannot go," he said, "but I'll fund the mission."

"Nor I," Grant said. "But I'll provide horses and other supplies."

"I must work my farm," Channing said. He settled back in his seat and crossed his arms.

"What about you, Seaton?" Callaway said. "Are you with us or not?"

Lleland thought quickly. Lydia was to go to the hill country with her family. But what if she'd returned to Storbrook alone? "I'll go, too," he said at last.

"Good, then it's all settled. I say we arrange our affairs tomorrow, and leave the following dawn."

Lleland listened as the men planned the details for the trip, but before they left, Scott drew him aside. "I thought you didn't want to hunt the dragons," he said.

"I don't," Lleland replied. "But I'll not stand aside while you do it. Perhaps I can convince you not to pursue this action. But how can you leave when you have a wife to support? How much longer till the baby comes?"

Scott frowned. "She says a few weeks. She's staying with her mother till she gives birth. And I have a little money saved that the wife doesn't know about." He grinned. "Besides, I'll be serving my country when I send an arrow through the heart of my first dragon and take a horn as a trophy!"

Lleland was at the north gate two mornings later, waiting for the other hunters to arrive. It was a cold and dreary day in early November, and the steady downpour of rain showed no signs of abating. Lleland was seated on one of Grant's horses, and its hot breath created clouds of mist in the cold air. The day before he had spoken to the Dean, who had reluctantly given his approval for his absence. Harold Dodds would teach his classes in his absence. His first choice was Zach, but he had left for the hill country. He had slipped a note beneath Lleland's door before he left, explaining his absence.

A sword was slung at Lleland's side, and in his hand he held his bow. He had not hunted with it since returning to the city, but it settled into his palm like a long-lost friend.

There was a clatter of hooves on the bridge and Lleland glanced up to see Elliott approaching, also carrying a bow, with an axe slung through his belt. Callaway was a few feet behind. "Eager to start the hunt, are you?" Callaway said as he drew closer. Lleland grimaced as he greeted the men.

"You know I don't agree with this plan. Those dragons are not a threat!"

"Now I've heard it all! Seaton saying that dragons aren't a threat! You and I both know that the only good dragon is a dead dragon!"

Matthew rode up. "Ready to go kill some monsters?" he said with a grin, before wheeling his horse around and starting down the road. After a moment, the others turned their horses as well and fell in behind.

They kept a quick pace, and were soon well clear of the city. The steady rain, combined with constant traffic, had turned the roads into a bog. The other men in the entourage pulled their hats low over their eyes and drew their cloaks tight around their chests. They traveled in silence, too uncomfortable for conversation. Lleland didn't mind the cold. The fires burned within him, keeping him pleasantly warm.

They stayed at a small roadside inn the first night, and were on their way again early the next morning. The rain had stopped, but the low clouds remained, and the air was frigid. Scott pulled his cloak tighter around his shoulders as he fell in beside Lleland.

"Cold, isn't it?" he said.

"Yes."

Scott gave him a sideways look. "Doesn't seem to bother you none."

Lleland shrugged. "I'm used to the cold. I'm a college master, remember."

"Hmm." Scott was silent for a few steps. "What are you going to do when you see the dragon?"

Lleland turned to face him. "What do you mean?"

"Will you kill it?"

"No."

"You still think the monsters should live?"

"I do. Despite what Hobbes says, they aren't interested in attacking the villagers."

"You're the only one who believes that."

Lleland shrugged. "Aaron Drake seems to agree."

"So you're basing everything on what Drake says?"

"Drake knows the dragons better than anyone. And his daughter is convinced the dragons would never hurt a human."

"His daughter, eh? Is she pretty?"

"That has nothing to do with it."

"Ah, so she is pretty! What else?"

"She's ..." Lleland paused, wondering how to explain Lydia. Courageous. Independent. Strong-willed. A monster. "She's different," he finally said, fighting the tightness in his chest.

"Different? Well, having a wife's not all it's cracked up to be!"

The days started to blend together as they traveled as fast as they could without exhausting the horses. The weather was cold, and a constant drizzle made the men irritable. Five days after leaving Civitas, Scott's mount threw a shoe. A passing traveler pointed them towards the nearest town, an hour's walk away, and as Scott delivered his horse to the blacksmith, the others gathered at the tavern across the road.

"What you here 'bouts?" asked the barkeep as he passed tankards of ale to the men.

Matthew leaned forward conspiratorially. "Dragons," he said.

"Dragons, eh? Saw one just last week. Flew over the town in a mighty hurry! Gold, but not as big as some I've seen. Perhaps it knew you were after it!"

Lleland stared into his tankard as the men laughed.

"Didn't stop to hunt?" Callaway asked.

"Nah. They never do."

"You've seen them before?" Elliott sounded surprised.

"Not often. Few times a year. They just streak over the town, and then they're gone."

"Hmm." Elliott frowned and tugged his beard.

"They have better hunting grounds in the north," Matthew said.

"Or they aren't interested in hunting humans at all," Lleland suggested. Callaway stroked his chin as he turned to look at Lleland, but he remained silent.

Scott entered the tavern. "The blacksmith said it'll be a few hours," he said. "It's market day and he has a queue of customers. Perhaps we should just stay the night and leave at first light?" He brushed wayward curls from his forehead and smiled at a barmaid as she walked past.

The men agreed, and soon split up to follow their own pursuits for the rest of the day. Taking his daybook and writing kit with him, Lleland wandered over to the old stone church, stopping to search for signs of the ancient foundation the church was said to be built upon.

As he was returning to the inn later that evening, he saw Matthew stop Callaway just outside the entrance. Matthew glanced around the yard, and Lleland stepped into the shadow of a tree. Water dripped onto his neck and steamed.

"I found something at the market today," Matthew said. Despite the distance of sixty feet, Lleland could hear him clearly.

"What?" Callaway said, sounding bored.

Matthew drew something from his pocket and opened his hand. "Wolfsbane. The most dangerous poison on earth. The hag who sold it to me says that just one drop is enough to kill a person."

Callaway glanced at the vial in Matthew's palm. "Must have cost you a pretty penny. Planning to murder someone, are you?"

"Just a dragon. A few drops on an arrow should be enough to kill it."

Callaway leaned forward. "Poisoned arrows, hmm? That may work."

"It will work! This one vial should kill all the monsters in the mountains."

A soft growl escaped Lleland, and Matthew glanced around. "What's that?" he said. He peered into the shadows, and Lleland closed his eyes as the flames blazed within him. When he opened them a moment later, Matthew was tucking the vial back in his pocket. Lleland left the shadows and walked towards them.

"Evening," he said as he drew near. "Enjoy your day?"

"Indeed," Matthew said with a smirk

"You two seemed deep in conversation," Lleland said to Callaway as Matthew sauntered into the inn.

Callaway shrugged. "Nothing important. The man's a bit dull, but I dare say he has his uses."

"Indeed?" Lleland said dryly. "I imagine even a dragon could find a more appetizing meal!"

Callaway's eyebrows shot up, then he laughed. "Probably!"

Lleland waited until he could hear the soft snores of the other men, before he rose from the bed and slipped from the room. It had been three days since he last fed, and he could feel the hunger rising in his belly once more. He glanced around before moving into the trees. He carried his bow and an arrow in his hand, and his dagger in his boot. Patches of snow clung to the ground, and his breath hung in the air. He sniffed, and turned towards the strong scent of fallow deer half a mile away, giving them a wide berth as he circled downwind. A snapping twig behind him made him pause, and he looked around, peering between the trees. He saw nothing, and after a moment, continued towards his goal. He could see the herd of deer between the trees, and he dropped to his knees and quietly strung his bow. He notched the arrow and lifted the bow to his shoulder as he picked out his prey. The arrow sprang from the string, and a moment later Lleland was kneeling beside a dead buck, lifting the neck to his mouth. He heard a slight rustling and paused, once more peering into the darkness. The darkness did not limit his sight, but still he saw nothing. He sniffed, but the tang of fresh blood blocked out all other smells. He dropped his mouth to the neck and drank.

The group of men clattered into a town in the shadows of the mountains two weeks into their journey, and it wasn't long before they were ordering ale at the local tavern.

"Do you see dragons around here much?" Elliott asked as the innkeeper slid a tankard down the bar.

"Oh, aye. There's dragons in those there mountains."

"They must be quite a menace."

"They don't bother us none."

"Do you send out a maiden every month to keep the monsters at bay?" Callaway asked dryly.

The man snorted. "They've never killed anyone."

"That's because they only hunt in the villages to the north," Matthew said.

"Oh, aye? Happens my wife's sister is married to a man beyond the mountains. Never heard her say anything about the dragons neither. Of course, that's not to say nothing's ever happened. There was that dragon in the city a few years back, and I heard a story once about a dragon that attacked a village in the north. But it was least a hundred years ago."

"My village," Matthew said darkly.

"Oh, aye? Well, I s'pect there's always something to be worried about. There was a man who killed his wife and children in their beds 'bout dozen years back in the next town." The man shook his head. "Terrible thing it was, too. My wife knew the woman – grew up with her, you know."

"So you don't mind the dragons?" Scott said.

"The dragons? Ah, no. The children like to watch them fly over. They run outside and wave their hands in the air, hoping the dragons will breathe fire."

Elliott raised his bushy eyebrows. "You let your children wave at the dragons."

"Oh, aye. Gives them a little fun, aye?"

Every night, Lleland dreamed, but it wasn't about Jack. Once he started feeding, those dreams had become less frequent, until they stopped altogether. It was another dragon that teased his mind as he slept these days. A beautiful, golden dragon, that beckoned him to join her as she soared through the sky. And in the morning when he woke, it took a few moments to get over the disappointment of realizing it was just a dream.

The men left the highway three days after the conversation with the innkeeper. The road, patchy with ice, was narrow and rutted, with only a few mean hamlets along the way. They hunted small game and cooked it over a fire, and slept beneath the stars. The other men shivered, and pulled their blankets close to their chins, but the cold didn't bother Lleland. They were sitting around a campfire one evening when Scott took a seat next to Lleland. He stared into the fire for a while, then turned to look at him.

"Where do you go at night when everyone else is sleeping?" Scott asked Lleland, his voice low.

Lleland glanced up in surprise, then quickly scanned the other men. No-one was paying them any mind. "What do you mean?" he replied, his voice just as low.

"I followed you, Lleland. I saw you kill a deer. Why would you do that?"

Lleland drew in a deep breath. "What else did you see?"

"You drank the animal's blood, then ate its raw, steaming flesh."

"Ah!"

"Who does that, Lleland? Who eats raw flesh? Did the

dragons do something to you when you were at Storbrook? Is that why you don't want to hunt them?"

Lleland was silent. He could feel Scott's gaze intent upon him. "I have a rare condition," Lleland finally said. "I need raw blood to survive."

Scott turned and stared into the fire. "Is that it? That's all you're going to say?"

Lleland nodded. "Yes."

"You'd better hope no else follows you," Scott said. He rose in disgust. "They might not be satisfied with such a dishonest answer."

CHAPTER THIRTY-SIX

After four days of traveling past small hamlets and shabby cottages, the men reached Matthew's village, and he led them to his house a little way past the market square. It was large, but clearly in need of some repair and maintenance. The front door opened into a hall where a thin, haggard-looking woman sat doing needlework. Two children played at her feet.

"You're back," the woman said, her voice flat. The children glanced up, then returned to their game. Matthew's eyes narrowed slightly.

"Yes, wife, I'm back. Now get us some food. We're hungry. And take the brats with you."

The woman stared at him for a moment then glanced at the others before turning away. She said something low to the children, and they followed her from the room.

"Your children?" Callaway asked.

"Yes. They take after their mother," Matthew said.

"How fortunate," Callaway murmured. Lleland coughed.

"Sit down," Matthew said, waving his hand expansively. "The woman may not be good for much, but she can cook." Callaway smiled sardonically as they sat down on a long bench drawn up to a table. Scott looked embarrassed.

"How far to Drake's residence from here?" Elliott asked.

"Thirty miles, or so I'm told. I haven't been there myself."

"You said the lair is at the castle. How do we reach it?" Scott asked.

Matthew shifted uncomfortably. "We have to find it. But it's just below the castle."

"There's no lair," Lleland said mildly. "I would've found it when I was at Storbrook. I spent plenty of time exploring the mountains."

"That Drake bitch made sure you didn't find it," Matthew said.

Lleland felt the heat rising, but he smiled blandly. "There were no limits to my explorations," he said. "I spent many hours on my own."

"Then where do you suggest we look, Seaton?" Callaway said.

"I suggest you give up this mission. Go back home. You've heard people say the dragons aren't a threat."

"Do you really think we came all this way, only to abandon the mission?" Elliott was incredulous. "You – who've killed three dragons! I don't know what's gotten into you, but we'll find the lair and kill every last dragon before we leave this place."

"And do you really think you can kill a dragon in the mountains? They probably already know we're here."

Matthew glanced at Callaway, then reached into his pocket and withdrew a small vial. "We'll kill them with this," he said with a smirk, holding the bottle up to the light. Lleland felt his chest tighten.

"What is it?" Scott asked.

"Wolfsbane. Enough to kill a dragon."

Elliott whistled through his teeth. "Smart thinking, Hobbes. Cover the arrows with the poison and let it do the rest."

"Exactly," Matthew said, placing the bottle back in his

pocket as his wife returned to the hall with wooden bowls clutched in each hand. Lleland rose to relieve her of the load, and she cast him a surprised glance. "What's this, woman," Matthew said as a bowl was slid before him. He sniffed the contents. "It smells burnt."

"We have nothing else," the woman said wearily. "I had no warning of your return and did not expect visitors, since no one else has ever graced our hall before. I had to scrape the bottom of the pot."

"Stupid whore," Matthew snarled as he rose from the table. He flung the bowl at her feet, and the contents splattered across the floor. "You offer this to me and my friends? Give it to the brats. We'll take our meal at the tavern." He marched from the room, and the others followed with varying degrees of embarrassment.

"Thank God," the woman muttered under her breath. Lleland smiled in amusement as he retrieved the fallen bowl.

"Thank you, Mistress Hobbes," he said, handing it to her. "Please forgive our unannounced arrival and the inconvenience we've caused."

"Thank you, Master." She met his gaze, her eyes wide, and an uncertain smile tugged the side of her mouth. She was pretty, once, Lleland thought to himself before turning to follow the others.

It was a short distance back to the tavern, and Lleland's eyes swept the dark interior as he followed the others to a large table. His heart sank when he saw Richard Carver glance up at him.

"Master Seaton! What are you doing back here?" Lleland could hear the suspicion in his tone.

"He traveled with me." Matthew came to stand beside Lleland, and Richard's eyes narrowed. Matthew gestured to the other men. "Them as well. They're all dragon hunters."

Richard's eyes flew back to Lleland. "You came here with him?" he snarled. "And brought hunters with you? What kind of monster are you?"

"I'm not —" Lleland began, but Richard cut him short.

"You're with him," he said, nodding at Matthew. "I hope the dragon takes his time killing you." He turned and stormed out of the room.

"And you want to save these monsters?" Scott said. He had come to stand next to Lleland during the exchange. "From the sounds of it, they'll rip you apart limb by limb."

"The dragons won't hurt me," Lleland replied. Scott snorted and walked away.

By the end of the evening Elliott and Matthew had decided that the best way to proceed was with as much stealth as possible, in the hopes that the dragons would not become aware of their presence. Callaway listened in silence, but Lleland had laughed. "Think you can hide from a dragon?" he said. "They can smell a man from miles away, and can see like an eagle."

"You seem to know an awful lot about dragons," Matthew snapped.

"I've hunted dragons for years, Master Hobbes," Lleland said. "And as you know, I spent many weeks with the Drakes, who are very familiar with dragons."

"You think you know everything," Matthew retorted angrily. "But dragons are not as clever as you suppose." Callaway raised an eyebrow and glanced at Lleland, who met his gaze with a shrug. Callaway turned away after a moment, but remained silent.

Matthew remained at the inn with the others that night, and early the next morning they followed him behind the church and onto the mountain path. It was late November and frost was thick on the ground, crunching beneath the horses' hooves as they rode silently in single file. A cold wind blew from the mountains, whipping the men's hair about their faces and tugging their cloaks, and their breath hung in the air. They left the open field behind the church and passed into the shelter of the forest. Lleland rode at the back of the group. Through the heavy, wet smell of the forest he could pick out Lydia's light summer scent. He could feel her presence in the air, and knew she wasn't far away. But when he searched the sky he found no sign of her.

The sun rose behind a blanket of cloud, and after a few hours Matthew ordered a stop. "The path gets much rougher ahead," he said. "We must rest the horses." Scott glanced at Lleland, and he nodded his agreement. Lleland slipped from the saddle and tied his horse to a branch. Again he searched the skies but saw no sign of Lydia. She was close by, though. He left the path and pushed his way through the trees, towards the sound of running water.

"Lydia, where are you?" he whispered under his breath as he pushed his way between the trees towards the stream. There was a soft rustling behind him, and Lleland breathed in the sweet scent of berries as he turned to look at Lydia. She wore a white diaphanous robe that hung loosely from her shoulders in long, flowing swathes, ending at her bare feet. Her golden hair rippled over her bare back. She stood with her arms crossed, but even so, Lleland could see she wore nothing beneath the robe. He swallowed hard.

"So it's true," she said. "You've brought hunters to the mountains. I didn't want to believe it when I received word from my grandfather, but you're a traitor to your own kind. Is this your revenge for what happened?"

"Lydia, please, you know better than that."

"You're here with Matthew Hobbes. Even if I hadn't seen him, I can smell his disgusting scent."

"I only traveled with them to try and stop them."

Lydia looked away. "I wish I could believe you," she said. "You think I'm a monster. A monster worthy of death."

"No. That's not true." Lleland stepped closer, and her eyes snapped back to him.

"Stop! Go now, before I'm forced to kill you."

"You don't mean that."

"I'm a monster, Lleland, or have you forgotten?" She pushed the robe from her shoulders, and it fell in soft folds at her feet. He stared at her standing naked before him. "Or maybe it's you that's the monster," she said as she spread her wings and flung herself into the sky. There was a flash of light, and the sleek, beautiful dragon rose higher in the air.

"You're wrong," he shouted.

There was a loud roar and flames filled the air. He started pulling his tunic over his head, but paused when he heard the sound of feet crashing through the undergrowth.

"What was that?" Scott asked panting as he came closer. "Who were you shouting at?"

Lleland yanked the tunic back on, and picked up the heap of white fabric at his feet. "No one," he said.

"You were speaking to someone. And then I heard a roar. Was it a dragon?"

"No." Lleland turned away, but Scott caught him by the arm.

"I heard something, Lleland. What are you hiding?"

Lleland shrugged off the hand and glanced at the robe. "It was Lydia," he said.

Scott glanced around. "Drake's daughter? Where?"

"She's gone."

"Gone where?"

Lleland laughed dryly. "She flew away with a dragon."

He stepped past Scott and walked back to where the others were still gathered. Callaway was rolling the small vial of poison in his hand. "Did you see the monster?" Elliott said.

"Yes. We should turn back now."

Elliott looked thoughtful. "Clearly we've lost the element of surprise."

"We never had it to begin with," Lleland said.

"We just keep going," Matthew said. "There're five of us."

"Four," said Lleland. "I didn't come to fight the dragon."

"Well, that doesn't surprise me," Matthew sneered. "I always doubted you were up for the task."

Scott glanced at Lleland then back at Matthew. "I'm sorry, Lleland," he said. "I know you don't believe we should hunt the creatures, but I came here to kill a dragon."

"Besides, Lleland," Elliott said, "you made an oath. An oath to rid the world of monsters!"

"I made an oath to rid the world of a threat. From all I've seen and heard, there is none!"

"Then you're a traitor to the cause."

Callaway looked at Lleland. "Of everyone in the League, Seaton, you and I are the ones who know what it's like to lose someone to a dragon. And now that victory is within our grasp," he held up the vial of poison, "you cower away?"

"You're wrong, Baric," Lleland said. "I'm not a coward, and the creature you saw is not the monster that killed your brother."

"They all deserve death," Callaway said bitterly.

"Are you sure?"

Callaway's face hardened. "Yes!" He swung himself into his saddle. "I'm going to kill a dragon."

"Yes, let's go kill that monster!" Elliott said. He glanced at Lleland with disgust. "You can do what you want, but nothing you say can stop us! Let's go, boys!"

"Come on, then," Matthew said, swinging himself into his saddle. "We've wasted enough time!" He kicked the steed forward as Elliott and Callaway did the same.

"I'm sorry," said Scott, before mounting his horse and following the others.

Lleland watched as they rode away, then mounting his horse, trailed the path behind them.

Matthew called another stop later that day near a patch of dead grass where they hobbled the horses and let them graze. A wall of mountain rose on the other side of the path. Matthew scowled at Lleland when he joined the group, but the others merely glanced at him as Scott passed over the wine and a hunk of bread.

The fragrance of berries and sunshine filled the cold air, and Lleland glanced around trying to see Lydia, but she remained hidden. That she was close by, he knew without a doubt. The cliff above the path was fifteen feet of sheer rock, but a short distance away a rock fall provided an easy means to gain the height. Leaving the others, Lleland headed over to it, and within moments was staring down at his companions from the rocky cliff. It was a narrow plateau, only a dozen feet wide, and the side away from the path dropped hundreds of feet into a deep valley, presenting a panoramic vista of the mountains. He could see Storbrook Castle above the trees, gleaming at the apex of the next peak. The huge windows in the vast wall of yellow stared back blankly, hiding the castle's mysteries from prying eyes. He stared at them, wondering whether Lydia was standing in the shadows, watching the hunters draw closer.

A wave of heat crashed into his back, and he spun around to see Lydia hovering in the air, her enormous body casting a huge shadow on the ground. Her attention was on the men on the ground, who were scrambling with their weapons.

"No! Get away," Lleland shouted at her. Callaway was stringing his bow, while Matthew held an open vial in his hand. Callaway dipped the arrow into the poison and lifted the bow to his cheek. "They'll kill you!"

She roared and started diving towards the men as Callaway notched the arrow. She was close enough for Callaway to make the shot. Callaway pulled back the string as heat ripped through Lleland. He saw nothing but Lydia as flames blazed around him. There was an explosion of light, and he flung himself off the cliff, soaring into the air towards Lydia, his tail streaming behind him. Dimly he heard someone shout his name. Callaway released the string and the arrow sped through the air as Lleland raced towards Lydia. He reached her moments before the arrow, and pushed her aside as the barb sank into his hide and buried itself deep within his flesh. He heard Lydia cry his name, while below, men were yelling and shouting – but already the sounds were fading. The arrow had penetrated deep into his chest, and he could feel the poison spilling through his veins as he started to fall. He pushed his wings against the air, but his strength was failing. Lydia's claws sank into his flesh, halting his descent.

"Wolfsbane," he whispered, "the arrow was poisoned." He struggled to keep his head up, but darkness was clouding his vision and his strength was fading away.

He awoke a few minutes later as an intense pain shot through him. He roared, then arched in agony as another stabbing pain followed. "Keep still." Lydia sounded far away. There was a wet, ripping sound and he ground his teeth as the pain intensified then dulled to a throb. "I think I have it all," Lydia said.

He opened his eyes cautiously to see Lydia standing over him. Blood was splattered over her jaws and down her chest.

"What were you doing?" he rasped.

"Getting the poison. I had to rip out the flesh before it spread any further."

"You could have been poisoned in the process," he said.

"I burned it," she said. He glanced down to see a hole in his chest. "It will heal."

"Where are we?" he rasped.

"Not far from where you were shot. Why did you do it?"

"It was my turn to save you."

She snorted dryly. "Why?"

"Because I love you."

She laughed bitterly. "I'm a monster, remember."

"No, you're not. You're the most beautiful creature in the world."

"I'm ..." She glanced around. "Someone's coming."

CHAPTER THIRTY-SEVEN

Scott was scrambling up the hill. His breath was shallow, and the smell of his sweat was sharp despite the cold day.

"We must go," Lydia said. "Can you fly?"

Lleland stretched his wings tentatively and flexed them. The pain in his chest throbbed, but did not impede his movement. He nodded. "Let's go," he said. He spread his wings wider and rose into the air, wincing slightly.

Scott reached the summit and glared at the rising figure. "Hey," he yelled. "Is that the only thanks I get after helping you?"

Lleland circled through the air, close on Lydia's tail.

"Lleland!" Scott shouted. "Come back here." Shock shot through Lleland as he glanced down at Scott. "I know it's you!" he yelled.

"How does he know?" Lydia hissed.

"I don't know." He dropped back to the hill and Lydia landed a moment later. Lleland cocked his head and stared at Scott, who stared back, eyebrows raised.

"You're incredibly frightening," he said. "Are you going to eat me?"

"How do you know?" Lleland finally said.

"I saw what happened. I was climbing the rock when there was a bright explosion of light. I had to cover my eyes, but when I opened them, instead of you, there was a huge black monster." He glanced at Lydia. "I mean, er, a dragon. Either the dragon had magically appeared and eaten you, or *you* were the dragon. I went with the latter."

Lleland groaned. "You cannot tell anyone," he said.

Scott rolled his eyes with a snort. "You have more important things to worry about at the moment," he said. "The others didn't see what I saw, but they were very excited when a huge black dragon appeared from nowhere. They are hoping to find your lifeless form very soon. By the way, I'm very glad to see that the poison didn't do you in. I sent them on a wild goose chase."

"Why do you care?" Lydia said.

Scott turned to her. "First off, Lleland Seaton is my friend" – he shot Lleland a glance – "despite what he looks like now. I'll admit it's all rather a shock, and it took me a few minutes to grasp all that had happened. But suddenly it all made sense – your newfound taste for raw flesh. Your unwillingness to hunt anymore. And I don't really want to kill you, Lleland."

"That's a relief," Lleland said dryly.

He looked at Lydia. "And this dragon's too lovely to kill!"

Lydia lifted her eyebrows. "What do you hope to gain by flattering a dragon?"

"My life."

"It was never in danger."

"All the more reason to tell you how beautiful you are!" Scott said, and Lydia snorted as he turned back to Lleland. "How did this happen? Should I be worried about turning into a beast?"

"It's a long story, but no, you have no need for concern."

"And you're not going to eat me?"

"I'm not sure – how much meat do you have on those bones?"

283

Scott laughed. "Just muscle and sinew. Not tasty at all. But you still have to figure out what you're going to do. It won't take Callaway long to realize he's on the wrong path."

Lleland nodded. "You're right. He and Hobbes will keep pursuing us. And neither of them will be satisfied until we're dead." He glanced at Lydia. "You must return to Storbrook."

Scott's eyebrows shot up. "Storbrook! So Hobbes is right – the dragons do have a lair there."

Lleland frowned. "Yes – and no." He glanced at Lydia. "Scott, meet Mistress Drake."

"Mistress Drake? You mean like Aaron Drake?"

"His daughter."

Scott's eyebrows drew together in confusion. "The dragon-slayer has a dragon daughter?" Lleland and Lydia watched him closely. "The dragon-slayer *is* a dragon," he said slowly. He looked at Lydia, then Lleland. "Am I right?" He laughed dryly. "It all begins to make sense. Their desire for privacy, their refusal to hunt." He paused. "Something happened to you when you traveled here, didn't it? Something that made you," he waved a hand, "this way."

Lleland nodded. "You could say that. But we don't really have time to have this discussion now." He turned to Lydia. "So you'll return to Storbrook?"

"No. I'm not about to run and hide. Besides, I'm a lot stronger than you."

"I know," Lleland said. "We're not going to fight our pursuers, just separate them. If we take different paths, they'll split up. Hobbes will want to follow you, and Callaway will want the dragon that looks like Jack."

"You're not Jack," Lydia said softly.

Lleland met her blazing gaze. "You're right," he said, and smiled. "I'm not." He glanced at Scott. "Elliott could go either way."

"What will you do with Callaway?" Scott asked.

"I'm not sure yet." He thought a moment. "Hobbes will follow you to Storbrook, Lydia, which is the best place for him. Order the portcullis closed, and when he arrives, have him locked in the tower. The Dragon Master can decide his fate."

Lydia frowned. "I can deal with him."

"I know you can, but should you? His history with your family reaches back to before you were born. Your father should be the one to decide his fate."

"And the other man?"

"If Elliott follows Hobbes to Storbrook, we can try talking to him. Just remember they still have poison, so don't allow either of them to get too close, especially Elliott. He's a hunter, whereas Hobbes doesn't have much skill with a bow."

Lydia nodded. "Very well. And be careful. I'd hate for you to die after all my efforts to keep you alive!"

Lleland laid his snout against Lydia's. "I have no plans to die today, love. There're some things I need to tell you before I go." He pulled back, brushing his jaw against hers, and felt her shiver. The sweet scents of berries, summer and fire filled the air, and when he met Lydia's gaze, her eyes had been swallowed up in flame. He breathed in deeply, filling his lungs with her scent. "Let's go," he said. He turned to Scott. "Climb on my back."

"How am I supposed to do that?" he asked. He walked around Lleland's huge side, then yelped when Lydia lifted him in her claws and dumped him at the base of Lleland's neck. He muttered something about dragons under his breath as Lydia swooped from the hill and Lleland followed.

"Over there," Lydia said, turning towards the east. Lleland followed, and soon he could see the three men heading towards the hill they had just quit. They dropped a little lower to get the men's attention. Elliott pointed in their direction, and Callaway lifted his bow as Lleland swept away from Lydia. He glanced down to see Callaway follow him, while the other two men went after the golden dragon.

"I never thought I'd be mounted on a dragon," Scott said,

as he clung to Lleland's neck.

"I never thought I'd *be* a dragon," Lleland retorted.

"Are you going to tell me how it happened?" Scott asked.

"This is hardly the time."

"Who's the Dragon Master?"

Lleland turned and met his gaze. "Aaron Drake." Scott started in surprise.

"Of course," he said slowly. He was thoughtful for a moment. "Can you breathe fire?" he finally said.

"I'm a dragon, Scott," he said. "Of course I breathe fire."

"Show me."

"No. I'm not a trained bear doing tricks at a fair."

Scott laughed. "Come on, Lleland, you're a dragon. And dragons breathe fire."

Lleland sighed, then blew out a stream of flame. It curled around his head, and he felt Scott pull back slightly as flames licked his skin. "You wanted flames," he said with a laugh.

He glanced down to see they were approaching the rocky outcrop where he had been shot. The horses still stood nearby, grazing unconcernedly. He landed on the ground and Scott slipped off his back.

"What are we doing?" he said.

"Showing Callaway that he's chasing the wrong dragon."

"You want him to chase Lydia?"

"No." He cocked his head as Callaway crashed through the trees. "Shh."

Callaway broke into the clearing and skidded to a stop when he saw the large, black dragon on the ground a few feet away. He lifted his bow and notched an arrow in one smooth motion. The arrow shot forward, and Lleland launched himself upwards as the arrow sliced the air beneath him.

"I'm not the dragon you seek," he said, as he dropped back to the ground. Callaway's eyes widened slightly, but he notched another arrow and let it fly. It scraped Lleland's side as he hopped sideways.

"Stop," Scott yelled.

Callaway glanced at him as he pulled out another arrow. "What are you doing here? Where's Seaton?"

"Seaton's, er, gone in search of Hobbes. But you need to stop, before someone gets hurt."

"The only one that will be hurt is this monster," Callaway growled as he notched another arrow.

"Callaway!" As Lleland roared his name Callaway stopped in astonishment. "I'm not the dragon that killed your brother." The arrow fell from Callaway's hand and clattered to the ground.

"How do you know …" He glanced at Scott. "You!"

"No." Lleland spoke softly, and Callaway glanced back at him. "It doesn't matter how I know. But the dragon that killed your brother is long dead and gone."

"Seaton told you, didn't he?"

"Seaton sought revenge, just as you do. He finally realized he was chasing a ghost. You could kill every dragon in this kingdom, but it won't bring your brother back."

The bow started to slip from Callaway's hand, but then his grip tightened and he pulled out another arrow. "I'd be a fool to listen to a monster," he said. The arrow flew from the bow, and hit Lleland in the same place as the poisoned arrow had an hour before. He felt it slip through his thick hide and bury deep in his recently healed flesh. He stared down at it for a moment, before carefully pulling it from his chest with a wince. Scott was running towards him.

"What have you done?" Scott shouted at Callaway.

"It's a monster," Callaway shouted.

"No, he's not," Scott said. "If he's a monster, why are you still alive? He could've killed you already."

Callaway stiffened as his arm fell to his side. "You're siding with a dragon," he finally said. "How did it seduce you? Did you drink its blood?"

Scott glanced at Lleland. "Of course not. But you do not want to kill this beast."

Callaway picked up the arrow that had fallen to the

ground, then looked at Lleland. "He's wrong, I do want to kill you. But since you've spared my life today, the honorable thing is to spare yours. But this isn't over, dragon, and next time nothing will stop me burying an arrow in your heart and cutting off your head." He stared at Lleland for another moment, then without another word, turned and headed down the path, taking his horse with him. Lleland and Scott watched as he disappeared around a corner.

"I thought he was going to kill you," Scott finally said.

"I'm not so easy to kill," Lleland said. He pointed to his chest. "Look."

Lleland's wound had already started closing, and Scott stared in surprise. "How does it feel?" he asked.

"Powerful." Lleland glanced up the path. "Now let's get to Storbrook."

CHAPTER THIRTY-EIGHT

It started to snow as Lleland flew towards the mountain castle. Large, wet flakes melted and dripped from his scales. He skimmed the tops of the trees as he flew, hoping to avoid being seen by the two men below. He made a wide arc around them as he soared up the side of the mountain towards Storbrook. Lydia stood at one of the windows, watching him. His gaze met hers as he glided past the window and into the chamber that had recently been his. He dropped onto the floor and Scott slid from his back. "Close your eyes," he instructed, then pushed the flame and heat from his belly as he exploded with light, changing back into human form.

"That's truly ..." Scott shrugged.

Lleland pulled on his breeches. A pile of clothes had been left on the bed, and Lleland pulled on one of the tunics. It smelled of Zach.

The door to the chamber opened and Scott turned as Lydia entered the chamber. She was wearing a dark blue gown, trimmed in gold, and her long hair glimmered on her back.

"Scott," Lleland said, "may I introduce Mistress Lydia

Drake? Of course, you have already met."

Scott's mouth was hanging open as he stared at Lydia. "Mistress," he finally stuttered. "I'm, er, it is my pleasure." Lleland grinned to himself. He knew how Scott felt.

"The others are close," Lleland said to Lydia.

She nodded. "I know. What happened with the other man?"

"He's gone. He decided to spare my life today, but threatened to kill me the next time he sees me."

"And when the other men arrive here, you think I should lock Matthew in the tower and leave him for my father?"

"I think it would be best, but the decision is yours, of course."

"Very well. I agree with you." She smiled. "This time!"

Lleland grinned, and ignoring Scott, pulled Lydia into his arms and pressed his lips to hers. Her lips curved into a smile and Lleland felt a moment's regret that he hadn't left Scott on the mountain. He stepped back. "Have you spoken to Thomas?" he asked.

"He asked me to bring you to Father's study."

"Should I be afraid?"

"Very!"

He took Lydia's hand. "Come along," he said to Scott. "You're about to meet a man who's fiercely loyal to his dragon master."

Thomas was in Aaron's study, working on some papers, when Lydia and Lleland entered. "You!" he said as Lleland walked into the room. "Do you realize that you've placed us all in danger by bringing hunters to the mountains?"

"I didn't bring them, but I know it is because of me that they're here. For that I apologize." He glanced at the man at his side. "This is Master Scott. He's one of the hunters."

Thomas frowned. "You brought him here? How much does he know?"

"I know that both Mistress Lydia and Lleland are dragons," Scott said. Thomas' eyebrows rose. "Knowing that, it seems I'll have to find other prey to hunt."

"You don't want to kill them?"

"No. Lleland's my friend."

"I'm sure you know that Matthew Hobbes is one of the hunters," Lleland told Thomas. "What you don't know is that he sought out the League and led the hunters back to the mountains. I accompanied them because I hoped I could change their minds."

"You failed."

"No, Thomas," Lydia said. "Already one hunter has turned back, and Lleland's friend here has changed his mind. Matthew Hobbes is still determined to kill us, to be sure, but Lleland and Master Scott think they may be able to talk to the other man."

"And what do you plan to do when they arrive here?"

"We'll place Matthew in the tower, and let Father deal with him," she said. "We'll entertain the other man and see what happens."

Thomas grunted. "Very well. But I hold you personally responsible for this mess, Master Seaton. If it wasn't for you, none of this would be happening."

Lleland hung his head meekly. "I understand," he said.

There was the sound of footsteps in the passage outside the study, and a moment later someone pounded on the door. "Master Thomas! Two men are seeking entry."

"Go," Thomas said to Lydia and Lleland. "I'll meet you in the hall."

"Thomas is right," Lydia said, her voice low, as they left the room. "This is your fault. If not for you, Matthew wouldn't have known about the League."

"*Mea culpa*," he said. "And it was your fault that I became what I am."

"But I didn't mean ..." She stopped when his expression turned quizzical. "Oh."

She looked away and he nudged her. "I still have the gown you wore this morning. Will you wear it for me again?"

Her eyes flew back to his, and then she laughed. "You're incorrigible," she said. Her eyes flickered with flame, and he wrapped his fingers around hers as they walked across the courtyard. Scott fell into step beside Lleland.

"There's a prisoner's tower here," he said. "Why would dragons keep prisoners, I wonder? Have your dinners hot and fresh, do you?"

Lleland shot him an annoyed look. "Perhaps you should be placed in the tower," Lleland growled. Scott laughed.

Hobbes and Elliott were standing outside, peering through the bars of the gate. "You," Matthew spat when he saw Lleland. "I should have known!"

"How did you get here?" Elliott said.

"Lleland knew a shortcut," said Scott.

"And Callaway?"

"He's gone."

Elliott's hands tightened around the thick bars of the portcullis. "Dead?"

"No. He changed his mind about fighting dragons. At least for today."

Lydia turned to the guard, who was looking at Lleland and Scott in confusion. "Let the men in," she said, "but take that one and lock him in the tower." She pointed at Hobbes, and the guard nodded. "Once he's been secured, search him for a small vial, and bring it to me. Be very careful – it contains a deadly poison. Escort the other man to the hall."

"Yes, milady," the guard said.

They returned to the donjon and entered the Great Hall, where they sat down with Thomas to wait. Elliott and the guard arrived a few minutes later. "Here's the item you wanted," the guard said, handing the vial to Lydia. She stared at the half-full bottle for a moment, then passed it to Lleland.

"Master Elliott," Lydia said, "please take a seat."

Elliott sat down. "Why have you locked up Hobbes?" he said.

"He seeks to harm me and my family," Lydia said.

"He only seeks to kill the monsters that plague this region." His eyes flicked to Scott. "I thought you were with us."

"There's no lair at Storbrook," Lleland said. "So what are you doing here?"

"Hobbes said that the Drakes are hiding the dragons."

"So you came here to threaten the Drakes?"

"We came here to find the monsters."

"What about the people who call Storbrook home? Do you think they would just stand aside while you searched?"

Elliott frowned. "Hobbes said they're terrified of the dragons, and desperate to see them dead."

Lleland turned to Thomas. "Do you want to see the dragons killed?"

"No," he replied.

Lleland turned back to Elliott. "It seems you're mistaken."

"Please, Master Elliott," Lydia said, "I have no fight with you. All I ask is that you extend to the dragons the same courtesy they extend to you. They have no desire to take your life. Why do you seek theirs?"

"They're monsters."

"What does that mean?"

"They kill and burn."

"Really, Master Elliott? The last time anyone was in danger from a dragon was thirty years ago in Civitas. And *that* dragon was killed by my father. Do you not see how mistaken you are? You've built your aims around a ghost. No dragon has attacked you or tried to harm you in any way. Instead, you've tried to kill them with poisoned arrows! Now, I'm happy to extend hospitality to you for tonight. Supper will be served soon, and I'll have a chamber prepared for you. In the morning, you can leave with Master Scott. But if you try to kill any of the dragons in these mountains, I cannot answer for the consequences. You have to decide what you value more, the hide of a dragon or your life."

Elliott glanced between Scott and Lleland, then back at Lydia with a sigh. "It would appear I have little choice but to retreat for now. But I'll consider what you've said."

"Yes, do that," Lleland said.

Supper arrived, and even Elliott started to enjoy himself as the evening wore on. The groundsman rose to tell a story, and later, Fritz brought out his fiddle and they all sang a few ditties, accompanied with much laughter, before retiring for the night. Lleland overheard Elliott asking some of the servants about the dragons, but like Thomas, they averred that the dragons were not a danger. "In fact," one man told Elliott, "we rather like having them around. Part of the family, you know." Elliott pulled his beard in confusion, but the man was already turning away, grabbing the hand of a maid who giggled and blushed furiously.

It was much later when Lleland finally found himself alone with Lydia. They had left the hall and were seated in the solar. Lleland glanced around the room with remorse. "I said some cruel things to you here," he said.

"You were shocked and angry," Lydia said. "I cannot blame you."

"You're too generous," he said.

She smiled and walked over to the window. Large flakes of snow tumbled gently through the sky to land softly on the trees. "Why did you come here, Lleland? You said you didn't know if you loved me. You said I was a monster."

"I was wrong," he said. "You're not a monster. You're a beautiful, incredible creature! I never stopped loving you. But I needed to love what I'd become before I could admit it."

"And do you? Love what you've become?"

"I've accepted what I am. A dragon." He walked over to the window and leaned against the frame so he could look at her. "I'm a fire-breathing, winged beast – a predator that needs the blood of other animals to survive. But I'm not a monster. And nor are you."

"Do you really mean that?"

He smiled. "I do. I've been fighting myself and fighting you. But I'm tired of fighting. I want to be a dragon. And I want to be with you." He slipped a hand around her waist. "I love you," he said. He brought his lips to hers and her mouth fell open. He groaned when his tongue slid along hers, and he wrapped his hand into her hair, holding her tight. He kissed her deeply, savoring her taste. When they broke apart, he moved his lips to her ear. "Marry me," he whispered.

She kissed his neck. "You'll have to drink my blood," she said.

"Gladly," he growled.

"And I'll have to drink yours."

"You can have it all."

"You'll be bound to me until you die," she said.

He pulled back and looked into her eyes. They were blazing, and he could feel the flames leaping in his own. "I'm a dragon," he said, "and I want you to be my mate. I want to feel the cords that tie us together, and know you are mine alone. I want to chase you through the skies, and be burned by your flames. I want your huge, heaving body beneath mine as I mount you like the beast I am. We'll blacken the walls of some abandoned cave, and smash the ground with our passion. I want to be wild and primal with you, Lydia. I want to be a dragon."

The blaze in her eyes grew brighter as he spoke, and when he stopped, she smiled. "I want to be yours," she said. "Your wife, your lover and your mate." She pulled his head back to hers, and kissed him as she wrapped her hands around his neck. He slipped his hands down her back, feeling the ridges of her wings, and she moaned slightly, pressing herself tighter against him. He breathed her name into her mouth, and the flames of their breath sparked and blazed between them as his hands roamed across the ridges of her wings, pulling her closer.

He broke the kiss and trailed his lips down to her shoulder.

"There's something you have to do first," she said. She was panting slightly.

"Anything," he groaned.

She pulled back slightly to look into his eyes, and Lleland felt his heart stutter as he saw how they danced with flame. "You have to become a member of the clan," she said. "I can't marry a rogue. You must give your oath, otherwise I'll be thrown out."

He nodded. "I'll take the oath. The moment your father returns, I'll offer him my loyalty."

"He won't be long. And as soon as it's done, we can be married."

His hands tightened around her waist. "It cannot be soon enough." They stared at each other as he lifted a hand and ran his thumb over her lower lip. She drew in a ragged breath.

"I'm going," she said. She pulled him closer and kissed him on the lips, then pulled herself free of his grasp. "I'll see you in the morning." His breath was uneven as he watched her walk to the door. She turned to smile at him, and he forgot to breathe at all for an instant, and then she was gone.

CHAPTER THIRTY-NINE

As Lydia disappeared around the corner, Lleland slowly breathed out a long stream of flame. He crossed over to the window and stared into the darkness. The snow was gathering on the trees, wet and heavy, shining in the moonlight. He stripped off his clothes and jumped onto the sill. Stretching his arms, he threw himself into the black night, unfurling his wings behind him. The cold air caressed his skin as he soared into the darkness, his arms and wings spread wide as he spiraled through the air. He fell back against his wings and drifted, his mind lost in the memory of Lydia in his arms. He rolled over onto his stomach, and saw fresh prints through the snow on the ground. He sniffed the cold air and caught the waft of a deer.

His stomach rumbled as he dropped silently to the treeline. He saw the creature between the trees, and could hear the sound of its beating heart. He pushed out the heat in his belly and exploded into his dragon form, then turned back to watch the deer. There were too many trees for him to be able to attack, and he waited as the animal slowly moved forward into a small clearing. Lleland dived between the trees and grabbed the creature around the neck. Hot blood spilled into his mouth, and he swallowed with pleasure. As the blood filled his veins and the flesh filled his belly, he could feel his strength expanding. By the time he finally returned to his chambers, it was nearly dawn. He collapsed onto the bed and fell asleep within minutes.

The sun was already high above the horizon when Lleland awoke. He lay on the bed for a moment, smiling at the promises of the night before. Lydia was the most glorious creature he had ever seen, a magnificent beast. That she would be his was almost more than he could believe. He could feel the power pulsing through him after his meal the previous night, and he blew out a stream of flame, watching as it curled through the air and burned out before it reached the blackened rafters. He rolled from the bed and dropped his feet to the floor. In a pile near the door were the clothes he had left in the parlor the night before. He picked up the tunic, and Lydia's scent rose from the fabric. He dressed quickly and went in search of her.

He found her in the hall, along with Elliott and Scott. Thomas sat across from them, tearing a hunk of bread. Lleland paused when he saw Lydia, drinking in the sight of her from behind. He could tell from the subtle change in her scent that she was aware of his presence, but she didn't glance his way. He walked over to the table and nodded at the men before taking a seat next to Thomas.

"Sleeping in again, Master Lleland?" Lydia said. Her golden eyes caught his, and for a moment he forgot to breathe. She smiled and turned to the two men. "Master Scott and Master Elliott are almost ready to leave," she said.

Lleland glanced at the men, and saw Scott watching him in amusement. "Has Master Elliott agreed to desist hunting dragons?" Lleland said.

"I won't hunt on the mountains. But come now, Seaton, you can't expect me to allow the monsters free rein around our kingdom. We were commissioned by the king to remove the threat of dragons."

Lleland nodded. "I agree." He felt Lydia's flare of surprise and disappointment. "But there are no dragons threatening the kingdom, are there?" he continued. "If a dragon ever threatens the people again, I would expect you, and all the other hunters, to be leading the charge against it; but until that time, there's no need to hunt creatures that haven't threatened you."

Elliott sighed. "This will have to be discussed by the League, as I'm sure you're aware. But for now, I won't hunt the dragons in these mountains."

"Thank you, Master Elliott," Lydia said with a smile.

"By the way," Elliott said, "what did you do with the wolfsbane?"

"I burned it," Lleland replied. "It seemed the safest thing to do."

Elliott gave a dry laugh. "Hobbes paid a year's worth of wages for that. He won't be a happy man."

"I think that'll be the least of his worries once Aaron Drake returns home," Lleland said. He glanced at Scott. "When are you leaving?"

"Right away," Scott said. "I don't suppose you can find a dragon to give us a ride?"

Lleland snorted. "No. You'll have to travel the hard way. But I'm coming too." He glanced at Lydia, who was frowning at him.

"I thought you wanted to see my father," she said.

"I do." He leaned forward across the table. "I think it's best that I await his return in the village." Next to him, Thomas nodded, smiling slightly. Lydia looked away as Lleland rose to his feet. "I'm ready to go whenever you are," he said to Scott and Elliott.

"But you haven't eaten," Scott said.

"I ate earlier," Lleland said. He saw Scott smirk and sighed. "Wait for me in the courtyard." He watched as the two men left the hall, then turned to Lydia and took her by the hand. "I don't want to go," he said softly as he led her to the passage.

"Then why are you?" she said.

Lleland moved his hands to her waist. "You're so beautiful," he said. "Your scent fills my mind, and I can't get enough of you." He trailed his fingers over her cheek and across her lips. "Just seeing you fills me with desire. If I remain here, I may not be able to restrain myself from taking you."

"You desire me?"

"More than anything." He leaned forward and brushed his lips over hers. "How could you even question it?"

"I'm a monster," she said.

"Mmm." He brought his mouth to her ear, and gently bit her earlobe. "You're the most desirable monster I've ever seen," he whispered. "We'll be monsters together." He felt her shiver, and slid his hand to her nape.

"You're leaving me because you want me?"

"I'm leaving because I can't resist you. But when your father returns, I'll return with him and take you as my mate."

She arched an eyebrow. "Maybe I'll be the one doing the taking."

He gave a throaty laugh. "Oh, Lydia, you can take me all." He pressed her against the wall and kissed her. When he pulled away, her eyes were blazing. "I love you," he said. "Like a fool, I tried to push you away, but I never stopped loving you."

"Will you stay in the village?"

"Yes."

"I often fly over it, especially at dawn," she said.

"You're trying to torment me, aren't you?" he said, his voice low.

She smiled. "Am I succeeding?"

He drew in deeply and heat spread through him. "You know you are," he whispered. He kissed her once more, then with a groan, pushed himself away. "I must go," he said. "I'll see you soon."

Scott and Elliott were waiting near the gates when Lleland arrived. Their breath hung in the air as they slapped their arms in an effort to keep warm. Elliott cast a look at the prisoner's tower as they walked by, but remained silent. They reached the village at dusk, after recovering the horses along the path, and made their way to the inn. Lleland was glad to have his satchel back, with his clothes and writing equipment. They walked into the common room to see Callaway seated at a table in a corner. He looked up as they entered.

"You're still alive," he said. "I was beginning to wonder." The men sat down and Scott held up three fingers to the barman.

"Why wouldn't we be?" Lleland said as three tankards were slammed onto the table.

Callaway shrugged. "You might have become a dragon's dinner. Where's Hobbes?"

"He was locked in a tower by the Drake woman," Elliott said. He scowled at Lleland. "She's the reason you started singing a different tune, isn't she? Are you hoping to get between her legs?"

Lleland's eyes narrowed as he stared back at Elliott. "Mistress Drake is my betrothed," he said, "and if you mention her again, I'll kill you." He crossed his arms and leaned back in his seat. "As for the dragons, any fool can see they aren't a threat."

"It isn't that long since you believed they were."

Lleland shrugged. "I was a fool."

"Where did you disappear to when the dragons appeared?" Callaway asked. "I didn't see you again."

"I went after the black dragon."

"I spoke to it, you know. It looks just like the dragon that attacked Civitas."

"It may look the same, but it's not," Lleland said.

Callaway grimaced. "The dragon said the same thing. But a dragon is a dragon."

"You won't stop hunting?"

Callaway clenched his jaw. "Never. Not until that monster is dead."

There was enough room at the inn for Lleland to secure his own chamber, and the next morning he rose as soon as the sun touched the horizon. He passed quietly through the passages, hoping to leave undetected. The front door squeaked on its hinges, and he winced, but nothing stirred. It was silent in the courtyard where a light breeze was scattering the snow over the icy cobbles. There was a large, open field behind the churchyard, and this was Lleland's destination. He was barefoot, and as he stepped through the snow it melted into puddles around his feet, then steamed into the air. The rising sun cast a pink glow on the snow, making the landscape rosy. Lleland turned towards the mountains and searched the sky for a sign of a dragon, but there were only a few wisps of pink cloud.

He lay down on the ground and placed his hands behind his head. The melting snow seeped into his clothes, but they would soon dry against his blazing heat. He blew flames as he lay on the ground, watching as they danced through the air before dissipating. A flash of gold a few minutes later caught his attention, and he watched as the dragon wended her way through the towering peaks.

With the rising sun glancing off her scales, she was more beautiful than anything he had ever seen, and his stomach clenched as he watched. He resisted the urge to leap into the sky after her, and followed her movements in exquisite agony as she came closer. Her tail swished slightly as she flew, and her horns glinted dangerously in the sun. A stream of flame escaped her mouth and he groaned. He wanted to feel those flames caressing him. She soared through the air, her wings open wide, until she was above him. She began to circle and when she swooped down low, her hot scent washed over him. Her tail brushed over his leg and he shivered.

"I love you," he whispered as she swooped back into the

sky and turned towards the peaks. "Soon, my love. Soon."

CHAPTER FORTY

Callaway and Elliott left the village that morning, but Scott insisted on staying. "I want to meet Master Drake," he said.

"What about your wife?"

Scott shrugged. "A few more days won't matter."

"You know I'm not planning to return to Civitas right away?" Lleland asked him. "You'll have to travel back on your own."

"I don't mind."

Aaron Drake returned four days later, on a gray, snowy day. It was late afternoon, and a fire roared in the tavern where Lleland sat with Scott. The door opened, bringing in a blast of cold air and flakes of snow that melted into puddles on the floor. Scott shivered as Aaron stepped into the low room, Zach and another man on his heels. Scott stopped what he was saying and gaped as Aaron walked towards them. All three men exuded strength and power.

"Lleland," Aaron said, "I wasn't sure I'd ever see you again," he said dryly. "You look well nourished."

"I thought about what you said, and decided that I rather enjoy life after all."

"I see. Well, I'm glad to hear it. Of course it doesn't

explain what you're doing here." Aaron pulled out a chair and sat down as the others followed suit. "This is Max," he said, nodding at the third man, "my brother-in-law. Richard says you arrived with Matthew Hobbes. He thinks you want to kill me. Of course, he isn't aware of certain changes since your last stay in the village."

"What do you think?"

"Matthew Hobbes seems like a strange traveling companion. I'd be interested in hearing what you were doing in his company." Aaron waved to the bartender, and took a seat across from Lleland. Zach and Max did the same. "Who's your friend?" Aaron asked.

"This is Master Scott. Another traveling companion."

"Hmm. And why exactly did you bring companions to the mountains, Lleland?"

"I came with the League."

Aaron leaned back with a frown. "Explain."

"Matthew convinced the League that the dragons here are a threat and should be hunted and killed. I hoped to convince them that this was not the case."

"You think people like Matthew Hobbes are a danger to dragons? He's been wanting dragons dead for years, and yet they still live."

"True. But there were other skilled hunters in the company. People like Scott."

Aaron turned to look at Scott, his eyebrows raised. "You're a hunter?"

"I was. But," he glanced at Lleland, "I realize now that it would be wrong to kill dragons."

Aaron stared at Scott for a moment, then turned to Lleland. "What does he mean?"

"He saw me change."

Aaron frowned. "That was careless," he said.

"He was saving your daughter!" Scott interjected.

Lleland sighed. "One of the men was about to shoot Lydia with an arrow dipped in wolfsbane. I intercepted the shot."

Aaron paled slightly. "Matthew's getting desperate," he said. He passed a hand over his forehead. "So you changed form and took the arrow?"

"Yes."

He leaned back in his seat. "You saved her life," he said. His gaze was intent as he watched Lleland. "How did you survive?"

"Lydia ripped and burned." Zach grimaced, and Lleland smiled grimly.

Aaron took a quaff of ale. "You're facing your fears. Your father would be proud." He met Lleland's gaze as he continued. "I think you'd better start at the beginning. How did Matthew know about the League, and how many hunters did you bring?"

The next few hours passed quickly as Lleland related the events leading up to his arrival at Storbrook. Aaron stopped him from time to time to ask a question, and once or twice Scott interjected with his own comments.

"Where are the other hunters now?" Aaron asked as Lleland finished his tale.

"Callaway and Elliott have returned to Civitas, and Hobbes is locked in the prisoner's tower."

"I see." Aaron paused. "And what about you? Why are you still here? Don't you have classes to teach?"

"I've been waiting for you. There are some things we need to discuss."

Aaron leaned back in his seat. "Master Former Hunter," he said, glancing at Scott, "can you please excuse us?" Scott glanced at Lleland, then nodded and slid off the bench.

"Well?" Aaron said when Scott was gone.

"I'm ready to give you my oath," Lleland said.

Zach leaned forward with a grin. "It's about time!"

"Why now?" Aaron said. Lleland glanced at Max. "You can speak freely," Aaron said. "Max already knows everything."

"I know what I am," Lleland said. "A dragon. And I'd like to take Lydia as my wife."

Aaron laughed. "Well, if nothing else, that certainly tells me you've accepted what you've become. And Lydia has agreed?"

"If I give you my oath," Lleland said.

"You understand what that means? You'll give me your blood and submit yourself to me. I'll be your Master."

"I understand."

"And you understand that Lydia can't bear children," Aaron said.

Lleland nodded. "I do."

"And you can accept that?"

"I love your daughter, Aaron. Before I knew what she was, I loved her. I'll admit I lost my way for a while, but there's nothing I want more in this life than to spend it with Lydia."

"Even if it means forgoing your human form entirely?"

"Even then."

Aaron nodded slowly. "Very well. I told you once that Lydia wouldn't be foolish enough to accept you, but you're no longer the man you were." He paused. "You'll be welcomed into the clan not only as another dragon, but also as my son."

Pleasure spread through Lleland as he met Aaron's gaze. "Thank you," he said.

"We'll do the oath tonight," Aaron said. He stood and turned to Max. "Keira and Anna will be wondering what's become of us."

"You go ahead," Zach said. "I'll bring Lleland."

Aaron nodded and strode out of the room, but Max paused to look at Lleland. "You may be a new dragon and not very powerful," he said, "but as the one who's won Lydia's heart, you have my admiration." He slapped Lleland across the back with a grin, then followed Aaron out.

"So you're finally ready to be a dragon?" Zach said when

they were alone.

"I am."

"Have you had human flesh?"

Lleland grimaced. "No. Nor do I intend to."

Zach's eyebrows pulled together. "You'll have to eventually."

"I don't think so. Since I wasn't born this way, perhaps I don't have the same needs as you."

"Perhaps." Zach's tone sounded doubtful.

Scott was loitering outside the inn, slapping his arms to stay warm beneath his cloak when Zach and Lleland emerged a short while later.

"Well?" he said when he caught sight of Lleland.

"I'm going back to Storbrook, and you're going home."

"I could come with you," he said hopefully, then raised his eyebrows when both Zach and Lleland gave a resounding no. "It was just a suggestion," he said. "But clearly I'm not wanted."

"No," Zach said. "You're not!"

"I'll see you back in Civitas," Lleland said. "Go home to your wife. And tell her you love her."

Lleland and Zach walked into the hall at Storbrook an hour later. Aaron and Max were seated at one of the tables scattered around the hall, while servants bustled in and out of the room. Keira sat next to Aaron, and a woman Lleland did not recognize sat beside Max. Her hand was on the table, and he played with her fingers as he talked with Aaron and Keira. Lydia sat next to her, their heads bent together in close conversation. Keira looked up as the two men entered the room.

"Lleland! How wonderful to see you again!"

"Mistress," Lleland said.

"Call me Keira," she said, "since you are going to be part of our family. I cannot tell you how delighted I am to welcome you as my son."

Lleland smiled and glanced at Lydia. Her face was still bent toward the other woman, but she was smiling, and he could smell her pleasure. "Thank you, Keira," he said, returning his attention to her.

"Lleland, this is my sister, Anna," she said, nodding at the other woman. She looked up from her conversation with Lydia and smiled. "And I believe you've already met her husband Max?"

"So you're Lleland," Anna said. "I feel as though I already know you!"

"Anna!" Lydia murmured.

"I can see why you're so taken with him," she said. "He's very pleasing to look at!"

Lydia groaned as Max turned to his wife with his eyebrows raised. "You should take Anna home to your brood, Max," Lydia said.

He looked at Lydia with a grin. "My sister is quite happy to watch our brood for a few weeks. Besides, I don't want to miss seeing you brought to heel, and Anna will forget all about your young man when I get her alone later."

Lydia laughed. "You should know by now, Uncle Max, that I'll never be brought to heel."

He nodded solemnly. "I know. Which is why I already feel unlimited admiration for your betrothed. He's either a fool or the bravest man I know."

"That's what we said about you once," Aaron said with a laugh. "In fact, we still wonder about your sanity at times!"

Max grinned and placed his arm around Anna as she glared at Aaron. He brought his lips close to her ear. "Still my little shrew," Lleland heard him say.

Aaron laughed and turned to Lleland. "You can give me your oath later tonight," he said. He glanced at Zach. "Perhaps you want to tell him what to expect."

Zach nodded. "Yes. Let's go, Lleland."

With one more glance in Lydia's direction, Lleland followed Zach from the hall. "Where're we going?" he asked.

"Hunting."

Lleland stopped. "Why?"

"You need to be at your strongest when you give your oath. And it'll give me a chance to explain what it entails."

Lleland nodded. "Very well. Let's go." He followed Zach into one of the chambers, and a few minutes later they were soaring from the castle over the deep forest below. Snow weighted the branches of conifers, and ice clung to the ground.

"There," said Zach, changing direction and nosing downward. "A herd of deer." He hung back slightly, allowing Lleland to pass him. He could see the animals in a snowy clearing below, and could smell their scent through the frigid air. They were still unaware of the danger above as Lleland dived towards them. He picked out a young female and increased his speed. One of the other deer glanced up and signaled an alarm as it started bounding from the clearing, but it was too late. Lleland slammed into his target and wrapped his jaws around its neck. Blood gushed into his mouth and he swallowed the hot liquid. Zach landed a few feet away, a larger doe in his jaws, and with a growl Lleland turned away, swinging his kill with him as he hunched over his meal. Using his talons he ripped open the creature's chest, then buried his snout in the warm flesh as he tore off large mouthfuls of meat. His tongue cleaned the last remains from the bones, then he fell back on his haunches and looked at Zach, who was cleaning his talons.

"Sorry," he said.

Zach shrugged. "You're a dragon, Lleland. It's what dragons do."

"Tell me what happens when I give my oath," Lleland said.

"You're binding yourself to the Dragon Master."

"Binding? I thought I was just pledging my allegiance."

"The tie of blood is stronger than your word. You'll have a connection with the Master that will only be severed by death, or if you submit to a different master."

"I thought Lydia was the only one I would bond with."

"The mating bond is different because it goes both ways, and your feelings for her are different. When you bind yourself to the Master, although you both drink the other's blood, the bond goes one way. You bind yourself in submission, but he's not bound to you. When he drinks your blood, it is to signify that your life is in his hands. If you disobey him, he can demand a renewal of your oath. But only after you've been soundly beaten in a fight."

"Have you had to fight him?"

Zach grinned. "The Master's my father! I had plenty of chances to disobey him growing up, and he beat me into submission each time!"

Lleland sprang into the gray sky and spread his wings. He was deep in thought as he skimmed the trees. Zach was silent as he flew behind. Lleland banked slightly and looked at Zach. "How's the oath given?" he asked.

"You'll each spill your blood into a chalice, then give it to the other to drink. Once he's had your blood, you'll offer him your fealty as your Master. From that time on, you will be subordinate to him, and he will command your loyalty. When you greet him, it must be with deference. You can follow our lead, but you'll know what to do quite naturally."

Lleland dived into a steep valley then surged up the other side. The air rushed past him, lifting his wings. Flames crackled and snapped within him.

"Are you ready to give your oath?" Zach asked as they crested a summit.

Lleland turned to look at him. "Yes."

"Then let's go home," he said.

Lleland smiled. "Yes," he said, "home."

311

CHAPTER FORTY-ONE

Lydia knocked on the door of Lleland's chamber a short while after he arrived back with Zach. "Let's go for a walk," she said. He followed her down the stairs and out into the courtyard. Snow had started falling, large soft flakes that melted as soon as they touched his skin.

"Where are we going?" he asked.

"Do you remember when you first arrived here? We climbed the cliff with the funnel."

"I couldn't believe how easily you managed to walk along the ledge," he said. "I should have realized then that there was something not right about you."

She arched an eyebrow. "Not right?"

"Actually, very right! Is that where you're taking me?"

"Yes. We can talk without anyone overhearing us there."

"Hmm, I like that idea," he said. He followed her as she led the way across the garden and to the small wooden door recessed into the wall. Lydia pushed it open and a blast of cold wind swirled her hair around her face. Her scent filled his nose, and he reached for her hand, but she stepped through the door and onto the rocky ledge beyond before he touched her. "We could just fly," he said, following her onto

312

the ledge.

"We could. But I wanted to remind you of the first time I brought you here. I think you were rather fearful of falling!"

"Can you blame me? I would have died."

"I would have caught you."

"Yes, but I didn't know that!"

"Would you have felt better if you had?"

Lleland glanced at the panoramic vista spreading before them. "No," he said softly. He could feel Lydia's eyes on him.

"Are you unhappy, Lleland?" she asked.

He turned to her with a smile. "No," he said, "I'm very, very happy." He brushed his fingers against her lips, catching his breath when a few wisps of flame escaped her mouth and curled around his hand. She stared at him for a moment, then turned and walked along the ledge as Lleland followed. The cold wind rushed around them and Lleland held out his arms to keep his balance, but he had no fear of falling, and easily kept pace with Lydia. They reached the place where the mountain ridge joined the ledge of the wall and jumped down.

They gained the cliff easily after that and Lydia led Lleland to the crack in the rock. He eyed it with resignation and sat down on the ground to squirm through on his back after Lydia. When he rose to his feet, Lydia was pulling on a pair of breeches beneath her gown. He watched with a smile as she loosened the laces of her gown and shrugged it off her shoulders, then tucked her chemise into her breeches. "You're not protesting my impropriety," she said with a laugh.

"I didn't know better last time," he said. "But I wouldn't dream of provoking a dragon!" Lleland glanced up at the funnel. "So you think I can get up there?" he said.

"Certainly," she said. "Just jump."

"Jump? I told you before I can't jump that high."

"Like this," she said. She bent her knees slightly, then propelled herself upwards, stretching out her arms and securing herself against the funnel walls. She glanced down at him with a grin.

"I can do that?" he said.

"Try."

She scurried upwards a few feet as he bent his knees as she had done. He drew in a deep breath and pushed himself off the ground. His arms shot out and he pressed his palms against the wall, securing himself so he didn't fall back to the ground. He looked up at her, a few feet higher than him in the tunnel, and laughed. She smiled back and scampered up the wall. It became narrower the further up they went, and at the very top Lleland had to lift his hands above his head and pull himself up.

Lydia was already on her feet and had walked to the edge, her posture pensive when Lleland pushed himself up. Snow covered the ground, and Lleland could see puddles of water where she had walked. He watched her for a moment. The wind whipped strands of hair around her face, and lifted the loose fabric of her chemise from her shoulders. He walked over to her.

"What's wrong?" he said.

She turned to him. "You're swearing your allegiance to a dragon clan this evening. Are you really ready to do that?"

"It's what I've become," he said. He lifted a wisp of hair from her face. "If I don't do this, I'll never belong anywhere."

"But does it make you happy?"

He wrapped his hands around her waist and pulled her closer. "Being with you makes me happy," he said.

She pulled herself out of his arms and turned away. "That's not enough," she said. "You can never undo your oath. If something happens to me, you'll still be bound to my father."

He placed a hand on her shoulder, and gently turned her around. "I know that," he said. "I confess I wouldn't have chosen this path, but now that I'm here, I find myself quite content to remain upon it. You know how I railed and fought against what fate had given me, but I see now that I have been granted far more than I could ever have imagined."

"So you really want to be a dragon?"

"Yes, with you at my side." He brought his hand to her neck and his lips to hers. He could feel her warm breath in his mouth and could taste her scent, and he deepened the kiss. He pulled away slightly. "We should be married as soon as possible."

"Tomorrow?"

He smiled. "Is that the soonest?"

She laughed. "Yes."

"Then tomorrow." He wrapped his hands around her waist and kissed her again. He could feel her smiling. She turned in his arms, and they stood at the edge of the cliff and stared out at the snow-covered peaks. "You're right," he said, "it isn't that high."

She smiled. "As I told you before, it's just a matter of perspective."

"I didn't believe you then," he said, "but now that I'm aware of what you are, I know better than to question you. I'd hate to see what kind of terrible monster you can turn into."

She turned back around in his arms and met his gaze with eyebrows raised. "Really?" she said.

"No," he whispered. "I can't wait to see the monster, and I'm anxious to know the dragon in every possible way." Her eyes started blazing, and he stared into them as the flames mounted within his belly. He traced her lips with his fingers, then replaced them with his mouth as his hands gripped her waist. He could taste the flames in her mouth and he pulled her closer as her burning fingers seared his skull and lit a path down his back.

Supper was served in the hall as usual that evening. The mood was festive, and when the last of the dishes were cleared away, one of the servants brought out a fiddle and started scraping a tune. The tables were pushed to the walls to clear the center of the hall, and a circle quickly formed.

"Come," Lydia said, pulling Lleland to his feet. Her hand was warm in his, and he squeezed it as they took their places within the circle of dancers. The music was lively and the dancers laughed as they swung their way around the hall. Finally Fritz put his instrument aside, and the maids started clearing away. Lleland and Lydia took a seat at the table with the others.

"So, Lleland," Max said, taking a seat across from him, "I hear you're a scholar."

"That's right," Lleland said.

"And you're a bit of a traveler as well, since you journeyed, on foot, all the way to Storbrook."

"I don't want all my knowledge to be from books," Lleland said. "I want to experience the country for myself."

"The whole world is at your feet now," Max said.

Lleland smiled. "I suppose it is. Have you traveled much?"

"Oh, here and there. I marched with King Alfred when he invaded Terranton."

Lleland frowned. "I didn't think dragons concerned themselves with human affairs."

Max laughed. "We don't. Aaron sent me to watch over Anna."

Anna, in conversation with Keira, turned at the sound of her name. "Aaron *sent* you, did he?"

"Of course! And you know how I have to obey my Master, as much as it pains me to do so!"

She leaned forward on the table and stared into her husband's eyes. "If I recall correctly, there wasn't much pain involved."

He gazed back. "The pain was watching you with the stablehand."

Aaron cleared his throat, and Max dragged his gaze away.

"My apologies, Lleland. You were telling me you wanted to expand your travels."

"Should the opportunity come along, certainly."

The hall had emptied, and apart from the dragons and their spouses, only Thomas remained. Aaron turned to him. "Do you have the chalice?"

Thomas lifted a package onto the table. It was wrapped in dark red velvet and tied with a gold cord. "Right here, milord," he said.

"Good." They watched as Thomas carefully untied the package to reveal a large goblet. It was made of gold, and inlaid with jewels. Beside it lay a dagger, with a hilt decorated as lavishly as the cup. Thomas lifted each item and handed them to Max.

"In the absence of any council members, Max will officiate our ceremony here this evening," Aaron said. He rose to his feet, and strode into the center of the hall, with Max a step behind. Lleland glanced at Lydia. She smiled, and reaching out her hand, squeezed his fingers. He stood, but before turning away, stooped to kiss her. His hand slipped from hers as he strode into the center of the hall and stood before Aaron.

"Are you ready?" Aaron asked.

Lleland nodded.

"Very well." Aaron extended his arm towards Max, but his gaze remained fixed on Lleland.

Gripping the dagger, Max slashed the blade across Aaron's wrist, catching the blood in the chalice as it spurted from the wound. Aaron did not flinch, but continued to stare at Lleland. The blood slowed, and Max slashed again, and more of the life-giving liquid flowed into the cup. It was three-quarters full when the blood slowed to a trickle, then stopped, and Max handed the chalice to Lleland.

"The blood of your Master," he said. Lleland took the cup in his hands, and met Aaron's gaze. He lifted the cup to his lips and drained the contents without breaking the stare. The blood tasted like a strong liquor that burned on its way down, filling him with flame. He felt the heat flare within him, and saw Aaron through a haze of flames. He could feel the depths of his being reach towards Aaron, securing him to the strength and power of his Master.

He lowered the cup and held it out to Max. "Master," he said to Aaron. He felt Aaron's stare probe his depths.

"Hold out your wrist."

Lleland extended his hand towards Max, but did not move his eyes from Aaron. He felt the sting of the dagger piercing his skin, and the cold metal pressed against his arm to catch his blood. From the corner of his eye he saw Max pass the cup to Aaron, and as Aaron downed the contents, he could feel his life-force slipping into his Master. He heard Max's voice as though from some far distance.

"You can give your oath now," he said.

"From this moment forward, I recognize you as my Master," Lleland said, "and pledge you my fealty and obedience."

"Welcome to Clan Drake," Aaron said. "We're now your family, and you belong with us. You'll never be without a home, and we'll not leave you wanting. You'll share in our successes and in our failures."

"Thank you, Master," Lleland said. He stared at Aaron for another moment. For the first time in his life he felt as though he belonged – that he had people, and they had him. He smiled and turned towards Lydia. She rushed over to him and wrapped her hands around his neck, pulling his lips to hers. He kissed her deeply, ignoring the audience, until Zach's laugh broke through his thoughts.

"It would seem that Master Seaton fits right into this family." He walked over to Lleland and slapped him on the back. "How does it feel?" he asked.

"Good! Very, very good! I feel as though … as though I've come home!"

"You have," Lydia said with a smile.

Lleland wrapped his arm around her as Keira and Anna walked over to them. "By tomorrow you'll be part of this family in every way," Keira said.

Lleland smiled, and pulling Lydia close, kissed her forehead. "I cannot wait," he said.

CHAPTER FORTY-TWO

Lleland awoke the next morning with a deep feeling of contentment. He rolled over in his bed and stared out the window. He could feel his bond with Aaron. It demanded nothing of him except loyalty, and offered a place to belong.

He rose from his bed and went in search of Lydia. He'd just started walking down the passage when he saw Max coming towards him. "If you're looking for Lydia, she's in Keira's chambers with Anna. They're getting ready for tonight's ceremony. In the meantime, Aaron wants to see you in his study." Lleland glanced down the passage towards the master chambers. He could hear Lydia laughing. He turned and headed towards the study.

The door was closed, but Lleland could sense Aaron inside and he opened it without hesitation. Aaron looked up at him from his desk, and waved him over to a seat.

"I hope you had a good night's sleep," Aaron said as Lleland sat down. "It may be a while before you have another." He laughed at Lleland's shocked expression, but then became serious. "You're a good man, Lleland," he said. "I know that becoming a dragon was not your choice, but I'm glad Lydia has found someone who can match her in strength and be her equal." He paused. "You've embraced what you've become. Now embrace all that Lydia is as well."

Lleland nodded. "I will."

Aaron leaned back in his seat. "Have you given any thought to your future?"

Lleland frowned. "I must return to Civitas to complete the year of teaching. Indeed, I've already extended my absence too long. I have no independent wealth and need to earn my living. I must also find a place to live. I'm sure you know I cannot bring a wife to the college, nor do I want to."

"I've already spoken to my cousin about you and Lydia living at Drake House," Aaron said. "And I have a proposition for you. You're a well-read and well-educated man. I have need of such a man to be my scribe."

"You already have Thomas."

"Thomas is getting old, and cannot travel as he used to. But what I have in mind is not the duties of a steward. I want someone to travel through our territories and create a record of our history. You'll meet all the dragons of the clan, and set down their records. My territory extends far beyond the human kingdom, and some dragons live in far-flung places. You'll travel to these locations and remain with the dragons as you transcribe their histories."

"What about Lydia?"

"She'll travel with you, of course. Her curiosity and adventuring spirit almost matches yours."

Lleland smiled. "I think you already know what I wish to say, but I won't make a decision without first consulting my wife."

Aaron smiled. "There's no rush to make a decision. Just let me know when you have. And now, I've been instructed to keep you away from Storbrook for the remainder of the day, so I'm taking you down the mountain with Zach and Max to see Richard."

"Master Carver? The man who thinks I intend to kill you?" Lleland had seen Richard a few times while he was staying in the village, but the man had refused to speak to him despite his efforts to offer an explanation. Instead, whenever he saw Lleland, he scowled and walked away.

"When he sees you with three dragons," Aaron said, "he'll realize that he reached the wrong conclusion. Now *I'm* just going to check if Keira and Lydia need anything before we go, and *you're* going to meet us outside."

Lleland gave a wry smile. "Very well, Master," he said.

A few minutes later he was launching himself through his large window into the frigid winter air. The snow of the previous day had stopped, leaving a glittering blanket of white over the towering peaks. Lydia's laughter flooded through the huge window of Aaron and Keira's chamber, but before he had a chance to draw near he saw a flash of light, and Aaron emerged from the room. He pulled back as Aaron glanced at him, his expression amused. "Let's go," he said. "Zach and Max are already waiting." He lifted his chin, and Lleland saw the two dragons circling high above the castle.

They landed in a clearing on the shores of a small lake a half hour later. Frost had painted the reeds white, and ice clung to the edges of the pond, trapping water weeds in its grip. The dragons changed form and pulled on some clothes before following a snowy path that led towards the village. As they cleared the thick canopy of trees, Lleland could see Master Carver's house in the distance, smoke rising from the chimney.

Zach fell into stride with Lleland as they walked. "When do you return to Civitas?" he asked.

"In the next few days. I've already been gone too long."

"And Lydia returns with you?"

"Of course! I'm eager to have her by my side."

"I'll come back with you."

"I'd rather you didn't," Lleland said dryly.

Zach laughed. "Fine. I'll return to Civitas without you. But I intend to stay at Drake House – my chambers at the college are rather cramped. I trust that meets with your approval?"

"Why didn't you stay at Drake House before?" he asked.

"I had a notion I'd enjoy staying with my fellow students."

"And now?"

"I'd prefer to stay with my fellow dragons."

They reached the Carver house. The door to the workshop was open, and Lleland saw Richard glance up. He left his worktable and came outside.

"This is a pleasure, Aaron," he said. He turned to the others. "Max. Zach." His eyes narrowed when they fell on Lleland, and he turned to Aaron with a scowl. "What's this man doing with you? You know what he is!"

"He's my future son-in-law."

"Impossible!" Richard stepped closer and dropped his voice. "He hates dragons!" he hissed. "You know he intends to kill you."

"Lleland's had my blood, Richard."

Richard looked surprised. "You've bound this man to yourself? Why?"

"He's given me his oath."

Richard frowned. "I don't understand. I thought only dragons gave an oath."

"You're right. And I confess I don't completely understand it myself. But this former dragon hunter is a dragon."

Richard's eyes flew to Lleland. "You hunted your own kind?"

"No." Lleland glanced at Aaron, who nodded. "I wasn't a dragon when you first met me. I am now."

"Show me!" Richard said. Lleland sighed, and flames spilled from his mouth. Richard stepped back in shock, and his eyes flew to Aaron. "How can this be?"

Aaron shrugged. "It doesn't matter. It is what it is. Now are you going to leave us standing outside all day, old man?"

Richard snorted. "Old, am I? What does that make you?"

Aaron grinned. "A dragon."

"Well, come in," Richard said. "Where are the women?"

"They're busy getting ready for a ceremony this evening."

"This evening? You dragons don't waste any time, do you?" Richard said dryly.

"What's the point of waiting?" Aaron said with a laugh. "We've been banished from Storbrook for the day, and we're taking you back with us."

"I think I need a strong cup of wine," Richard said.

Max laughed. "That's an excellent idea, Richard. Make sure it's unwatered!"

"I don't water down my wine!" Richard exclaimed.

Aaron laughed. "You know better than to take Max seriously, Richard," he said. "And besides, it's only my opinion you should be concerned about, and you've never offered me watered-down drink."

Richard smiled at Aaron, his eyes intent on the tall dragon. There was something about his demeanor that went beyond mere familial affection, and as Lleland watched, he realized what it was. Richard's bond to Aaron had been forged in blood.

It was a few hours past noon when the men returned to Storbrook. Lleland was sent directly to his chambers, with strict orders to remain there until summoned. Zach came by a short while later with a pile of clothes in his arms. "You cannot marry my sister in those peasant clothes of yours," he told Lleland.

"They're not peasant clothes," Lleland protested, but when he saw the garments Zach laid on the bed, he had to agree that nothing he owned could compare to such attire. A crimson doublet cut from the finest cloth and embroidered with gold thread, a silk shirt of snowy whiteness, doeskin breeches cut in the latest fashion and moulded perfectly to his legs. Woolen stockings and polished leather boots completed the ensemble.

"Where do these come from?" he asked as he dressed

himself in the fine attire.

"We always have extra garments on hand," Zach said. "And Mother ordered the seamstress to alter these for you."

"Your mother is an enterprising woman."

"She is. And here's a cord for your hair." He handed Lleland a ribbon that matched the doublet, and he pulled his hair from his shoulders and secured it at his nape. Zach nodded. "Very good. Now that you're suitably dressed, I've been instructed to accompany you to the chapel. Are you ready?"

Lleland nodded. "Absolutely! Lead the way!" He followed Zach from the room and down the stairs. As they passed the hall, Lleland saw that it had been scrubbed clean. Scarlet berries and boughs of greenery decorated the tables, and the room was ablaze with candles.

"The whole castle will be celebrating your nuptials this evening," Zach said. "Cook has not left the kitchen since yesterday. Your haste to marry my sister has sent everyone spinning."

"I wasn't expecting a grand feast," Lleland said.

Zach stopped and turned to him. "You're marrying the Dragon Master's daughter. Even if there are only a few in attendance, do you really think he would allow such an event to go uncelebrated? Word will reach the other dragons that, despite the impatience of the groom, it was celebrated in style."

He turned and continued down the stairs, Lleland a few steps behind as he considered Zach's words. By marrying Aaron's daughter, he was stepping into the ranks of dragon royalty.

They reached the courtyard and walked across the icy flagstones to the small chapel across from the prisoner's tower. Lydia was not there yet, but Keira stood with Anna and Max near the stairs, and the priest stood shivering in his surplice at the door. Richard stood a short distance away. The priest nodded at Lleland as Zach led him to the bottom of the steps.

"You look very handsome," Keira said with a smile. "I was right in thinking those garments would become you."

"Many thanks for your care in ensuring I was properly prepared, Mistress," Lleland said.

Lydia's scent wafted through the air, and he turned to see her step into the courtyard, Aaron at her side. She was dressed in a long, sweeping gown of pearl gray. A gauzy veil, decorated with tiny seed pearls, hid her face while on her brow rested a thin circlet of gold. Lydia looked up at Lleland, and through the thin veil he saw her golden eyes shining as she stared at him. The breath caught in his throat as his gaze met hers, and he stared as she made her way towards the chapel. She stopped a few steps from Lleland, and turned to look at Aaron.

"You look lovely, my daughter," he said. He lifted the veil and kissed her forehead. "I love you," he whispered. He lowered the veil and turned to Lleland. Their gazes met and Aaron nodded, then stepped back to stand beside Keira.

Lleland took Lydia by the hand and gently caressed her fingers. "You're so beautiful," he whispered. "Ready to become my wife?"

She smiled. "Yes," she said. She turned towards the priest, and Lleland led her up the chapel stairs.

"Dearly beloved …" the priest began. He barely paused when he asked if there was any impediment to hinder the marriage, then led Lleland through his vows.

"I do," he averred, his gaze on Lydia. When she answered the same, it took all his effort not to sweep her into his arms then and there.

"You will now share a bond of blood," the priest said. Lleland glanced at Lydia in surprise – he had not expected the dragon binding at a human ceremony. The priest held a small knife, and he gestured to Zach to step forward.

"Extend your arms, please," the priest said.

Lleland followed Lydia as she held out her hand, palm up.

The priest nicked each of their wrists, bringing a drop of blood to the surface. Lleland smiled. The blood bond they were participating in was an ancient pagan ceremony – perfect for a dragon wedding.

The priest stepped back as Zach tied their wrists together with a gold cloth. The wounds had already healed, but the drops of blood mingled and smeared on their skin. The priest opened the door of the chapel, and served them the nuptial mass in private, then led them back out to the courtyard. "You may kiss your bride," he said.

Lleland stared into Lydia's eyes for a moment before lowering his lips to hers and kissing her softly. Their hands hung at their sides, the cord still binding them together, and he twisted his fingers around hers as he trailed his mouth to her ear. "Later," he whispered. He pulled away to see the flames burning in Lydia's eyes, and knew that they mirrored his own.

"Yes," she breathed. He stared at her a moment longer, then turned to grin at his new family.

CHAPTER FORTY-THREE

Lleland kept his fingers around Lydia's as they walked across the courtyard back to the hall. The loose knot in the cloth was already slipping, and Lydia pulled it free as they walked. They entered the hall to see the servants lined up in two long rows on either side of the doorway. They clapped as Lleland and Lydia entered, and threw grain over them as they ran, laughing, through the rows to the dais, ducking the showers of grain. The room glittered from the many candles that flickered and shone around the walls, and the huge fire that roared in the enormous fireplace. The main table had been decorated with holly and pine, and wide swathes of fabric tied into bows lined the sides. In one corner of the room a small group of musicians were tuning their instruments, and Lleland glanced at Thomas, wondering what wizardry he had used to bring them to Storbrook in such short order.

Lleland and Lydia took their seats at the raised table, while around them gathered Aaron and Keira, Max and Anna, Zach, Richard and the priest, who remained on his feet until silence fell in the hall. He lifted his hands and blessed the meal, then took his seat as the hubbub rose once more. Servant girls, laughing and smiling, brought in huge trays laden with delectable dishes and spiced fruits. Fish followed fowl, and when that was cleared, succulent roasted venison was placed on the tables. Wine flowed freely into the cups on the tables, and laughter and gaiety filled the hall.

Aaron rose to his feet as the venison was cleared away. "People of Storbrook," he said as those in the hall fell silent and turned to look at him, "you have loyally served the Drakes over many years. You have seen and heard things that would have sent lesser souls fleeing, but you have remained faithful. Many of you have watched my daughter grow up, and have loved her, as we do." He lifted his glass and turned to look at Lydia. "You've grown into a strong and determined woman, and I am proud of you." Lleland glanced at Lydia to see her watching her father intently, her eyes shining. "I am happy to release you to your chosen mate – I couldn't have chosen anyone more worthy." He glanced at Lleland, then turned to face the crowd. "Join me in the toast to my daughter and her husband."

There were cheers as glasses were lifted and they drank Lydia and Lleland's health. Lleland's hand snaked around Lydia's waist, and he kissed her cheek.

"I love you," he whispered.

She turned to face him, then spun around when the door to the hall was suddenly flung open. Lleland looked up in surprise as a huge man strode into the room, with blazing red hair that hung to his shoulders and eyes as blue as sapphires. He was flanked on one side by a man who was clearly his son, and on the other by a petite woman. The two men were dragons, and they froze as they stood at the threshold to the hall, their gazes ranging across the room and settling on the dragons on the dais. The woman smiled slightly as she saw Keira, then moved on to Lydia, but both the men narrowed their eyes angrily.

"It's him," said the younger man, staring at Lleland. "And he's a dragon." The words were spoken softly, but to Lleland it seemed as though they were shouted across the hall. He recognized the man who had been with Zach at the inn. Lleland glanced at Zach, who was staring at the young man, his face set.

"Favian," Aaron was already at the door to greet the new arrivals. "Welcome to Storbrook."

"What's the meaning of this, Aaron?" Favian's voice was angry. "I came here looking for a hunter, and stumble on a wedding. Your daughter's getting married, and you keep that from me? And who's she marrying? A rogue? A hunter?"

"Favian." Aaron's voice held a note of warning. "Remember who you're speaking to. If I kept things from you, you of all people should know I had good reason to do so."

"This doesn't look good, Aaron." Favian's eyes swept the room and settled on Max. "I see the pup knows all your secrets," he said bitterly.

"We can discuss this later, Favian, but right now we're celebrating a marriage. You're welcome to join us, or leave peacefully, but I'll not have you ruining Lydia's wedding."

Favian looked back at the dais, his gaze settling on Keira for a moment then moving on to Lydia. "Very well, Aaron, for Lydia's sake I'll hold my peace. I cannot remain here, but Cathryn and Will are free to do as they choose. And as soon as this is done, you and I will have words."

"Of course, Favian." Aaron waved at Thomas. "Please show Master Favian to a chamber where he can cool his heels."

"Yes, Master," Thomas said.

Favian turned to the woman. "I suppose you will remain," he said.

She smiled and laid a hand on his arm. "I know you're angry, but I'll stay. I'm sure Aaron has a very good reason for his actions, and I wish to see Keira and Lydia."

He nodded, then glanced at Will. "And you?"

"I'll stay," he said. Favian stared at his son for a moment, then strode from the room without another word.

Lleland glanced at Lydia. "Who is that?" he asked softly.

"Father's cousin. And his closest friend." She turned to look at Lleland. "How is it Will recognizes you?"

Lleland looked at Zach. "He was with Zach when I saw them in the hills," he said wryly.

"In the hills? Did you … were you hunting?"

"Yes. And later I saw them both at the inn." Lydia shot him a horrified look. "It was a different life, Lydia," he said softly. "I did things I wouldn't do now."

"I know," she said. She stared at him a moment longer, then smiled. "Now you're mine."

He returned the smile. "And you, my beautiful dragon, are mine! But we've only been married a few hours, and already I'm causing problems for your family. I'm sorry."

"Uncle Favian will forgive Father once he's had a chance to cool down and Father's explained."

Except for those seated near the door, few in the hall were aware of the tension that had momentarily swirled around the dragons. Their conversations had been low, heard only by those with exceptional hearing. The musicians had continued their playing, and the conversations had continued unabated. As Favian left, Aaron greeted Cathryn with a hug, then turned to Will.

"Next time you speak to me first, understand?" he said.

Will hung his head. "Yes, Master," he said.

"Good. Now come join us for what's left of the meal."

Will joined Zach on the dais. Zach's expression was set, and he immediately began an earnest conversation with Will, his voice so low even Lleland could not hear over the other noise. Will glanced at Lleland with a frown then returned his attention to Zach.

Aaron resumed his seat, and Keira left the dais and hurried towards the woman.

"Cathryn! What a to-do! But Aaron will explain all to Favian."

Cathryn smiled. "I know. Now let me see the bride and

331

groom."

Keira led her over to the table. "Lleland," she said, "this is Cathryn."

Lleland nodded. "Mistress."

"Cathryn," Lydia said, "this isn't the way I wanted you to come to my wedding, but I'm glad you're here."

Cathryn smiled. "You look lovely, Lydia. And may I wish you many years of happiness."

Lydia glanced at Lleland with a smile. "Thank you. I think we'll be very happy."

"Come, sit down," Keira said. "We're halfway through the meal!"

The meal resumed, and a few minutes later Will left Zach and came to where Lydia and Lleland sat.

"I'm sorry about this, Lydia," Will said. "It's just …"

"I understand, Will. But you must know there's a reasonable explanation."

Will sighed. "Yes, so I've heard. Anyway, I wish you the greatest happiness." He glanced at Lleland. "You too, I suppose!"

The hall was cleared for dancing after the last course was served, and the musicians struck up a lively carol. Lleland rose to his feet and led Lydia into the center of the room. Her hands were in his as they twirled around the floor, but they were soon joined by others who pushed between them with a laugh, forcing them apart. Lydia swung her skirts and moved her feet to the lively rhythm, and her scent drifted across the hall. The music ended, and Lleland made his way to Lydia's side as the first notes of a line dance were sounded. Taking Lydia's hand, Lleland led her into the line of dancers, while Max and Anna took their places beside them. Zach and Will led their mothers into the line with a laugh, and Lleland glanced around to see that Aaron had disappeared from the hall. Next to Zach and Keira, Richard danced with a serving girl. Lleland watched them a moment. Richard didn't look older than fifty, but he was over seventy years in age. The wonders of dragon blood, he thought wryly.

It was after midnight when Lleland finally had a chance to draw Lydia aside.

"Please tell me you're ready to leave this joyful gathering and go to your chambers?" he whispered into her ear. The musicians had laid down their instruments, although Fritz was accompanying those still with enough energy to dance on his fiddle.

She smiled as a line of dancers circled around her. "I'll meet you there," she murmured. She moved away and joined the circle of dancers as Lleland watched. She wound her way through the hall, but when the line of dancers swept past the door, she fell from the circle with a laugh, pleading the need for refreshment. She stood on the sidelines for a moment, then slipped into the shadows and out the door. Zach glanced at Lydia as she left, then looked at Lleland and made his way to his side with a grin.

"Not thinking of leaving us, are you?" he said. "There're some girls who would be devastated if they didn't have a chance to dance with the groom."

"I'm sure you can keep them well occupied," Lleland said. "In fact, I doubt they'll even notice my absence."

"Even so," Zach said, dragging him towards Cook, "you cannot leave without showing Cook your appreciation for all the work she's done." Lleland shot Zach an annoyed look, but he gallantly held his hand out to the stout woman and led her into a circle that was forming. She was red in the face and panting slightly, but she beamed at Lleland as she placed her sweaty hand in his. Lleland glanced at the wine table – how many glasses had she had?

Another quarter of an hour had passed when Lleland slipped through a side door, and making his way along the passage, he headed towards the stairs.

CHAPTER FORTY-FOUR

Lleland mounted the stairs three at a time and fairly ran down the passage, but slowed his step as he neared the chamber. He stepped into the room to find Lydia standing at the window, staring out across the pristine mountains. She turned as the door closed behind him, and their gazes collided. In another moment she was in his arms, and his lips on hers. Flames swirled into his mouth as her lips parted, and he groaned as a need, more desperate than the need for blood, swept through him. He pulled her closer, tasting her fiery, sweet flavor. Her hands slipped around his waist and slid up his back, caressing the ridges of his wings, and she pulled slightly away to look into his eyes.

"I want to taste you," she whispered. "I want your blood."

"Yes," he moaned. "Taste me. Drink me." He bent his head back to hers and kissed her again. When they broke apart, he saw she had a knife in her hand.

"Take off your shirt," she said.

He slipped the doublet off his shoulders and yanked off his shirt. He watched as she placed the point of the knife against his chest, a few inches above his nipple. The breath caught in his throat as she looked up at him, meeting his gaze, and he nodded.

The blade pricked as it slid into his skin, bringing blood welling to the surface. Lydia tightened her grip on the handle, and Lleland gasped when she pulled the knife downward, slicing his nipple and sending a searing pain through his chest. Her lips covered his skin, and his blood flooded her mouth, filling him with the sweetest pain. His fingers gripped her shoulders as his wings sprang open, stretching into the furthest reaches of the room. He could sense her spirit reaching towards him, like an invisible cord that wound around his heart, and he gave himself to her, melding his spirit with hers. He threw back his head and roared, filling the room with flames that curled around them.

The pain in his chest had already eased as the wound healed, and he was filled with the deepest need to know her in every possible way. He ripped off her gown and sent it to the floor, then roughly pushed the chemise from her shoulders. His lips found hers as his hands tentatively touched her breasts, becoming bolder as she moaned into his mouth. His hands slid around her back and slipped to her waist as he picked her up and carried her to the bed.

"I want you," he rasped. "I can't wait."

"Take me," she groaned. "Make me yours."

He kicked off his breeches, and covered her with his naked body. "I love you," he gasped as he took her. "You're mine."

They collapsed onto the bed a few minutes later, panting heavily. His wings had disappeared, folded against his back, and flames swirled through the air, dissipating as they neared the ceiling. Lydia's eyes were blazing when she turned to look at him, and he gazed at her in wonder. He traced his fingers down her face to her neck, before bending forward to nibble her earlobe. Golden hair tickled his nose, and he wrapped a long silky strand around his finger.

"You're so beautiful," he whispered.

She smiled. "Let's get away from here," she said. She slipped off the bed onto the floor and turned to him. "Come."

"First show me your wings," he said.

She smiled and shrugged her shoulders, unfurling the massive appendages. They shimmered in the low light of the moon shining through the window. He stared at her, then pushing himself from the bed, stalked towards her, stopping a foot away. He reached out a hand to stroke the smooth surface of her wings, and a shudder passed through her, making them quiver. He glanced at her to find her staring at him, her eyes blazing.

"Show me yours," she said.

He opened them, and they filled the room, huge and black. Lydia stepped closer and reached above his shoulders to touch them. Her soft touch made the heat flare again, and he grabbed her and pulled her against his hard frame, kissing her deeply. Her hands slid down his chest and around his waist, molding their bodies closer together. Their feet left the floor as they circled slowly through the air. Cold air brushed against them from the window, and Lleland broke away to glance at the darkness beyond. He looked back at Lydia and she smiled, and without another word they angled themselves towards the window and sped into the darkness.

Lleland rolled beneath her and wrapped his arms around her, capturing her mouth with his. She folded her wings while he wrapped his around them both, and they were free-falling through the air. Lleland knew, without thinking, when the ground was close, and he spread them to stop their crash fall. Arms clasped around each other, they straightened and shot towards the heavens, spiraling as they rose higher. They kissed as the wind rushed past them, and Lydia wrapped her legs around his waist. His hands slid down to her thighs and clasped her, supporting her as he claimed her again. Her hands tightened in his hair, holding him close as their passion soared, and when he felt the exquisite release, he lifted his head and roared, spilling a trail of flames that lit the sky.

He fell back against his wings as she collapsed against him. The earth was far below, and in the sky, the stars glittered far away. Her fingers trailed over his chest, while her legs lay tangled in his.

They drifted, twisting and turning languidly through the air in an aerial dance as they separated and then came together. They dozed for a while, floating through the air, then found pleasure as they joined together once more. They touched one another, learning the curves and contours of each other's body, and Lleland felt as though he could not be more complete.

The eastern horizon started to grow lighter, and he looked at Lydia ruefully. "I don't want to go back," he said.

She smiled. "We don't have to. I know a place we can go." She pushed herself away from him, but he grabbed her hand.

"Where?"

"A cave. We'll get there faster if we change." He held her for another moment, then let go. She drifted away, and a bright light flashed through the air. She turned to look at him – wonderfully huge and beastly. Her horns glimmered in the early morning light, and her scales glowed. He felt another wave of desire wash through him, and he pushed the heat away from his belly in a blast. She was already soaring away as he started to follow her. Her tail flicked near his face, and he watched with awe as the enormous creature glided ahead of him. How was it possible, he wondered to himself, that such a magnificent beast belonged to him?

They flew in silence towards a distant peak, but as they grew closer, Lleland could see the dark entrance of a cave high in the tall wall of rock. Excitement filled him as he looked at Lydia, and he could sense hers mounting as well. He slowed down, allowing Lydia to pull ahead of him. She flew into the mouth of the cave and landed on the floor a few yards from the entrance. Her tail swished over the hard, stone floor, but she did not turn around to look at him. Lleland glanced down at himself. He was huge, primed and ready to take his mate, and a wave of satisfaction washed over him. She might be an enormous creature, but he was her mate. He landed behind her with a growl, and did not wait before mounting her.

His talons sank into her sides, and she lifted her head and roared as she writhed beneath him, sending him deeper. Her huge frame heaved under him and her roar dropped to a growl. He sank his talons deeper into her flesh, and the tension ran from her body as she lowered her huge form onto the ground and stretched out her long neck. The growl became a purr that vibrated through her as she yielded herself to him. He stretched his neck and dropped his jaws to her shoulder, then sank his teeth into her skin. He felt a thrill pass through her, and he swallowed the blood that flooded his mouth, as sweet as berries and summer sunshine. He drew more, reveling in the exquisite pleasure of tasting her. Her blood was weaving through his body as his soul reached out to hers, and he could feel her reaching back, strengthening their bond. The wound he had made was already beginning to heal, and he ripped it open again, desperate for more. He pushed himself deeper and filled her with his passion. As the last shudder subsided, he slipped off her and lay beside her, his neck draped over hers.

"You're the most exquisite creature," he whispered. "Your blood has made me into a powerful beast, and taking you as a dragon is the most fantastic thing I have ever experienced. If you want me to forgo my human form completely, I'll happily do so, as long as you'll remain with me forever."

"Whatever you are," she said, "you'll always be my dragon."

He groaned. "I love it when you call me that. Tell me how I'm your beast."

"Like this," she said, digging her claws into his hide and

yanking him closer as her jaws ripped through his neck and his blood spilled into her mouth.

CHAPTER FORTY-FIVE

They dozed, and later they hunted. Desire filled him again, and he mounted her on the soft forest floor as their roars echoed between the mountains. They slept side by side, or in each other's arms, and when Lleland watched her, he marveled silently at the incredible gift he had been given.

They remained in the cave for the next three days, until finally the harsh realities of life could no longer be ignored.

"I have to return to Civitas to finish the rest of the school year," Lleland said to her on the third morning. His arms were wrapped around her as she sat between his legs at the lip of the cave, their feet dangling over the edge. They watched the rising sun, making the pure white snow glisten.

"I know," Lydia said.

"Your father offered me a job as his scribe when the year is done," he said.

Lydia turned in his arms to look at him. "Do you want to work for my father?"

"I want to travel and experience the world. But only if you're by my side."

Lydia laughed. "Do you really think you could pry me away? I'll remain with you wherever you go."

"It'll mean living as wanderers, never being in one place for long."

"We have a long life ahead of us," Lydia said. "There's plenty of time to settle down. So let's go see the world!"

He smiled. "How long do we have?"

"Well, Father is ..." – she paused as she calculated – "a hundred and forty-two."

"What?" Lleland pulled away from her in shock.

"Max is only seventy, or so," she said.

"How old are you?"

She smiled impishly. "A perfect age."

He grabbed her back into his arms with a growl. "Tell me!"

"Twenty-eight," she said with a laugh.

"Twenty-eight! Good thing I came along when I did," he said. "You were in danger of becoming an old maid."

She pushed herself free of his arms and slipped off the ledge. Her wings spread and she turned to face him.

"Old maid, am I?" she said. She scowled playfully as he stared at her. They wore no clothes, and he gazed at her small, firm breasts, flat stomach and shapely legs; her golden eyes shone as she laughed at him. He reached for her, and she glided away; he launched himself from the rock and she turned and fled. He caught her a moment later, and wrapping his arms around her, nibbled her ear.

"Mmm, my mistake. You taste as young and fresh as a maid of sixteen."

"What do you know of sixteen-year-old maids?" she said, struggling to free herself from his teasing mouth.

"Nothing," he said, dropping his lips to her shoulder. "But I have eyes to see, and nothing I've seen pleases me as much as you."

He moved his lips to her mouth and kissed her. He could feel his desire mounting, and he drew away reluctantly. "So are we agreed that I should accept your father's offer?"

She nodded. "Yes."

"Then we should be on our way. I've already over-extended my leave of absence from the college. But I couldn't bear to leave this place any sooner."

"Good," she said, "because nor could I. But there are caves near Civitas. We'll claim one for our own and escape there whenever we feel like it."

He smiled. "Then let's get going," he said.

They took their time returning to Storbrook, and it was already late morning when Lleland left Lydia and returned to his room, where his clothes still remained. He dressed quickly, and returned to Lydia's chambers by way of the passage to find her brushing her hair.

"I missed you," he said.

She turned to him with a laugh. "How will you manage teaching all day, if an absence of twenty minutes is too much to bear?"

He walked up to her and took the brush from her hand. "You'll just have to become a student."

"But Master Seaton," she said, smiling demurely, "I think I'd prefer private lessons."

"It'll be my pleasure to give you lessons in any subject you please," he said, pulling her into his arms and kissing her. They pulled apart when the door opened and Aaron stepped into the room.

"Papa!" Lydia said. "You could have knocked."

He shrugged. "Why? I wasn't interrupting anything."

Lleland felt Lydia's ire rising, and took her hand. "Master," he said.

Aaron looked at Lleland. "You left in a hurry."

Lleland grinned. "So we did."

Aaron snorted. "Have you considered my offer?"

"We have. I'd be happy to accept."

Aaron nodded, then smiled. "I'm very glad to hear that." He clasped Lleland's shoulder. "Welcome to the family, son."

Lleland's heart swelled at the word. "Thank you, Aaron," he said.

"Is Uncle Favian still here?" Lydia asked.

Aaron smiled wryly. "They left yesterday, along with Max and Anna. Favian still hasn't quite forgiven me for keeping him in the dark, although he understands why I needed to. He asked me to apologize to both of you, though, and hopes he didn't ruin the evening for you."

"Of course not," Lydia said.

"Actually, once we left the hall, he quite fled our minds," Lleland added.

Aaron laughed. "Quite! So what are your plans? Christmas is only a few weeks away – you can remain until then."

"We can't," Lleland said. "I must get back to my responsibilities."

"Of course," Aaron said. "But there's still one more matter that needs to be dealt with before you leave."

Lleland lifted an eyebrow. "Oh?"

"Matthew Hobbes."

Lleland drew in a deep breath and released it through his teeth. Sparks sputtered through the air. "What do you have in mind?"

Aaron started pacing the room. "The way I see it," he said, "there are two options. One is to kill him."

"And the other?"

Aaron stopped and turned to face Lleland. "He can be bound to one of us."

Lydia gasped. "You can't do that. If the Council found out –"

"They would know it was the best option," Aaron said.

"What will happen to him if he's bound to a dragon?" Lleland asked.

"That depends on him. A weak mind will quickly crumble beneath a dragon's will. You remember how you only wanted Jack, while he was still alive?" Aaron said, and Lleland nodded. "He'll feel the same way, only it will be much worse for him. You were just a child and didn't question why you felt as you did. But Matthew will remember his previous revulsion for dragons, even as he desires nothing but the dragon he's bound to."

"He'll become a slave to the bond?"

"Yes, although the dragon can loosen or tighten the cords as much as he chooses."

"What about his family?"

"He'll forget about them. And from what I've heard, they won't miss his attentions." Lleland thought of the woman at Hobbes' house, and had to agree.

"And this is what you think you should do. Bind him?"

"I do," Aaron said. "But I think it should be you who does it."

"Why not you? Surely that would be a greater punishment since he already hates you."

"True. And in the deep recesses of his mind, he'll know he's bound to the dragon that killed his brother."

"Then why?"

It was Lydia who answered. "Because of Jack," she said.

He looked at her in confusion. "What does Jack have to do with this?"

"You're the only one amongst us who knows what it feels like to be bound against your will," Aaron said. "By binding Hobbes, you'll break the last chains that hold you to Jack and find your own salvation."

Lleland was silent for a long moment. "He must be given the choice," he finally said. "Life or death."

"Very well. Let's go."

Lleland gripped Lydia's hand as he followed Aaron down the passage and across the courtyard to the prisoner's tower. Aaron nodded at the guard, who took a bunch of keys from his belt and unlocked the door.

"Which one, guv'nor?" he said.

"Hobbes."

The guard led them past three doors and stopped at the fourth. He found another key and inserted it into the lock.

The door swung open as Matthew turned to look at his visitors. His eyes narrowed with hatred as he looked at Aaron, then moved on to Lleland. "You!" he snarled.

Lleland nodded. "Hobbes."

"I knew you were siding with the Drakes. You're a traitor."

"Master Seaton is my son-in-law," Aaron said. The stench of loathing leaked from Matthew's skin, and Aaron glanced at Lleland with a wry grin. "It seems he regards you with as much affection as me," he said. He turned back to Matthew, and his expression grew hard. "We come to offer you a choice. Life or death."

Wariness flitted across Matthew's face. "What do you mean?"

"You came to exact vengeance against the dragons, not caring whether you hurt or killed my people. Your sentence is death, but I'm offering you a reprieve. If you drink the blood of a dragon, you can live."

"Never!" Matthew spat. "I'd rather die."

"Very well!" Aaron turned to the guard. "Feed him to the dragons at dawn."

"Wait! You said nothing about being fed to dragons."

Aaron turned back. "Your death might as well serve some purpose," he said. "If the dragon feeds on you, it might be less tempted to torment the poor people of your village." He paused. "That was your motivation in coming here, wasn't it? To protect your fellow villagers?"

"What'll happen if I drink dragon's blood?"

"Well, you'll live longer, for one thing. And heal faster. And if your mind is strong, you'll overcome the other effects. But the will of a weak mind can be bent by the dragon. A weak mind will worship the dragon he's bound to."

"My mind's not weak."

"Then you have nothing to worry about."

"Fine! I'll do it. Give me the dragon's blood."

"Lleland?" Aaron turned to him with eyebrows raised.

Lleland nodded. "Good," Aaron said. "Use your wrist." He handed Lleland a knife as Matthew watched in confusion.

"What're you doing?" he said. "I thought you weren't going to kill me."

"I'm not," Lleland said. "You're going to drink my blood."

"*Your* blood. But I'm supposed to drink ..." His voice trailed off as Lleland's eyes flashed with flame. "You're a dragon!" he hissed.

"He is," Aaron said. He took Matthew by the tunic and yanked him closer. "But I'm the dragon that killed your brother." He pushed Matthew away, and he stumbled to the floor as Lleland slid the knife across his wrist. He crouched down and held his wrist to Matthew's mouth.

"Drink," he said.

Matthew stared at him, then slowly pulled Lleland's wrist to his mouth. His lips sealed over the wound, and he swallowed the liquid as the cut wove back together. "Do you want some more?" Lleland whispered. He watched as Matthew nodded hesitantly, and sliced open his wrist again. Matthew pulled the wrist to his mouth and swallowed, licking the drops from his skin. Lleland pulled back in revulsion. "That's enough," he said.

"No, more," Matthew said. "Please, I want more."

"You came here to hunt dragons, Matthew. You brought poison to kill them. Why should I help you now?"

Matthew dropped to the ground and covered his face. "I'm sorry, Master," he sobbed. "I didn't know what I was doing. I'll never do it again!"

"No, you won't." Lleland rose to his feet and started towards the door, but Matthew crawled towards him and wrapped his arms around his legs.

"Don't go," he said. "I'll do anything. Anything at all. Just give me a little more."

"Let me go," Lleland said. Matthew dropped his arms and scooted backwards. "You'll stay here," Lleland said.

"But you'll come back? You mustn't leave me here. Please, don't leave me."

Lleland sighed. "I'll come see you before I go," he said. He took Lydia's hand and followed Aaron from the room.

"Does he know?" Lleland said as the guard locked the door. "Does he understand what's happened?"

"A small part of him does," Aaron said. "But his desire for you overwhelms his reason."

"Wonderful!" He glanced at Lydia. "If your love for me wears off, I can come here and find continual adulation."

She grinned. "The perfect punishment! If you make me angry, I'll send for Matthew and leave you to mend your ways."

He growled. "Try that," he warned, "and I'll ..."

"Ahem."

Lleland stopped as Aaron cleared his throat, but he smiled at Lydia in a way that threatened punishment, and she shivered in anticipation.

CHAPTER FORTY-SIX

The following morning Lleland went to the prisoner's tower, where Matthew was curled into the corner of his cell. He jumped to his feet as Lleland came into the room. "Please, Master," he said, "take me with you. I'll do anything you want."

Lleland turned away, unable to look at the man. "You should've chosen death over this," he said. Matthew's eyes narrowed, and for an instant, hatred leaked through a crack in his emotions. It was immediately replaced by a beseeching expression.

"I want to be with you."

Lleland sighed. "I must go. And you cannot come with me. You must listen to Master Aaron." Matthew's features hardened slightly.

"I hate Aaron Drake! He killed my brother!"

"Yes, he did. But it was not without reason." He paused. "Do you want to return to your wife?"

"My wife? That bitch?" He spat on the ground. "Pah! Never want to see her again."

"Then you'll stay here. You'll be fed and clothed, and you'll do what Aaron tells you to do. That's what I want."

348

Matthew dropped his head. "Yes, Master," he whispered. "Can I have some blood?"

Lleland was about to refuse, but the desperation in Matthew's voice held him back. Is this what he had sounded like to Jack? But he'd only been a child, and this was a grown man. He took his knife and slashed his wrist, and Matthew pounced like a rabid dog, pulling the wrist to his mouth and drawing as hard as he could. Lleland pulled away when the wound closed. "I'm going now, Matthew," he said. "Do you promise to be loyal to Aaron?"

"I promise," he whimpered.

Lleland nodded. "Good. Because if you aren't, I'll have to kill you."

He left the room with a shudder and returned to the chambers he shared with Lydia. "There's something I have to do before we leave for the city," he told her.

"Does this have to do with Matthew?"

"It does. I met his wife. A poor, miserable woman."

"It'll probably be a relief to her that Matthew is gone."

"I think so. But she's lost her only means of existence. She has no other income."

"Ah! You want to help her."

"Yes. I don't have much, but I would like to give her what I can. But by giving to her, I'll be taking from you."

Lydia smiled. "Our needs are not great! We are beasts, after all, able to survive in the wild. Do what you must."

Lleland wrapped his arms around Lydia's waist and kissed her. "Thank you," he said.

Their plan was to leave Storbrook after dinner. Zach was leaving at the same time but, he told Lleland and Lydia, he would follow his own route and meet them back at Civitas. "Being around the two of you will be too much for me to bear," he said, and Lleland had punched him good-humoredly. He was very glad that Zach was not traveling with them.

As dinner finished, Aaron motioned Lleland to join him in his study.

"Sit down, Lleland," Aaron said as Lleland closed the door behind him. "You're now a member of my clan," he said, "and I'm your Master. There'll be times when I call on you to render me service, and I'll expect your obedience."

"I understand," Lleland said.

"As a clan member, you'll share in our prosperity and our misfortunes. If someone like Jack threatens the clan again, you, too, will be threatened. But it isn't just dragons that threaten the clan. Humans are also a threat, and the information they possess can be our downfall. You know that better than anyone. So you'll also understand how important it is that our secret be kept at all costs."

"Yes."

Aaron nodded. "Not only are you part of my clan, but you're now also my son. I'm proud to call you that, Lleland – you're a fine man."

"Thank you."

"I look after my family, Lleland, and that includes you. You'll never be alone, and you'll never be left wanting." He took a small sack from his drawer and dumped it on the table, where it landed with a heavy thud. "This is yours."

Lleland frowned. "What is it?" He opened the sack and looked at the glittering coins inside. "I can't take this."

"Why not? It's a gift from a father to his son."

"But – it's too much!"

Aaron snorted. "Then think of it as Lydia's dowry."

"I –"

"All you have to say is 'Thank you, Father.'"

Lleland looked up and caught Aaron's gaze. His own was covered in a haze from the flames leaping in his eyes. He smiled. "Thank you, Father," he said.

Lleland and Lydia left Storbrook a little while later, after an emotional farewell between mother and daughter. "We'll be back soon, Keira," Lleland assured her. "As soon as the school term is over."

"I know," she said tearfully, "but it's just that Lydia's … married!"

Aaron laughed, and wrapped his arm around her. "Lleland will take good of her, my sweet. And we can visit anytime."

She sniffed. "I know."

"And just think, we'll have the place all to ourselves at last!"

Keira burst into tears again, and Aaron shook his head in confusion.

"Ready love?" Lleland said to Lydia.

She nodded. "Yes."

They left by way of the chamber, soaring from one of the windows, but instead of heading south, they flew north to the village, where they landed and made their way to Hobbes' house. Mistress Hobbes was in the hall, and she rose as Lleland and Lydia entered.

"Master," she said. "How can I help you? Do you bring news of Matthew?"

"I do," Lleland said. "He's not returning."

"He's dead?"

"No."

"Then how do you know he won't be back?"

Lleland paused. "He's been placed under arrest," Lydia said. "He was found guilty of a crime."

"I'm not surprised," Mistress Hobbes said. "Thank you for bringing me the news."

"There's something else," Lleland said. He held out a bag of coins. "This is for you."

The woman frowned. "I won't accept money from you."

"It's not from us," Lydia said. "It's from, er, Matthew. He didn't want you to be left destitute." The woman's eyebrows flew up in disbelief, but she remained silent as she eyed the bag.

"Take it," Lleland said. "As my wife says, it's from Matthew. There's just one thing you need to do."

Her expression turned wary. "What's that?"

"Tell your children the truth about dragons. That they aren't a danger and want to live in peace."

"That's not what Matthew said."

"I know. But Matthew was wrong. It wasn't completely his fault, because his father hated dragons too. But their hate was based on fear, not on truth. Tell me you'll teach your children the truth."

Her eyes flew back to the bag of coins, and after a moment she nodded. "I will." She took the bag. "I'll tell them we were saved by dragon gold!"

Lleland glanced at Lydia, eyebrows raised, but Lydia just smiled. "That's right, Mistress," she said. "Dragon gold."

They arrived back in Civitas three days later, after a slow, leisurely trip that involved many stops and detours. As they walked into Drake House, a voice was heard from the parlor. "Took you long enough!" Zach called. "I was beginning to wonder if I needed to send out a search party."

"Zach! How marvelous to know you're here!" Lydia said, walking ahead of Lleland into the parlor.

"You always were happy to see me, sister," Zach said with a laugh. He glanced at Lleland. "I saw your friend when I was traveling back. Scott."

"Did he recognize you?"

"He did! He waved and shouted at me as I flew overhead, and when I landed, he wanted to know when you were returning."

Lleland laughed. "What did you say?"

"I told him you were thoroughly occupied, and then offered him a ride back to the city."

"Really? Well, that was generous of you!" Lleland poured a glass of wine and handed it to Lydia. "Have you attended my classes?" he asked Zach.

"I have. Your students will be overjoyed at your return. They're probably wondering what they did to cause you such displeasure that you'd choose Dodds to stand in for you. The man is excruciatingly dull!"

"You could have taught in his place."

"And miss watching the boredom on the others' faces? But I did pose a few, er, interesting questions."

"I'm sure you did," Lleland said wryly.

They passed the afternoon pleasantly, and a few hours later there was a knock on the door. Hannah bustled into the room.

"There's a man outside who wants to see you," she told Lleland. "His name's Scott."

"Thank you, Hannah," he said. "Please show him in."

She disappeared down the passage, and returned a short while later with Scott a few paces behind.

"You don't waste any time, do you?" Lleland said as Scott entered the room.

"It's your wife I wanted to see," Scott said.

"You have your own."

Scott scowled. "You don't need to remind me," he said. He accepted the glass of wine Lleland held out to him. "Callaway and Elliott will be back soon," he said. "We should speak to Grant before they do. Make sure he understands our side of things."

"You can't mention who any of us are," Zach said.

"I know!" Scott said, his tone exasperated. "But he needs to know why we don't have a head on a stake!"

"I agree," Lleland said. "Do you know if Grant's in town?"

"He is." Scott grinned. "In fact, I can tell you with complete certainty that he'll be at home alone this evening. His steward happily gave me the information in exchange for a silver coin. Which you need to pay me back!"

"Tonight? Very well. Meet me outside his residence at eight."

Grant was, as Scott had discovered, home for the evening, and the two men were quickly admitted. "Ah! Seaton. Scott. Back already? What happened? Where are the others?"

"Callaway and Elliott are still en route. Hobbes remained behind," Lleland said.

"What happened? Did you see the dragons?"

Lleland glanced at Scott. "We did. But as we traveled, it soon became clear that they weren't a threat."

"No-one we spoke to seemed in the least concerned about them," Scott said. "Even the people in Hobbes' village were unconcerned."

"The aim of the League is to remove dragon threats," Lleland said. "These dragons are not a threat."

Grant frowned. "So you let them be?"

"We did."

"And what about Elliott and Callaway? What do they think?"

"Elliott saw our point," Lleland said.

"And Callaway?"

"There's a black dragon in the mountains," Scott said.

"Like the one that plagued Civitas?" Grant interjected.

"Exactly," Lleland said. "Callaway was, er, distracted by the resemblance."

"Did he kill the dragon?"

"No. He will, if he can. But he's no longer interested in the others."

"I see." Grant frowned in thought. "What about you, Seaton. Do you want to kill this dragon?"

"No. I've finally come to realize that the dragon that killed my father is dead and gone. The other dragons had nothing to do with his death."

"Hmph! So you no longer wish to hunt?"

"No."

"You made an oath, pledging to give your life to our cause. And you've been our most successful hunter."

Lleland hid a grimace. "I know, Master. And I've served

the League faithfully for ten years. I ask you to release me from my oath, but even if you don't, I refuse to hunt any longer."

Grant nodded thoughtfully. "What about you, Scott? Are you also reneging on your oath?"

"I want to remain in the League," Scott said. Lleland frowned, but was silent.

"Very well. Seaton, I release you. Scott, you'll receive word soon."

"What are you doing?" Lleland said angrily when they were back on the street. "Surely you don't wish to kill me?"

"I don't, Lleland," Scott said. "But someone needs to know what the League is up to."

Lleland glared at Scott for a moment longer. "You're going to be our spy?"

"Yes."

"Why?"

"Because I agree that dragons shouldn't be hunted. Besides, I need the money."

"You want me to pay you?" Lleland was shocked.

"Of course! You don't expect me to serve you for nothing!"

Lleland laughed wryly. "I can just give you my blood!"

"Ah, but you won't! Come now, you must admit it's only fair."

Lleland sighed. "Very well!"

Zach laughed when Lleland related the incident later, but Lydia was concerned. "Do you think we can trust him?" she asked.

Lleland had been wondering the same thing. "I think so," he said.

"We'll smell a lie," Zach said. "There's nothing to worry about."

"When are you going to introduce me to your mother?" Lydia asked Lleland a few days later. He'd returned to class, and as Zach had predicted, his students were thrilled to have him back.

"She's terrified of dragons," Lleland said. "After all, her husband was killed by Jack."

"She needn't know what we are," Lydia said. "But you cannot hide me away forever!"

"I know, my love. And I don't want to. It's just that last time she saw dragons, she had nightmares for weeks, even though they were in human form."

"You still need to introduce me," Lydia said.

"You're right. We'll go on Sunday."

Drake House was closer to Tottley Alley than the university, and it didn't take long for Lleland and Lydia to reach the house on the following Sunday. Anabel was busy in the kitchen when Lleland pushed open the door, but she stopped what she was doing when she saw Lydia at his side. Her eyes flew back to Lleland as she took off the apron tied around her waist.

"Lleland, who is this?" she said.

"Mother, this is my wife, Lydia." He took Lydia's hand. "Lydia, meet my mother, Dame Seaton."

"Dame Seaton," Lydia said with a nod as Anabel's eyes flew to Lleland.

"Your wife?"

Lleland nodded. "Yes, Mother."

"Oh, my!" She sat down on a chair. "Lydia, is it?" Lydia nodded. "Well, my dear, welcome to the family. I cannot tell you how thrilled … but when did this all happen? I didn't know you'd even met someone."

"I've known Lydia for some time now," Lleland said. He squeezed her hand. "Her brother is one of my students."

"One of your students? Well! And who are your parents?"

Lydia glanced at Lleland before answering. "My father is Aaron Drake," she said.

"Aaron Drake?" Anabel paled. "The dragon-slayer?" she whispered.

Lleland knelt down beside Anabel and took her hand. "Aaron Drake only killed one dragon, Mother," he said. "The one that killed your husband. But he doesn't hunt others."

"He doesn't? But what about you, son? Does he know–"

"I don't hunt dragons any longer, Mother," Lleland said. "Lydia has shown me that not all dragons are monsters."

Anabel looked at Lydia. "You have? Oh, thank God! I've been so worried." She rose to her feet and pulled Lydia into an embrace, startling her. "Oh, my child, that's the best news. I know you will be perfect for my Lleland." She pulled away and placed her hand on Lydia's forehead. "You're very warm, my dear. Are you with child?"

Lydia blushed. "No, Dame," she said.

"Ah, well, all in due time."

Lydia glanced at Lleland as he wrapped his arm around her. "You're all I want," he whispered as Anabel hurried from the room to fetch some wine. "Our lives could not be any more complete." She smiled, and flames flashed in her eyes.

"I love you," she whispered.

They spent a few hours with Anabel, and left as it was growing dark. Lleland took Lydia's hand as they walked along the street. "I'll admit I was rather nervous introducing you."

"I know."

"The thing is, she kept warning me about dragons. That they were all around me, but that I couldn't see them."

Lydia smiled. "She was right."

"So I thought she might recognize you as a dragon. That somehow she'd know!"

"Her fear was for you. As long as you were hunting, you were in danger. She knows you're no longer in danger."

He wrapped an arm around her waist and stared into her eyes. "I heard there's a dragon lair somewhere in the hills. Should we go hunt it down?"

A slow flame started to burn in her eyes. "What will you do when you find the dragon?"

He laughed low. "Oh, my love, I intend to devour it."

"Let's go," she whispered.

A few weeks passed before Lleland saw Scott again, but one evening there was a knock on the door, and Hannah ushered him into the room.

"There was a League meeting last night," he said as Lleland passed him some wine.

"Oh? What happened?"

"Callaway and Elliott are back. Callaway has convinced the others that the black dragon is a threat and must be hunted."

"What about the rest of us?" Zach asked.

"They're no longer interested in you. But they're determined to hunt Lleland down and kill him."

Zach nodded. "Well, brother," he said. "It seems we'll have to stay hidden in plain sight. But remember, no matter what happens, we're on your side."

Lleland nodded. "Thank you," he said.

"Now pay your spy," Zach said, "and let's go hunting!"

EPILOGUE

Lleland stared down at Lydia as she lay spread out on the cave floor, her tail stretched in one direction, her neck in the other.

"Are you sure you want to stay here?" he said. It was early spring, and the scent of crocuses drifted through the hills into their hiding space.

"I'm sure," she groaned. "I'm too exhausted to move."

"Hmm." Lleland cocked his head as he took in Lydia's form. Her belly spread over the hard floor of the cave, bulging on either side. "I'll return when my classes are done," he said.

"Bring me something to eat when you come back," Lydia said, closing her eyes. "An elk, perhaps."

"Maybe that's why you're feeling so tired," Lleland said. "You've been eating constantly."

Lydia's eyes opened as she flashed him a blazing glare. "Are you telling me I'm getting fat?"

Lleland backed away, almost tripping over his tail. "Of course not," he said. "Nothing of the sort."

Her eyes closed again. "Good. I'll see you later."

Lleland watched her for another moment, then turned

and flew out of the cave. It was deep in the hills, hidden by a pile of rock. He changed a few miles from the city, and walked the rest of the way to the university. Only a few weeks remained before the term was done and he was free to start his role as Aaron's scribe. Hopefully Lydia would be back to her usual self by then.

He entered the university building and headed towards his classroom, almost walking into Zach in the process. "*Bonum mane, Frater,*" he said. "Nice to see you again." He cocked an eyebrow. "Have you taken such an aversion to my presence that you stay away from Drake House so much?"

Lleland sighed. "Lydia didn't feel up to returning."

"Ah! Blame it on Lydia." Lleland mustered a small smile, but remained silent. "That's not it, is it?" Zach finally said.

"Lydia's been feeling … unwell," he said.

"Unwell?" Zach's eyebrows came together as he frowned. "That's impossible."

"She's always hungry, sleeps all the time, and says she's too exhausted to move."

"Where is she?"

"In the hills?"

"Should I send for Aaron?"

"Not yet. Give it a few more days, and let's see what happens."

Lleland returned to the cave that evening, a deer clamped in his jaws as he flew. Lydia smiled at him sleepily. "Is it already evening? I think I slept all day! Did you bring me something to eat?" Lleland dumped the fresh carcass in front of her and watched as she heaved herself up. If possible, she looked larger than she had that morning. She crawled forward and sank her jaws into the still-steaming flesh, ripping it delicately. She licked her claws when she was done and lay back down on the ground. Her stomach was definitely spreading over the rock more than it had before. "Mmm, that was good, but I'm still hungry. Can you get me some more?"

"You can't be serious! You've fed every day for the last week."

"But I am." She turned to look at him. "Please, Lleland."

"Very well! Stay here."

She smiled. "I won't be going anywhere."

Lleland was back an hour later, this time with a small doe. As he landed in the cave, he saw Lydia scratching the ground with her claws. "What are you doing?" he asked.

"I was getting bored," she said. "Did you get something?"

He dropped the carcass on the ground and watched as Lydia ate. She closed her eyes when she was done, and immediately fell back to sleep. Lleland lay down next to her with a sigh.

He woke a few hours later to the sound of groaning, and turned to see Lydia on her feet, her body hunched over her stomach. "What is it?" he said. "What's wrong?"

"My stomach. It hurts. I can't lie down."

He rose to his feet. "Can you change?"

"No," she moaned. "I tried, but it's impossible." She groaned again as Lleland watched helplessly. "What can I do?" he said.

"I don't know!"

"I'm going to get Zach."

"No! The pain's passing. I'll be fine." Slowly, the tension eased from her body and she lay down on the ground again. "There, I'm already feeling better."

He lay down next to her. "Something's not right," he said. "Perhaps I should send for your parents." But she was already asleep.

The next morning, Lleland was woken by the sound of scratching. He opened his eyes to see Lydia scraping sand out of the hole she had started making the night before. She smiled guiltily when she saw him watching.

"How're you feeling?" he asked.

"Hungry!"

"Are you going to hunt with me?" Her smile vanished and

her expression grew pleading. He sighed. "I'll be back in an hour," he said.

When he returned, Lydia was on her feet, panting. Wisps of flame curled through the air with every breath. She groaned and hunched over her stomach. Lleland dropped the animal in his jaws and landed at her side. "Lydia!"

"It's … all right," she panted. "Just a … passing pain."

A spasm shook her body, and she lifted her head with a roar. Her tail flicked through the air, arching down to the ground, and her eyes grew wide. The spasm passed, but a moment later she was rearing back onto her hind legs, roaring again as another gripped her. Lleland saw her stomach tighten, and she gritted her teeth. "Must get … it out," she panted.

"What?" Lleland said.

She turned to him with a snarl. "This thing inside me," she roared. Lleland pulled back slightly, surprised at her ferocity, and glanced at her back end. Her tail was raised, and beneath it he saw something gleaming white. His eyes widened as his glance flew back to Lydia. She gritted her teeth as another spasm racked her body, and her whole frame shook as a roar tore from her throat, and then she relaxed as something slipped from her onto the ground. It rocked slightly as Lleland and Lydia both turned to stare at it.

"You laid an egg!" Lleland finally said. "My wife laid an egg."

"I can see that, Lleland!"

He reached out a claw towards it, but drew back hurriedly as Lydia growled. "Don't touch it," she snarled. She dropped to the ground and pulled the egg to her side with her tail, wrapping herself around it. He stepped backwards, and her expression changed to remorse. "I'm sorry," she said. "I'm being a dragon!" Lleland smiled as she uncurled her tail. "Come look at our, er, egg." Lleland stepped forward and peered at the object. It was a brilliant white, and from one end to the other, measured about two feet.

"How's this even possible?" he said.

"I don't know."

"How long do you think it will take before something, er, hatches?"

"Something?" He looked up to see her eyes glittering dangerously.

"Our child." She smiled. He tentatively reached with his claw, pausing to see if Lydia protested, then touched the smooth, white surface. It was as hard as stone, and rocked slightly beneath his touch. He withdrew hurriedly, glancing at Lydia, but she just smiled.

"You can go now," she said. "We'll be fine without you."

"Are you sure?"

She nodded. "Just make sure you hurry back."

He leaned forward and touched his snout to hers. "I love you," he said. "You're amazing." He pulled back with a laugh. "You laid an egg!"

"How's Lydia this morning?" Zach asked later that morning, joining Lleland as he walked towards his classroom.

"Well …" Lleland started. He turned and met Zach's gaze with a grin. "She laid an egg!"

"What?" Zach's expression turned incredulous. "You're jesting."

"No." Lleland's grin grew wider. "My wife laid an egg."

"Well." Zach stared at Lleland. "I'm not sure I have the words."

"Quite!" Lleland said.

Lleland rushed back to the cave after his classes were done to find Lydia sleeping, her body curled tightly around the egg on the ground. She had moved it to the shallow hole she had dug the previous day, and nestled it in some furs. Her body had lost the extra weight of the last week and was back to its usual, sleek form. The egg rocked slightly, and Lydia opened her eyes. "You're back," she said with a smile. She glanced at the egg. "He's been doing that all day."

"He?" Lleland settled down next to her, his head next to hers, and his body curled around both of them.

"Yes. Definitely a boy."

He smiled and tapped lightly on the egg. "Are you a boy?" he said. It started to rock, and Lydia smiled.

"He knows your voice," she said.

"You think so?" Lleland placed his paw on the egg and leaned forward to whisper against the shell. "You took us quite by surprise, but I'm looking forward to meeting you." The egg began to rock more violently, and a tapping sound was heard from within. Lleland's eyebrows flew up and he looked at Lydia. She looked as surprised as he felt.

He leaned forward again. "Are you as eager to meet us?" he said. The tapping grew louder, and a crack appeared on the hard shell, spreading along the surface. There was another loud knock, and the shell fell open. Curled within, eyes blinking furiously, was a baby dragon, as white as glistening snow. It lifted its tiny wings and gave a little yelp as sparks fluttered through the air. A long neck uncurled, and it looked up at the two dragons staring down at him in shock.

Lleland glanced at Lydia, then back at the hatchling. "Hello, son," he said.

GLOSSARY OF TERMS

The setting for this story is the Medieval period or the High Middle Ages, which covers roughly the time period from AD 1000 to 1300. In the course of the story I have used terms that not everyone is familiar with. Below is an explanation of these terms.

Bower – a private study or sitting room for the lady of the house.

Cabinet – a study or library.

Carol – a dance (not a song) where everyone holds hands and dances in a circle.

Doublet – a tight-fitting jacket that buttons up the front.

Great Hall – a multi-purpose room for receiving guests, conducting business, eating meals, and when necessary, sleeping.

Kirtle – a gown worn over a chemise and laced across the front, side or back.

Reeve – an overseer of a town, reporting to the local lord. (In this story, Aaron Drake is referred to as 'milord', a title used for someone of superior social standing. However, he is not the lord of the district, and the reeve does not report to him.) The word 'sheriff' comes from the word reeve. The reeve carries a white stick as a symbol of his authority.

Solar – a private sitting room used by family and close friends. The word solar does not refer to the sun, but rather to the fact that the room has sole or private use.

Tunic – a garment pulled over the head that reaches around mid-thigh. It is worn over a shirt and cinched at the waist with a belt.

A note about meals. During the Early and High Middle Ages, the entire household typically ate meals together. There were only two meals a day, although the working classes would usually eat something small, such as a piece of bread, when they first arose and before they started working. The first meal, called dinner, was served at around 11 a.m. and was the larger meal, with numerous courses. A second meal was served in the late afternoon.

If you are interested in learning more about the Medieval period, head over to the author's website, www.lindakhopkins.com.

ACKNOWLEDGMENTS

Thank you, Tara, for so diligently reading my books and providing valuable feedback! Couldn't do it without you!

ABOUT THE AUTHOR

Linda K. Hopkins is originally from South Africa, but now lives in Calgary, Canada with her husband and two daughters. Head over to her website, www.lindakhopkins.com, to learn more about the author. Sign up for updates, and be among the first to hear when the next story from The Dragon Archives will be released.

BOOKS BY LINDA K. HOPKINS

Books in *The Dragon Archives* Series
Bound by a Dragon
Pursued by a Dragon
Loved by a Dragon
Dance with a Dragon
Forever a Dragon

Other Books
Moondance

11010743R00211

Made in the USA
San Bernardino, CA
03 December 2018